Song of the Crocodile

Caroline Lisa

First published in Great Britain in 2020
by BOLDvoice press

Copyright Caroline Lisa 2019
authorcarolinelisa.com

Under the Copyright Designs and Patents Act 1988, Caroline Lisa has asserted her right to be identified as the author of this work.

A CIP catalogue record for this book is available from the British Library

ISBN 978-1-9161827-6-9 paperback
ISBN 978-1-9161827-8-3 ebook

Printed and bound in Great Britain

BOLDvoice press is committed to a sustainable future for our planet. This book is made from Forest Stewardship Council certified paper.

BOLDvoice press
boldvoicepress.com

(Caroline Sakala trading as BOLDvoice press)

Dedicated to all women,
who have faced the Crocodile

You are beautiful and brave.

About the Author

The story of SONG OF THE CROCODILE was inspired from Caroline Lisa's year living with the Mandinka tribe in The Gambia. She wrote the novel between juggling her full-time job within children's social care and family life, raising two active, amazing boys; and saw sunrise on far too many occasions. It was a novel she felt compelled to write to help colleagues understand the issues the story raises, and in doing so, she hopes that professionals, families and communities will be better equipped to protect the girls they love. Caroline Lisa lives and works in London, but often lets her imagination take her to warmer climates. Her next novel is likely to be set in Africa again.

A Note of Caution

Within the pages of this book, readers may find some scenes upsetting. Details of a graphic nature have purposefully been included – not to traumatise, but to demystify – but in their very nature, the issues raised may trigger feelings associated with traumatic experiences. There are organisations that are detailed on the following website if Binta's story resonates with your own experience and you would like further support.

authorcarolinelisa.com

For The Gambia, our homeland
We strive and work and pray,
That all may live in unity,
Freedom and peace each day.
Let justice guide our actions
Towards the common good...

(From The Gambia National Anthem)

Prologue

Binta

The thought of the machete sends a cold shiver down my spine, and I glance in the direction of the town where I was born. Until yesterday, it was my home. People will be searching, rushing from one compound to another, asking if anyone has seen me; and, of course, Ma will be frantic, crying like women do when someone dies. She'll give up eventually.

The *Ngansimba* will be looking for me too; or rather, hunting me. I have no illusions she wants me dead. She nearly killed me once before, which is why I had to run. And now I've done something I know she won't forgive, something that will make sure she comes after me – but I had no choice.

If I squint against the sun I can just about see the land disappearing around the corner towards the town, where the outline of palm trees fades together – it's more than a day's walk away, but I still look to see if anyone appears around that headland. The *Ngansimba*'s powerful. She'll have help from the spirits to find me, but for now the beach is empty. Nobody comes; not just yet.

Not long now and it will be dark. The sun is quickly slipping into the ocean turning the sky to a brilliant orange. Before the last light fades I'm aware that I need to find somewhere to rest – not that I will able to sleep with these terrifying thoughts that are racing around in my head, filling every part of my mind.

If the Ngansimba *catches me, will she kill me quickly? Or torture me?*
Again.

Amie

'Binta! Binta!'

She's not here. But she has to be.

'Binta!' I call her name again and again, hurrying from her room where she should still be asleep, jumping down from the veranda and across to the other side of the compound.

'Binta!' Emptiness is rising from the pit of my stomach as I push open another door.

'Amie, what's wrong?' My sister-in-law holds onto my elbow as I turn to try another room. It's the first time I've taken time to pause. Although it's only been moments since I've realised, it feels as though an eternity has passed. I scan the yard quickly before I answer, because I don't want it to be true and when I voice what I think has happened, it will be more certain; terribly real.

'She's gone, Marokie. Binta's gone!'

'What do you mean? Where?'

'She's gone!' I put my hand to my mouth to suppress the sudden sobs that come. My body reacting, even if my mind cannot comprehend. There is a weight that seems to descend upon my shoulders that I know I will never be able to shake off if I can't find her.

I close my eyes to fight the awful facts and sense Marokie's arm around my shoulder trying to comfort me. I appreciate her gesture, but it is futile.

I was told there were three pains a woman bears in her life: that much is true beyond doubt. But nobody prepared me for this. Of everything I have ever endured, this is by far the worst.

My daughter is gone.

The worst thing is – I know it's because of what I did. I only have myself to blame.

PART ONE

- Before -

A Year Ago

Chapter 1

Binta

I manoeuvre my way amongst the market stalls, through the stench of fish and the buzz of flies, and into the square where I take a deep breath of fresh air, the deafening negotiations of the traders left behind. I head across to the concrete steps that raise Mr Janneh's shop away from the dusty main road. It's the perfect location to watch the bustle, right on the corner of the crossroads and, as I expect, Jena and Isatou are already sat on the steps, each with a half-empty bottle of Coke in their hands.

'Left some for me?' I call to them, pausing for a goat to amble past aimlessly, then making my way up the steps where Jena shuffles along to give me room to sit in between her and Isatou. This is our usual hangout on a Friday – holy day – the best part of the week when school finishes early.

'Here, but don't drink all of it. I know what you're like!' Jena eyes me, then smiles and hands over the warm bottle.

We've been friends since before I can remember. I think we probably even knew each other as babies. I don't actually know my birthday, but Jena knows hers. Jena's mother told me though that we were born in the same rainy season, thirteen years ago. All of my memories, even before I started primary school, include her. It's as though she's part of me; every thought I have of my childhood she's there, and by default, Isatou has occupied the space of a substitute older sister.

Everyone's hurrying to mosque, the grandiose building opposite with smooth white walls that towers over the far side of the square, and the multicolour minibus 'bush taxis' park with a sense of urgency. Soon after, women disembark with oversized baskets on their heads, rushing home quickly to prepare an early meal, while the men walk across the road with prayer mats rolled under their arms to pray. Rows of shoes line the outside walls, as the men join short queues for the outside tap to begin their ablutions and enter the mosque barefoot. It looks kind of funny, the shoes just lined up against the wall as though people were standing there one minute and then they disappeared into thin air.

Often, when Ma passes the mosque, she recalls our town's history – our proud history, she says – insistent that I absorb it. I copy her in my head, ad verbatim as she says the same things each time. When she's not looking I repeat under my breath, making sure she doesn't see me roll my eyes, mouthing the words, 'Mandinka have been settled here for over four hundred years. Two hundred years ago our town was a very important place during the Holy Wars.' At that point, Ma usually pauses to enquire, 'Binta – can you imagine?

Are you listening?' I then look up quickly and smile, nodding attentively. 'Your history is important. It's because of our town that Islam became established in the whole of this region.' To emphasise it, she throws her arms wide. 'The whole of this country.' It gets boring hearing her tell me over and over; does she not think I know it by now? Actually, our country is one of the smallest in the whole of Africa, but if I tell her that, she'll likely clip me around the ear for being rude.

With this position here on Mr Janneh's steps, we have the best spot to witness the commotion around the bush taxi that's just arrived. A couple of white tourists debark awkwardly out of the rusty doors and immediately children swarm around them like bees to their hives, shouting in the only English they know, 'Toubab, Toubab! Any pen?' It feels like a lifetime ago that we did the same. The pens were all good and all, but I liked the sweets best, which I'd scoff down quickly, otherwise Musa would try and steal them from me.

I can see now that the *Toubab* woman is much fairer than even the *Fula* couple that rents the shop in our compound from my father. I know they pay too much money for it, but I'm old enough now to understand that things are more difficult if you are a stranger – if you haven't always belonged to our community. The *Toubab*'s milky skin is peppered with brown spots dotted all over her arms and face, like someone has flicked mud – something Musa would do to me after the rain stirs up the earth – but when she walks past I see the spots are part of her actual skin.

'Do you think she's ill?'

'It's sun kisses,' Jena says.

'Sun kisses?'

'Where the sun burns the skin. Their skin is weak.'

'The man just needs a red bottom and he would be like a baboon!' I say, making Jena and Isatou laugh, enough that they need to hold their stomachs. I like that about the three of us. We're always joking around.

'Did you know the women are different to us?' Isatou whispers, once she has stopped laughing.

'What do you mean?'

'Isn't it obvious? Scared to show their breasts for a start!'

'Perhaps because they don't want them getting little sun kisses on them.' Witty and quick-minded – that's what Ma says about me.

Isatou looks around, seeming to make sure nobody can hear, and I lean in closer expectantly. 'They have bits between their legs that keep on growing like a man's, and their private parts always itch!'

'Urgh! That's horrible,' I say, giggling to displace a little embarrassment at what she's just said, and Jena sucks her teeth in the way that elders tend to do when they are disgusted by something.

'Anyway, how do you know that?' I ask Isatou.

'Something I heard Grandmother saying to Ma – they didn't know I was listening. Ma wasn't happy with her – they were arguing, as usual.'

After taking a sip from the Coke, I hand the drink back to Isatou and nod agreement. Words of the elders are esteemed – they hold secrets and truths that only we can imagine; therefore, if Isatou's Grandmother, Mamamuso, said it, it must be true. My eyes glance towards the *Toubab*'s trousers and it's as though a blindfold has fallen from my eyes and I'm seeing things clearly for the first time. How could I not have realised before? That's why the *Toubab* women dress like men – they can't wear skirts, not with the issues they have. I've always envied the white women coming here with their money, but not now: not with that kind of embarrassing problem and where there was envy before I now feel pity and, to be honest, a little disgust. Errgh!

'Look at their fair skin. You know, men like fairer skin.'

Jena turns with raised eyebrows to Isatou and smirks at my comment.

'Why are you thinking about what men like?' Jena asks, sucking her teeth again.

'Men? More like what Yaya likes!' Isatou jabs my side, grinning.

'What do you mean?'

'I see how you look at him.'

'I do not,' I answer, feeling the heat rise in my face. 'Anyway, it's okay for you, Jena. Look.' I put my arm next to hers to compare, our warm skin touching. 'Mine's much darker. You two never have to worry about getting nice husbands.'

'Ah, poor little Binta!' Isatou jeers, while I resist the urge to push her down the steps.

'You could try bleaching cream, Binta.'

'Don't let Mum hear you talk like that! She hates the stuff!' Isatou reminds her, placing the bottle of Coke to her lips and the last of the brown liquid disappears.

'But it doesn't work miracles – it won't make you a *Toubab*!' Jena giggles.

I hit her on the arm, just enough to set her off balance, and then the *Toubab* woman catches my interest again. She makes her way through the crowd of kids towards a battered old Ford taxi that goes the short distance to the beach. My eyes focus on how the woman walks, the way she carefully weaves through the children, looking uncomfortable at them getting too close – I can see now how she tries to cover up her affliction. I'm watching her every step, amazed at how obvious it is now that I know how different *Toubab* women are.

Thank Allah I was born Mandinka.

Chapter 2

Yari

At the sound of *her* voice there's a nauseating churning in the pit of my stomach, and the day hasn't even begun.

I keep my eyes closed, pretend I'm still asleep and hear Sarko sigh at his name being called for the third time. The bed creaks as he sits up and manoeuvres out of his side followed by a shuffling against the tile floor as his tired legs reluctantly move.

'SARKO!' her voice echoes, booming across the yard, finding its way through the cracks, permeating the fabric of our home.

'Coming!' he shouts. The first word he's uttered today. Our day.

I block out the muffled voices, roll onto my side and draw up the blanket over my head wanting this day to start over; without her voice being the first thing I hear. But as much as I try, it feels as though my head has been contaminated already and I know for the rest of the day I'm going to feel a little unsettled. Like the many other times where she's seeped into my mind and dominated my thoughts. Today is destined to be no different.

13

It's not until the mattress dips with Sarko's weight that I realised I must have drifted back off to sleep for a moment. There's the warmth of his body as he snuggles along my back and puts his arm over my shoulder. His lips brush against my cheek and I open my eyes, feigning waking for the first time. His eyes crease in a smile and I turn my head, hold his face in my hands and kiss him. This is how the day should have started.

'I haven't forgotten, Yari. I remember today is the day we married all those years ago,' he whispers and immediately presses his lips against mine again. I'm glad he doesn't give me chance to say anything, because amongst the things I want to reciprocate – telling him how blessed I am that he's my husband, how kind he is, how much I love him – there's something else percolating on the edge of my tongue that would ruin the moment. Something I've asked with increasing frustration, but less frequency, for over a decade.

Are we ever going to leave this place – and his mother – behind?

By late afternoon I feel less of the unsettledness I woke with this morning, of the frustration of still living here. It was only supposed to be for a few months – a year tops. Not forever. The familiar niggling of feeling trapped in my own home has lessened throughout the day – but not enough for me to let the conversation be buried. Not any longer. As it's our anniversary I've decided that today is as good a day as any to reflect and discuss where we are; where we are going – our future. Yes, it's good timing. The more I think about it, the happier I'm feeling – a lightness lifting from where I normally feel a pressing weight. Tonight we need – we *have* – to talk.

'Hey, what's all the nonsense?' I ask, and my thoughts are suddenly put aside hearing the ensuing argument between my offspring. All I can decipher is that they're debating over who has done the homework correctly. There's an anticipated quietening as I approach the table and peer over Jena's English workbook. I see straightaway what I need to see to resolve the tension, but I make out that I'm working it out in my head just for a little longer. The girl's eyes are attentive on my expression, the tension easing away for a moment. But it's not just the lull in the arguing that causes me to linger over their books, it's the way it reminds me of who I used to be. What I used to have. Status. Belonging. That life of teaching; a life before motherhood that now seems so surreal that I have to remind myself it did actually occur. There was never an opportunity to return to work. It wouldn't have worried me that it would have added to the eyebrows rising and voices muttering around town; I've never fitted into the mentality. Never ticked the boxes others thought I should fit into. If we lived back in the city, nobody would care if I took a job; they wouldn't say I was too educated and too full of myself. And there would have been the opportunity to do it. Instead here we are.

Tonight Sarko and I will talk.

'You are doing it just right—' I take the seat next to Isatou and turn her book towards me '—but ...' I continue before new fuel starts fresh bickering between them '... your sister was only trying to encourage you. Sometimes, though, you need to let Jena do her work in the way she wants.' The girls glance at each other, both reluctantly resigned to letting the matter drop. They are aware of me watching closely, waiting to notice small

15

antagonising gestures that will reignite the squabble. With their heads both turned back towards their books, the pens poised to write, I have them focused once more. If only I had such control and respect in every area of my life.

'Yari!' Inwardly I groan at the sound of her voice, but in front of my girls I make an effort to remain neutral. As much as education with books is essential, it's more important for me to demonstrate respect for the elders to my children. I push my chair back, ready to head outside – though not before catching the look Isatou and Jena give each other. So much for me trying to set a good example. Let's just say, it's not often Mamamuso and I communicate, and if we do the atmosphere is often left charged. Nevertheless, I embrace the pretence for their sake that their grandmother just wants a nice little chat, but I make sure I close the front door behind as I leave the house and step down into the yard.

Mamamuso is leaning up against the frame of the panelling that runs along the veranda. 'Come!' she says, turning and walking a little way to the back of the house. I sigh slightly, close my eyes for the briefest of moments then force a smile.

'Mamamuso, how are you?' I begin, all polite preamble nonsense that I don't feel. My heart speeds up as I wait for the reason she wants to speak. She's not known for her pleasantries towards me but I walk calmly in her direction, trying to settle my emotions. It took me a while to realise that Sarko had her mouth – hers is usually pursed and tight; his is often full, the corners gently arching in a smile.

'I've got something to tell you. I know you don't want to hear this, but you have to.' My defences are immediately up. I don't have to do anything. 'For too long – all this speak of new ways of doing things with my son's daughters – but you know that's not our way. It's wrong.' She's done it now; I'm not having this conversation again with her and I say exactly that and begin to turn.

'Isatou is getting too old – you aren't doing her any favours,' she says with contempt seeping from every word. There's something in her voice that makes me pause and I turn slowly to face her.

'They are not your daughters, they are mine. I know you don't understand, but we will never agree on this. Never.'

Then she inches forward and raises her voice, telling me the crazy reasons for what she believes, things that I've heard over and over from the Imam and the elders since I was a child. However loud she tells me, it makes no difference; our realities are poles apart. If only she'd realise that she is saying things that don't have any basis in truth. But she believes she is utterly, emphatically right, and arguing with her about this again is as good as trying to move an elephant. Exasperated and angry I turn and walk away, but coldness grips me when she utters resolutely, 'The *Ngansimba* is in town.'

There is only one reason the *Ngansimba* comes. The same reason I met with her. Why I have nightmares even now. And why my daughters will never meet with her. I begin walking towards the house, but slow my pace when Mamamuso continues, 'The *Ngansimba* – I've told her about Isatou.'

17

Chapter 3

Binta

Immediately on opening my eyes, something feels different about this day; there's a tangible expectation in the air. A cockerel crows, probably the one that usually perches on the wall around the side of the compound near the well, followed by a goat bleating a few roads away. The noises seem to combine in my early morning foggy head. Then it comes to me – today is *Tobaski*. In the early-morning light, I lie lazily, watching the dust particles drift around, dancing in slow motion, excitement building in the bottom of my stomach as I think of the day ahead. The cockerel sounds again, louder than before, as though it is determined to wake as many people as possible.

'I'm awake already!' I mutter, sitting up and dropping my feet to the floor, searching with my toes for the flip-flops I kicked off under the bed last night. Most of the town will have woken at the sound of the Imam's call to pray when the sun broke, and it's just a few others who cling onto sleep, like me, that the cockerel disturbs. At the other end of the bed there's a snuffled grunt, a momentary pause in my grandmother's snoring. She needs more than the Iman's speaker or a noisy bird to rouse her; usually it's her full bladder that does the trick, and everyone has to make sure she has a direct path to the loo otherwise she pushes us to the side with surprising strength saying, 'Out my way, quickly, quickly!'

I walk over to the corner of the room and pick up the blue plastic bucket with the metal handle and step down from the veranda towards the back of the compound, swinging it as I go. The cockerel is startled and it flaps its wings madly to rebalance on the wall as I laugh. 'Serves you right for waking me!'

In competition with the cockerel, goats and sheep begin to bleat in unison, which fills the air with noise every few minutes, because at this time of year there are as many animals as there are compounds. Tomorrow it will be quiet again, but the bleating only adds to the anticipation of the day ahead. My father bought our goat a few weeks ago at Ma's insistence because 'I don't want to be left with a scrawny one again, like last year, Ousman.' It should really be a sheep, but a goat is the next best thing and my father is never one to part with money if he doesn't have to.

Our goat is right there along the fence by the well, looking at me, waiting for food – anything goes – and I find myself automatically stretching towards it to stroke the coarse hair on its back as I pass by, but I immediately stop myself, my hand midway in the air. I can't bear to touch it today – to feel the warmth of its body, to feel it move and breathe – only to imagine it as meat on my plate at lunchtime. I turn my back on its expectant large eyes, deliberately ignoring it and fight the thought of what is going to happen.

I set the bucket down by my side and take the long fraying rope resting on the waist-high crumbling wall of our well. It takes skill to get the water, but I've done it for so long that I've nearly forgotten how difficult it is. It's only when I see the younger children struggling to draw water, getting frustrated bringing up a dry bucket for the hundredth time, that I recall how it's not as easy as it looks.

I wrap the end of the rope around my wrist then rest my knees against the wall and peer carefully over the top towards the dark bottom of the well, then drop the bucket where it lands bobbing on the top of the surface. The next part is the tricky bit: getting the floating bucket to dip beneath to fill with cool water. I take the rope in both hands and move it slowly to draw the bucket from side to side then lift it slightly, careful to keep it horizontal before dropping it quickly. A satisfying glug emerges up from the damp walls of the well and water pours in, the weight pulls on the rope in my hands, which signals for me to begin lifting the bucket; one hand over the other I gather the rope and soon my arm muscles burn with the effort.

The distance I need to travel is only a few steps away, not far enough to bother lifting the water onto my head, but the handle still digs into my fingers as I cross the compound. A drop spills, spreading out onto the dry concrete when I step up onto the veranda that leads in to the house. Then a few more splash across the bedroom floor leaving a trail showing my path to a rickety wooden door, where behind is an enclosed courtyard. A high wall blocks off the view from anyone; I set the bucket down on the floor and rub my aching arms before undressing to wash.

The early-morning sun is pleasant on my naked skin, not like it gets before lunch when it is too hot and there are no shadows to offer protection. As I pour the last water from the bucket over my head a goat bleats from the other side of our compound wall and another replies. I wonder if they can sense today is *Tobaski*? That they only have a couple of hours left to live?

Chapter 4

Amie

The sunlight streams through the window in a continuous beam. It seems fitting that the room is bathed in glorious light on such a special day. I've always loved *Tobaksi*, but since I've become a mother it has taken on something more. Respite from the ordinary, from the normal stresses of day-to-day life. A time for us all to be together, to remember and celebrate who we are. It's a day aside from working, providing and surviving and it makes the other days of the year easier, knowing that they are heading to this one.

We have it easier than most families with Ousman's job in the city, but there are still times we have to decide between fixing the corrugated iron roof before the rainy season, or meat to add to the rice and the vegetables that I provide from the field. From time to time I think there is a glimmer that life will become easier without the stress of having to choose what is most pressing for our money, but then something comes along to keep us vigilant. With that responsibility comes stress. Worry about where school fees will come from, or praying that the children don't get ill. It's the worst feeling having to wait an extra day for medicine when your child has fever, waiting for enough dalaisi, hoping that you won't see them die before your eyes. And the fear and guilt that because you didn't have enough dalasi it's your fault. I know too many mothers that has happened to. Thank Allah I have been spared that burden.

For that fact – that money is already tight – as well as other reasons, I am glad that Ousman's second wife has never given him children. Of course I'd never voice that. Can you imagine if I did? The next time she had a miscarriage all eyes would be on me thinking I'd gone to the marabout to curse her!

Binta comes into the room and the sunbeam shines on her. It perfectly reflects her beauty as she slowly spins in front of me, showing off the new outfit that I've just given her for this special day. The best of it is – the thing I consider most as I take a moment to watch her – is that she's unaware of how remarkable she is. That makes her even more beautiful, and I feel pride rising in my chest as though on wings.

Ousman appears next to us and he smiles at Binta and me and comments on how pretty her dress is. It's on rare occasions like this that I'm also grateful that Ousman doesn't have children with his other wife. Times like this when it feels as though we are important to him. Just us.

A thought quickly comes to mind and I ask him to take a photograph because there is a feeling that catches me off guard for a moment. The realisation of how different Binta looks from a year ago, when she excitedly jumped up and down in her then-new outfit.

Time suddenly feels as though it is racing as I compare this same scene in my mind from only last *Tobaski*. In this last year, she has grown so much.

I don't expect the sense of worry this thought brings, as though something clicks inside at the very instant Ousman takes the picture. Immediately I long for things to stay the same, for life to be static – like the photograph. Then, in the next minute, Ousman ushers us out of the house to make sure we're not late for the ceremony.

Laughter, chatter and excitement for the day ahead: life moving forward. I can't even stop it for a second.

Chapter 5

Binta

The road outside of our compound runs in a straight line to the prayer ground, which seems (especially on days like today) to lead to the centre of all that is important. My father pants as he walks quickly in front of us, inhaling a long drag of his cigarette. Usually the place is empty, just a clearing surrounded by ancient trees, but, even on a normal day when I walk to school, the area holds a sense of holiness when I look up at the sky through the branches that sway gently in the breeze, up to the blue expanse; I sense God's enormity.

Today the clearing accommodates rows upon rows of people; hundreds are here, kneeling, ready for the Iman to commence. My father heads to the front where the men are; my mother heads further back. There seems to be a tangible awesomeness about the place and for a second I have to pause before taking my next breath; it's amazing seeing everyone here – to feel such a part of something – somewhere special like this.

'Binta,' she tells me, 'go to the far side of the ground with the children. I'll meet with you later. And be on your best behaviour!'

'Yes, Ma!' Thankfully she doesn't notice me roll my eyes as she eases her way toward her *Kafo,* her intimate, special group of friends. For years, all through my childhood, I have seen them together, her *Kafo* that are closer to Ma than anyone, even closer than her own two sisters that live in the next village. I've never really thought about it before, but, as I wander over to find Isatou and Jena, that's the thought that occupies my mind: how did Ma get to be in a *Kafo*? Did she choose her friends to be with? We should be a *Kafo* together – Isatou, Jena and me – to be special friends forever. I mean, I know we'll always be really special friends, but being a *Kafo* makes it...I don't know...a completely unbreakable bond. That's it. An unbreakable bond. I find them leaning up against the bark of a large tree, shading from the hot sun.

'*Salam Malikum!*' I say, aiming for a greeting that's dignified, feeling that the place and day demands a level of formality.

'Happy *Tobaski!*' Jena hurries over and hugs me.

'Happy *Tobaski!*' I giggle.

'Hey, are you coming to the cinema with us tonight?' Jena asks, excitedly.

'Of course! Where better to spend our *Tobaski* pocket money?'

'Our neighbours always give us lots of money on *Tobaski* – don't worry, we'll have enough for you too if you end up empty-handed after going round your stingy neighbours.' Isatou laughs.

'They're generous too,' I say, sucking through my teeth, mocking offence. 'Hey, do you know how you get to be in a *Kafo*?' I ask, glancing back towards where I can see my mother merged in close proximity to hers; the same faces I've seen all my life, there at every special occasion.

'Maybe we just choose who our best friends will be for the rest of our lives?' Jena smiles, shrugging slightly.

'Maybe,' I reply. 'It's okay for you two – being sisters, you'll always be together.'

'Don't worry, Binta – we'll be friends with you for ever,' she says and links arms with me.

'Shhh! We have to be quiet now,' Isatou says, and although she is only slightly older, it still makes her our elder and we listen – at least this time. From here I can see all the people – I reckon the whole town must be assembled. The Iman calls everyone to prayer using his tannoy, and there is an instant hush and a combined patter as everyone prostrates to the floor, their backs to us moving downwards in absolute harmony; rows of various bright colours, with everyone wearing a new outfit – every colour that I can think of in unified motion. I watch in wonder, longing, as I do every *Tobaski*, for the time when I can join in too but it feels as though it will never come.

The Iman prays and then I can tell by the way people are watching that the first animal has been brought to him to be slaughtered. We are too far away to witness it properly, and, really, I can't say I'm that disappointed. Next to me, Jena stands squinting, trying to see, like she does in class at the blackboard.

'Today we commemorate when Abraham was willing to sacrifice his own son, Ismail, in the name of Allah,' the Iman says; his authoritative voice carries loudly across the ground on the still air, demanding absolute attention.

'Every year each family is required to sacrifice an animal in remembrance of Abraham's obedience.' The last word hangs, settling in people's minds.

27

I try to imagine my father pinning my younger brother, Musa, down to cut him up. It's preferable to my goat being killed, but I doubt Ma would be as happy. Perhaps if he could just be threatened with being killed, like Ismail was – that might do something to his meanness.

Prayers come to a conclusion and there is a growing murmuring as people turn to each other to talk again. Amongst the colourful kaftans, I spot Ma.

'I'll see you tonight,' I say to Jena and Isatou, adjusting my headscarf.

'See you tonight – by Mr Janneh's. The film starts around eight o'clock,' Jena reminds me.

'Come as soon as you hear the last call to prayer. Have fun getting your *Tobaski* pocket money from your stingy neighbours!' Isatou teases.

'I will, don't you worry – I'll collect enough money to last me a whole year! See you later.'

'Remember, just after the last call to prayer,' Jena says, the excitement bouncing off her words.

Chapter 6

Amie

'It's hot today,' Mariatou says, inching closer to the bark of the tree where there is still a little shade. 'You look beautiful in your outfit, Amie.'

I smile and thank her, though she is being gracious. She always carries off the outfit better than I do, but I don't mind. Since we became a *Kafo* all those years ago, it has been our tradition to wear outfits made from the same roll of material. At every ceremony, every occasion we come individually, but find each other out amongst the crowd. Through the array of bright colours we spot each other easily, variations of each other; parts of a whole. Today we stand under the tree, purple and white outfits, our headpieces tied on the left, as we always do.

We emerged from that time, eight of us brought together as a *Kafo* – but as we have journeyed through life – childbirth, malaria and a violent husband have reduced our number to five.

'Your Binta is growing quickly now, Amie. Have you arranged things yet?'

I glance over Mariatou's shoulder and pause in answering her question. The sight of Binta walking towards us silences my response to the expectant ears from the rest of the *Kafo* who are all now poised to join in this conversation. My response is on hold – not just because it's not for Binta to overhear, but also the way she carries herself across the prayer ground catches me by surprise. The clumsy steps of a child are now morphing into the elegant movements of a young woman. There are curves she didn't have a little while before. Mariatou's question about my daughter's future rings loudly in my head, seeming to demand a response, and makes me feel uneasy as Binta approaches.

'My, Binta, you are getting tall now. All that sweet potato and yam!' Mariatou laughs as she reaches for Binta's bicep and squeezes it gently. 'Look at your strong arms – all that lifting water from the well. You will make a good wife.'

'Strong arms to keep your husband in check if he gets out of line!' Fatoumata adds. As they talk and joke, they both knowingly smile at me and I suddenly feel the need to run and hide Binta. In reality I just try and laugh away their words, whilst Binta is blissfully unaware of what their talking means.

'Ladies, don't be giving her such bad advice. She's a good girl,' I say, desperately wanting them to stop their focus on her. I want them to stop because I have a feeling that there's an acceleration of things I am not yet ready for.

'She sure is. Look how she's grown,' Mariatou says. 'Nearly a woman now.'

Chapter 7

Binta

By the time we arrive back at our compound, my father is in the middle of the yard straddling my poor goat with his hand under its jaw, lifting its head to fully expose the neck where his knife is pressing.

'Ousman, were you not going to wait?' Ma says loudly, the annoyance diminished slightly in her voice probably because of the semicircle of relatives that are standing around my father ready to witness the event.

He laughs. 'Just timing it for your arrival!'

The goat's wide eyes are looking straight at me, bleating desperately, seeming to plead with me; I quickly walk across to the house, take one big step onto the concrete veranda and head inside. I can't watch my goat die. Then there is no more bleating, only silence.

For a while, the excitement of the day is squashed with a heaviness that seems to restrict the joy that I experienced earlier and I flop down onto the sofa in the lounge. I think of my goat, and I know it's silly, but I feel sad for it. I didn't want to watch it bleed to death, or to see my father quickly peel the skin from its back, which will be carefully cut and laid out to dry in the hot midday sun. It will become a new prayer mat – particularly sacred, seeing as it was from the *Tobaski* sacrifice. It will feel strange to touch the coarse hair of the mat and not think of the times I stroked the animal as I fed it.

After skinning it, my father will then turn the goat on its back and cut vertically from the wound in the neck, over the enlarged stomach, to the back legs. The bowel discarded, the intestines removed in one pile. Then my father will take the heart, lungs, liver, kidney and place them on a bowl. In another he'll place the legs and cut the hind into chunks. Within an hour of the goat bleating its final breath, the animal will already be prepared to distribute as gifts to friends, family and poorer neighbours who only have chickens to sacrifice. We end up with just as much meat as we start with – hopefully some will bring sheep to give us variety. If we're lucky, we might even get beef.

'Binta, go and take this to the *Fula* shopkeeper,' Ma says, coming into the room carrying a large white ceramic plate. When she lifts the lid to show me the raw meat, I immediately imagine the aroma of sweet stewed meat drifting up from inside, and, with a pang of guilt, realise I'm already looking forward to our evening meal. I swing my legs to the floor and take the plate from her and make my way across the compound to the *Fula* shop.

Knock, Knock', I say, tapping on the corrugated-iron shop door. After hearing the *Fula* answer, I step into the room and put the plate down on the shop counter, and lift the lid to show Ibrahim what's inside.

'This is from my father.'

'Thank your father, Binta. Here, take a handful of these,' Ibrahim says, smiling. He holds out a large glass jar of multi-coloured wrapped sweets. As I turn to leave I see his wife, Mariama, sat on a stool in the corner of the room, plucking the feathers from a chicken.

'*Salam Malikum*,' I say, stuck for anything else to say to her as I know she doesn't speak Mandinka. She looks up, and, although she looks tired, she smiles. Then she wipes her hands on some material and gets up, motioning for me to stay. Just as her toddler is about to crawl through the feathers on the floor, she returns, picks him up, putting him on her hip. Shame, I smile to myself. He would have looked funny with feathers stuck to him, like an oversized chicken. She comes over to me, and holds out a leather necklace with a small shell attached. It's beautiful. Mariama says something in *Fula* and then puts the necklace over my head. I feel inept; unable to express my gratitude in her language. Instead I say it in Mandinka and hope she understands.

Later when the call for prayer travels clearly through the warm evening air, I make my way towards the market, passing others. It's busier than any other night of the year with everyone out celebrating, which adds to the excitement in the air.

'I like your necklace,' Jena says as soon as she sees me.

'Thanks. How much did you get today?'

'Thirty dalasi. How about you?'

'Twenty, but I got this,' I say, holding the shell around my neck, 'and sweets too.'

'Told you that you had the stingy neighbours!' Isatou teases.

'Well, this necklace is worth a hundred dalasi!'

'Maybe if you sold it to a naïve *Toubab*!' Normally I'd rise to the banter, but I feel a tinge of sadness at Mariama's gift being the subject of ridicule and choose to ignore her.

The crowds are milling around the entrance where we buy tickets for the film and a brown bag of groundnuts each. Through the entrance of the wall, which is the only structure of the roofless cinema, plastic chairs are set out in rows and there is a screen at the front of the enclosure. Isatou, being the eldest, and having been to the cinema more often than us, leads the way. Without a bright moon, I stumble over someone's feet spilling most of my groundnuts from the bag. I'm embarrassed; the saving grace is that it's dark enough that I hope nobody has seen.

'What are we watching?' I ask, sitting down on a wonky chair.

'James Bond. Double-o-seven,' Jena says, holding her ticket right in front of her face, squinting in the dim light.

'Is that a good one? Is it Bollywood?'

Isatou laughs. 'No, English.'

The stars in the sky are glistening bright, not a cloud in sight, creating a perfect canopy above. Jena leans close to me and whispers, 'Look, Yaya is over there – can you see him?'

Instinctively I follow her finger, but can't distinguish him amongst the shadows in front of us. I'm glad. I don't want him to see me, especially after stumbling when I arrived and now with heat rising in my cheeks.

'Hey, Isatou – did you see Yaya is sitting there? Binta should move and sit next to him. You know she likes him!'

'No, I don't!' I say, digging her in the ribs with my elbow.

'Yes, you do!'

I'm sure Yaya is just about to turn around when the generator whirs into action behind us. A small tunnel of light cuts across our heads beaming, attracting moths and insects to the bright screen where one settles on the actor's nose, making us giggle. Before long, I'm forgetting the teasing, forgetting Yaya and I fix my eyes on the film. As I glance down the row to my friends, I feel a sense of complete happiness.

Chapter 8

Yari

It requires all my resolve not to run the last few steps back towards the house; to sprint up the steps onto the veranda and into the living room. Knowing that Mamamuso is still watching me I walk calmly, despite the fact my heart is racing and there's a building ball of emotion inside that makes me want to scream. I put my hand on the handle of the door and take a deep breath; my girls need to see me composed. They mustn't see the fear in my eyes.

When I enter the house my daughters are bent studiously over their books.

'How are you getting on?' A small cough to clear my voice and I continue with forcibly cheery words, 'Good – that's good handwriting...well done.' They don't seem to notice the façade I have – either that, or they have learnt the art of discretion. I spend some minutes pottering around the room, lifting up a pile of material on the side and sorting through items that need mending. It's a chore I've already done, but I have to keep my hands busy; keep the thoughts away, at least with Isatou and Jena in the room.

What did Mamamuso mean when she said the *Ngansimba* knows about Isatou? She couldn't have meant that she's told her that Isatou is to be on her list. She doesn't have the right. Perhaps she was just giving her the heads up – for the *Ngansimba* to come and talk to me, like she's done in the past. She knows there is no room for me to move from my views and she knows I don't care about what others think. I can't believe she'd bother to come and meet with me again. She did once before after that day last year. That education day I ran at the library trying to bring the elders together to open up a new discussion about our ways. Mamamuso stood in the corner at the time, her arms folded defiantly and I could almost imagine steam rising from her ears from the anger she felt towards me. Everyone knows my views. How dare Mamamuso think I could be swayed? Unless...suddenly I feel a weight descend in the bottom of my stomach and I have to sit down quickly. *Unless... she is planning to do things without me? No. Surely she wouldn't try to do that?*

'Ma – are you okay?'

I look up and see the concern in Isatou's face, and Jena glances up to see what Isatou is saying. I force a smile and slowly fold the material I'm still holding, placing it on the sofa next to me. 'Just a little headache. Nothing to worry about.' I stand up and head over to the sideboard to find my handbag with the brown purse inside. 'Here, you have both been working hard.' I pull out a couple of coins and walk over to the table. 'Why don't you go and get yourselves a fizzy drink at Mr Janneh's?'

'Thank you, Ma,' they say in unison, quickly folding their books closed, standing up and coming over to me in case I might change my mind and decide more homework is needed. I love my children equally but in that moment, as they both give me a brief hug simultaneously, I squeeze Isatou a little tighter and kiss her on the top of her head, feeling the lines of her plaits under my lips.

After they're gone, I collapse into the dining-room chair and push my hand into my mouth to silence the scream that threatens to escape. In its place, tears wet my cheeks. Although I am alone, I quickly wipe my face with my sleeves because I can't risk the girls returning for something and finding me like this. And not that Mamamuso is likely to come into my home, especially without Sarko around, but my moment of vulnerability worries me. If she sees me as anything other than stoic then she'll use it as leverage.

My mind is spinning. I've got to think straight, but my emotions are making my thoughts numb. The *Ngansimba* is coming to town, but she's not here yet. I've got time to find out what Mamamuso meant. Sarko can speak with her; he can remind her that she is living in his compound. She'll respect him, even if she doesn't see me as anything more than an annoying fly. I dismiss the fact that as a man Sarko shouldn't have that kind of conversation with his mother – our daughter's life is at risk.

Chapter 9

Binta

The walk to the beach takes us through a meandering path into the forest. It takes longer this way, but the trees offer welcome shade from the incessant heat beating down from the sun. It's peaceful, unlike the main road from the town where local bush taxis seem to try to run people over, whichever side of the road you stand. By bush taxi it doesn't take long from outside the mosque to arrive at the entrance of the smoke houses drying out the fresh fish right on the beachfront, but we'd rather spend our dalasi on other things, like Cokes and the cinema. This way takes about an hour to walk, which I know because Isatou timed us last month when she first had her new watch; the forest path disappears under the deepening sand until it becomes part of the beach.

Jena is the first to run toward the sea, shouting over her shoulder for us both to join her. As I reach the surf, she's ready to flick seawater at me with her feet, spraying it up so that I can taste the salt on my lips as the drops fall. Just at the moment when a wave breaks over her knees I attempt to push her into the sea, which wouldn't have worked if Isatou hadn't come to help and we get her down, right in time for the next wave to crash over her. Isatou and I fall into the sea laughing hysterically, the ocean pushing around my arms and legs, drawing me powerfully back towards the beach.

'My watch!' Isatou cries out, the realisation immediately dawning. She jumps out of the water, sprints back to the shore and unstraps it quickly from her wrist as she goes.

'Is it still working?' I ask, splashing through the water towards her, but already from the look on her face I can see it isn't. As I look past Isatou and eye the trees, I have an idea, although I'm not that sure it will work.

'Lie it out on this – the sun might dry it out,' I direct her as I drag a large palm leaf to her and Jena joins us.

'Do you think it will work?' Isatou asks hopefully, handing me her watch.

'It's worth a try.'

We sit together in quiet empathy and stare at the precious watch laid in the centre of the leaf; it feels like forever – and ironically if the watch was working we could see how long we've been waiting – willing it to work again.

'I'm sorry, Isatou, it doesn't look like it's going to happen,' I say, stating the obvious. Isatou looks as though she might cry. She wraps her arms around her knees, hides her face and mutters, 'Pa got it for me.'

'Will he be cross?' I ask, mentally putting myself in her situation. I'd dread to think how my father would react – not that he would buy me a watch in the first place.

Isatou unbends her legs and stretches them so that her feet make identical lines in the sand, and she puts her arms behind her to support her weight as she leans back. 'No, probably not cross – more sad than anything.' She wipes her eyes with the back of her hand. 'He got it for me for my exams at the end of term – he said I could use it to do well, to make sure I answer all the questions in time.'

I'm struck by how different our families are; I doubt my father knows that I have exams coming up and I can't imagine he would think about helping me do well in them. I wish my father were like Isatou's.

High in the sky over to where the fishing village is, the dark shape of a vulture circles before descending. I watch it for some time, the way it soars, how its wings keep it suspended in the air. Imagine being so high above the earth, being able to see far in the distance, to go anywhere. Sometimes in my dreams I fly. It's not like the birds – it's more clumsy and with effort – but I really do fly. I've never told anyone that.

'I'm thirsty,' I say, in an attempt to distract Isatou from the despair of her watch. 'Do you think we could find water at the fishing village?' I point in the direction where the vulture was, no longer in the air.

'Yeah, there'll be water there,' Isatou answers slowly; easing herself up off the sand, she picks up her watch and wistfully reattaches it to her wrist.

The repugnant smell of discarded fish parts is strong all along this part of the beach. This is where the bush taxi arrives once an hour, right past the fish-smoke houses. On a bad day, the smell drifts as far as the tourist lodge the far side of the beach heading south to the next town.

We weave our way between people, through the various production lines going on before us on the beach; there are pairs of women collecting fish in large plastic containers holding a handle each, then there are other groups descaling and gutting fish. I guess you could also include the vultures too, who come and clean up the discarded bits. I hold my nose to block the stench; we head over the other side of the only road to where there are several long concrete buildings. The large concrete blocks make up a patterned wall that hints at what's inside; white smoke drifts out into the open towards the sky above.

'We can ask for some water in there,' Isatou says. 'I've also got a couple of dalasi on me. Want to get a fish?'

Inside the concrete building the dull hazy light permits only enough light to see the brick ovens running the length of the wall where fish are crammed on racks being smoked and those already prepared are hung high from the ceiling.

With our thirst quenched and a couple of smoked fish in our possession we meander through the fish sellers and turn south on the beach. Isatou picks at the dried skin of the fish, handing us both some meat as we walk towards a few large boulders of rocks that are set into the sand where the shoreline curves dramatically.

The boulders are smooth and worth the effort required to climb up onto them. I claim one, lying down along the length of it. The warmth is pleasant underneath me from where the sun has baked the stone since morning.

'You'll get too hot there,' Isatou points out.

'I'm only going to lie here for a minute,' I tell her, but I don't explain how I love the smoothness of the rock under my hand, the way it's shaped and how connected I feel with this place. I've come here since I was little and the rocks are different to the transient sand that only visits these shores. To the rocks it's me that is passing by, a mere few years against their ancient age.

'I'm going in the water,' Jena says, untying the material around her waist. She folds it and places it near my feet, standing there in just her T-shirt and underwear.

'What if someone sees you?' I ask, looking around.

'They won't,' she says, and runs into the water, laughing.

I lie back down on the rock and rest my head on my hand and watch Isatou clamber across the smaller bounders to my side. Every few moments she stops and bends over a pool to look at the array of creatures that have been caught up in the retreating tide. After watching her for a while I sit up and try to decide whether to join Jena in the sea – she's there jumping over the rhythmic waves, absorbed in her own game – or if I should join Isatou to see if she has found anything interesting.

It's while I'm watching her that out of the corner of my eye I become aware of a couple of other figures: two teenage boys. They aren't that far away, but for clarity, I need to squint to focus, which is when I recognise one of them. Standing in the shallow water, droplets glisten against Yaya's skin like diamonds shimmering, and I'm enticed to stare. For a moment I gaze at him and watch how his muscles curve underneath his skin; I notice his shoulders, his broad chest narrow towards his abdomen, and how the shape changes to reveal other muscles in different places as he moves.

'Are you coming in?' Jena shouts to me. Heat immediately rises in my face and I quickly jump to my feet, leap carefully from the boulder onto the cushioning sand and sprint into the sea, hoping she hasn't noticed what I was doing.

The waves are powerful. One second the gentle push around my knees, the next the force of water over my shoulders, salt over my face. I'm not sure if it's the sea that is intoxicating, each wave almost hypnotic with the sound of the water crashing onto the beach and then retracting back in itself, or the image of Yaya still playing in my head.

'It's getting late,' Isatou says, appearing at the shoreline and pointing at the sky. 'The sun won't be long going down.'

'Imagine what it would be like here, seeing the sunset!' I say, but I know that it is something I won't get to see for a long time yet on account that Ma doesn't allow me to be out late far from town. 'Just a couple of more minutes.'

'I guess she's right – we better go soon,' Jena agrees.

Before I can argue there is a searing pain across my thigh that makes me lose my footing and I fall into a wave. The intensity takes my breath away, causing me to swallow a mouthful of salty sea and another wave washes over my buckled body. I let out a long scream, as though trying to push the pain away, but it stays.

'Binta, this way!' Jena screams. 'There's jellyfish!'

I look around, desperate to move away. 'Where? I can't see them!' I shout, panicking, and another wave unexpectedly fills my mouth, causing me to splutter.

'Walk straight towards me!' Jena shouts. Coming to meet me she puts her arm around my waist. I have to lean all my weight on her because my leg is numb with burning pain and she guides me to the shore where I collapse.

'What happened?' Isatou asks, running towards us.

'Jellyfish.'

I'm trying not to cry; I grit my teeth together in an attempt to wrestle the pain. If I move my knee the burning increases and I almost expect to see flames coming from my skin.

'I've got an idea.' Isatou grabs me under my arms and drags me up the beach towards where the sand is at its hottest from the day's heat and starts to bury my leg.

'What are you doing? This isn't time to mess around!' Jena says.

'The hot sand will help the pain. I saw Ma do it once for a little girl a long time ago when we came here. Grab some sand too – the hotter, the better. It will help stop the poison.'

At the point when I am no longer fighting the pain I look at Isatou and say, 'Thank you. I'm so glad you knew what to do.'

'You know, Isatou wants to be a doctor,' Jena tells me.

'Really?' I try to move my knee. The pain now lessens. Then I look at Isatou and try to figure out how serious she is. 'But can girls be doctors?'

'Ma's always told us we can do anything,' Isatou says, as she removes the old sand and replaces it with hotter grains. 'My parents want us both to go to secondary school in Serekunda next year. Perhaps one of the international schools; that's if Pa gets a better teaching position.' She pats the hot sand down and pushes the heat to my skin, easing the pain.

I watch Isatou, confident in what she's doing; her words seem to press down on me as much as the warm sand on my skin.

'Can girls really do that?' I ask while I clutch at my throbbing stung leg.

Isatou looks to me, her eyes bright, and she smiles. 'Of course!' she says, and she helps me to stand.

With each of my friends holding me up under the arms, for the first time I properly consider that this time next year they will be heading to secondary school and we will no longer be together. As it is, Isatou should have gone last year. If it wasn't for her having malaria and needing to repeat the year, she would have already left. At least we've had another year together, but in this moment there is a throbbing in my chest that has nothing to do with a jellyfish; just the understanding that we are on the crest of change, which I don't want to happen.

I glance quickly back to the rock and envy it, never changing.

Chapter 10

Yari

He spoke to her – I somehow managed to convince him. They didn't speak for long: I know because I was peering around the corner of the yard, watching their body language in the absence of words that I could hear.

'She understands your views,' he said later in the evening.

'And yours.'

'Yes, and mine.'

I sighed, not knowing how much he had emphasised that they were his views as well, and not just mine: the daughter-in-law she can't stand. 'What did your mother say?'

'You know what she's like – her views are stuck in the past. She doesn't understand the new ways of doing things, and there's no reasoning with her.'

Which is why you didn't try, I wanted to say, but instead I bit my lip to keep the words away.

'But she does know you're against it too?' I said desperately. 'She only listens to you.'

'Yes, Yari. Don't worry. She understands.' There was frustration in his voice.

I can see that he's caught in this difficult position between his wife and mother – I truly can – but this only fuels my own frustration. After all, this is about *our* daughter. I have to trust now that he's said the right things…said enough to keep her from our business.

'She was only saying what she thought – there's no possibility that she'll do anything without our say.'

'You sure?' I asked, moving towards him, allowing him to wrap his arms around me to confirm it was true.

'Yes. She's under our home; she has to listen to my views – even if they don't make sense to her. Isn't that what we've always said to her? She's wanted this for years and we've always told her no, haven't we?'

I nodded and agreed, though deep inside I felt more unsettled than ever: that because we've gone against what Mamamuso wanted for so long, it makes her more determined … more dangerous.

I've felt anxious over the last few days, but Mamamuso hasn't said anything further after Sarko spoke with her, and now a week on the worry has began to subside – until a moment ago.

The noise of the market around me suddenly silences as my ears immediately pick up snippets of a quiet conversation to the side of me. I turn my head and my eyes fix on the words forming on Fanta Jammeh's mouth as she speaks to the woman beside her. She nods and repeats the phrase and although the words are hushed between them, it is as though the words are being shouted because of the weight of what they mean. It makes me want to scream the way they tear me inside: 'The *Ngansimba* is in town. She's here.'

All the way home my heart races and a new wave of anxiety comes over me. When I arrive home, Mamamuso is there, sitting under the shade of the tree in the middle of the yard. She looks up and definitely sees me, but she doesn't bother to get up and bombard me with her views again, which is what I'm expecting. I close the door behind me and lean against it, wanting to close everything out, wishing we didn't live in this town with the petty gossip, the talk that drags your reputation for everyone to comment on. Days like today I long to be back in Serekunda: Sarko and me doing things independently from small-minded neighbours.

I take a deep breath and assure myself that Mamamuso has taken on what Sarko said. She's still not bothering me about taking Isatou to the *Ngansimba* for her to do her worst. Like the *Ngansimba* did to me. It was a different *Ngansimba*, but the results will be the same if she gets her hands on Isatou. With the memories that I try to forget comes a pain that sears into my mind that will never leave – and a fear that is always there in the quietest of dreams.

I become aware of the time. The girls will be coming in from school in a moment, which makes me head away from the door and into the kitchen. I need to take my mind off this. The onions don't need cutting yet, but I grab one and peel off the first layer of skin, take a knife and chop it in half and half again, then dice until my eyes cloud over. The sting in my eyes is actually welcome, the tears flow easily, the reason hidden by the squares of white vegetable.

'Look, Ma – my test paper.' Jena suddenly appears behind me, her happy voice filling the room. 'I got eighty-three per cent.'

'I didn't hear you come in,' I say, picking up a cloth and dabbing my eyes as I turn around. 'That's wonderful, Jena. Aren't you clever?' I push the worrying thoughts from my mind. It's just the kind of news I need to lift my mood and I hug her close, smiling in contrast to what I've been feeling since I came home.

'Ah, Ma,' she says laughing, 'you smell of onions!'

'Sorry.' I smile and release her from my embrace.

'Can I go and buy that little bracelet I saw in the market before the stalls pack up for the day?'

'With results like this, I should think so, but remember to be back to finish any more work you have. Don't get complacent. And don't be too long; your father is coming home early tonight.'

'Okay.'

For some time after Jena leaves my mood has lifted. The joy you see in your child's eyes is one of those moments that makes the difficulties of parenting worth every second. I hum to myself, tidying up the house, preoccupied with Jena's good news when I suddenly realise the time. It occurs to me that Isatou should be home and stop humming. The silence that seems to immediately fill the room leaves me uneasy; a tingling moves up through my arms and my chest tightens for a second, as a pang of dread rises in me. Jena left some time ago to go to the market and they are usually only moments apart when they arrive home. The train of thought – that Jena went to the market – seems to bring an antidote to the worry as quickly as it came. Isatou probably saw Jena on the way to the market and went with her. The thought draws me back to my humming and tidying up and I don't think anymore about where she is.

Until much later: too late.

Chapter 11

Binta

Ma calls for me. I edge over to the entrance of the cooking hut where I find her bent over the charcoal fire, stirring a stew in a large pot blackened by years of use. Smoke fills the place, making my eyes water. She eases upright, wipes her brow, looks over and smiles at me. Even on a good day, the dark, hot, smoky cooking hut is uncomfortable, but Ma seems to be finding it harder because of her conspicuously growing stomach. It makes me wonder if she's pregnant again.

'I need some yam and sweet potato,' she says, producing a note from within the folds of her *fanu* – a type of skirt made from one piece of material. She hands over the money and tells me that if I negotiate well in the market, I can keep a couple of dalasi. From the smell drifting from the pot, I can tell it's her speciality: the one with all the chillies. Inside the darkness, a cough breaks through the haze and, from the corner of the hut, out from the shadows, my little brother appears and Ma glances across.

'Take him too, Binta – he's getting in my way toddling around. If we're not careful, we'll end up with Lamin stew!'

I join with Ma laughing, amused at her own joke. Lamin's standing there, naked as always, looking up at me with his arms hanging limply beside his enlarged stomach where a small juju is tied around with a string. I wear mine around my neck. The tiny leather square amulet protects me from evil powers, especially at night when they are at their strongest. Everyone knows about the dark evil that roams at night. That's why I never take mine off, because the spirits bring nightmares and worse.

Lamin's staring at me, but all I see when I look at his face are flies buzzing around his nose where the two lines of snot reach his upper lip. I lift him up, put him onto my back and tie him with a long strip of cloth like Ma taught me to do. When he was very young I worried about dropping him, but now I am as quick as any woman; picking him up by one arm, swinging him behind me to balance him on my back before attaching him quickly into place with the cloth. His feet stick out either side of my waist when I tie him on – it's much too tempting – I tickle his stubby toes until I think he might fall off my back because he's squirming madly.

Before I head towards the market, I quickly go into Ma's room where there is a large earthen jar in the corner and I remove the lid. Using the plastic cup that belongs on the lid, I scoop up the water from inside. Most of the grit has settled to the bottom of the jar, but the dusty flecks remain and I flick away a dead fly before drinking it. I adjust Lamin on my back and replace the lid to the water jar, determined I'll drive a good bargain for Ma's groceries at the market. I can almost taste the cold, sweet Coke on my lips from Mr Janneh's shop.

Chapter 12

Yari

'It's pretty, isn't it? What do you think? Do you like it?' Jena asks expectantly. She bounds towards me through the front door and holds her wrist for me to examine the small shells that dangle daintily from her new bracelet. But it's not her jewellery that my eyes settle on, but the empty space behind her where I had anticipated Isatou joining her.

'Where's your sister?'

Jena shrugs. 'I don't know.'

'Didn't she bump into you on your way to the market?'

'No.'

'You've not seen her?'

'No.' Jena shakes her head slowly, noticing the creeping worry across my face.

'Do you know if she went home from school with anyone?'

'I've not seen her since the lesson before last. I went to help Mrs Darbo in the garden with some of the others.'

Although there's a series of likely explanations – she's seen a friend, perhaps stopped off outside Mr Janneh's shop and Jena didn't see her, or did an errand for an elder on the way home – the fact that my heart is pounding with increasing ferocity triggers the fear that has been surfacing since Mamamuso confronted me last week. There is a ball of terrifying energy that pulsates up through my stomach, which makes me feel giddy and numbs my thoughts so much I can no longer think logically. The only words I hear echoing in my head are '*Isatou has gone*'.

Somehow I find myself storming down the steps to the yard and across to where Mamamuso is sat on an old wooden chair outside of her room on the other side of the compound. The way I'm pacing towards her, focused on where she is, my eyes narrowed and fixed, alerts her to the battle that's about to commence and she stands quicker than she normally manages. She's hardly out of her seat when I scream, 'Where is she? Tell me now! Where?'

For the first time since I've known her there is a slight look of bewilderment on her face, not at what I'm asking, but the absolute unwavering demand with which I approach. In all these years, despite our disagreements, our open awkwardness, I have still shown her the respect of an elder. But not now. There is no respect due and she is going to have to answer without the unequal authority she's been used to.

'Answer me!'

'You are too late,' she says in a voice that is half the volume of mine, not in defiance, just matter of fact.

'Where have you taken her?'

'You know.'

'Where?'

'She was taken to the *Ngansimba* after she came from school. They've been gone a couple of hours already. I don't know where exactly they were heading.'

'You had no right,' I say my finger close to her face and tears prickle behind my eyes, but I'm determined that she will not see them fall.

Inside I am crumbling, but until I am alone I will not collapse.

Chapter 13

Yari

Mamamuso's words ring in my head as I find myself sitting on the edge of my bed, bent over with my hands over my ears trying to force that sentence away. Isatou's gone and I'm too late.

The tears run down my face and I grip my stomach to dispel the nausea that is rising. It can't be too late. I've got to find her. I quickly head from the room, past Jena who looks up questionably from a book as I rush past, down the steps onto the yard and out onto the street.

My heart is pounding; my head is numb. I have no idea where to go but allow my feet to aimlessly guide me. After circling the town a couple of times I cross the market place and head near the fields. The initial energy that surged through me to walk in every direction is settling and I sit on an upturned log by the side of the path. Where can I go? Where is she? The air has changed, the intense heat of the afternoon dipping, which is what first makes me aware of the time. There's not much longer before the early evening sun disappears, giving way to night. As though reading my thoughts, once decided the sun quickly dips into the horizon. The realisation suddenly motivates me to rise; I brush the dust off my skirt from the log and walk again. Somewhere. Anywhere.

This time I make my way along the path near the school. Deep down, I know there is little chance of finding clues, but it seems the first place to try and as I make my way there I hold onto the shred of hope it gives me – using it like a knife to cut away the building fear.

The schoolyard is silent but I strain my ears to hear the secrets it might reveal. When they took Isatou, did the older women entice her: tell her to come somewhere with her, perhaps say I sent her? With that thought my hand flies to my mouth and I let out a small gasp. What if Isatou thinks I'm responsible?

I turn and start to leave the schoolyard, but then I notice something blue dangling from the makeshift fence to the side. I didn't really think I'd find anything, but I lift my hand to the piece of material that is obviously torn from a uniform – a pinafore dress – and handle it carefully as though it is treasure. It could be anyone's. How many children rush past here when the bell rings at the end of the day? In the distance I can hear the Imam's call to pray, birds rise squawking in response from the trees, their shapes emphasised against the orange glow of the dimming sun.

My eyes drift to the ground and I notice the wide circular shapes in the dust where it looks like it was pushed under foot and there are footprints on top of footprints. In the same moment I picture what has happened – Isatou was taken in a struggle – I also feel the weight leave from thinking that Isatou had been told I had sent them. There is no question in my mind now what has happened; the marks in the dust seem to graduate around the back of the school and into where the bush thickens, leading to where the trees mark the start of the forest. Time is against me, crickets are increasingly noisy in their evening call as I push against the long grass and the orange sky is now glowing red. It doesn't take many minutes to reach the edge of the forest. The shadows from the branches above dramatically reduce the dusk light, adding to the sense of foreboding I have, glancing before me into the forest. It's already too dim to make out any patterns in the dust that might give me the way forward, but I still bend low, touching the grit between my fingers willing the ground to speak to me.

For a second I look back over my shoulder and up to the last uncovered fraction of burning sky and then back to the darkening forest. I have to try. I have to find her and I walk forward, desperately shouting my daughter's name – not because I think she'll answer, but because it settles my nerves and I don't feel alone in the place where spirits congregate in the night.

Chapter 14

Yari

I'm not sure how long I've been gone. I don't know how long I walked in the darkness – tripping on branches, bumping into trees – but the moon now fully illuminates the road home.

I pass through the entrance of the compound and notice the residual fragrance from the white flowers that hang over the gate. The kerosene lamp from inside the house brightens the veranda – a welcoming glow – and for a moment I will myself to imagine Isatou there waiting: safe.

But as I open the door, it's Sarko's and Jena's concerned looks that greet me.

'What's happened?' Sarko asks, his eyes glancing the length of my body where my skirt is dirty and ripped in parts, then he takes my hands turning them palms up and back over, examining the cuts.

'Is Isatou with you?' The worry shrouds each of Jena's words and I take my eyes from her to look at Sarko and shake my head.

'Jena, you need to go to bed. I have to speak to your father.' She immediately complies and doesn't ask questions. The atmosphere that arrived with me is tangible and she must be aware of something very wrong, something out of the ordinary is happening, and she quietly retreats to the back of the house.

I wait for a moment longer before I allow myself to fall into Sarko's arms and I sob, making the shoulder of his white shirt wet. With his arms around me I take a moment to regain my emotional strength, the words I have to tell him will make it all so real and I want it to stay a figment of unreality for just a breath longer.

'The *Ngansimba*'s taken Isatou.'

'What?'

'She's gone, Sarko. She's gone.' Then I unpeel myself from his arms as a sudden awareness clears my thoughts. 'I told you this would happen. Your mother orchestrated it all. Mamamuso. I told you, Sarko.'

He lets me vent at him, the words coming easily – thoughts I didn't know were there but they must have been simmering away for them to be spilling quickly like this. He sits on the edge of the wooden dining table, his shoulders bent and his hand covering his eyes in a futile attempt to block it out. But the truth is there.

'I can't believe she did that, to go against what I said!' he mutters angrily and bangs his fist on the table, knocking a spoon off, which clangs onto the floor. A quiet settles in the room, our fears seeming to fill the air.

'I'm sorry, Yari. I'm sorry,' he begins, edging tentatively towards me, and puts his arms around me. Initially my body tenses in anger that he didn't stop this, but the longer he holds me the more my muscles relax and I allow him to comfort me. I place my head on his chest and hear the quick pulsing beat of his heart, my eyes wet with fresh tears.

'I don't know where to look. I tried the forest, but it got too dark. Sarko, time's running out.' I feel my resolve dissolving as I speak my worst fear; my lips press against the cotton of his shirt. 'I don't think we are going to find her before it happens.'

I close my eyes and focus on the strength I feel being in his arms. He kisses the top of my head gently and whispers, 'I'm sorry, Yari.'

His words don't seem to reach me and the only reason I'm still standing is because he has me in his arms.

Chapter 15

Binta

A short time later, I quickly pass through the stalls swinging a blue plastic bag with Ma's groceries in one hand, fiddling with the coins in the other and hurry across the market. A motorbike swerves past me, throwing up dust while their passenger holds a chicken from flying away with a string attached to the bird's feet. As I look up towards the shop I see Jena with her head low resting on her bent knees. From the way she's sat I know she's upset but I can't run to her because of the three goats that idly walk across my path. They come up to my waist and I have to lift the grocery bag up to zigzag between them until I'm next to the uneven concrete steps, then I run up them to Jena and sit next to her.

'Hey! What's wrong?'

She raises her head slowly, blinking at the bright sunlight. Jena's eyes are swollen where she's been sobbing; she wipes her eyes with the back of her hand and smudges the two perfect lines of wet that have run down her cheeks.

'It's Isatou.'

The noise of the market suddenly diminishes and my heart begins to race as I imagine what terrible thing might have happened.

'She's gone!' Jena cries.

For a moment the action of the market seems to still, the noise of the bush-taxi engines disappears, the boys chasing each other down the road silences.

'What do you mean, Isatou's gone?' I ask and put an arm around Jena's slumped shoulders.

'She hasn't been home for the past two days. She's never been away before – not without Ma.'

'Have you asked your mother where she is?'

'Of course!' Jena wipes her face with the sleeve of her white T-shirt, leaving a mark.

'What did she say?'

Jena shrugs and looks towards the boys that are running around, narrowly avoiding the newly arrived bush taxi. 'She told me not to worry, but didn't say anything more – she's not herself. I know something isn't right, Binta. Why would Ma not tell me where she is?'

I mull over the information and begin to wonder if Isatou has been sent to a new school already, one of the ones in the city – one of the good schools, like the ones she told us about when we went to the beach. Although she's in our year, she's bright and she should be a year ahead already, but I can't see why Yari wouldn't tell Jena if that was the case.

Malik, my cousin, stays with us during term-time because the journey would be too far each day for him. 'Do you think Isatou has gone to stay with a relative of yours to go to school?'

'No.' Jena shakes her head. 'Ma would have told me, wouldn't she?'

I nod my response. Yari wouldn't have any reason to keep that kind of information from Jena. But what other reason could there be? Being at school out of town is the most logical explanation. I remember the coins in my hand and immediately I have two plans. One to cheer Jena up, if only slightly; the second is to get information.

'Wait here a minute.'

I adjust a now-sleeping Lamin on my back as I stand, turn and walk up the uneven steps to the shop and greet Mr Janneh who is leaning on the counter.

'Malikum Salam.' He beams back.

He has constant smile lines around his eyes, which crease often and easy – as I say, I can tell a lot just from somebody's eyes. The way he smiles gives him a youthful look, but from the wrinkles in his face and his receding hair I know he's old. Not as old as my grandmother, but still old – older than my father.

'The usual?' He smiles, the creases join together on his face. He opens the fridge – the door is slightly stiff, which causes a brief clinking of bottles inside and he reaches for a Coke. In the background the generator whirs away in the shop's storeroom. It is working today. It doesn't always, but today I watch Mr Janneh's hand on the cold bottle anticipating the cold sweet taste.

'Your last year of Middle School, isn't it – back to school soon?' he asks and hands me the drink.

'I don't know. My father hasn't decided yet.' I shrug, giving him my dalasi coins.

He briefly frowns and then asks, 'What's your favourite subject, Binta?'

I put the ice-cold bottle to my lips and consider his question, holding the fizziness in my cheeks before swallowing and then answer honestly. 'I find them all a bit hard. They are all in English.'

Normally I might be evasive, embellish how good I am at school but Mr Janneh puts me at ease making it easy to be open. I don't know why. And I don't regret it afterwards either; which is often what happens with other adults when I wish the words could come back into my mouth the instant they leave. But Mr Janneh is different. When I say that I find English hard, he chuckles, not teasingly, but in a way that makes me think he understands.

'Don't worry. You're clever – like your mother. How is she?' He's known her for ages, since she was a girl. 'How many children does she have now?'

'Four.' I half turn and motion to Lamin sleeping snuggly on my back. There's Musa, my younger brother by a couple of years, whom I avoid as much as possible. He's not amicable and entertains himself by throwing stones at little lizards as they dart up trees. They usually dart fast enough to avoid his aim, but sometimes he's spot on and they drop to the ground, dead. But mostly he spends his time thinking of ways to get me into trouble. I sometimes picture him as the lizard running up the tree and me throwing stones at him instead. See how he'd like it.

Loli is my little sister, but I don't see her much. Aunt Loli, my sister's namesake, adopted her when she was still small: one of our Mandinka customs. Aunt Loli didn't have children of her own, and after Loli was weaned she went to live with her. Sometimes Loli visits, but I wished she lived with us because I've got to tolerate my brothers instead. That's why I envy Jena and Isatou – how amazing it would be to have a friend who is also your sister.

I'm certain Ma is going to have another baby soon, but I can't ask her about it; or anyone else for that matter. To speak about an unborn baby brings a curse and I don't want to chance being the one that causes a death. Witches are always listening. Last time when Ma lost a baby I tried to figure out who'd been responsible. It was frightening, thinking how evil spirits had been around our compound at night – Ma told me she thought it might have been her co-wife. Ma believes my father's other wife is cursed because she doesn't have children herself, even though she's even older than Ma. I think she's okay, but I keep opinions like that to myself.

'I remember your mother – about the same age as you.' Mr Janneh smiles.

I don't actually know how old my mother is; if it wasn't for Yari telling me that I was born thirteen years ago, when Isatou was just walking and she was heavily pregnant with Jena, I wouldn't even know how old I was for sure. When I asked my Ma which month I was born, she just told me it was during the dry season. Later I realised that she didn't know the months of the year. Musa knows how old he is because my father took the time to register his birth – unlike mine.

'It just seems like yesterday. Your mother was clever, like you Binta,' Mr Janneh says. At his compliment my cheeks feel hot, but I don't think he notices.

'Your mother would have done well with education – with your opportunities. But then, of course, she was married off to your father instead.'

I sip on my Coke, not sure how to respond and taken aback by the way Mr Janneh describes Ma. In my mind, she's always been married. Always been a mother. Mr Janneh looks towards me and I wonder what he is thinking for a moment as he puts his head to one side and looks to the floor. Then he looks up with a smile and says, 'I'll talk with your father. Leave it with me, Binta. See if he will let you continue school.'

'Thank you!' I reply happily and immediately turn to tell Jena the news. That's when I remember the second part of my plan and stop to face him again.

'Mr Janneh, what schools are there in Serekunda?'

'Well—' he pauses, leaning back on his counter '—there are many schools: some state ones, quite a few private ones, a handful of international ones.'

I try to hide my disappointment: I thought there would only be one or two, like here in Kenji.

'Why do you ask?'

'As you say, it's my last year. Maybe my father will decide not just to let me finish middle school, but to go onto secondary as well!' I say, half lying, half hoping that might actually happen.

Mr Janneh laughs. 'Good for you, Binta, that's the attitude to have! Anyway, let me speak to your father first about just this year. A step at a time, hey?'

I settle next to Jena and offer her the Coke, which achieves my first aim – the tears have stopped and she smiles a little. 'Do you know what? The more I think about it, the more I reckon Isatou could already be starting secondary school and it would be in Serekunda, wouldn't it?'

'Do you think so? I guess it could be. Ma loves Serekunda, the urban life and all. I can't remember much of when we lived there; I was only little when we left. Did you know my dad had a job in an international school lined up, but then my grandfather died and they ended up having to come to Kenji.'

'Didn't your ma also teach there before you were born – I remember she told me?'

'Yes.'

'Do you know which one?'

'Why?'

'Just wondered.'

Jena's brow creases as she thinks. 'I can't remember. I just know it was near the beach somewhere.'

'Hey, don't drink all my Coke!' I tease and put my arm around Jena. 'Don't worry, we'll look for Isatou. We'll find her.' I wish I were more certain and that I had more to go on apart from the smallest threads of a clue. She could be in Serekunda at school, but that clue almost seems pointless when I've never travelled there by myself and cannot hope to prove it.

Chapter 16

Binta

Steam rises from the small pot that I carry over to where Grandmother sits on the concrete veranda, legs out with her ankles crossed. When my grandmother sees me approach, her lips wrap around her toothless gums: a smile without teeth.

'I've brought you some food,' I say and settle down next to her. I've got to be careful taking out the bones from the fish, because I don't want her to struggle with eating and I especially don't want it to be me that ends up choking her accidentally. I mash the fish on the side of the bowl and mix it with the rice and then blow some of the steam away. Then I put it carefully to her lips. She mushes it a bit more against her gums before swallowing.

'Do you like it?' I ask loudly, on account of her deafness. Grandmother nods and with effort puts her wrinkled hand on my arm. Her skin feels fragile when I put my hand on top of hers. Everything about her body seems to be failing, which makes me think of how old she's getting. Sometimes, from nowhere, a terrifying thought crops into my mind about how she's not always going to be around, which makes me hold her hand longer – until I can discard the thought again.

I stay with Grandmother until I hear Ma calling me over for another chore. Ma is always too busy to sit together like this. Slowly I unwrap my fingers from Grandmother's, disappointed I have to leave.

'Your father's work shirts are ready to collect from your auntie.'

'Can't it wait until tomorrow, Ma?' I say watching her un-shell groundnuts into a small pile, not expecting her to agree.

'Don't be lazy!' she says and half-heartedly throws one of the shells at me, chuckling. I don't feel like reciprocating the humour. 'Anyway, it won't take long,' she adds.

Not that it makes me feel any better, but she's right. Soon I'm on my way back home with a full basket of clean clothes balanced skilfully on my head, my hands relaxed at my side. The first hint of trouble comes at the sound of a rock hitting the ground. Another comes, barely missing my feet.

'Hey!' I turn around awkwardly and try to keep my neck straight, though I have to put a hand up towards the basket. I catch Musa's head disappearing behind a wall.

'Stop it!' I shout and turn back around. I curse him under my breath with every bad word I can think to call him that I've learnt listening to how the elders scorn us over the years. When I feel satisfied I've reprimanded him enough I resume my walk home. Certain the basket is properly balanced, I remove my hand, but then in an instant it tumbles from my head, too quick for me to realise Musa's rock has hit it off; a bigger target than the moving lizards he usually aims for. I scream at him and bend down pick to pick up a stone to throw it madly in his direction, although he's sprinted far enough away to avoid it.

'MUSA! You idiot! You baboon! Look what you've done!' My father's white shirts are strewn across the path and a panic rises inside as I pick up the first. Red dust – that's not good. I feel dizzy with worry and I frantically try and rub it off, but it only serves to rub in the dusty stain and it stands out even more against the cotton. While I pick up the other shirts I try to think of excuses, of a plan to get me out of this mess, but a growing anxiety hampers any inspiration. I should blame Musa, but I know from experience that's not going to get me far. Perhaps I'll say I tripped? As soon as the excuses come, I imagine my father's face. He's only going to be concerned with the state of his shirts and he won't care how they got ruined. Once all the clothes are back in the basket I head home quickly – at this time of day my father won't be home – and hope it'll give me some time to think how to get out of trouble.

I step up slowly onto the veranda and take a deep breath before pushing the door open. Ma isn't around, nobody is inside; I sigh in relief. Before anyone comes in, I dash across to Ma's bedroom and place the basket in the darkest corner and for good measure, I take a piece of material from the bed and place it over the laundry. I need time to figure out a plan. At least I've got until evening to come up with something and I make my way quickly out of the house. I need to find Ma; if anyone can talk my father around, it's her.

It's a long way from the city on the bush taxi and sometimes my father doesn't even bother coming home at all, but when he does he usually arrives after dark when the other men have come back from the mosque. Things are not going well today and I begin to wonder if there's some kind of curse on me, because tonight he arrives before evening prayers. I see him walking across the compound, stopping to greet my uncles, sharing some story from his day before he enters the house. I wish I'd had time to find Ma, but now it's too late and my heart begins to beat quickly. When I get my hands on Musa he is going to be sorry.

For a second when my father goes into the house I look around the compound for Ma to help me, but before I can find her I hear him shout my name from inside and I know I'm done for. He's found the shirts. I'm in big trouble. He's calling me to come and I know to disobey will make things worse, but I can't bring myself to walk to him and instead I turn to where I've just spotted Ma, my widening eyes begging her to rescue me.

I sense the rush of angry footsteps behind me. He grabs my hair, spins me around and hits me across the face. A sting erupts from my cheek and with the next one I scream before I land on the floor in front of his feet in the dust. I draw my knees up in an attempt to dampen another blow.

'Stop! Enough, Ousman!' Ma screams as she rushes towards us.

'Don't tell me to stop, woman!' he shouts back. The beating stops, but I still cower just in case he changes his mind and resumes hitting me again.

'It's your fault she's like this. What kind of wife are you raising? At this rate I won't be able to get a decent dowry, I'll be paying someone to take her off my hands!' For a moment I think he's going to hit Ma as well. There is a ringing in my ears where he hit my head, but I clearly hear him say to her as he pushes past, 'Sort her out.'

It is difficult to tell if the warm liquid on my face is tears or blood and I'm too angry and confused by what my father has said. Ma helps me sit up and I look straight into her eyes for an answer. 'What did he mean? It wasn't me, Ma, it was Musa.'

'I know,' she replies and holds me close to her chest.

Ma's arms wrap around me and I bury my face into her and try to stop my tears from coming.

Chapter 17

Amie

It must be the stress of this afternoon that has tired me like this. My back and pelvis ache, my feet are hot and swollen in competition with my growing abdomen. Ousman's words add a layer to the uneasy thoughts that have already settled in my mind since *Tobaski*. Since my *Kafo* began to question me again about Binta's future. Until now I have managed to set the question aside, avoid the inevitable. But Ousman has never reacted like this – he has never broached the subject before.

I sit heavily on the bed; massaging my stomach at an attempt it will also soothe the worry that's filling me. As though in a timely response I feel a push under my palm at my hand. At its movement I'm reminded of the joy that will soon come: another precious child in my arms. My thoughts drift and I have to consciously set aside the knowledge of what comes before that joyful moment: hours of agonising labour. All those years ago I was taught it was the third pain a woman must bear in her life. The final necessary pain that we embrace, being a woman. In all of the things we go through there is a power that men are not aware of. That secret is passed throughout the generations. Generations that we give birth and life to.

My thoughts focus again on Binta. I am now used to the pain that brings unspeakable joy. Maybe not used to it – I'm sure the sixth time around will be no different – but experience has taught me that I will overcome the long hours ahead and reap the reward of holding my baby.

But this is the first time that I've had to consider Binta's future and what that entails. Another push against my hand, this time I think a tiny foot. It reminds me that life is a cycle. Pain and joy. Soon I will face the third pain a woman bears. I close my eyes and sigh. If only Binta didn't have to face the first pain. Another wriggle from the baby and I smile. I will meet this new person soon. I need to be strong. Binta will miss out on all this wonderment if I am not strong. How will she be allowed to marry? She'll be an outcast. Then how will she feed herself and where will she live if she doesn't have a husband? I wish there was another way.

I allow myself a moment to dream of something different, my thoughts skip to the future, but I find it hard to imagine any other future apart from Binta being married. What other future is there? Ousman won't have her living here much longer, less so if she is shunned for not having things done properly. I've heard about woman living on their own and working, earning enough money for themselves in the city – but those are the ones that have had chance of a good education. Even then, there's talk about how they are like the *toubab* tourists, easy women with the men: the sort of talk that brings such shame. Perhaps a man would marry her as she is. But, I can still imagine the gossip at their wedding – people whispering, asking why would a man want Binta like that?

Another little push against my hand brings my mind back to the present. The reality is, there is no choice. There is no other way. I have to be strong now. Otherwise, what kind of mother does that make me?

Chapter 18

Binta

I lie on my bed unable to sleep, listening to the chorus of frogs and crickets. My swollen eye causes me to wince and at this moment I hate my father – even more than my brother. I look over to the door where the moonlight shines under the crack and I think of ways to get Musa back. Ma's words keep popping into my head, 'If a donkey kicks you and you kick back, you are both donkeys.' I don't care if it makes me a donkey too; he's going to get it – something with some ground-up chillies down his pants will be a good start.

The final call to prayer echoes the half a mile or so from the mosque's speaker. Other noises from the town quieten down as people head to pray until, aside from the increasing song from crickets and frogs, there is a hushed silence. Before long, Grandmother comes into the darkened bedroom and awkwardly climbs onto the metal bed, which creaks under her weight. I've shared this bed with her since I was little. It's useless saying 'goodnight' to her, as she can't hear, and in this darkness she can't even see whether I'm awake or not. Within a few moments her snores resonate, which makes the bed vibrate. I can make out her silhouette and imagine her chest rising and falling. The snores get louder with each exhale; I grab the pillow and squish it between my hands but resist the urge to throw it at her. 'Be quiet!' I mutter under my breath.

Instead I push the pillow over my ears to muffle her noise, which it does but not enough. Somewhere in the distance a drum begins a rhythmic unceasing beat: probably someone's wedding party, or a naming ceremony. Crickets, frogs, drums, heat, snoring – it's a wonder I ever sleep.

A heaviness presses down on me like a thick blanket when I replay the incident with Musa and the beating it lead to; and to add to it, I can't sleep. I sit up and throw the pillow at Grandmother and for a second it makes me feel better. It bounces off her arm and lands near her knees and she stirs; her leg moves to rest on my pillow and she snores even louder. While she's in mid-snore I yank my pillow determinedly from beneath her and put in under my head again. I lie awake in the hot room and focus my breaths to match hers in the hope that her sleep will become infectious.

My mind calms, but sleep doesn't come. Instead I concentrate on where Isatou might be and how I can possibly find out where she is. Has something really happened to her? I'm sure Yari would have said – wouldn't she? And other people would be gossiping about some illness or accident, but there's been no word from anyone. The more I ponder, the most likely explanation is that she's been sent to secondary school. I can't believe it – I don't want to believe it – only the other day I was contemplating how awful it would be for us not to be at school together anymore and that was in a year's time. Could it really have happened already? I begin to feel cheated; denied my friend for another year, denied a proper goodbye.

Yari is different. Other women, I know, talk about her; they say she's too educated, too full of herself. Doesn't understand the traditional ways, they say, whatever that means. Maybe Yari and Isatou are trying to find out if she could really become a doctor? Yari would do that kind of thing. It makes sense Yari wouldn't tell anyone – she wouldn't want any more gossiping; people knowing her business and undermining Isatou's dreams. For a moment I feel guilty for wanting Isatou to stay with me instead of fulfilling her ambitions but the growing lump in my throat overwhelms reason and I just want her back.

But where would they go? The international school? Perhaps Jena's father is due to start a job there soon and they didn't want to tell Jena just yet? Tears prick the back of my eyes as I consider the possibility that Jena might also leave me and it makes me even more determined to find out if it's true. Not only do I want to find out where Isatou has gone, I need to know if Jena is moving too.

Grandmother's snores seem to catch in her throat and she turns over again, this time bringing a moment of respite from the heavy breathing. This is my small window of opportunity to drift to sleep too and I close my eyes. A trickle of a solitary tear escapes, tickles gently as it travels across my cheek and pools onto the pillow.

What would I do without Isatou and Jena? We've always been together.

Chapter 19

Binta

By mid-morning the sun has already sucked up every shadow. I'm sitting on the veranda and watch them disappear like water dried out by the sun. It's already too hot to move and wisely Grandmother has taken herself into the bedroom to sleep.

'Binta!' Jena appears around the corner of the house and steps up on to the veranda towards me, pulling two lolly sweets from the top of her skirt. 'Look what I've got!' she says, handing one to me, then sits down and puts hers in her mouth.

'Thanks. Any news about Isatou?'

She shakes her head slowly. I think back to when Isatou told us about the *Toubab* woman at the market – she knows more about things than we do – she said she'd overheard Yari and Mamamuso talking.

'Has your grandmother told you anything about Isatou?'

'No,' she says, the lolly removed and held in front of her, poised. Her tongue has gone blue. 'My mother doesn't allow me to speak with her – they have fallen out more than ever about something.'

'But I bet Mamamuso could tell you things. It's got to be worth a chance to find out?'

Jena shakes her head. 'Ma would be furious with me if she knew I'd been speaking with her.' Her words are slightly displaced with the lolly back in her mouth.

'Well, then, let me speak to her instead!'

Jena's quiet for a moment. Her eyes focus on me, she lifts one shoulder in a half shrug and then says, 'Okay. I guess that would work. When?'

'How about now?' I say quickly, getting up and brushing specks of dust from the back of my *fanu*.

'Now?' she asks and looks up at me, bewildered.

I offer her my hand for her to get up, 'Yes – why not? Is Yari around?'

'Not until later.'

'Sounds like as good a time as any!' I say, jumping down from the veranda on a resolved mission.

Chapter 20

Binta

A few minutes later and we are at her compound. The old lady, Mamamuso, is sat alone on an armchair under the shade of a tree at the far corner of the compound. She seems to be asleep, but like a cat she's aware of our presence almost immediately and then instantly alert.

'Come, Jena. Come and sit with me,' she calls over to us. 'And your friend.' She gestures, drawing us over.

It's convenient because I hadn't thought through how we would start talking to Mamamuso when we got here. It's not like I could just waltz into the compound and casually start some dialogue with her.

We approach and greet her with the respect demanded before we sit on the spare plastic chairs that are usually reserved for Mamamuso's peers. Other than the initial greeting, Mamamuso doesn't say anything more and I find myself wondering again how we might find out the information we need. Mamamuso sits back in her chair and closes her eyes; her skin is loose around her mouth and neck, and it's hard to see any of Jena's features in her. The two tribal marks on each of Mamamuso's cheeks glisten as the sunlight catches the scars. How did she get those scars? Did they hurt? They are too defined to have been accidental. I'm still staring when the old woman opens her eyes and I quickly look away.

Mamamuso begins, as though already partway through a conversation. 'Our Mandinka ways have been passed on to us from generation to generation.' She sits forward in her chair, puts her hands on her knees and looks at us. 'We are a great tribe and this is one of the most respected of all the towns. Many famous Mandinka warriors come from here. We are at the heart of this Mandinka heritage.'

She brushes a fly away and carries on. 'Our ways have been passed down from the elders to the younger generation since the beginning of time, not through the written word, but like this, through the spoken word.'

I wish my grandmother would sit with me like this, but she's too frail to talk much. When she does it's hard to hear what she's trying to say and I don't like to ask her to repeat just in case it frustrates her.

'Did you know the Mandinka are one of the largest and most respected of the tribes in West Africa? It is a great honour to come from our tribe, did you know that?' I listen carefully for any clues Mamamuso might give us about Isatou. It's the same history Ma tells me when we walk past the mosque, but it seems to sound different coming from Mamamuso's mouth.

'But our ways are passed down in a special way.' Mamamuso places her hand upon Jena's. 'It will be your turn soon to learn these ways – like your sister.' My eyes suddenly focus on Mamamuso's lips, on every sound coming from them, aware that she's about to explain something important to us and I edge forward, captivated.

'Haven't you done enough damage?' Yari yells, rushing over to us. I immediately wish I wasn't sat here now. I glance across at Jena, her eyes widening, her mouth ajar.

'I did what I had to. How could she remain like that? Don't you want your daughter to marry, to have healthy children? What kind of mother does that make you?' Mamamuso retorts back at Yari loudly.

Yari ignores the old woman and lifts Jena and me up by the arm. 'Come! This is no place for you.' She pushes us across the compound into the house. I didn't expect her to be so cross and now my heart is beating fast, but Mamamuso's words ring in my mind and Yari's actions make me more curious. If only she'd come a few minutes later. Mamamuso was just about to tell us something – something important. Secret.

'Stay away from your grandmother from now on!' Yari says to Jena, her words clipped and annoyed. I'm waiting for her to shout at me, to tell me to go home, but she doesn't.

'I'm sorry, Ma. I just wanted to find out where Isatou is.' Jena looks at her mother and asks quietly, 'Why won't you tell me, Ma?'

Yari hesitates. The creases on her forehead disappear and her eyes soften. 'I just can't, Jeneba. But stay away from Mamamuso. Trust me, it's for your own good.'

They are definitely hiding something. I know it.

Later, as I walk home, I'm adamant that if they won't tell us, we'll have to find out for ourselves.

Chapter 21

Amie

This baby is making my mind wander. I'm sleepy at strange times of the day and my thoughts often drift. Usually my mind just flits from one thought to another without any thread or any depth. I can't concentrate for long enough and, sometimes, even words escape me. It's not just when I'm thinking things quietly to myself, but also in the midst of a conversation – forgetting names, even.

Today is different though. I heard a name mentioned at the market place, which I can never forget and it made my skin feel momentary electric. I wasn't sure if the brief nausea was to do with the pregnancy or because of the utterance of it. I joined in with the hushed speculation of what her presence means, the odd excitement in their voices reminded me of the depth of what I belong to. But now I'm here on my own, my thoughts are visiting memories I believed had been buried long ago. Back in the field where they were made; under that tree.

I've heard the *Ngansimba* mentioned many times over the years. Why would it have this effect on me now?

I first considered it's because I heard the news at this time – life about to arrive from my belly again when my mind is vulnerable to wondering. But now I realise it's not that. It's because Binta is getting to the age where she will know the name too. I don't want to think about what that means. At least for now I don't have to. That is not the plan for the *Ngansimba's* visit to town. She is not coming for Binta – not this time. I shut my eyes and force both the memories and the thoughts for the future far away.

Chapter 22

Yari

It's been many nights now that I have laid in bed looking at the way the moon shines onto the ceiling, casting a series of different shadows. I'm exhausted, but every time I close my eyes a darkness closes in that comes from deep within. The nightmares I've had since a child are as fresh as they were the first time I had them, stirred from knowing that Isatou will return with the same struggles.

Five days she has been gone. Five days! Each morning I've gone at first light while Sarko and Jena are still asleep, back to the forest, going north to where it eases away into fields towards town and then by late afternoon I walk miles back on myself to the beach in the south. I do this in a futile attempt to do something, though I know the worst would have already happened – and I've been powerless to stop it.

Today I started my search early as dawn was rising. It was when I had my hand on the front door handle, turning it without waking anyone, that I heard a shuffle on the sofa and I turned to find Jena huddled up under a blanket.

'Hey, what are you doing out here, love?' Sunrise was some time away and the room was still bathed in a grey light.

'I'm waiting for Isatou.'

'Oh, love,' I said, sitting next to her on the sofa.

'Is she ever coming home?'

'Yes.'

'When?'

'Soon.' I touched her cheek, feeling the dampness of a stray tear.

'Where has she gone? I heard Mamamuso say she'd gone to get educated.'

I had to bite my lip before answering after hearing Mamamuso's name mentioned. 'She'll be home soon. Come, let's get you back to bed, otherwise the mosquitos will munch on you out here,' I said, trying to lighten the heaviness of her worry.

Sarko stirs in the bed and turns in his sleep towards me; his arm rests across my waist while I close my eyes and listen to his subtle snores. We failed her. Then a new worry fills my mind in the stillness of the night. What's to stop Mamamuso doing the same to Jena too?

'Yari?'

'Sorry for waking you,' I say between sobs. The bed squeaks as Sarko sits up and leans against the old metal frame. I sit up too and wipe my eyes. There's something I have to address, the only thing I can think that will make any difference. 'Sarko, we need to think about moving back to Serekunda.' I allow the possibility to settle, the reasons why obvious but as I listen to him in the dark, breathing without responding, I venture further. At least he hasn't immediately dismissed the idea.

'It will only be a matter of time before she tries to take Jena too.'

'I know.' He sighs and rubs his head. Then he gets up and walks across to the corner of the room where the stone water container is. He lifts the lid and places a cup into the jar, I hear the stray droplets falling. He puts the cup to his lips and stares out of the window into the dark night. From his silhouette I can see his shoulders drop, then he turns and walks back to the bed.

'Perhaps you can go to Serekunda on Saturday and see what you can find out from your friends there. Take Jena with you; we shouldn't leave her at home at the moment.'

'Really, we can leave Kenji?' I put my arms around his shoulders.

'Yes.' He turns and kisses me. 'We'll make plans to leave as soon as I can get a job there. Perhaps you can think about teaching again? We'll start afresh.'

I kiss him back, but the relief of a fresh start is only partial.

'Thank you, Sarko,' I whisper and kiss him again, trying to block out the guilt that we didn't manage to protect Isatou.

Chapter 23

Binta

Grandmother snores loudly, oblivious to the Imam's early morning call to prayer, ignoring it as she does every day – and every morning she blames the mosque's speakers for not working properly. Most days it seeps into my dreams but I've learnt to drift over the sound to keep it from fully rousing me. This morning it's accompanied quickly by my mother's voice near to my pillow.

'Come, Binta, wake up! Come with me.'

Curiously I follow Ma out of my room to the final echo of the Iman's call and rub my eyes as I walk out into the early light of day, over to the cooking hut. Ma's picked her tomatoes from the field – lots of them, nearly spilling over the bucket she motions to. 'I need you to sell these for me in Serekunda. I can't go today.'

I stretch and yawn to clear my mind, needing to process the information that is loaded in her request. It dawns on me that if Ma wants me to travel for her, she might be close to having a baby. I know it seems obvious, with her stomach growing like it is, but I've seen many women's stomachs grow and next time you see them they look different, but without a baby in their arms. Before I allow myself to work out how I feel about that – about having another sibling – a thought distracts me.

A mixture of excitement and nerves bubbles in the pit of my stomach at the thought of travelling all the way up north – and on my own! I take a quick deep breath to steady the growing energy churning around inside and ponder how opportune this is. This is too much like a coincidence – this has to be fate. And if that's the case, Isatou must be there.

It's not long before we are in the market square with the other few people mingling around, waiting to catch the first bush taxi of the day. It is so early that even Mr Janneh's shop is not open yet. The sky is turning from midnight to dark blue – nearer the horizon it's lighter blue tinged with yellow, reflecting across the few wisps of stationary cloud. Dawn is breaking, already taking the edge off the chill that was there when I awoke. Ma takes my arm and hurries over the road.

'*Salam Malikum*,' Ma greets Yari, who seems to be expecting us.

'Amie, how are you?'

'Thank you for allowing Binta to accompany you. She won't be any bother.' I return Ma's expectant glance with a reassuring smile, which is also partly due to feeling a little relieved that I'm not travelling alone.

'Mrs Sarr has a stall in Serekunda. I told her Binta would be coming. I mentioned to her last week when I went to market I'd be sending her next time instead of me.' Ma exchanges a look with Yari that seems to explain more than her few words, but before I can try and read into what that means I feel fingers pressing over my eyes, hiding the rising morning light.

'Guess who!' The voice is as known to me as my own, which is why the fingers release immediately because she knows that too and there is no puzzle.

'You're coming too?'

'Of course, I'm not missing out on a trip! Especially when I heard you were going!' Jena beams in that way she does when she's excited.

Once the vehicle is full to bursting with passengers, the driver turns on the engine and simultaneously there is a sputtering from the exhaust and white smoke fills the fresh morning air. The bush taxi seems to come alive, vibrating so much that I think the windows could easily fall out. The plume of smoke disappears and we ease away; the sun breaks over the horizon and Ma watches as we disappear down the long road towards the city.

On the way we hit pothole after pothole, dust filters through the windows, adding to the red tinge on the glass and the torn fabric seats, which I hold onto tightly in order not to be thrown off into the aisle. A chicken breaks free and vigorously flaps its wings as it jumps on people's heads, trying to find an exit while people grab at it frantically. By the time it's caught my sides are aching from laughing hard. Even Yari's laughing so much that her eyes crunch shut, her arms wrapped across her stomach trying to contain more from erupting. She wipes away tears with the back of her hand and sighs deeply, still smiling.

A couple of hours later we arrive and the day is already hot. I stare out of the dusty window, wiping it to get a better view of the market we are pulling up at and in the process smear the red flecks over the glass.

The market stretches out in every direction. From what Ma has told me on our handful of trips together, this is the largest in West Africa and I reckon it must be the size of a small village.

Laden with Ma's tomatoes, I balance them precariously on my head and follow Yari closely, determined not to get lost. Soon we are surrounded by a multitude of people hurrying past in every direction. I'm immediately struck by how everyone rushes without greeting each other, very different from back home. There are rows of stalls with only narrow alleyways between for us to pass. Everything is for sale, every kind of food, tie-dye cloth, cassette tapes, animals and jewellery. I try not to look too long at the traditional wooden masks hanging ready for tourists to buy, just in case there is a demon waiting to find its way into me. We work our way through the stalls and I recognise the occasional Wolof greetings, 'Nanga Deef'! There are also words from languages I've never heard before, motivating me to keep closer to Yari, as I'm scared at how easily I might get lost in this place amongst all these people.

Once we are inside the maze of stalls, the noise is deafening. People are shouting and it takes all my effort to keep the tomatoes balanced against the crowd pushing past me. Then Yari stops. 'Binta. Here. This is Mrs Sarr's stall.'

The woman quickly directs me underneath the table, lifts a cloth and then returns to negotiating a price with a customer. I'm glad to be able to get the tomatoes off of my head, as I wouldn't want to have to explain to Ma later how they ended up squished under everyone's feet.

'I'll be back later, after you hear the Imam's call for afternoon prayers. Work hard and make your mother proud,' Yari says, and quickly disappears into a sea of people with Jena.

It's not until mid-morning that I formulate a plan, borne from the fact that I seem to have a knack for selling and the tomatoes are going quickly. If I can keep selling at this pace they should be gone by midday, giving me time before Yari is due to come back for me.

When the basket is empty, and the sun's high in the sky, Mrs Sarr allows me to leave for the afternoon and I head confidently through the stalls in front, turning right and then left. It's hard to tell one part of the market from another, I thought this was the way, but the flowing crowd draws me forward and down another alley. After a few minutes I feel myself being taken deeper into the heart of the market by the push of the crowd and I begin to panic; I am completely lost.

It's then I notice the briefest motion of a bush taxi at the end of the row of stalls in the distance and aim for it, brushing past bodies flowing past me, stopping as others come to a halt to negotiate at a stall in front of me. Out from the depth of the market the air flows freely, my body no longer trapped by others. I look over my shoulder – I don't know how I'll find Mrs Sarr's stall later, but I push the thought to one side. Time is ticking and I need to work fast. Thankfully I've arrived out in the middle of the taxi rank on the edge of the market. Ma gave me a five dalasi note for the day, for food – but I've got other uses for it.

'Excuse me, does this taxi go to the beach?' I ask a man in jeans and a dirty grey T-shirt dragging the last bit of tobacco from the remnants of his cigarette.

'Which one? Kaloli Beach, Bakau, Fajara, Cape Point?' he asks, and flicks the end of the cigarette, which lands some distance to his side and blows the smoke near my face.

I pause and feel stupid for the lack of forethought. How did I think I could find Isatou on my own in this huge town?

'Do you know the international school, by the beach?' I tentatively ask.

'Marina School?'

I don't know, but will it to be right and nod.

'The cars parked alongside that far wall, they head in that direction,' he points.

I head over, squeezing into the back of a worn silver and rusty Mercedes and find myself the last of six passengers in a car designed for only four. Out of the partially lowered dirty window, which does little to keep the dust out, I absorb everything. It's vibrant. Women selling watermelons, men flagging down buses and taxis, cars everywhere, high-school students in smart uniforms.

I look closely at the groups of students and scan the faces for Isatou. We pick up pace on the smooth asphalt road, which pushes a fresh warm breeze into the car. The driver said that he would tell me when we got to the school, but I doubt we've arrived when he stops outside a beautifully landscaped two-storey cream building. It looks like one of the many exclusive hotels that we've just passed, but he assures me that it is the right place.

When the taxi drives away, I venture towards the path next to the sign for the school towards the glass pane doors at the entrance, where an occasional pupil walks by in a neatly pressed blue and white uniform. After a day in the market the heat has made my skin sticky with sweat and I suddenly feel scruffy. Any confidence I might have had wanes, but I put my hand to my hair and try to tame some of the loose ends that have escaped from my plaits and then straighten out the crease of my skirt. My heart is beating fast, but now I've made the effort to get this far, I'll keep going. Beyond the entrance there is an oak reception desk where a woman in silver-rimmed glasses looks up at me quizzically, as I tentatively push open the door.

'*Salam Malikum,*' I attempt in my nicest voice. She looks over the top of her glasses at me, unimpressed.

'I've come to give my sister a message from family.' The receptionist removes her glasses and looks at me without saying anything. It was the opening I'd rehearsed in the taxi on the way here, but now it seems lame and I'm expecting the woman to see right through my pretence.

'Her name is Isatou Darboe from Kenji town,' I continue, willing my words to be listened to. The woman puts the arm of her glasses to her lip, but remains silent – it doesn't seem as though the name resonates with her, or perhaps she's not prepared to give her my message. 'My sister is new here, she came just over a week ago.'

The receptionist looks at me for a moment longer and then returns her glasses onto her nose and opens up a filing drawer next to her knee, bringing out a small blue cardboard folder. She opens it and runs a neatly manicured red nail down a list of names. 'Are you sure it was this school?'

I nod, to save my voice from failing.

The woman looks again and says, 'We haven't had any new students since last term. There's a waiting list you know – not many spaces come up during the term. You must have the wrong school.' There is a subtle tone of contempt in her words, but I thank her politely.

I'm about to turn away when I'm suddenly inspired and question, 'Are any new teachers due to start next term?'

Unsurprisingly, the woman looks at me strangely – I know it's an odd question, but I have to know if Jena's dad is going to start working here and if they are going to move. I don't care what she thinks of me for asking.

'Yes.' My chest instantly feels heavy as though something is pressing on it. 'Mrs Patel – teaching science.' And just as quickly, the weight lifts.

'Thank you.' I walk away and feel relived: I may not have found Isatou, but at least I don't have to worry about losing Jena as well.

On the journey back across town, I am so preoccupied with where else Isatou might be that it only occurs to me once I have paid the driver and found myself on the edge of the huge market, that I might have missed Yari and have no way of finding my way back to Mrs Sarr's stall on my own. Just on this side of the market alone there are five entrances. I stand on the perimeter and can sense the hustle from inside, much like a beehive: I don't know what to do. Once I head inside, I will be swamped by the mass of people and it will only be chance that I find the right stall amongst the thousands. My heart begins to pound with worry.

It's as I'm looking backwards and forwards between the different entrances that I spot Jena and Yari are close by and sigh at this stroke of luck – if that is what it can be called – and touch the juju around my neck thankfully. They have stopped across the taxi rank to look at the tie-dyed material and I move quickly, before they stir, and head into the maze of stalls. Between the empty bush taxi labelled for Bakau and the full one for Brikarma a small boy stops me with a tray of frozen coloured ice in a triangular-shaped plastic transparent bag. I glance over his shoulder and see Yari start to make her way, but the boy blocks mine. 'Ice?' he asks, holding his metal tray up to my face. I still have enough change for two ices and give the boy my last dalasi, which is the quickest way to get him to move and head towards Jena before I lose her and Yari.

'Here!' I say and tap her on the shoulder. 'Have an ice!'

Jena hugs me and laughs, surprised. She may be smiling for now, but I know she won't be as happy when I tell her that Isatou isn't in Serekunda after all. At least, not at the international school and I don't know where else to try.

After Yari takes us back to Mrs Sarr's stall to collect Ma's money, I expect us to get on the bush taxi back to Kenji – already filling up with people – but instead she directs us outside of the square, through a small gap in the bricks where there's a line of men urinating against the wall.

'Where are we going?' I ask Jena while I try not to inhale the strong ammonia odour.

'We're going to see Ma's friend in Bakau,' she says, as Yari flags down a car. We quickly hop in before it's taken by anyone else and within moments we pass roads lined with hotels; the affluent tourist district near where I was earlier, not far from the International School.

I glance across at Jena and wonder how she's going to take the news that Isatou isn't at school after all.

Yari tells the driver to stop at what I can see is a barren piece of land. There's nothing here, but Yari still gets out. '*Abaraka*,' she thanks him, and hands over a few dalasi.

Cars travel by quickly, this being part of the main highway to the city and one narrowly misses us as we follow Yari out of the taxi. There doesn't seem to be anything here, just the road to Banjul, but then I can see the roofs of some buildings in the distance across this wasteland. As the car drives away, Yari stretches and adjusts her full kaftan outfit – I think it might be her best one – and leads the way through the ankle-high, dry grass in the direction I'm looking. For a moment I wonder if Yari is taking us to Isatou – perhaps she *is* staying with relatives after all?

'Stay close.' She points to the dusty ground and waves her hands around to where the path is barely visible. 'Stay on here. There are scorpions around.'

Yari's heel lifts from her flip-flops and with each step they make a rhythmic shu-shu-shu-shu sound. As I follow, my eyes fix on her heels, completely focused on her feet, on watching for quick movements in the grass, before a series of shouts distracts me.

'Hey, sexy sister!'

Yari doesn't slow down – she even speeds up – but I do. I stop. Against the late afternoon sun, I have to use my hand as a shade, but when I do I can make out where the shouting is coming from.

'Sweetie girl, come here!'

Like a swarm of insects when a nest is disturbed, hundreds of voices begin to whistle and jeer, merging together – angry voices, very obviously directed towards us. My heart begins to race as fear creeps up my skin and around the back of my neck.

'Don't stop, keep walking,' Yari says. She grabs one of my and Jena's hands and pushes us forward.

On the right – where the voices are coming from – there is an odd-looking building stretching across the length of the wasteland. A mass of arms reaches out from each of the small square gaps in the brickwork, beckoning us.

'What is it, Yari?' I ask under my breath, trying to keep up with her.

'Nothing; just follow quickly.'

I'm not satisfied with her answer, but hurry along.

As we continue I spot a noticeboard with large black letters on it, which stands out against peeling white paintwork on an ageing wooden frame. It's large enough to read, even from here. Despite the heat, a chill runs through my body. 'A prison!' I blurt out, hardly believing the sign that I've just read.

Now I squint to try and see how secure the walls are. Yari looks over her shoulder at me, and, without slowing her pace, says, 'Don't worry. They're not much of a threat to us at Jeshwang. Not like those in Mile Two Prison.'

Whistles echo around the wasteland and I think we're never going to get out of their sight; the worry of the scorpions is now forgotten. Not a moment too soon we arrive on the edge of a housing development. I wouldn't want to live close to the prison like this; it's strange how expensive compounds are so near. It doesn't make sense to me, but perhaps the high walls and metal gates help them forget about what's just over there?

When we stop in front of a compound a few roads from the wasteland, far enough away that I can't see the prison anymore, Yari knocks on the large green metallic gate set into smooth white-painted walls. The hollow tin sound resonates and immediately I hear a voice from inside in response.

'*Salam Malikum*. It's Yari from Kenji,' she calls to the voice the other side.

A bolt slides into place the other side and the gate squeaks open. Yari is obviously expected and the woman embraces her, then she motions to Jena. 'Look at you! A miniature Yari!'

I haven't really thought about it before, but the woman's right: Jena's got her mother's round face.

'Girls, this is my old friend, Fanta.' Yari introduces us and I'm just as warmly welcomed before we step over the gate's threshold into the compound. The middle of the yard is paved with large square blocks where there is a mature tree shading a good part of the outside space. A few small children are sitting on a mat underneath it playing some kind of game, and an old man is asleep on a chair. But from here, it doesn't look like there is any sign of Isatou. Fanta leads us across the yard, up some steps into the main house, into a living room where a television flickers in the corner.

At *Koriteh*, a feast marking the end of Ramadan, Mr Ceesay – who lives near the market square – allows several families to come and watch his television. He brings it outside and we all sit on the floor eagerly awaiting the screen to flicker on, like insects drawn in to the warm light. We watch Mr Ceesay's television until it gets late, although it's difficult to hear over the noise of the generator. This is the first time that I have actually seen a television in a house. Actually inside.

'Can I get you a drink?' Fanta offers, which is when I notice a fridge in the corner of the room. I'm seriously impressed.

I sink comfortably into the sofa, drink in my hand, ready to watch television with nobody blocking my view, no excited chatter and no noisy generator that cuts out just at the best bits.

'That's the president, isn't it?' Jena points at the young man in military uniform, on the screen. I've seen posters of him around Serekunda – I recognise him too. Yari comes and joins us on the sofa and, as she does, sucks her teeth although I'm not sure what exactly she's disapproving of.

'Indeed.' The comment belongs to a tall man just coming into the room. Fanta takes another bottle of Coke, opens it and hands it to him. 'Thanks.' Then he greets Yari and tells her, 'I'm Mohammed, Fanta's brother – the cleverest of the six.' He chuckles, before he takes a seat in an armchair. Then he motions to the television with his drink. 'Do we really need a commemorative arch to celebrate his coup?'

The footage on the news channel is showing the president with his convoy driving to the construction site of the new arch in Banjul. The newsreader details how much they're spending on the project. That comment gets a response from Yari and Fanta in unison: 'A million US dollars?'

'It's crazy to think we never even had a proper election!' Yari continues.

Mohammed stands up to find a packet of cigarettes in his back trouser pocket. He takes one out, puts it to his lips and lights the cigarette, and the paper glows red followed by a small cloud of smoke that drifts into the room when he exhales. 'I have a friend, a human-rights lawyer. He's talking of founding an opposition party. As you say, we still haven't had an election. We're looking to get supporters. You interested?'

Yari doesn't answer straight away.

'There's a gathering happening at the end of the month. Come along,' Mohammed continues. My attention is drawn to the newsreader and I wonder if Jena has noticed that she's probably used bleaching cream. She must have with that kind of fair complexion. She's mesmerising, sat talking to people across the country with such confidence.

'I'm not sure about getting involved in politics,' Yari answers.

A picture appears filling the whole television screen for a moment of an oddly dressed man who's wearing grasses and dyed red bark that cover his head and body. The newsreader expounds that there is an investigation under way about a *Kankurang* who beat a man to death.

'Witchcraft cannot be put neatly into jurisdiction; *Kankurang*s are an essential part of our culture and cannot be expected to limit their work, for fear of reprimand. They represent a violent but benevolent beast that chases away harmful, evil spirits when children are at their most vulnerable,' a witness of the attack is saying to a journalist on the newsreel. Although he's speaking in Mandinka, I don't quite understand what he means when he says the *Kankurang* protects children. I think they look really frightening.

I've sneaked a glance at a *Kankurang* a couple of times with the other children in town. He's so scary, the way he bangs his machetes together. We're always careful for him not to see us, otherwise he'd come and chase and hit us. Thankfully they only appear in the town occasionally.

I stare at the footage on the screen of a *Kankurang*, this figure with machetes in each of his hands as he jumps up and down, banging them over his head. Then he walks unfazed from the crowd that is following him into a small fire that is burning in the centre of the road. It doesn't burn him; he spends a moment dancing in the fire where the flames jump up to his calves and then steps out and runs towards the crowd that disperse in partial delight at the display but also with fear. I remember feeling like that when I've seen one – it's kind of fun and scary all at the same time – trying to sneak a look at him, without him seeing and chasing us. I never really thought one would actually kill someone though. Next time I see a *Kankurang*, I think I'll just be scared.

Chapter 24

Amie

It's humid today. Thankfully it isn't my turn to cook this week, the heat in the cooking hut makes me dizzy now. Hopefully the baby will come before I'm due to cook again. Everyone is out, but even as I come inside the house, it still feels claustrophobic in this temperature. I ease myself inelegantly into Ousman's armchair. It's a little firmer than the sofa and Ousman won't find out I'm in his precious seat. As soon as I'm sat, I'm disappointed that I'm just as uncomfortable as I was stood up. I consider kicking off my flip-flops, but decide the effort of trying to get them back on my swollen feet isn't worth the bother.

Flies hover over my head, seeming aware that I haven't got the energy to shoo them away and it seems they are here to annoy me on purpose. I look around near me to see if there is anything to use as a fan, but there isn't even one of Binta's school books lying around for me to use. Oh, this heat is unbearable!

I sit forward and put my hands on the top of my abdomen, just under my ribcage and push down. My stomach is as hard as a rock, but I push again willing the baby to start its journey into the world. There seems to be a constant building of pressure – both inside my own body and around me. This humidity has to break soon; there will be rain. I close my eyes and picture huge, refreshing drops of water falling from the sky when it comes.

I open my eyes again and notice the silence of midday. There is no noise from vehicle engines across the compound where my brother-in-laws – mechanics by trade – fix their customers' cars. The laughter of children playing in the street outside has quietened. The heat is slowing everyone and there seems to be an eeriness to the calm. For a moment it makes me feel uneasy. Perhaps it's because I feel alone and what if the baby does suddenly come, obedient to my wishes after all? The thought prompts me to awkwardly manoeuvre out of the chair. As I stand, my hips and back ache.

'Come soon baby!' I say, looking down hopefully. Out the window I can see my sister-in-law. She's close enough for me to call if the pangs of labour begin, but I still feel uneasy. There's a growing anxiousness that I can't shake. I cannot place what I'm afraid of, or why I should worry. Just that deep inside, I know: life is going to change and it's going to shake me, challenge me to my core. Not just because there is another baby on the way. Other changes. The uneasiness makes me wonder for a second if this baby will be another stillborn. Is this what the growing dread is about?

I smooth one hand over the top of my bump, cradle the other hand at the bottom and deliberately dismiss these thoughts.

Everything is going to be all right. I close my eyes and repeat it in my mind until I can almost believe it.

Chapter 25

Binta

The Imam's voice is loud and clear over the speaker when we arrive home in front of the mosque, signalling the evening prayers are due. As we get off the bush taxi, men hurry past to the mosque and some of the passengers quickly jump down to join them.

The sun is already low in the sky and there is little daylight left.

'Binta, it's getting late – come to ours for dinner.'

'Thanks, Yari.' I'm starving after the long journey and I also don't quite want this day to end yet. It's been fun.

It's not long before we are at Yari's home and she heads straight to the far corner of the compound where the cooking hut is, to help with the final preparations of the meal. I follow Jena up into the house and into her bedroom. Books are placed neatly on a wooden bedside table and a net curtain hangs perfectly still in the stifling evening heat. I jump up onto her bed, envious at how she doesn't have to share it with a snoring, ageing grandmother.

The sound of the dinner being brought into the living room along the hall makes me acutely aware of Isatou's absence and that she won't be there sharing a meal with us tonight.

'Have you heard anything more about your sister?'

'I asked Ma again – she keeps telling me not to worry and that Isatou will be home soon, but then doesn't tell me anymore. She obviously knows where she is, Binta, but I don't understand why she won't tell me.'

'I checked out the International School today.'

'You did what?' Jena asks, and immediately sits upright attentively. 'When? How did you get a chance to do that?'

'I finished early at the market and got a taxi there.' She looks at me, expectant and hopeful, which makes it difficult to tell her. 'Isatou wasn't there.'

Jena doesn't say anything, but her shoulders drop slightly and I can tell how disappointed she is.

'Don't worry, we'll keep looking.'

'Perhaps it doesn't matter – Ma said she will be back before too long.'

'But I know you are just as curious as me to find out where she is, aren't you?'

'Of course, but where else could she be?'

'I don't know,' I say; my mind runs over any possibilities.

'Hey, guess what I've got from Serekunda?' Jena suddenly whispers excitedly, joining me on the bed. I'm too tired to do any guessing and just shrug. Jena loosens her *fanu* and pulls out a tub.

'What is it?' I ask, but I instantly recognise the blue-and-red label, like the ones advertised on the billboards in Serekunda.

109

'You're not the only one that was resourceful today,' Jena says, handing me the tub of cream. A broad grin grows across her face. 'Bleaching cream!' she exclaims, confirming what I know already.

I take it from her and turn the tub around in my hands like one of the precious china cups that Ma has – the ones in the cupboard she never uses, just in case they break. I unscrew the lid. 'Where did you get it?'

'It was at Fanta's house...'

I think back to our visit. 'When did you manage to get this?'

'When I used the bathroom.'

Inside, finger imprints have left indents in the yellow cream. I hold the tub up to my nose expecting a fragrance like Yari's flowers at the entrance of her home—

'Ah, it reeks!' I say through sputters, and the odour actually stings my eyes. 'What do we do?' I hand it back to her quickly to distance myself from the smell, but place the lid next to me on the bed.

'It can't be too difficult. It is only cream.' Jena says. She lifts the tub and screws up her nose when she smells it, before she studies the writing on the side.

'I'm not quite sure what it says, but you must just put it on. Here—' she puts a good amount on her fingers and scoops up a large dollop. She covers all her fingers and rubs the cream on the back of her free hand, then works it up towards her elbow before she repeats the process on her other arm. Replicating her, I rub it into my face and arms.

'You look like you're getting ready to pray,' I say, giggling, thinking of Ma. The odour is worse out of the container. When I look up at Jena she's covered in the white cream. '*Any pen, Toubab?!*' I tease, holding out my hand mockingly. It sparks a question in my mind. 'Why do you think *Toubab* women come here for a husband?'

I laugh hard, thinking about that *Toubab* baboon man we saw at the market. 'Maybe *Toubab* men are lazy...or ugly. Hairy white legs and red arms!'

Before Jena has time to respond I suddenly feel a rapidly growing burning sensation across my face. It continues with an intense tingling across my arms, as though a million ants are biting. 'What's happening?' I cry and rub at my face.

Jena jumps up and waves her arms around and cries out too. She runs out the room, leaving me on my own in a confused stinging pain.

A moment later, which feels like forever, Yari appears at the door and although her voice is panicked and angry, I immediately feel better that she's here.

'What have you done?!' She moves towards the bed and picks up the bleaching cream. 'You idiots!'

I brace myself for a beating, but instead Yari yells for someone to fetch water – and my ma. I suddenly feel worse at the thought of her coming; if I missed out on a beating with Yari, Ma is sure to do it. By the time I hear her angry voice outside I feel dizzy from the pain and rest my head on the pillow to stop the room from spinning.

It must be some time later when I become aware of a pink glow instead of darkness through the lids of my eyes, which refuse to open. I lie still, listening to the sounds in the compound. I know the smell, the touch of silk bedding. It's Ma's bed. If it wasn't for the burning sensation all over my face, I might think I was dreaming. I hear the familiar sound of Ma, the way she shuffles, the little humming she does when she's busy and I sense her warm breath near me.

'I can't open my eyes, Ma, I'm blind!'

'Nonsense, child; your eyes are just swollen.' Her voice is soft, calming and I instantly feel better.

I couldn't see properly by the time Ma arrived, my eyes burning hot. I can't remember much about the walk home, apart from crying while Ma led me through the back roads until we got back. She directed me into the house and onto a bed.

'You look better than last night. Let me see your hands.'

She takes them and turns them over gently. I wrap my fingers around her hand because her touch is comforting.

'I'm worried about these blisters; they could turn nasty.'

It's not difficult to picture Ma's face, brow creasing, drawing lines across her forehead, eyes narrowing with that worried look that she does.

'I'm sorry.'

'Oh, Binta! What were you thinking? Bleaching cream! You don't need anything like that – a beautiful daughter of mine – you are already beautiful as you are.' I feel her warm lips kiss my forehead. 'Momodou Ceesay will know what to do,' she mutters and then I hear her leave the room. I hope not for long.

Momodou is a *marabout*. Not a pious, religious one, although he's studied the Koran diligently and he's very powerful. He's proved his ability many times over the years, with his knowledge about how to heal people – as well as other things – by using his spiritual powers.

People come to him for potions: to heal; for fertility; to seek revenge; to find out if a spouse has been unfaithful.

Whenever I brush my hair I'm always careful to put any strands down the latrine, like Ma has directed me to do, and not leave it lying around for anyone to find to take to the *marabout*. I'm concerned about someone wanting to do me harm, but Ma is more concerned with a boy using it to get me to fall in love. 'Remember, get rid of your hair properly, we don't want you falling in love with just any boy,' she used to nag. That was before. At one time I didn't think it such a bad thing to fall in love, but that was before Fansu started making wide eyes at me, pursing his ugly lips in my direction. After that I make sure I'm careful and she doesn't have to nag anymore.

An experienced *marabout*, Momodou can tell if someone has an evil spirit in them when he talks with the ancestors. When I was very young, I visited the *marabout* with Ma and sat very quietly on the armchair while she bowed before him, taking several dalasi notes from inside her *fanu*, all folded neatly. I was afraid because I knew then that he must have a lot of power if she was willing to part with that much money. I feel bad that she'll have to spend her money on me like this – the money probably from the tomatoes I sold for her today – to make me well, and it adds to my guilt.

There's a clanging. I guess Ma has returned and is struggling to bring the gas canister into the room. Before too long I can hear the water bubbling away and as the leaves boil, an overwhelming stale odour fills the room.

'Is that you, Ma?' I ask, managing to open my eyes enough to allow a sliver of light in.

'Yes. Momodou gave me these.' She's forgotten that I can't see, but I hear the rustle of plastic bags.

'What is it?'

'Leaves…medicine.'

The foul steam rises and seeps into every crevasse of the walls. I have a horrible feeling she will make me drink it and I know it's going to happen when I feel Ma lifting me under the arms to sit up.

'Careful, it's hot!'

I don't open my lips – the vapour now so close to my nostrils makes me want to vomit.

'You must take it. It will help with the pain…' I know she only wants the best for me. She always does. I open my lips enough to allow her to pour the concoction into my mouth and try not to smell it as I taste it on my lips: bitter. When it settles in my stomach it takes all my effort not to retch it back up. Ma lowers my head again onto the soft, welcoming pillow.

After a few minutes the bitter taste on my tongue travels to my lips, causing them to become numb. Soon the numbness works through my face, down my neck, into my body, across my shoulders; like a constricting snake, the numbness works its way around my body – almost pleasant. I don't want to fight it, even if I could. Gradually it takes away the stinging pain and the tingling numbness reaches my head, then my thoughts, and then I drift to sleep.

A different kind of tingling wakes me and I open my eyes and blink at the afternoon sun streaming into the room from the open back door. The sense of relief that I can now see is short-lived due to a fierce itching and my hands are bleeding from where I've already scratched; I guess my face too.

'Try not to do that,' Ma says, as she comes into the room. 'Momodou said you'd scar for life if you give into it.'

I don't care at this moment, but she takes my hands and moves them away from where I really want to dig my nails into the skin and then perches on the bed, caressing my temples, soothing me.

Ma helps to calm me and before long I am aware of this unusual moment we have of just being together on our own. I glance at her stomach and wonder how much longer it will be before I share my mother with another sibling. The train of thought leads me to ask her: 'Ma, Jena's sister – Isatou – has gone away. Have you heard anything about it? Do you know where she might be?'

'Don't fret, she'll be home soon.'

'Where is she, do you know?'

She strokes my head for a moment before she answers quietly. Although she's sat right next to me, I have to strain my ear to hear. 'Sometimes it's time for girls to become women and they are sent away for a little while.'

'Like school?'

'A little. But don't tell anyone I've told you anything. It's a secret.'

'Okay.'

'Promise me?'

'I promise.' A secret? My intrigue is heightened. I want to assure Ma that I can be trusted with it and gently squeeze her hand. I feel suddenly better, the sores on my face forgotten for a moment, and I mull over the thing Ma has just said and sense a special bond between us.

'See! Momodou Ceesay is a good *marabout*. The blisters are going down.' Ma turns my face from side to side, changing the subject, perhaps feeling aware that she has told me too much.

'What does it look like?' I say, aware that the conversation has altered, and I picture my face swollen, blooded, scratched, scarred.

'It's fine. It's your hands I'm worried about, but Momodou said you would heal in time. And, if not, he's powerful. He will know how to get you a husband, even with scars. It will cost a lot of money, but if that's what I have to do, in sha'Allah!' she says smiling, probably joking.

'You could always use my hair and get a boy to love me, Ma,' I suggest, the corners of my mouth rising, just in case she really is worried and needs to go back to Momodou.

She laughs and rubs my head. 'Get some rest!'

A couple of days later I venture out of the house, desperate for fresh air after the stench of the medicinal leaves. At the edge of the compound on the veranda Malik, my older cousin, is sitting with Musa. I head towards them, hopeful that they might feel generous and give me a sip from the bottle of Coke that they are sharing.

'Look, it's pinkie!! Are you trying to be a *Toubab*? You missed a bit!' Musa points and laughs, but I ignore him. I expect as much from him, but then Malik – older, sensible Malik, who helps me with my schoolwork – says, loud enough for everyone to hear, '*E Solima*!', which stops me dead in my tracks.

I stop walking towards him and cough to clear my throat so that I can say something clever in response to his derogatory insult, but I have no answer for him. It's an insult we've all used, though I don't actually know what it means. Apart from that you are a little child, stupid, that you don't belong.

'*E Solima!*' he says, again.

For the first time though, I hear it differently. As though the word means something new. It's not just teasing, like we've said to little kids when they do silly things or we don't want them spoiling our game, when we want them to go away. It means you can't join in – you are not wanted. Before I can deflect his words, Musa runs around me in circles repeating it in an annoying sing-song way: '*E Solima, E Solima!*'

Instantly, with anger, shame and embarrassment boiling up inside I clench my fist and hit him as hard as I can. Immediately he stops, yelps and grasps at his face where blood pours out his nose. He looks as shocked as me at the accurate punch I've landed him. I wait for Musa to cry, but he doesn't – he just remains stood there, looking stunned.

It also shuts Malik up because he doesn't say it again, although he looks at me sternly. Even though the boys have been silenced as I turn to walk over to Ma, the words continue to fill my head: '*E Solima – E Solima*'.

'Ma, it's not fair!' I say, when I get to her. 'Musa and Malik keep teasing me.'

'That's boys for you, Binta.' Ma is awkward with her protruding abdomen and doesn't look much like she wants to talk, but I need her to listen.

'Ma, they keep calling me, "*E Solima*"!'

She looks up; I've got her attention now.

'They mean nothing by it.'

'But it's not nice, and they're saying it loud. People won't want me around if they keep saying it. Will they, Ma?'

'Nonsense,' she says and adjusts Lamin on her back, then she looks at me. Her lips part to say more, but she pauses before she mutters, 'It just means you're still a child.' I think about the secret she told me, about how girls become women.

'Well, I don't want to be anymore, Ma. I don't want them to call me that anymore! Please! Get them to stop calling me that!'

She doesn't reply, but just unties the material tied across her chest and lowers Lamin down to the floor.

'I need you to take Lamin now, Binta.'

I expect her to ask me to go with him to market or somewhere, but then she says, 'Lamin is no longer a baby. He needs to be with you *dindingo*s now. With you children.'

Pot-bellied, with just his juju around his waist, he looks at me as Ma turns and shuffles back inside the house. It's deeply unfair: Lamin gets a new status, but I have to keep being called childish names.

'Come, *dindingo*,' I call to him under my breath. Flies swarm around his snotty nose.

He still looks like a baby to me.

Chapter 26

Binta

Lamin joins Grandmother and me in our bed – them at one end, me at the other. When he pees himself that first night, the warm liquid seeps around and over my feet. It's not the best way to wake up and adds to the annoyance I already feel. A few days later it's not Lamin that disturbs me in the early hours, but my auntie shaking Grandmother.

'Grandmother,' she says and taps the old woman on the shoulder. 'Your daughter-in-law had a baby in the night. Your son has a new baby,' she says, louder.

'I heard you! I heard you. Why are you waking me? He's already got children. Tell me about it later,' Grandmother says, and turns back over. Within a couple of breaths, she's snoring again.

'Boy or girl?' I ask my auntie in a whisper.

'It's for your mother to tell you. Come and see!'

It goes without saying that I'm hoping for a sister, but even at the prospect of meeting a new brother, excitement grows and flutters in my stomach as I walk towards the house. I hesitate before entering Ma's room, as I catch sight of the small naked baby curled up, like a tiny ball in the middle of the bed. Ma sees me and she has a broad, ecstatic smile that remains fixed across her face long after I come in. She picks up the baby, holds it against her chest, her chin rests delicately on its head. The baby remains in a ball shape, with its legs all curled up.

'Here, would you like to meet your sister?'

Excitement rushes up from my stomach, into my chest and for a moment I am overcome with such intense joy that I have to keep myself from crying. Instead I rush over to the bed, desperate to hold her.

'A girl! She's so beautiful! So perfect!' I say and examine her little fingers, her sweet toes. Ma hands her to me when I sit next to her on the bed, shows me how to hold her wobbly head, where there are wisps of soft silky hair. As her small fingers wrap around mine, I have an overwhelming instant love for my little sister.

Exactly one week later it's my new sister's naming ceremony. Ma isn't expected to do chores, because she's just had a baby. Instead, my relatives busy themselves and get everything ready for the naming ceremony. From the first call to prayer at dawn, they dice onions, cut the tomatoes from Ma's field and pound rice ready for a day of continual feasting – peanut rice pudding, *Benachin*, *Domada*, sour milk with cous cous and fizzy drinks.

Later in the morning, my father appears at the entrance of the cooking hut, pulling a reluctant goat by a rope. It's strange to see him home during the day and stranger to see him look so cheerful, especially when he throws me a smile and ruffles my head.

'You're not stopping there, are you?' my aunt asks him and looks up from where she's bending over, washing a large bowl of rice.

'Why not?'

'It'll be too messy and you'll be in our way here.'

He looks around, the goat bleats loudly behind him seemingly in agreement with my aunt.

'No, no, it's fine.'

My aunt throws him a stern look, which he seems to notice because he compromises by saying that he'll make a hole in the ground. It is useless for her to try to argue – once my father has an idea he is stubborn. Ma says I'm like that too at times.

My father holds the goat tight while he directs Malik and Musa to dig the hole for him. The boys attack the dry earth, carving out a small hole, until their foreheads are saturated with perspiration. It's good to see them work hard for a change, I consider, with a smug satisfaction. Then my father gets Malik to hold the rope while he gets his knife. The sunlight glistens on the silver blade and the goat seems to sense danger, because it struggles to step back.

'Ah, mind the onions...' my aunt gasps, as they spill out everywhere.

I bite my lip, I want to laugh, but I don't think my aunt will appreciate the humour – not just at this moment. My father puts his legs either side of the goat and his weight forces it to drop onto its front legs.

'Musa, push down at the back,' he says.

The goat falls completely to the ground. My father pauses and wipes the sweat from his eyes. A lump forms in my throat because as funny as the onions were, I know what is coming next, although I am not attached to the animal like I was my *Tobaski* goat, I still feel a little sadness.

'Come boys, hold it down.'

With the goat now held by Malik and Musa, my father gets off the animal's back and moves towards the head. The goat's eyes widen and it bleats in what sounds like desperation and fear. Just like my *Tobaski* goat did, but this time I watch as my father faces towards Mecca, gives thanks to Allah before forcing the blade hard into the goat's throat.

Blood suddenly pours and flows. It turns the ground red and the hole fills with blood like a small river. The goat's back legs kick furiously at the ground, throwing up little plumes of dust, while my father strokes its head, speaks softly and mutters, 'In sha'Allah.' Soon the goat settles, bleeding to death quietly.

It is hard to believe it's the same creature an hour later with Musa chasing me around the compound with the goat's testicles.

'Enough, Musa,' I pant and lean over with my hands on my knees, trying to catch my breath. A sharp pain stabs my side. He shoves the revolting smelling meat close to my face.

'Kissy, kissy!' he jeers.

'Musa, go away!' I push him, which is enough for him to go and find younger children to annoy. It's a good job I belted him across the nose before, because he's quicker to get out of my way.

Malik is in charge of music. The speakers vibrate with the booming base, which draws people to our party in the same way the Imam does to the mosque. When Momodou Ceesay, the *marabout*, arrives, it's time for the main part of the party – the ceremony – to begin.

The baby is brought out to my father, who handles her awkwardly, unlike how Ma holds her. This is probably the first time that he's held her. It's not normal to see a man holding such a tiny baby, but today is special and the music dies down and the guests hush to watch. Waiting, like me.

Quiet and oblivious to her surroundings and the party, my baby sister is laid on a goatskin mat – the one made out of my *Tobaski* goat – on the veranda and my father is handed a razor blade. All eyes, I can sense, are watching him as he bends over. He carefully draws the blade across her head and the wisps of silky soft black hair drop away and she begins to cry, although I know she's not hurt. My father hands my bald-headed sister back to the *marabout*. Momodou seems more comfortable handling my sister and after praying he attaches a juju to her small wrist, before passing her back to my father, his role complete.

The crowd is now even quieter, anticipating the climax to this tradition. It is meant to be a father's greatest honour. Just as his father had done with him, and his father and all the fathers until the beginning of time, now my father holds my sister up in the air for all to see. Then he brings her ear to his mouth and whispers her name. It's only right that she'll be the first to hear it, but I'm stretched up on my toes straining to hear.

I suddenly realise how intimate and significant this moment is; passed through the generations – my father would have done this with me too, and in this moment I'm surprised to feel a special connection with him. He speaks loudly and addresses the crowd, projecting his voice in order for everyone to hear.

'This is – Mai!' he says proudly.

Ma is smiling. I'm glad she likes the name, as I do. Mai. As the initial excitement dies, I mingle amongst the guests and find Jena.

'How great is that? I've got a sister called Mai!' I say and sit down next to her, but then realise it was an insensitive thing to say, considering that hers still isn't home. 'Sorry, I—'

'No, it's fine,' she says with a smile that doesn't seem to reach her eyes.

The atmosphere in the compound is jovial: groups of men are sat in small groups pouring bitter tea into small glasses; women sit together eating and passing around my sister; a group of boys are dancing next to the speaker to a mixture of Tata Dindin, Yusen Dor and Michael Jackson. My aunt brings a bowl of sour milk and cous cous for Jena and me to eat, and, as I put the creamy liquid to my lips, I'm suddenly aware of how familiar and comforting these things are to me – I've been to more naming ceremonies than I can remember. This is part of who I am. This is our culture – and I feel a thread pulling me close to the generations gone before.

'I'm going to go home,' Jena says after finishing her sour milk. She stands up, straightening her *fanu*.

'Why so soon? Stay.'

'It's just – being here without Isatou – I miss her more.'

I suddenly feel a bit selfish for being so happy. 'I understand.'

In this moment, seeing how despondent she is, I desperately want to tell Jena what I know, but I'd never betray such a special secret that Ma told me; I can't. Although I can't disclose what Ma's told me, it occurs to me that I could find out for myself where Isatou is. Then I could tell Jena without breaking my promise to Ma. I watch Jena leave and resolve to look harder for her sister. Then I turn back to the music coming from the heart of my compound, back to the rejoicing over my own sister.

As it grows darker the activity around me increases, people that were busy earlier in day are arriving for a night of dancing and laughter. In the shadows my confidence grows and I join my aunts in dancing to the latest *Kora* beats. The rhythm vibrates through my body, and, as I relax, it seems the beats take over and tell my limbs what to do and it's a wonderful feeling of being lost and found all at the same time.

After dancing for what must be hours, I tire and realise how exhausted I am and reluctantly decide to head to my room to sleep. I manoeuvre through the crowd and it takes time to get past, with people stopping to talk to me.

'Binta, what do you think of your little sister – little Mai?' an aunt asks. Her width blocks my way and I politely stop.

'She's lovely, Auntie.'

'Good name.'

'Yes, I like Mai.'

'Your mother said how proud she was of you today, helping with all the preparations.'

'I'm glad she was happy.'

'Some girls, they think they will make a good wife but are lazy. You know what they say, Binta? A log can float in the river all it likes; it will never become a crocodile – but not you, Binta. You will make a good wife some day.'

'Thank you, Auntie,' I say, and ease myself through the women, towards my room at the end of the compound.

The noise of the party will go on for hours more, but my eyes already feel heavy as I go to step up onto the veranda.

A hushed whispered voice causes me to pause: 'Binta – hey, Binta!'

It's too dark to see, but, when it is repeated, my senses make me aware of someone by the outside wall, near the well. I turn and step back off of the veranda and move towards the voice. It's familiar. It's one I know I've heard before, but I'm still trying to place it when he appears in the dimmed lights.

'Hi Binta,' Yaya says, and puts his hand behind his head, seemingly nervous.

'You going to join the party?'

'Yeah,' he says without heading over. The longer he remains the more a flutter rises in my stomach at the hopeful anticipation that he might say more to me. After a moment of waiting, I decide he doesn't want to talk, and I turn to leave, feeling embarrassed at thinking he wanted to.

'I just, um—' he coughs '—I, uh, wondered if you wanted to get a Coke sometime at the market?'

The pause between him asking and me replying seems to indicate that I'm not interested, but it couldn't be further from the truth. I don't answer straight away because I'm stunned he's asked me and for a second I wonder if I'm dreaming. Quickly I come to my senses and hurry to say, 'That would be nice – sure.'

Although it's dark, in the kerosene lamplight I see the dimples appear as he smiles, which triggers another flight of butterflies inside of me. As he passes to go to the party, our eyes fix on each other for an instant and I smile back shyly.

Lamin is already asleep when I get in my room, although Grandmother, who is usually first to bed, is still enjoying socialising outside. I drop onto the bed and continue to listen to the voices outside, the quietened music, the laughter, and the crickets. I absorb every sound and long to etch this night into my memory forever. When my baby sister is all grown, I'm going to tell her all about this night: the night I fell in love – and I'm sure that it's happened without any *marabout* potions.

A few days later, I am on my way home with Ma, crossing the dusty path leading down the side road to our compound. It's very late, but the moonlight lights the path ahead, enabling me to look out for sticks that move, which are really snakes. I'm ready to grab hold of Ma's hand at any moment. In the other hand I hold an empty pot of stew, which Ma took to the party we are coming back from. The handle squeaks as I swing the pot in time with my steps.

Then Ma stops suddenly, her body tense and she puts her hand out to halt me; my initial reaction is that she has spotted a cobra.

'Give me the pot,' she whispers, the urgency obvious in her voice. She places it quietly on the ground and puts a hand over my mouth and, half dragging me, takes me to the side of a haphazard fence. I have no idea what she is up to, but I can see her eyes in the bright moonlight and they are serious and afraid. There's enough silently spoken in her expression that I don't have to ask more.

Ma's warm breath brushes against my neck; she relaxes her fingers from my mouth when I nod, showing her that I know to keep silent.

A loud metallic banging and a high-pitched whistle startles me and prompts Ma to stare through a small slit in the fence. I shuffle over to look too and make out a shape of...*of someone? Something?* Actually I don't know what it is, and press my face right to the crack in the fence to see more clearly.

In the full beam of the moonlight I catch my breath. Suddenly I recognise the figure is a *Kankurang*. His back, arms and legs are covered in red bark, while my eye is caught by the glint of what is in his hands. Machetes.

Every subtle noise immediately seems to intensify – Ma's breathing, Mai's little cough, the tap of the pot, which my foot knocks. The *Kankurang* bangs the machetes together, turning in frenzy as he does so. For a second I think he's heard me, but, thankfully, he doesn't move our way. Unfortunately for us, he is stood at the crossroads of our compound and to get home, even if we go through the back of the compound, we have to cross his path. I copy Ma and sit with my back to the fence and wonder how long I can stay silent, unmoving. I doubt I can stay here until morning without being seen, but Ma doesn't seem as scared as I feel.

The machetes bang, their echo resonates in the night, even seeming to silence the crickets for once. For a while the banging stops and I shift my body quietly to take another look through the gap in the fence. The *Kankurang* is still stood in the middle of the crossroads, but is now still. Waiting.

Only when he has moved further down the road does Ma push herself up to stand. That is when baby Mai begins to stir: not a good time for her to wake. Ma takes my hand and peers around the fence where the sound of the machete's clashing grows quieter by the second.

'Now!' Ma says, and we rush across the road onto the path leading behind our compound, leaving the pot where it is. With the jiggling up and down, Mai begins to cry. It brings back the unmistakable sound of the machetes: the clashing noise coming closer, and faster.

'Quick, Binta!'

We speed across the yard and I can now hear the *Kankurang*'s feet just outside the compound wall. I desperately follow Ma up onto the veranda, where we scramble into the living room. She slams the door shut. Panting heavily, she leans against the door and laughs, which surprises me.

'Were you not scared?'

'Maybe a little! I forgot the *Kankurang* was out tonight. But they look more scary than they are – we weren't in real danger, Binta.'

'Then why were you hurrying?' I ask, catching my breath. I remember the news report about the one that killed someone and I'm not as convinced as she is that he wouldn't have done something.

'Well, I still didn't want to take the chance and stop and ask a machete-wielding *Kankurang* how friendly he really is! And when they come out at night they are more serious – not like when you see them entertaining the crowds in the daytime.'

'Why was he here?'

Ma hesitates, as though she's not sure whether to answer me, then straightens up and puts a hand on the door to balance, still gasping for air.

'Why do they come to town, Ma?'

Perhaps she feels that I deserve to know, after being so scared, because she says, 'The *Kankurang* is around during initiation.'

'Initiation?'

Ma pauses before answering, seeming to weigh up what information she's prepared to divulge.

'He's there to keep children safe as they become women,' she continues. 'Keeping evil spirits away. This is the time when the children are at their most vulnerable to witchcraft.'

'What do you mean Ma? How do they become women?'

'Nothing, Binta, nothing. I've said too much as it is. Don't ask me anything more.'

My head is full of questions, but as hard as I try, Ma doesn't say anything further, making me wish that I didn't know anything at all because I wouldn't be as frustrated. Better no information than half of something.

Tonight Ma lets me sleep on the sofa in the living room outside of her bedroom, in order for me to avoid going back outside, down the veranda to my room. She says that the *Kankurang* won't come into the compound but she doesn't argue with me when I ask to stay. I close my eyes and listen to the sporadic clanging of metal against metal as the *Kankurang* bangs the machetes together and wonder if perhaps Ma is right: if Isatou's gone to become a woman, and if the *Kankurang* is here – she must be near.

130

I draw the blanket over me, squished against the narrow row of cushions on the sofa and consider how Jena and I could now find out where Isatou is. She probably isn't in Serekunda after all. From the corner of the window I can still see the bright moon – it gives me the inspiration I need and I turn over with a plan already formulating in my mind.

After what Ma told me about the *Kankurang*, instead of feeling afraid, I fall asleep quickly knowing that it's just outside my compound keeping evil spirits away. And that it means Isatou is probably nearer than we thought.

Chapter 27

Yari

She's avoided me and I haven't had to set my eyes on her until now.

'Yari, wait.' There's a tone in her voice that I've not heard before. I don't know if it's because she's approaching with trepidation at my response, but, instead of walking away as I thought I would do, I turn and wait for Mamamuso, shuffling, to catch me up, and cross my arms. I don't say anything to her when she gets to me. It's as though my mind is numb; all those things I had thought about lying in bed at night, the venom that I would spout towards her.

'They are coming this afternoon.' She waits for my reaction, but when I remain silent she continues, 'Isatou is coming. I'll take you to where the celebration is.'

I never want to speak to Mamamuso again, apart from this last thing. 'I will not be attending any celebration. There is absolutely nothing – *nothing* – to rejoice. Bring Isatou home to me immediately.' Then I turn and walk away.

There is an emptiness, a sadness, that I feel in the core of my being that I've not protected my daughter, and I wonder when she sees me if she is going to hate me – because I do.

'She's asleep,' I say, easing myself down next to Sarko on the sofa.

'Did you tell her that Isatou's coming home?'

'No, I thought it best not. I didn't want her to stay awake and ask Isatou too many questions when she comes back. Do you think they'll be soon? It's late already.'

I don't need Sarko to answer; I know how it goes: the celebration the elders will put on will go on well into the night.

'I told Mamamuso to bring her quickly though,' I say. We sit for a long while quietly, eager for Isatou's return, but I'm also nervous about how she will respond. Louder than the past few days, the words ring in my head that we let her down.

'I went to another meeting at lunchtime today, when I was in Banjul,' Sarko says after some time. I can tell it's his effort to help me focus on something else. 'Support is gathering against the president; you should have heard them, Yari. I think it might only be a matter of time before we have some decent elections.'

'What's the point of elections, though, if they end up being duped?'

'No, I don't think that will happen. Not with the amount of support that there is; it will have to be fair.'

We both look up as we hear footsteps ascending the steps outside. I jump up and open the door. Mamamuso is in the shadows, keeping her distance and I barely sense her, I'm so focused on Isatou. I hug her tightly and bring her inside the house, shutting the door quickly... shutting out Mamamuso and all the horror she has imposed.

Sarko suddenly seems awkward. I can't blame him; all of this he shouldn't really know about and neither of us want to make Isatou more uncomfortable. He gets up from the sofa, kisses her on the head and hands her a packet of biscuits. 'I was in Banjul today and thought you might like these.'

'Thank you,' she says quietly. My heart races quickly at the sound of her voice again.

He starts to head to the bedroom, but then turns back and adds, forcing a smile in an attempt make the moment less tense, 'Maybe you could share some with your mum. You know how she loves them. Anyway, see you in the morning.'

I stand, holding Isatou for a long time, relieved that she's back with me, hoping that through my arms she can feel my sadness for what's happened, my regret, but most of all I hope she can sense the depth of my love.

Chapter 28

Binta

Under the tree in the middle of the compound, taking shade from the sapping afternoon heat, Yari is sat washing rice in a large bowl. Next to her is Jena who springs up when she sees me approach and runs over. I've been desperate to tell her about my encounter with the *Kankurang*, although I've been wondering how I will keep it to myself – that I think it means Isatou is near.

'Isatou is home!' Jena laughs.

'She's home?' I'm so excited to hear the news that all thoughts about telling Jena about Ma and me having to run away from the *Kankurang* at night completely disappear from my head. 'Where has she been? Was she at school?'

'I don't know exactly,' Jena says. 'I've asked, but she won't tell me and my mother said I mustn't probe her anymore. She was really cross for some reason when I wanted to know – it's annoying not knowing, but she was very clear that it's the end of the matter. Come, I have something for you!'

I follow Jena into the house, across the living room down the hallway, into her room. She hasn't been this relaxed and happy since before Isatou went away. Although I feel glad Isatou's back and Jena's no longer worried, I'm also frustrated. There is no explanation where she was. Somehow it felt that I was on the verge of finding out some important information, something that was nearly within my grasp – not just about where Isatou was, but the way Ma spoke, it seemed there was something much more to it. Now it feels as if that information is like water, something that you can put your hand on, but not hold in your fist.

'I've got some little shells. Come and have a look,' she says. 'Here. What do you think? Choose some and I'll plait them into your hair, if you want. You never know, Yaya might like them.'

'Hey!'

'What do you mean, "hey"? I know you like him, Binta.' Jena carefully drops a few small shells into my palm.

'They're pretty,' I remark, quickly changing the subject away from Yaya.

Before too long, Jena has combed out my hair and separated it into sections, plaiting it into rows from the front to the back of my head, causing my scalp to tingle from where she has plaited it tight.

'So, Isatou didn't say anything then about where she's been?'

'Just that she had to go away. She didn't say more – and you know what my mother is like, I can't ask again. What is strange though, is that Isatou doesn't want to tell me. I thought she'd be full of stories about where she's been.'

It confirms Ma's secret and I'm intrigued to find out more; even if Jena can't ask more questions, I want to.

In the distance we can hear Yari's voice calling for Jena. She gets up and leaves me to admire my new hair in a compact mirror on the bedside table. In the reflection I briefly catch a glimpse of Isatou passing by the bedroom door. This is my opportunity. I'm not sure how long Jena will be gone for, but I ease myself up off the floor and turn to go down the hallway to Isatou's room. Through the coloured hanging beads from the door, I can see her sat on her bed, reading.

I draw a handful of the beads to one side and ask, 'Hi! Can I come in?'

'Sure.'

'What are you reading?'

'Not much.'

'We missed you,' I say, tentatively. All the questions in my mind are fighting to be voiced, but my throat is dry. Somehow I know I am about to ask things I shouldn't – even though I'm not asking an adult – but I am too desperate to know. Yari hasn't said for me not to ask, she only spoke to Jena.

'Where did you go?'

She keeps looking at her book, as though she hasn't heard me. I try a different, approach, one I feel nervous about. My throat dries more before I can get the words to form, then I force them out and they come quickly. 'I've heard that girls go away to become women.'

'Who told you that?' Isatou asks, and I'm surprised by her harsh tone.

'I don't know.' I lift my shoulders and look down at my hands to avoid her stare. 'Sorry. I just missed you – I wondered where you'd gone.'

'Nowhere for you to worry about,' Isatou says, her tone a little gentler. 'Really, trust me.' She smiles but it doesn't properly reflect in her eyes, and I don't push the matter any further. 'Anyway, what's going on between you and Yaya now?'

'Oi!' I respond and laugh, attempting to ignore a sense there's this underlying awkwardness that has settled between us, like I've just pulled at a piece of thread and something is coming undone.

PART TWO

- The Crocodile -

A month ago

Chapter 29

Amie

I've timed it well. I've waited patiently for days for this moment. That's why for once I feel calm. Empowered. I am here to wait on him, to meet his every need, even those things that sicken me to my core.

It's the second of the three pains that a woman must bear.

I've learnt now that dismissing the pain – hiding it – makes him happy. And so I do. Like the third pain, I have learnt how it can be overcome. The power that comes by embracing it. I've also learnt that men seem stronger than they really are. Women harness hardships that men cannot imagine and in doing so we have a hidden strength that they are only tentatively aware of.

I have decided I can use this time; a window of opportunity – a moment that can shape my daughter's future. The thought makes it bearable knowing any moment he will open the door and spend the night with me; the first after being with his other wife for the last week. I sometimes lie here thinking of her. I wonder if she feels the same as me, or if she prefers his arms around her to an empty bed. The nights he is with her are the nights I rest and sleep deeply. When he is with me I spend the nights counting when he is due to be with her again.

Instead of pretending to be asleep – not that that stops things, just postpones it for a few moments more – tonight I lie on my side watching the clouds drift serenely across the bright, beautiful moon and I wait. Not with apprehension, but with anticipation of what I can do for Binta.

The moonlight shines a light across the room and I can see Mai's face, deep in a blissful baby sleep at the foot of my bed. How I'd love to be in that point in life again with no worries. The wonderful innocence we must all have started with.

I hear his cough, his signature approach from filling his lungs throughout the day with the smoke of tobacco. Again he coughs, part clearing his throat and then the bedroom door opens. Closes. I calm my breathing. Tonight I will be in control. This is an opportunity for me. I turn over and watch him approach.

Afterwards, before he falls into a sleep, I rest my hand on his rising and falling chest and say quietly, 'School is starting back soon, Ousman. I was wondering, could you allow Binta to attend one last year?' He turns and rummages for something in his trousers that are discarded on the floor next to the bed. I'm not sure if he's heard me, or if he's just ignoring my question and I immediately feel frustrated. The moment has gone and I've blown the chance.

Then he sits up in bed, puts a cigarette in his mouth. The sudden flame from the match lights his features and I can see he's thinking. The flame dies with the shake of his hand and is replaced by the red glow from the end of the cigarette, which intensifies as he takes a long drag. I hold my breath, not because of the smoke that travels over my face, but because I need his answer. If he is going to respond, it will be now. Then he says, 'I'll allow her this one, last year.'

In the darkness he is unable to see the happiness on my face. For a moment I am delighted and I put my arm on his shoulder and watch the cigarette diminish with each inhale. It is almost hypnotic. Then, in the darkness, in the quiet, he follows up his answer further and says, 'One more year, but there's something that needs to happen. You know what it is, Amie.' I remove my arm from his shoulder, trying to comprehend the words he has said. Hoping I've misunderstood. But from the pounding in my heart, I know what he's said. He turns his back on me as he presses the end of the cigarette into the ashtray on the bedside table. 'Make sure it's done by the time her schooling finishes. No more wasting time. You have to do what mothers have to do.' With those words, I feel a dread immediately descend and I'm glad the darkness hides my fear from his eyes.

Chapter 30

Binta

For the first two weeks of the new school year, the days are occupied with fixing the classroom roof with palm leaves from the forest. Lessons don't begin until that task is complete, towards the end of the third week. By the time I eventually sit down in the classroom my hands are chapped and sore. There is a small hole in the hem of my new dress. I look up at the ceiling in my classroom and feel I know every strand of the palm leaf above my head; there's a deep satisfaction that comes from sitting under something that I've created from hard work. My eyes drop towards the door where a teacher makes an entrance.

I don't recognise him from past years. From the way his hair is beginning to grey, I imagine he's the same age as Mr Janneh, although this teacher's eyes lack the same amiable glint that Mr Janneh has. He doesn't have any of those lines that Mr Janneh has from all his smiling; there are only creases on his forehead from frowning, which he is doing as he steps alongside the blackboard. A silence settles upon the class as he stares intently over our desks, not bothering to hide his antipathy towards us.

The teacher takes a stack of thick textbooks from the table at the front and walks slowly up and down each of the aisles, throwing a book onto each of the desks, the frown on his face barely easing.

'My name is Mr Darbo,' he says, and drops another book. Although I'm anticipating it, I still feel my stomach flip when it lands with a slap onto my desk. It spins but I catch it, with relief, before it slides and falls on the floor. The pages are yellow and curled at the edges and the word on the front cover is starting to fade. My finger follows the letters before me. 'MATHEMATICS,' I silently read.

He sits down at his wooden desk, underneath a large blackboard at the front of the class. Mr Darbo's voice fills the air: 'Page nine. You have half an hour.'

The only sound is a rustle of paper as we open the books, but we don't utter a word: we've already sussed out his type. The type that you dread having each year, the kind of teacher you feel sorry that others have, but secretly relieved you don't.

I quietly turn the pages, but the English and the numbers merge together and don't make any sense. Thankfully, I'm sat next to Jena, which is the best thing about being at school.

'*I don't understand,*' I whisper and lean over closer to her.

Before she replies, the newly familiar voice immediately bellows from the front. 'Stand up, girl!'

It is so loud that I imagine I can hear the palm roof I helped make rustle. It sends an instant shock through my body. My heart speeds up, even though I'm not sure it's me he's addressing. The classroom is even quieter as he makes his way towards the back of the room – towards me. I know he's coming my way, even though my eyes are fixed on the blurring words in the textbook. Heat rises in my cheeks, and my body tingles in dread with each footstep he makes.

'STAND!' Mr Darbo shouts again and when he towers over me there's no doubt whom he's addressing.

I struggle to fight the urge to freeze and move my chair back slowly. Mr Darbo grabs my arm and marches me to the front of the class while all eyes watch me intensely. At least Jena's are friendly, if not anxious for me.

'What is so important that you not only interrupt my lesson, but you are using vernacular?'

I'm confused.

'Well?' he says, and reaches for a large stick, balanced carefully on a ledge above the blackboard. I eye the cane and have a sudden urge to pee from the fear that's building up with each moment. Being embarrassed is more awful than the anticipation of the pain that I know is coming, and I close my eyes and try not to imagine wetting myself in front of everyone.

'Let me clarify. No talking and certainly no vernacular. Let me see your hands, girl,' he says, and uses the stick to turn them over.

The force when it comes down a second later on my palms brings instant tears to my eyes. The red welt across my hand throbs intensely and then another stinging pain comes. Again and again he hits me. It takes all my energy not to cry in front of my classmates, but I can't help but let out a gasp with each hit. As I stand in front of the class and the pain burns through

146

my skin, I wonder why I was so desperate for my father to agree for me to return to school.

When Mr Darbo finishes, he sends me back to sit down. I look to the floor to avoid all the stares, still unsure what I did wrong, but feel guilty nonetheless.

'Stop!' I now hate that voice, and hold my breath. 'Sit down where you are.'

I sit quickly and long so deeply for the incident to pass that I don't notice the girl next to me until later. I just want to hide, for the stares to stop. I close my eyes for a brief moment, hold onto my juju and think this is an excellent time to vanish.

Only when I hear the light scratch of pencil on paper from around me from others focused again on their work, do I open my eyes again. I'm still holding onto my juju when another teacher peers around the door. 'Mr Darbo,' he says. 'Could I trouble you for a moment? I need your assistance with my unruly boys.'

'Of course,' he replies. Obviously his reputation is not just with the pupils. It does actually surprise me that the juju's worked for once. I might not have disappeared, but this is the next best thing. When Mr Darbo goes out of the room, it gives me chance to rub my hands together to ease the stinging.

'That looks painful,' the girl next to me whispers and glances towards the door.

I know her face, but I've not been in a class with her before. Before I respond, I check Mr Darbo hasn't suddenly reappeared and venture, '*Ebe kairato?*'

'I don't speak Mandinka,' she replies.

'What's your name?' I try again, this time in English. I feel a bit foolish for assuming she'd understand

Mandinka and, as I wait for her answer, hope she doesn't think I'm stupid.

'Esther.' She smiles and asks mine.

The knot in the pit of my stomach starts to untie. 'Binta.'

'Mandinka?'

'Yes.'

'How are your hands?' Esther asks, reaching towards them to turn my palms upwards. As she does, I see that the tip of her middle finger is missing. I look away quickly and hope she hasn't noticed me glancing.

'I'm not sure what I did so wrong,' I say and rub my hands, looking over to the classroom entrance.

'Because you spoke in vernacular.'

I'm still confused, which must be obvious, because she continues, 'You spoke Mandinka, not English.'

'Oh,' I say, but I still don't really understand. I don't want to come across as stupid, so I just ask her what tribe she's from.

'*Karoninka.*'

There are only a handful of them in town. I don't know any – well, not until just now – but I do know they are Christians. Esther smiles warmly. She doesn't look much different to us Mandinkas, same dark complexion – unlike the *Fulas*...they are very fair. But her nose is smaller than mine and she has a beautiful smile, which makes me feel we're friends already.

My father's words form in my head. '*What can a* Karoninka *know about our Islamic traditions, about our Mandinka ways? They don't believe our holy prophet Mohammed – peace be upon him – is the last prophet. Instead, they think Jesus is God's actual son! Crazy thinking – it gives me a headache. How can God have a son? Blasphemy!*' Other people don't have a problem with Christians, but my father always has his own ideas on things. He can be stubborn like that. As I said, Ma says I take after him, but I don't see it. I'm not like him at all.

I smile quickly to reassure Esther that I'm happy to be her friend too and she offers me her hand to shake. I go to, but then remember the missing top part of her finger and hesitate. She must realise, because then she shrugs and says, 'It's okay. It happened ages ago, when I was little.'

'What happened?' I ask before I can stop myself.

Esther doesn't seem to mind my question. 'I was playing on a gate. I was standing on the bottom rung, and my brother swung it shut. Only, he didn't know that my finger was next to the hinge.'

'Ouch!'

'Yeah, I guess! But it was a long time ago. I can't remember much about it. Unless I want to tease my brother!' We both laugh and it seems to cement the beginning of our friendship. It's one of those friendships that I can just tell will be special, which is why I immediately decide that I won't mention it to my mother, in case my father finds out she's a *Karoninka* and thinks we shouldn't be friends.

Chapter 31

Amie

I watch her reading, wondering how she makes sense of the black marks against the white. Sometimes, when she has left her books on the table and I'm alone like I am now, I lift the pages carefully and run my finger across the words. I whisper under my breath what I think they might say. There are some I remember from school, but most I don't. These extra couple of years of schooling will help Binta remember those things, it will allow things to settle properly and to grow – rather than vanish as they did for me. I'm so proud of her. Everything I missed out on, I treasure seeing in her.

A thought suddenly appears in my mind. I think how the year is quickly moving on, her time at school coming to an end. As though shutting the thought away, I close the book quickly, as though it will somehow make a difference.

Ousman is expecting me to keep my promise soon. I've spent time over the months trying to think how to get around it. He really shouldn't have even mentioned it and the fact he did means that it will happen, even without me. I'm not sure how; perhaps he'll speak to his mother, or sisters. I shudder at that thought. The shame and the discussions that people will have behind my back that I'm not doing my duty as a mother. I feel trapped. I don't want to do this. But if I don't it will happen anyway – Ousman will make sure – and the consequences will be worse.

Chapter 32

Binta

The school year passes quickly; the season transitions without much notice into the dry season until the air is noticeably cooler. The searing heat of summer is replaced by the Harmattan wind that travels from the Sahara Desert that blows grit and deposits grains into every pore of skin, and when I blink it scratches my eyes. The dust also gives me an irritating, lingering cough. I get it every year. Once I thought I was dying – Ma had to take me to the clinic and I got an injection in my buttocks, of all places – the embarrassment worse than the sting of the needle. It stopped my cough, but the memory of standing in the middle of the waiting room, having that injection, gives me reason enough to tell Ma I'm okay, even when my chest burns.

Harmattan is with us again when Esther invites us to her home. We meet at Mr Janneh's but I notice that Isatou isn't with Jena.

'Where's Isatou?'

'She's not feeling so well. Stomach ache, she said.'

'She often seems to be unwell these days. Do you think she's just not wanting to hang around with us as much?' I ask. Immediately I feel that I'm being unkind, that if she's unwell, I should be thinking about how she is, but I also wonder if she really is as sick as she is saying. 'Maybe she should see a doctor,' I say.

'That's what I said, but my mother said it's just women's things.'

We walk along the road that leads to a far part of town that I don't recognise, and although I want to ask more, Jena's comment seems to have finality to it. I'm not satisfied with her explanation of women's things – what does that mean?

A bush taxi races past, kicking up dust around us. On a quiet side road, we pass a shop owned by a man with fairer skin than even Ibrahim, the *Fula*, but his features are very different. He has an angular nose that reminds me of *Toubabs*, with high cheekbones.

'He's a Moor – from Mauritania,' Esther says to us.

'Where's that?'

'North of Senegal. Blacks are still slaves there, you know.'

'Really?'

'Yes, they tried to make it illegal, but there are loads of black slaves there still.'

'Do you think they take them from here?'

'Like the Kunta Kinta story, Binta?' Jena laughs.

'What's so funny? You wouldn't be laughing if you were taken as a slave!' I say, and pick up my pace as we walk pass the Moor's shop. I'm not taking the chance.

Esther tells us we're nearly at her home, just as there's a piercing scream that resounds in the air, causing a small flock of birds to take flight from a tree. We stand still and look at each other; I'm not sure if they are as scared as I am, but this isn't good. Esther walks slowly and we follow her around the corner.

There's a man running around in circles, flapping his arms and screaming again and again, in a way that men never should do. Possessed.

'What's he doing?' Jena asks and crouches behind me.

'He's tormented by a demon,' I say. The beat of my heart is hard in my throat. My body is tense, ready to run away from the evil spirits. I wish we hadn't come. For a moment, I wonder if my father might have found out about me being friends with Esther, and put some kind of bad juju on me – getting a witch to follow us. Then, as I eye up the road we've just come from to find somewhere to run, I spot a group of boys sprinting away, waving sticks in their hands. Their laugher mingles with the man's screams. There's a broken bees nest high up in the tree with a few buzzing, still hovering above. It's clear now what's happened. There's no bad juju and I exhale, relieved. I look over to the man where I can now see the faint haze of the swarm attacking him.

'Bees!' I shout and duck under a wall. Esther and Jena quickly follow me and huddle tight against the bricks, our heads low.

'What are we going to do?'

The man runs into the nearest compound, stripping his clothes off as he goes, and continues to scream. When Esther tells us that it's her compound he's run into, we don't dare venture out. We remain behind the wall until my legs tingle from inaction and the deadening numbness in my legs becomes uncomfortable.

154

After what seems to be an age, with no more buzzing in the air, we decide to make our way across to Esther's home. The bee-stung man is lying on the veranda, groaning. A couple of men are seeing to him – probably Esther's relatives.

'Will he be okay?' Esther asks as she approaches a man and woman sat in armchairs outside, under the shade of a tree.

'Poor man was embarrassed, after removing his clothes. We've come over here to give him some dignity while your uncles see to him. He was very lucky.'

'These are my friends from school. This is Hannah, my mother – Moses, my father.'

'Welcome! Come and join us for tea.' Hannah gestures to empty seats.

Hannah hands me a cup – a china one, like Ma's – with a pattern of red roses delicately sweeping around the handle; only Ma never gets it out to use. A young man comes through the gate with a bag slung over his shoulder.

'Good evening, uncle.'

'Isaac. How are you? You're just in time! Come and join us for food.'

'This is my cousin – Isaac,' Esther says. 'He works in the bank in Serekunda, though he never brings me any money!'

Isaac searches in his trouser pocket, throws a 5 cent coin at Esther, and playfully pushes her back into the seat.

'Little sister, if you want more, you need to earn it yourself!'

'You'll have to forgive my rude cousin,' she giggles. 'His name means "to laugh at".'

'Eat your food, little one; otherwise you'll stay small.'

'So what brings you here, Isaac? I thought you weren't due to come until the weekend?' Moses asks.

There's a pause, then Isaac leans forwards and says, so quietly that I can hardly hear him, 'Uncle, I wanted to come and tell you about what happened this morning in Serekunda. Have you heard?'

'Heard what?'

'There was an attempted coup in the army barracks at Farrafeni. About half a dozen men stormed the barracks in the middle of the night. Gunshots were heard and reports on the radio this morning said several soldiers had been killed.'

'That's awful,' Hannah mutters.

'Do they know who stormed the army barracks?' Moses asks.

'No, but the word is it's probably Sanyang supporters. The coup failed and the armed men are on the run.' Isaac looks at Moses. 'Uncle, I came to let you both know the army is looking for the men and things may become dangerous for people who might sympathise with them. You need to be careful now.'

I catch Jena looking across at me anxiously and it is enough to trigger the memory of hearing Yari in Serekunda – when she said she'd be interested in knowing more about those opposing the government. We'll have to let Yari know what Isaac's said: the sooner, the better. I don't like what Isaac said about it becoming dangerous for some people, and I have a feeling Yari counts as one of those.

Chapter 33

Amie

Sometimes it feels as though nothing changes, one day spills into another. There are the daily chores, the washing and cooking, cleaning and going to the fields. Day after day as time edges forward it's easy to dismiss how change is on the horizon. I look down at Mai, the way she pauses in her suckling at my breast and she glances up and giggles in delight. Moments like this I want to capture forever. There is so much that stays the same around me that I wonder if the promises I made to Ousman – the way Binta is heading towards being a woman – will be forgotten somehow.

I wish that would be the case, but know it's not true.

But Mai also reminds me that things are changing; my baby no longer has the smell of a newborn, her teeth cutting through her gum. The niggling certainty that change is coming. My children are growing. That is what motivated me to be here today. The library isn't a place I've been to since it was opened when Binta was a baby.

In the centre of the room is a semi-circle of wooden seats where the elders sit already in a heated discussion.

People are stood tightly packed, making the air stifling. I stay near the door, not just because the dust is heavy where half-open boxes of books are placed around the room, but because I don't feel brave enough to enter further in. I see Yari at the front and others that seem equipped and confident to be in those positions. I'm half in, half out of the building, as though only tentatively exploring the discussion that is happening here. Along with the heat in the room, voices raise in discord and disagreement. The elders join together in their individually frail speech to shout down the voices of a newer generation.

I'm forced a few inches closer into the room as others arrive behind me, straining to hear the discussions about our traditions. This is a first. I've heard about these kinds of meetings in the city, but to have this happening in our own town is something else. Part of me is excited that it's even happening. Something about this room being full of people discussing things that we never speak of feels both exhilarating and unsettling. I catch the opinions of Yari and her fellow campaigners and hear the murmurs jeering her on around me, before the elders dispel her views. Along with words, the room is heavy with the attitude of the town. It almost feels like a physical force fighting against two sides. It is powerful.

That's what makes me resolved. I came interested, a little intrigued perhaps to hear what the campaigners wanted to say. What their arguments were. But even those educated and powerful people cannot stand up to our ancient ways. As more people arriving push me, I can no longer see Yari or the other campaigners. I can't hear their voice anymore above the rumble of people talking them down. I turn and force myself into the fresh air again and leave, taking the phrases with me that I've always heard. That this is our way. It can't be changed. This is how it has always been.

As I walk home, my head feels as though there are bees flying all around in my mind. I can't think clearly. I am now aware that by going to the library today I had hoped there was a different way. I hoped that others would be strong enough for me. But all I know now is that I am certain of what has to happen and nothing will stop it.

I walk over to sit under the baobab tree at the side of the road when Mai begins to cry. I unstrap her from my back and sit for a moment to rest under the shade of the ancient tree and feed her; to rest and to allow peace to come in my head. I look at the bark and think how old this tree is, how long it has been here. I have no more strength to move it than the ways of old. I know I'm hoping for a miracle. I look down at Mai suckling at my breast, unaware of my worries. Miracles are all around. You never know. I just wish time could slow down to give change a chance.

Chapter 34

Binta

Grey clouds, indicative of the imminent deluge of rain, cover the sky completely. There is a tangible, building electric tension in the air. Older students with longer legs walk past me quickly on the way to school, keen to avoid being caught in the downpour. I can't believe the rainy season has come around again so soon. In fact, today is the last day of term. As I pass through the quiet, sacred prayer ground, under the thick covering of ancient trees, I hear the distant rumble of thunder. Before I'm the other side of the holy place there is an immediate, instantaneous deafening noise above me, of water cascading onto leaves. In less than five minutes the ground has turned a terracotta colour, sudden large puddles forming rusty-looking water; I'm ankle-deep in the rainwater and drops run down my face and cover my eyes, blurring my vision.

Thunder sounds again, closer, which seems to intensify the torrent and motivates me to walk faster. To my surprise, the palm-leaf roof of our classroom has lasted through the increasingly frequent rainstorms that mark this time of year. As I take refuge at my desk, I watch the droplets find several places to pour through and wonder if it will last the last few hours of the academic year. Eyeing it suspiciously, I'm not convinced. The continuous dull thud on the roof draws my attention from the monotonous droning of Mr Darbo's teaching, his back turned to us as he writes equations that I never understand on the blackboard with white chalk, the dust floating gently on his shoes. I can't see that from where I'm sat, but I've noticed in the past the white speckled chalk as he walks up the aisles checking our work.

The pelting on the roof, the different timings of water streaming from the leaves, is quite hypnotic. Minutes have disappeared and I immediately panic that I am not aware of what Mr Darbo has been saying. He is now quiet, facing the blackboard with his back to us, and the class bent over desks, writing equations from the textbook. I have no idea what I'm meant to be doing. I sense that he will ask me a question any second, and with Isatou sat too far away to ask today, my heart speeds up and my mind quickens, thinking how I'm going to save myself from another barrage of humiliation.

Impulsively I tear a piece of paper from the corner of my exercise book, roll it tightly and take aim. A tiny paper ball bounces off of Jena's back and she turns around. Her creased brows silently question me.

'What are we meant to be doing?' I whisper; I mouth the words, emphasising them so that she might understand without me being louder.

Jena's brows narrow further, trying to understand, oblivious to what I'm trying to convey even when I attempt to ask her again.

Neither of us, or anyone else in the class, expects the board rubber to come flying through the air, which knocks against her chair leg and drops to the floor.

'You, girl. Why are you talking?' Mr Darbo directs his question to Jena, who has quickly turned back around to face the right direction.

My heart races, my face suddenly feels hot and I hold my breath in hope that it will stop the inevitable punishment that is bound to follow. Jena doesn't say anything as he walks towards her. She remains quiet when Mr Darbo asks her again. She's silent out of loyalty to me, quietly brave.

I'm silent out of fear.

My words could stop her having to be pulled out from her seat by her ear and marched to his desk at the front; my voice could stop him reaching for the cane on the blackboard. If only I could force my speech, it would stop him from bringing the stick hard across her hand in a beating that should be for me. I cannot bear for her to exchange a knowing glance and drop my eyes to the book on my desk. Inside I feel awful – horrible as I hear the cane connect with her palm, the slight gasp as she inhales with pain. I listen to Jena's slow footsteps back to her desk and sense Isatou looking at me with disdain.

The lesson concludes subdued; nobody else wants to chance Mr Darbo's wrath. The rain has stopped and the bell for the end of the day rings. Although this is our last lesson with him, I don't feel elated. I just feel heavy with guilt, ashamed at the way I've let my friend take a beating that she didn't deserve. I remain in my seat until the class is empty, watching Esther and Jena ease out of the door with the stream of others until I am alone. I stay in my place, feeling too empty to move.

After a few moments, I resolve I must leave, push my chair back and despondently walk out of the room. The late-afternoon sun breaks through the dispersing clouds, but the bright warm rays don't reach me – I have my own internal perpetual storm. Jena and Isatou are underneath the tree in the centre of the yard, which I have to pass. I consider avoiding them by walking around the back of the school, but decide that I owe it to Jena to apologise; take a breath and walk towards her. I expect Jena to shout at me, call me names or at least ignore my presence but when she sees me, she doesn't do any of those things.

'I'm so sorry, Jena. I understand if you don't want to be my friend,' I say quietly, as I tentatively approach.

'Don't say that. You would have done the same for me.'

I don't answer straight away. After today I don't know – my actions have spoken, have shown what type of person I am: a coward, a lousy friend, selfish, self-preserving. Then Jena takes a step forward and wraps her hands around me, hugging me. 'It's okay, Binta.'

'I'm sorry,' I say and squeeze her tight, relieved. I nearly lost our friendship. I then step back from her hold and tell her determinedly, 'I won't let you down again, Jena.'

'In that case, you've got to come to the end-of-term disco tomorrow.' At my hesitation, she continues. 'You have to come, Binta – we're finishing Middle School! And you owe me!' Any of the sadness from being beaten by Mr Darbo has evaporated and Jena is just excited to leave school – who wouldn't be after today? For Jena – and Isatou – it's an end of a chapter, going from one school to another. For me I think it's the end of a chapter in a different way. I've overheard the usual arguments between my parents about my future; my father has decided that this is now it, for me. No more education; Ma has argued all she can.

My mouth starts to form my response to tell her that I've got to ask Ma's permission first, which I know isn't going to be straightforward because she's always saying how it was never respectable in her day to go to a dance. I can hear her voice in my head saying, 'just girls on their own, without their families, gyrating their hips, asking for trouble.' I'm not quite sure what trouble she means. Instead, I smile and tell Jena, 'Of course.'

It is easier to slip out of the compound than I envisioned. Ma is busy trying to settle baby Mai, who is thankfully particularly grouchy – when I tell her I'm visiting Jena and Isatou, she doesn't think to ask me questions. I take the opportunity to head off quickly, before she has a chance to ask where we are going.

The disco is a simple structure, a cemented dance floor surrounded by a ten-foot-high wall. There isn't a roof, which is why the place is located along the quiet road on the outskirts of town because the music drifts up and over the walls into the night sky. Initially, the bubbling inside me was because I knew Ma won't be happy if she found out, but now the feeling is excitement, heightened by the anticipation of having to wait our turn to pass through the small green metal door.

'Binta, Jena…Isatou!'

I look around and see Esther running towards us; she quickly edges into the queue to be with us. We shuffle through the door and on the other side there's a desk, which looks like it has been 'accidentally borrowed' from our school, where a tall man in his early twenties sells tickets for two dalasi.

'Good thing I had generous neighbours at *Tobaski*!' I nudge Isatou, and hand over my money.

Once I'm inside, a string of green-and-blue lights hanging from the walls illuminates the place, attracting mosquitos and moths, which seem to court each other in time to the music. Jena takes Isatou by the hand as she hesitates to enter the crowded place. Isatou used to be the first to try things, the boldest of us, but these days she seems more timid. I don't know why? I dismiss the thought and follow tightly behind, not wanting to lose sight of them – it's not a big place, but there's a lot of people and the token lights aren't bright enough to find each other easily. Ma's words ring in my head that this place can bring trouble and I don't fancy getting caught up in any fights or anything.

'These look like the last couple of seats,' Isatou says and takes one, but Jena looks eagerly at the dance floor, 'Come on, let's dance!'

'Yeah, come on, I love this song,' Esther says.

'We'll lose these seats though.'

'We didn't come here to sit, Isatou.'

I'm surprised to see how determined Isatou is gripping onto the chairs, her eyes cautiously scanning the crowded dance floor.

'It's okay. I'll stay here and look after the seats,' she offers, and sits down quickly before any of us can encourage her to dance. 'But come back after the next song,' she immediately adds. I begin to follow Jena and Esther, but when I glance back to Isatou she is sat on the edge of her chair, sat on her hands looking anxious and her demeanour draws me back.

'Want me to stay with you?' I ask and she looks up at me and smiles. She removes her hands from under her lap and her shoulders relax.

'Please,' she replies. 'Just for a song, I'll be fine in a minute.'

'What's wrong?' I ask.

'Nothing. I just don't want to dance – but I just don't want to be on my own either.'

I turn my head to trace where Jena and Esther merge into the crowd on the dance floor, so I know where to look for them if Isatou doesn't want to dance after the next couple of songs. I feel a bit torn. Isatou doesn't seem too keen to do anything but sit, but I didn't come here to do that; I came to dance! From the corner of my eye I sense a figure approach.

'Can I sit here?'

'It's for my friends,' I say, putting a protective hand on one of the two empty chairs, but then I turn as I recognise whom the voice belongs to. The green light shines against Yaya's face and gives him a surreal glow. The dimples in his cheeks appear as he smiles.

'Just until they come back?' he asks.

'Sure,' I say.

I absorb every second of the move he makes to come around and to sit down opposite me, the way his forearm tenses as he takes the chair, the way the tendons in his wrist contract. I feel a prickly heat rising in my neck and I suddenly turn to watch the dancing. Instead of seeing people flowing to the rhythms of the music, in my mind I'm just seeing Yaya and I remember the time on the beach when I saw him in the sea. Water droplets that looked liked diamonds on his skin. I'm aware Isatou's probably watching my reaction to Yaya and

166

I feel a little embarrassed, but I try to ignore that for a minute because I'm also enjoying his attention.

'Do you like Yussan Dour?' he asks.

Although he is wearing a short-sleeved shirt, the image in my mind remains and my eye drifts to the open top buttons, revealing a hint of what I saw that day on the beach. Consciously I blink hard and cough to clear my throat. 'Yes, I love Yussan Dour.'

'Want to dance, then?'

'I've got to look after the seats.'

'How about your friend? Can she look after them?'

'What do think, Isatou?' I ask as quietly as I can above the booming bass from the music filling the air. She hesitates, but then looks over my shoulder and nods. I turn around and see Jena and Esther heading back towards us.

I don't need any further convincing, 'Okay,' I say to Yaya, and try to stifle the excitement in my voice as a familiar fluttering rises in my stomach.

His hand feels strong, warm against mine. I wrap my fingers around his and my heart pounds hard in my chest; I can't believe that we are on the dance floor together and I have to resist the urge to shout for joy, because I'm sure that would ruin the moment. Instead, I walk composed with him past the thundering speakers to the far corner, as though I've done this before, feeling grown and mature.

My fingers reluctantly uncurl from his hand as we begin to dance. The music slows the introduction to my favourite ballad, four notes repeated having the effect of switching the atmosphere on the dance floor, and I notice many of those around me are couples. Yaya begins to dance, his feet shift from one to the other in gentle steps to the beat, his arms sway from side to side and then I copy. For the first few moments I feel conspicuous, but then, as the music crescendos, I close my eyes and allow the notes to flow over me. My arms wave to the beat; my feet find a rhythm as my body interprets the emotions that are bubbling from inside. I open my eyes and look up at the sky where the stars shine brightly and I feel I could live this moment forever.

Chapter 35

Amie

I've not been here for many months. The taxi stops and I balance Mai on my lap as I manoeuvre out of the vehicle. There is a different atmosphere here than at the beach. At the side of the river fishermen still bring in their catch, a few women sort through the baskets seeing what they can barter to take home. The price is better here than at the market, but it's the women that live close to the river that take advantage of that. Two hours walk here from Kenji is too far to make the deal worthwhile. Even with a sister in this village, I don't visit often and each time I walk down the road to her compound, the building guilt that I've been away too long increases with every step. On my return to where the taxis drop people, I know later today I will have the familiar feeling of renewed resolution to come back again sooner – but really I come as often as I can and I won't be coming any more frequent. I know that deep down, but I'll tell myself otherwise. But like me, her main support comes not from siblings, but from our *Kafos*. With that thought in mind, it eases the sense of duty I have to come and see her more than I can.

Evening is nearly here. I look out across the river to the other bank where mangroves curve around the meandering shape of the water. The sky hasn't changed, but the birds are more active, different species dancing in harmony to alternative rhythms in the sky. Some flock in a line, others move in perfect synchronisation. Up stream a singular dug-out canoe gently drifts with ease as the fisherman paddles slowly to shore. It makes me think of the many times, like now, that I have stood on the banks of the River Gambia, mesmerised by the gentle flow of water with birds chirping in the trees along the mangroves.

But there have also been times when I've seen the river after storms. That's when it takes on a new life. The swollen brown water rapidly charges forward. It pushes heavy logs along with ease in its power. Nothing withstands its force.

I'm not sure where the feeling comes from all of a sudden, but the image of stormy water fills my mind. As I rock side to side, tapping Mai gently on the back to settle her, I think of the power of the storm coming in my own life. The water might look calm here, but that doesn't mean the rain isn't already building a terrible flood upstream. I can sense how although my life looks calm now, something is happening in the distance that will come against me with overwhelming power. It's already started and I am helpless against what will come.

It feels as though I'm being swept away by something greater than me, like the river. A momentum that I can't stand up against that has flowed from generations long ago.

Chapter 36

Binta

I open my eyes and carefully assess things – was I dreaming it? My mind retraces the night before and the excited bubbling in my stomach immediately returns. It really did happen – dancing with Yaya. I replay each moment and savour it. It's a good thing that I'm still lying down because I feel a bit giddy from joy. I think of how we danced together, becoming more comfortable with each other so that we began to mirror each other's moves. Then Esther needed to go, so Jena, Isatou and I walked her to the crossroads before doubling back to the market square. After saying goodnight to my friends, Yaya reappeared, out of breath from running. 'I thought I'd missed you,' he said. 'Can I walk you home?'

Can I walk you home? I say the words again in my mind and replay how long it took us to travel the short distance from the market, walking slowly as we chatted. As I stumbled on a pothole, Yaya reached out to balance me, but afterwards left his hand in mine until we were outside my compound. I close my eyes and touch the side of my cheek where his lips rested for a wonderful moment as he leant forward to kiss me.

My moment of enjoyment is rudely disturbed when Musa jumps onto the bed to sit. He squashes my leg as he does so. 'Oi!' I shout. 'What are you doing?'

He's got a grin on his face, which makes me cautious.

'I know,' he says.

'You know what?'

'I know.'

'Go away, Musa; I'm just waking up.'

'I know.'

'Leave me alone,' I say and turn over. I bring up the blanket around me in the hope that it will make him disappear. I have to pull it hard because he's still sat on it, but it does the trick and he stands up.

'Well, if you don't want to know what I know – Ma will,' he says and starts for the door.

I remove the blanket from around my head and prop myself up. Already dreading what he's got planned, I tentatively ask, 'What is it, Musa? Tell me then.' It gets him to stop and retract a couple of his steps.

'I saw you last night – with that boy.'

'What do you mean?' I ask and my pulse quickens.

'The boy who kissed you.'

'You did not!' I say and attempt to sound nonchalant, which isn't easy when there is a rising panic inside of me. He's too far away for me to grab him and before I can get out of bed, Musa has spun around and runs out of the room singing, 'Yes, you did!'

I fall back onto my pillow and stare at the ceiling and wonder how bad this is. Why should I feel bad about Yaya kissing me? Why should I feel bad about something so lovely? Although my reasoning tells me there is nothing to worry about – it is just Musa being Musa – the excitement I had has turned to nervousness about what Ma is going to say. Perhaps I should tell her first? Musa is bound to exaggerate, make something seem bad even when it isn't. Ma has told me before that there is a right way of doing things and that I shouldn't hang around with boys, which I've never done; but now I'm getting older, surely she'll change her mind. And Yaya is a nice boy. I'm sure she'll understand. I just have to tell her before Musa does. But it doesn't help, I suddenly remember, that I didn't tell her that I was going to the disco in the first place.

It isn't until late afternoon that I find Ma on her own after she comes from the fields with Mai on her back. She looks tired. I follow her into the house and offer to unstrap Mai off her back. She sits down on the sofa and removes her headscarf. 'Oh, Binta, it was hot out there today.'

Mai is asleep and I take her through to the bedroom, place her on the centre of the bed and then go to the water jar in the corner of the room to get Ma a drink.

'There you go, Ma,' I say. I come back into the living room and hand her the cup.

'You are a good girl, thank you.'

I sit next to her on the sofa and wonder how I'm going to start the topic about Yaya. Every time I go to open my mouth my throat feels blocked. Has Musa told her already? If he hasn't, then I don't need to worry about this. Then again, he could tell her anything – tell her Yaya's not a nice boy – someone I need to stay away from. After what seems like an eternity I ask her, 'Ma, what would happen if one day a boy liked me?'

She's taking a sip of her drink and the water seems to go down the wrong way as she sputters, 'If a boy likes you, Binta?' She puts the cup on the coffee table.

'Yes, I mean, you know – one day.'

'Well, there are ways – things have to be done in a certain way.'

'How?'

'When you are older you will find out.'

'When will that be, Ma?'

My nervousness has turned to frustration and I feel cheated, both because Musa has put me in the position of asking – and he obviously hasn't told her anything yet – and because Ma isn't giving me any answers.

'I want it to be as long as possible.'

'I don't understand.'

'I don't want you having to worry about these things yet.'

Through the frustration I become bolder in my questions and ask her, 'And what if I like a boy?'

She pauses, her eyes narrow slightly in the way they always do when she wants to find something out from me. It's like a key to my soul, that narrowing of the eyes. They always seem to prise open the truth. 'Is there a boy you like, Binta?'

I shrug, knowing how fruitless that is. She's still staring at me a moment longer and I can't stand the narrow eyes trying to pierce my layers. 'Kind of,' I admit, and shrug slightly in an attempt to undermine the importance of it.

She puts her hand on my arm, sighs and says, 'My Binta, you are growing up too fast. Much, much too soon.'

'He's a nice boy, Ma. I know you will like him.'

She squeezes my arm gently and says quietly, 'That may be, my love, but there are things that have to happen before boys get interested in you – and you in boys.'

'What Ma?'

She doesn't answer. It looks as though she is trying to stop a tear from falling, but I don't understand how I've made her upset. Then she kisses me on the head. 'Whatever happens, always know that I love you.'

'I know that, Ma.'

Then she gets up slowly, probably from the effort of working at the fields and tells me, 'I'm going out for a while – keep an eye on your sister.'

I watch her leave and I'm not sure how to feel or what to make of what we've just talked about. She wasn't angry, like Musa implied she'd get, but I also didn't get any answers. In fact, I am more confused. What things have to happen? If that means I can be free to like Yaya then I want to know.

But why, if she didn't shout at me, or get angry, did she also seem sad?

Chapter 37

Amie

Now things are in motion.

I feel guilty in many ways. There is the guilt I feel that I have to do this – and that there is no other way. Then there is the guilt I feel that I nearly didn't act and that I would have let her down. A guilt I feel for acting – and guilt I feel for not acting. But it is fear more than guilt that is the catalyst now. A fear of what might have been. Binta wouldn't have been prepared for the future and I would have let her down in the time I've delayed things by questioning and hoping for a different path. I've come here, letting my feet lead me without thinking; the fear pulsing through my veins moves me forward.

I tried to ignore what needed to happen, wished for there to be a different way, but I can see that wasn't going to be. I have to ensure my lack of action until now doesn't have a lasting impact for Binta. She doesn't know all that she needs to yet. Telling me about that boy made me realise how I've nearly failed her. She doesn't understand what boys want – what it might lead to. She's not prepared.

The time has come for things to be put in place. If she doesn't know what she needs to, she could end up getting into difficulties. And it would have been my entire fault. Can you imagine? – in trying to do right, I could have easily lead Binta into a place of being ostracised for the rest of her life.

It was a close call. At least I found out in time.

I had to act quickly for that reason – and also if I don't act quickly, I might find it impossible to act at all.

'Amie! What can we do for you?' I know the woman coming towards me, but not well.

'Is the *Ngansimba* coming soon? I heard she was due here.'

'That's right,' the woman is a little hesitant, seeming to read my expression to see if my enquiry is genuine.

'Let me know when she comes,' the words come easier than I thought they would. The words I have fought in my head for months. I swallow to ease the dryness building in my throat and say, 'My daughter Binta is ready.'

Chapter 38

Binta

'Do you like these little shells?' I ask Loli. Jena gave me the idea before and showed me how to tie them into plaits. Her eyes seem to sparkle as she smiles widely, showing her bright white teeth.

'Do you want me to put them into your hair?'

She nods while she sits as still as her body allows. I attach the first of the shells at the end of her plaits when Ma passes by.

I look up, surprised to see her returning from the fields. 'Why are you back so soon?'

'Nothing for you to worry about.' She pauses briefly to answer, before she disappears into the cooking hut; she's humming a tune I've not heard before under her breath.

I finish the plait that I'm currently working on, and then think whether I ought to ask Ma if she wants my help. I notice she suddenly seems really busy preparing food – and it's not even her turn to do the compound chores. I leave Loli for a moment and go over to the cooking hut. Half of Loli's head is in neat rows, while the other half sticks out in all directions.

'I won't be long, Loli. I'll be back – I just need to speak with Ma.'

Instead of accepting my help, Ma chuckles, though her eyes don't shine as they usually do, and she nods across to Loli. 'Perhaps you should finish off that for your sister first!'

She's got a point. I look over to poor Loli, with her hair pointing up, all over the place. I'm quicker than Ma doing hair, because I don't want to pull too hard and hurt Loli. When Ma does my hair I usually complain. She says something like how it's preparing me, although I never quite work out what for.

After I finish Loli's hair, I suggest a game we can play. 'Okay, you have to get to the other side of the compound without me catching you. Ready?'

She jumps up quickly and claps her hands together, excitedly.

'Can I join in?' Musa's voice drifts across the yard. I don't want him to spoil our fun, but as he shuffles from one foot to the other, I feel a bit sorry for him. Perhaps he can make things more interesting.

'Okay!' I tell him. 'You can go first, but listen to my rules. Stand in the middle. You've got to try and stop us getting to the other veranda. You're a crocodile!' I duck low, dodging Musa's attempts to trip and run in a different direction. There's no way the crocodile is going to get me. I'm much too fast. My legs move quickly. We have so much fun that my sides ache from laughing, and for once, Musa doesn't even ruin things.

Later, I'm the first to bed. No squirming toddler, no snoring grandmother. I light a candle, allowing the hot wax to drip onto the bed frame, then I push the candle into the wax as it hardens so I can let go of it to get into bed. The little candlelight illuminates the whole room, with a flickering, soft yellow glow. An occasional breeze blows the flame gently, from side to side.

Ma stops at the doorway and calls in, 'Goodnight, daughter. Sleep well.' She doesn't often do that. Tonight she even comes in to my room, sits on the edge of my bed and kisses me on the forehead. She hesitates and caresses my face with her hand. 'Time to sleep my daughter.'

'Goodnight, Ma.'

She kisses me on the head again, smiles, then turns to leave.

The mosquitos are already attacking. I can hear the way the buzzing comes close, right next to my ear. It only helps a bit, but I wrap a cloth around my shoulders and most of my head. Then I place it on the soft, frilly, silk pillow. It had been Ma's best bedding. Although there are a couple of holes in it – and the pink has faded – I like how the material slides smoothly under my hand. The nearly extinguished candle still manages to make shadows dance around the room. In the distance, I can make out deep rhythmic drumming: perhaps it's a wedding, or maybe the end of a naming ceremony. The repetitive drumbeat soothes and hypnotises me to sleep.

Chapter 39

Amie

All afternoon there have been ripples of talk passing between a network of ears that know the secrets and what to listen for. Hidden in the sentences of ordinary words. 'The crocodile has come,' they say. 'None can hide,' they whisper. My stomach churns in anxious anticipation as eyes glance my way because they know I'm Binta's mother and that she is included. 'She is coming for her own,' they mutter, nodding with wisdom as I pass. It amazes me how others are deaf to the sounds announcing the importance of this night. All the worry from before is seeping away; instead Binta is on the brink now of understanding.

For her it will be like seeing for the first time, understanding a depth of belonging that she didn't even know was possible. She will hear the talk and understand. She will have a level of support around her for the rest of her life – even after I die. She will have support that she didn't know existed. She will marry. Have babies. Our women will care for her. When she needs carrying through life's challenges – when food is scarce or people are saying nonsense about her – she will have her *Kafo* alongside her to make her strong.

All that is on offer for her starts tonight. But as I walk along the veranda to wake her all I feel is a growing dread in the pit of my stomach and I know in my innermost place that the kind of belonging that occurs through this ritual is just a compensation, rather than the true reward. More is taken than is given through this.

The fear builds in me of what she has to face. What I have to do. I have to stop and put my hand against the wall of the house to steady myself and I tell myself to be strong. I am a woman. I know how to be strong because of what I have faced. I have managed to bear the pain of childbirth and other things because of what my mother had to do for me. I now realise how it must have been for her too. Over the years I battled with many feelings, struggled to understand. For a moment there is a slight gust of wind, which brushes against my face and suddenly I am reminded of the ancestral spirits. They will know if I am weak now and don't carry on the ways of our people. It has happened forever. Who am I to change the course of the future, even just for my own daughter? I take a deep breath, stand up tall and walk again in the direction of Binta's room.

It's time.

Chapter 40

Binta

It only seems a moment later when I feel hands on my shoulders, shaking me awake. The night is silent, apart from intermittent snores and the continued distant beating of drums. From the greyness of the sky, I can tell the darkness of the night is nearly over. It's Ma that's shaking me.

'What's wrong? Are you okay?' I say and rub my eyes.

'Binta!' she whispers. 'Nothing is wrong. Come with me. Bring your shawl – it's cold outside.'

My flip-flops are right next to the bed and my feet slip into them in an instant. I follow her across the room. Ma takes my hand and leads me out into the night. Her excitement is contagious and my stomach begins to feel light while I walk next to her.

'Where are we going, Ma?'

'They are expecting us at Touray Kunda.'

I can hardly see. 'It's early, Ma! What's at Touray Kunda?'

She slows, and turns to face me. 'My *sungkuto* – my daughter – you will find out soon.'

I throw questions at her as we go through town, but she just ignores them. She's humming that tune again, under her breath. It's hard to avoid the large cracks in the path made by the scorching sun, which will appear again in a few hours.

As we head across town, I realise we're heading towards the drumming; the sound I've heard since I went to sleep last night. When we get closer, the ground vibrates and as we enter a compound I can make out the silhouettes of several dancing women. At our arrival they become ecstatic, which is strange. I don't know them – perhaps they think I'm someone else, or perhaps they're dancing for my ma.

The women cheer as I walk towards them, and then part, making a path through their group. I hold Ma's hand tightly and my mind races as I try to make sense of my surroundings.

For a moment, I wonder if I'm still dreaming but when I stub my toe on a stone I know I'm not. I'm definitely awake. But why are the elders dancing like this for me? And there's that tune Ma's been humming all day.

As I pass through the women, they are singing it, and I hear the words clearly.

'The crocodile is coming,
Underneath her tree,
Coming with surprise,
Coming with her teeth
The crocodile comes to take what is hers
Who can run? Who can hide?
The crocodile makes you brave
Do not cry

Coming with surprise,
Underneath her tree,
Coming with her teeth
Who can run? Who can hide?'

I follow Ma to a room at the far side of Touray
Kunda. The subdued atmosphere in the room is a
contrast to the increasing drumming outside. It's just
large enough for three double beds, which are placed
along the walls and on each bed there are girls of
various ages, sitting quietly. I can see it in their eyes that
they are trying to figure out, like me, why we're here.

I step over four young women who are sitting on
the floor, too busy drinking tea, chatting and laughing.
They are not like the older women outside, who paid
attention to my arrival and danced for me.

'Come, sit here!' Ma pats a space on a bed and I jump
up onto it.

'Binta!' Ma cups my face in her hands. She looks
at me in a way I can't place, but it feels good. I sense
her pride, and affection. And love: her deep love for
me. 'Binta, my daughter. Next time I see you, you
will no longer be a *dindingo*.' She leans forward and
kisses me gently on the cheek, squeezes my hands and
turns to leave. I'm not sure where she's going, but I'm
immediately excited by the information she's left me
with and would desperately love to join in the dancing.
Instead I focus on sitting properly, quietly on the bed,
like the others: grown-up.

Chapter 41

Binta

Ma disappears into the frenzy of activity and drumming outside. No more being a *dindingo*! No more being teased, or always being the one to get the water for everyone. As a grown-up, my opinions will be considered, my questions answered. There will be no more reprimands for being a silly child. Best of all, there will be no more of Malik and Musa calling me, '*E Solima!*' That will teach them!

On a bed next to me are the Touray twins, Awa and Adama. Their younger sister, little Aminata, is asleep on Awa's lap.

A girl, perhaps a couple of years younger than me, keeps wandering to the door to watch the women dance. When she thinks someone might see her, she runs across the room and jumps back onto the bed, laughing. The younger women on the floor carry on their chatting, and only when the girl spills a cup of water, on her way back, do they raise their voices.

'Make the most of your nonsense, Ida!' one of the women shouts. 'Your time is coming to put this silliness away!'

Ida doesn't seem bothered, but something about it makes me feel uneasy. There's something unpleasant in their tone. The fluttering in my stomach turns from excitement to a growing apprehension. Then I turn my attention to a young woman sat on the next bed.

'*E tondi?*' I ask.

In an accent similar to the *Toubab*s, she replies and sounds each word deliberately.

'*Ntomu Sara leti.*' My name is Sara.

'*E bota minto le?*' I'm puzzled and wonder where she's from with such a strange accent. She looks dark enough to be a Mandinka, but her words don't sound like they belong. The woman shrugs her shoulders and looks apologetic, not able to answer me.

'Where you from?' I try in English, thinking of the first time I met Esther; maybe she's not Mandinka after all.

'You speak English! Oh, I'm from London.'

'London? Not Mandinka?' I'm confused.

'Yes, I am – but I grew up in England. I've come here a couple of times growing up, to visit my grandmother.'

'You speak Mandinka?'

'Not much. I understand more than I can speak. My mother speaks it sometimes at home, but my father is Wolof. We mainly speak English.'

Thankfully in the past year, since hanging around with Esther, my English has greatly improved, but it isn't until this moment I realise how much. 'How old are you?' I ask, sitting cross-legged. I'm twisting a loose piece of hair just above my ear, until it stands upright.

'Eighteen.'

As we talk, a little girl on the bed next to Sara shifts along and climbs onto her lap. 'This is Hawa, my cousin,' she says and stokes the little girl's hair fondly.

'How old is she?'

'Six last month.'

Hawa pipes up, smiling. 'I had a party with all my class. I had a Barbie cake!'

I have no idea what a Barbie cake is, but instead I ask, 'From England too?'

'Yes.'

'I'm six!' The little girl holds up fingers for me to count: four on one hand; two on another.

Just then, Ida, rushing back to her bed again, trips over one of the women sitting on the floor.

'You will soon learn to get rid of your childish ways,' one of the women scorns. She catches the back of Ida's leg, landing a resounding smack. 'Your time is coming to meet the crocodile!'

Crocodile? The word seems to settle heavily in the air and now I'm worried.

Just outside the next town there is the sacred crocodile pool that's hundreds of years old, where people – especially tourists – come to visit. When there is no sign of the crocodiles, people brave bathing quickly in the pool, because of the strong fertility magic in the water. That tune suddenly comes into my head again – the one the women were singing, about meeting the crocodile. A tight ball begins to form in the pit of my stomach and I wish Ma would come back in the room in order for me to ask her. I'm adamant that I don't want to go to the crocodile pool. I'm not brave enough to take a dip in the water.

Little Aminata stirs from her sleep, sits up and rubs her eyes. She looks around, still sleepy. Hawa puts a small hand on my shoulder to clamber across the back of me to sit next to Aminata.

'Hello. I'm Hawa!' I know Aminata can't understand what she's saying, but the two little girls instantly look like friends.

Sometime later, the drumming changes rhythm. The women sing louder and then the twins' mother comes to the door. Addressing the young women, she says, 'It's time. Bring them!'

They usher us out of the room. We go through a dancing crowd of women, who have formed a circle and they make a path for us to walk through. We head out in a straight line and follow an ensemble of women. When we are out on the street they hush their singing.

We head out past the main road, and cross over to a small path that leads towards the fields and forest. Hawa holds her cousin's hand, until the walk becomes too long for her small legs, and then Sara carries her on her back. I'm guessing there are close to fifty women walking with us to...to – well, wherever that might be. I spot Ma following some distance behind, and I desperately try to remember...

Is this the way to the crocodile pool?

Chapter 42

Amie

$\mathbf{M}$y stride falls in step to the pace of the beat from
the drums. Away from the town, whispered,
hidden hums break into articulated definite words.
With only just the women in earshot now, the verse
crescendos and I join in and sing:

> *'The crocodile is coming...*
> *...Coming with surprise...*
> *...The crocodile comes to take what is hers*
> *Who can run? Who can hide?'*

I sing loudly in order to force the words deep into my
being, where I feel a growing fear of what my daughter
is to face. There are too many conflicting thoughts
screaming in my head to be heard.

How can I do this to Binta, my beautiful Binta?

But if she doesn't go through this, how will she know
what it is to be a beautiful wife? Who will want her then?

What kind of mother does that make me?

And what kind of mother am I, if I don't?

I dance with renewed vigour, pounding my feet into the ground, making dust clouds rise up around my ankles. I stamp my anger into the earth, this damn earth where I have nothing more to give than frustration at our ways. This is how it has always been.

'Who can hide?' I sing the words, forcing the tears back. 'Who can hide?'

Who did I ever think I was, to think I could have kept my daughter from this?

The crocodile takes us all eventually.

Chapter 43

Binta

The path is narrow, which is why we walk in single file. The sky is still grey, dawn just about to break through, but although the sky looks like any other morning at this time, there's anticipation in the air. This day is special in a way that I've never experienced and it feels for a moment as though I've never seen a true sunrise. As we head further from the town everything seems quiet and peaceful after the noise of the drums in the compound, but my heart still pounds, beating its own rhythm to emotions of anxiousness and anticipation.

From the fields that we pass at the side, I know we're heading further away from town, where the path gives way to denser bush and twigs, stinging my legs with each thorny scratch. We walk fast and it takes all my concentration to focus on where I'm stepping, careful to avoid the bigger thorns. It's only when we slow that I notice – I assume we've arrived.

We're at a small clearing in the bush; this has got to be it. I lift my head and take in the location.

My shoulders relax, I breathe easily and I smile quickly – it's not the crocodile pool. Relieved, I assure myself there is nothing to be scared about; no crocodiles after all, and I feel foolish for working myself into a worry.

There's a basic compound surrounded by a circular fence constructed from palm leaves, and we arrive to another reception of ecstatic women dancing and drumming as we enter through the small gap in the fence. The anxiety now gone, I'm full of excitement and expectation.

At the centre of the clearing there is a small hut, made from logs, palm leaves and grass, where we are lead inside. It smells musty from the dried leaves and grass. Inside a candle burns, but it's still dim inside and it takes a second for my eyes to adjust.

'Sit here!' we are told and I join the others on the dusty floor. Away from the town, the mosquitoes buzz around, jostling for position with the flies for a place on our bodies. Although the drumming is loud, the other girls' breathing fills the thick stifling air inside the hut. Now we just sit and wait.

I watch the wick on the candle dwindle until the flame is clinging to the last drop of wax and then it diminishes in a moment and disappears into nothing. The light of the candle is now replaced by the early dawn light. The young women, the same ones that had been in the room with us at Touray Kunda, come into the hut. 'Stand up!' the fat one says. 'Take off your clothes. All of them. Your *fanu*s too.'

Ida and I look at each other. I've not been naked in front of people since I was as small as my little brother Lamin. It must be some kind of test – to check how modest, respectful, we are – because a woman, a

193

grown-up, would not take her *fanu* off. Never. But there's a growing confusion in my mind, which makes my palms sweat and it's not just that it's hot in here.

'Quickly now. All your clothes.' The woman points a stubby finger at me with so much authority that I nearly expect my clothes to drop by themselves. I stare back at her, which I know is rude to do, but I'm too cross and indignant and don't move until I notice the others undress. The other women's eyes bear down on me, making me feel uncomfortable, even more uncomfortable than if I was naked. I take my T-shirt off first. Then I turn my hand slowly and untie my *fanu*, keeping myself covered even after I've undone it.

'Do you think you have something special that we haven't seen before? Don't we have all this in common?' the fat woman jeers at me, pointing at my newly forming breasts. It creates amusement for the other women at my expense. I glare back in an attempt to express how much I despise their laughter, to make them feel some of my anger, but it has the same effect as a fly on a goat.

As heat rises in my cheeks, so does my anger. What does she know? It's not right to be naked. I'll tell Ma when I see her and Ma will reprimand her fiercely, but unfortunately there's nothing I can do right now. My cheeks burn hot when my *fanu* drops to the ground around my ankles; I am naked and feel more vulnerable than I have ever felt before.

Then I'm directed to sit in the corner next to Sara, which I do really quickly so that I can try to cover myself with my hands. Sara is quietly staring at the wall. 'Are you okay?' I ask. For a moment I forget my embarrassment and think about Sara, how hard it must be, being so far away from home and missing family. This environment is strange to me, so I can't imagine what she's making of this, already being in a different country – even if this is where her heritage is.

Sara looks at me and whispers, 'I'm fine...just nervous.'

'Nervous?'

Being naked isn't great, but I don't think that can be Sara's reason. A lizard runs across the floor and up onto the walls. Within a second it's scampered all the way to the roof. The lizard sparks a memory, the one where Ma's *Kafo* came to Mai's naming ceremony, when I stopped Musa throwing stones at the little creature. *Kafo*.

Something niggles my thoughts. Of course! The *Kafo*: Ma's special group of friends. They always dress in the same kaftans and *fanu*s when they meet together, to show they're a *Kafo*.

'Don't worry, Sara.' I can't believe I didn't realise before. Being from London, Sara won't know and when I explain she'll understand why we are sat here like this without clothes on.

'We're going to be a *Kafo* together.' Sara turns, but there isn't the excitement in her face that I was expecting, after I tell her. I'm going to have to explain. 'We're going to have new outfits. Special *Kafo* clothes.' She's still not responding right. 'That's *why* we had to undress – to get our new outfits. I hope it's a blue and white one; do you like blue and white? Actually, that's like my school uniform...maybe purple would be good instead. Purple's a good colour too. What do you think? Do you think we'll get to choose?'

Sara's just listening. She's not happy, not smiling and I wonder if it's because she doesn't understand my

English now that I'm chattering quickly in excitement. She's got to get how great this is and, with a slight sigh, I try one last time to explain, slowing down.

'It's special being a *Kafo* together and we're going to get new *fanu*s. Once we get them I'm sure we'll be allowed to join in with the dancing and there's going to be some good food to go around. Peanut rice pudding, cous cous and sour milk, *Benachin* rice. Have you had *Benachin* before?' I'm too excited, still talking too fast to let her answer. I notice how she keeps looking over to the entrance of the hut.

Suddenly Sara's body tenses. An older woman walks in. See, she's going to get us to try our outfits on, but I don't mention this to Sara. The woman walks past us towards Aminata, who is sitting on Awa's lap, sucking her thumb. A woman takes her gently by the arm and raises her up onto her feet. Aminata takes her hand and follows her outside. I watch, wondering why they've only taken Aminata and how unfair it is not to take us all out to try our outfits on. Perhaps Ma will be here in a minute and let me join in.

Sunlight streams in the entrance of the hut, which is getting stuffy, even though the sun is only just rising. I really want to go outside for fresh air and to join in with the dancing; then, as my stomach churns in hunger, I focus on when they are going to bring food for us. I think about it more – about being a *Kafo* – and I take time to look around the room to take in who will be part of this special group. It's not what I thought. I assumed Isatou and Jena would be part of my *Kafo* group and I suddenly feel disappointed that they're not here with me. I'm sure it won't make a difference in our friendship, but I just always imagined my best friends being in my most intimate social group as I became an adult.

Through the noise outside there is suddenly a sound that doesn't belong. There it is again. Again and again it fights through the barrier of drumming, growing louder. I try hard to place it and the best I come up with is that it's an animal being slaughtered. That means we're going to have some meat – maybe for lunch. It's been ages since I had anything other than fish, and I imagine the succulent flavour. In the meantime I hope they'll bring in some hot bread for our breakfast, I'm hungry.

The woman arrives at the doorway again but she doesn't have any food with her, no bowl of fish *Benachin*, or even some nice warm loaves. She heads towards us. I look up at the woman coming over, willing her to take me next.

'Come!' the woman says, to little Hawa, who is now sat on Sara's lap.

Hawa bounces up excitedly. 'I'm going to join the dancing!' She grins and I can see she's got a front tooth missing.

Sara touches her arm and whispers, 'Be brave for me.'

'Are you coming too? Are you coming to dance? Come on! Come and dance with me!'

'Maybe in a while,' Sara says. Then Hawa disappears outside, holding the woman's hand, skipping as she goes.

'She'll be okay outside with the woman,' I reassure Sara, wondering briefly why she told her to be brave. 'Don't worry, she'll be fine.'

Sara responds by closing her eyes and covers them with her hands. She's acting strange, but maybe because she doesn't know what to expect, being from England.

'Don't worry. The food will be good.' Sara opens her eyes and looks at me. I don't know what else to say because she doesn't look any happier by that.

Again the same odd sounds break through the pounding of the drumbeats and I wonder why they are slaughtering more than one goat. We only had one at baby Mai's naming ceremony. One is enough. I think about that day when I watched my father slaughter the goat and how it bled silently to death. Silently! It hadn't made a sound.

I'm then suddenly aware that the noise outside isn't an animal being killed, and I strain my ears to hear the sounds that constantly battle even over the loudest drums. Then I know what it is, and swallow hard.

Screams.

Agonising screams.

The next one resounds through to my bones and makes me feel sick, because I am suddenly aware of what is making them. Hawa.

I draw my knees up under my chin and wrap my arms around them. From the way Sara's shoulders are moving up and down, I can see that she's sobbing into the crook of her arm. Holding myself tight, I'm fighting a growing, overwhelming fear and my body begins to shake with each scream.

Ida begins to cry quietly. Evidently I'm not the only one who has heard and her cries make me more scared. I must be right. Aminata, Hawa. They are going out in order of age. I look over to Ida, not hiding my fear. We look at each other, our eyes wide. She is next. In the next moment two women arrive in the doorway to the hut, blocking out the sunlight.

198

When they make their way into the hut, Ida shuffles back on the floor, but there is nowhere to go and by that time another woman is already behind her, lifting her up onto her feet. Ida's crying louder and drags her feet, kicking the dust as she is pulled along.

'What are you doing, girl? Stop being difficult!' The women are large and strong but they struggle against her flailing legs. One of them hits her across the face, which makes a loud slap. 'It's a good thing you are visiting the crocodile. You're too stubborn!'

They drag her out of the hut, into the sunlight, towards the drumming, towards whatever is going to make her scream. My mind is numb.

The hut is more stifling than before. In an instant I become aware of my rapid breathing, there is no air left in here. The drums immediately crescendo to block out Ida's screams and my heart seems to join in, pounding heavy against the wall of my chest. An internal drum, wanting to block out her screams from entering my head.

It's no good – I can still hear her. I move my hands, which are tightly wrapped around my knees, and put them over my ears. Screams still reach me however hard I press my hands to silence them. I make a low humming sound so that, with my eyes closed, nothing outside of my head is real. No sounds get in. I'm dizzy and nausea washes over me in waves. When the screams stop I am painfully aware of what it means. I want to throw up, but only manage to retch.

It's time for another.

And I know it's going to be me.

Blood is splattered across the women's clothes when they reappear at the door. This is what I see, when

I open my eyes briefly. Blood on their clothes, as they walk towards me. I close my eyes again and hold onto my juju. If there is ever a time it's got to work, it's now. I hold the breath in my lungs, willing to vanish, until my chest burns. Then I sense the women in front of me.

'Come!'

I open my eyes and look up at them and slowly breathe out. If I could have left the breath in there longer – to be my last ever – I would have done so.

'Come!' one of them repeats louder.

I don't want her to hit me. I try and stand, but my legs are weak. 'Be brave,' Sara said to Hawa. How did she know about this? My legs give way and buckle. The women grab me under the arms. I look down at Sara; she's looking at the floor. I hold onto the words she said before to Hawa as they drag me outside.

For a moment I'm blinded by the brightness. Squinting, I take in the scene. I'm led to the far side of the compound to the baobab tree. Aminata is lying on her mother's lap, her eyes closed. Lines on her dusty face clearly show where tears have flowed. I cry out at the sight of Hawa and Ida lying quietly in the corner, on a mat. Both no longer naked but covered with blood-soaked *fanu*s.

Frantically I look for Ma in the crowd.

She must be here.

The women hold onto me tighter, pushing me forward to the baobab tree. Directly underneath I'm lowered down, onto a pile of freshly cut palm leaves, which have been laid carefully on the ground. A new level of fear rises in me when I notice the pools of blood soaking into the dust and a pile of leaves are crimson, attracting flies. My mind is numb through frantically trying to understand, to piece together what has happened. Where has the blood come from?

I look around desperately. 'Ma!' I shout.

The women now push me down and place me on the leaves, holding my arms. Other women suddenly come rushing forward to hold my legs. I'm pinned down so hard that the palm leaves dig into my back. I don't know what is going to happen, but I know somehow that my blood is going to soak into that soil too. Bile rises in my mouth.

'Ma!' I cry out again, tears streaming down my face.

Faces press in, I scan every one to see if it's Ma.

I can't see her.

'Ma! Ma!' I force my voice over the drumming. She's got to be here.

There! For a second I no longer feel the uncomfortable leaves, or all the hands on my naked body. All I'm aware of is Ma, working her way through the crowd. She's coming!

'Ma!' I cry, relieved.

But something isn't right. Ma ignores me and kneels beside the others. I feel her fingers on my skin, gripping my thigh.

Look at me! I beg her with my tearful eyes, but she continues to look away; instead I feel every one of her fingers pressing harder. In that moment I feel numb with confusion and fear.

'Ma,' I plead, lifting my head up as much as I can, the only part of my body I still have any control over. If she just looks at me she'll see how frightened I am.

Why is she not looking?

Through blurred vision, through tears, I watch an elderly woman walk towards me. Space is made for her.

She is helped down carefully onto the palm leaves, and kneels awkwardly. They push my thighs apart. Spreading wide my legs, the old woman shuffles in between, close to me. I glance over her shoulder to Ma. She is making a point to avoid my gaze.

Then I look into the eyes of the old woman bending over me.

It doesn't matter that I don't know what exactly is about to happen. Fear still fills every nerve of my being. The screams of the other girls play in my mind, and as she edges closer, I cry.

'I am the *Ngansimba*. The crocodile! Don't cry,' she demands.

My eyes widen and fix intently on her, watching her wave a finger. Time moves slowly and I notice the detail of her long yellow nails.

'You must face the crocodile with courage!' the *Ngansimba* says. 'Make your mother and your grandmother proud. Your crying will bring evil spirits on you, so be sure to be brave and no tears. No crying. Courage will bring blessings from your ancestors for the generations you will bear.'

I continue to cry.

The crocodile's words wash over me; they are distant. My mind is in a fog but I lift my head a little more and watch her take out a safety pin from a small tableware box. An involuntary sound comes from my mouth and I try to move back. Hands hold me firmly in place.

Then the *Ngansimba* – the crocodile – takes a small piece of flesh, the delicate bit that is right in between my legs, with her long nails. Then she takes the safety pin and pierces me.

Every last gasp of air expels from my lungs. I scream, competing against the drums to be heard, pain searing through me from between my legs, ripping through my body.

She pulls on the pin, lifting my flesh. She holds it up with one hand. With the other, she reaches for something in her little box. My breathing is rapid. I don't know what to do with this pain. Crying and screaming is doing nothing to stop it.

Breathe slowly – focus. It doesn't help. My eyes, wide with terror, are fixed on her, anticipating her next move.

From the box she lifts out a razor blade.

When she brings it towards me, I urinate in fear. The warm flow doesn't bother the *Ngansimba*. Doesn't stop or slow her. I'm not ashamed of my involuntary act in front of her or all these women; I don't feel anything but an overwhelming terror. I watch her move the blade, down between my legs. Blood splatters across her arms, as she cuts into my sensitive flesh. I scream and feel liquid pour out. Warm and sticky, it flows over the inside of my thighs. The pain is so intense. Thoughts no longer exist. I can't even feel the hands holding me down.

Except, perhaps, Ma's.

The faces of the women began to disappear in a blur, but I do feel the *Ngansimba*'s nails move to hold a larger piece of my flesh. She begins slicing it. Over and over she cuts. I knew the screams must be mine. Pain fills every pore of my body, from the outside in, even to the core of my soul. The crocodile continues to slice. When she finishes on that part, her nails find another piece of me.

The drumming becomes distant. The screams eventually belong to someone else. Pain consumes me completely. My mind drifts to another place, where the jaws of a crocodile open wide – coming for me. It pauses long enough for me to see the evil in its eyes. I try to scream but there is no sound. The crocodile opens its mouth to eat me. To bite me in two, coming down towards me where I already feel pain.

Then there's only darkness.

Chapter 44

Binta

My thoughts are foggy, in a blend of consciousness and frightening sleep. A crocodile drags and pins me to the ground. Opening its mouth, the sharp jagged teeth bite into my flesh. Blood sprays all over the creature's snout; its jaws crunch down on bone. I open my mouth, but my voice is silent in place of a scream.

Suddenly I am fully awake, acutely aware that I cannot breathe – not easily anyway. My breathing is so fast that it hurts. I gasp for air and try to sit up, which is when the intense stabbing pain shoots up from between my legs and increases each second I am awake. Confused, because I know I'm awake and the crocodile was just a nightmare, I cannot place why I'm in agony and struggle to think. I try to order my memories. They don't come easily and I have to force them.

I barely notice the tears roll down my face, but I don't cry aloud. Within moments, scenes of yesterday flit through my mind – the musky hut, the other girls, the women dancing, drumming...being taken to the tree, the *Ngansimba*. Ma.

None of the images make sense. I try to reason it is part of the nightmare I've just woken from. But when the pain doesn't go, I have to conclude that it actually happened.

My throat hurts. It doesn't ease when I rub it and when I swallow it feels like thorns sticking inside. The answer to why it is sore is instantly clear in my mind, and does more to confirm this sickening reality: it is because of my screams. Empty screams that brought no relief to what the *Ngansimba* was doing.

The room I'm in is quiet. I lie back down on the pillow, more aware of an occasional cry or groan, but mainly the room is subdued, cloaked in quiet sadness.

I stare at the wall. Nothing could have prepared me for this secret. I always knew there was something untold, kept from us until we were old enough. I was so keen to find out what it was, jealous of older girls who knew what I didn't. It suddenly occurs to me that this is what Isatou went through too. Why didn't she say anything? Now I understand why she seemed to have changed. Nobody can ever be the same after this. Then I feel a wave of renewed sadness. I'm not sure if it's for Isatou, or for me. Perhaps it's for all of us? What is the point of this? When I think of Ma – I stop myself there. I cannot think of her. How can I call her Ma? Tears flow freely, quietly and they don't stop.

The pillow becomes damp under my eyes. If I lie still perhaps the pain won't get worse. I will myself not to move, keeping my legs straight, frightened to bend them. When the pain increases I groan and add my sorrow to the other voices in the room.

At some point, after I've woken, I am given something to drink. The foul-smelling liquid is the same one as my mother bought from the *marabout* when I used the bleaching cream. I drink without caring whether I'll vomit it back up; I don't care about anything. The liquid numbs the pain in my body and mind and I drift back to sleep...

The crocodile walks slowly up out of the water, onto the banks of a river. 'Binta, Binta,' it calls, and comes towards me. I can't run, because it's already eaten my legs. I push myself back with my arms, towards the bush leaving a trail of blood soaking into the sand. It calls my name again and again, thrashing its tail...

I wake, sweat pouring from my forehead, still facing the wall and I hear the crying of a young girl. It's either Aminata, or Hawa, which immediately brings thoughts of the *Ngansimba* and I long to fall back to sleep, to stay apart from this reality. The advancing crocodile is better than the real memories, but pain stops me from returning to the place of sleep. Eventually, I move myself a fraction at a time to face the others.

I scan the dark, stuffy room that has a stale odour of sweat, blood and urine, and I try and work out which one of the other girls is crying. I don't know why I want to know. Perhaps it's to feel that I'm not alone, or maybe it's to offer some comfort. No, it's not that. I'm too numb to care even for anyone else. I just want to see something other than the wall. Something to look at that will stop these memories filling my head. When I put my hand underneath myself to shuffle around, I notice the wet, sticky bed sheet. My hand is covered in blood. I'm scared. I no longer want to call for my mother. I'm alone.

Awa is laid down. Adama has her back against the wall, sat with her legs outstretched on a bed. Little Aminata lies at Adama's side, crying. That's who it was. The crying aggravates me and I'm surprised at how little I care about anyone else. That's not like me. Am I different? Perhaps I am – I don't feel like me anymore. I wonder if I will ever be me again. I try and feel some compassion, but it doesn't come. I just want silence, nothingness. No thinking, no feeling. Nothing.

Little Hawa is sat huddled next to her cousin. Sara's arms are wrapped around her, though Hawa doesn't look like she will ever be comforted. Her eyes are distant with lines down her dusty face, where tears have made paths. But there are no more tears. She's all dried up, like me.

Another dose of the *marabout*'s potion takes me away from here...

I'm hiding behind a bush. Not a bad view of the river. There are no ripples. The water is still. I watch, waiting for the crocodile to come out. A crane flies down and lands on the bank – the water doesn't explode, as I'm expecting. The crocodile has gone. Then there is a crack – a broken branch – behind me. I turn and put my hands to my face, as the crocodile lunges, each one of its yellow teeth ready to tear at my flesh and as it opens its mouth, its face morphs into that of the Ngansimba, *her teeth the* Kankurang's *machetes...*

The morning sun rays flood into the room, but it's out of place. How can it light up this sad room? For a while, I watch dust particles float up, caught in that ray of light. Then a familiar sensation comes over me. For the first time ever, it fills me with dread. I've got to pee. The harder I try to quell the urge, the more it comes.

A woman comes to help. I don't know her. One of many faces that blend together. First of all, I've got to get out of bed and stand. Once I'm on my feet, it takes some moments to overcome the pain between my legs. The journey to the latrine – out the room, across the compound and around the back yard – really is no distance, but I need to sum up all my energy just to put one foot in front of the other.

Outside, there are a few women doing jobs in the compound, just like any other home, getting on with their daily chores. Just as though nothing has happened. Everything is normal – life is carrying on as it has always done. Maize is being pounded. One woman is carrying water on her head from the well. There's the usual laughter and chatter.

'STOP!' I want to shout at them. How dare they act like nothing's happened! Are these the same women that held me down? I don't recognise any of them. From now on, I'm going to always wonder when I'm at the market, or pass women in the street: Did you hold me? Did you? Or you?

The only faces I actually remember are the *Ngansimba*'s and my mother's and I think of them while the woman helps me balance over the latrine, holding my *fanu*. My mother's face looking at me while the *Ngansimba* cut me is the image that I see in my mind, all the time while the urine burns.

In the evening, the room is dimly lit with just a single candle that burns in the corner. The flame dies out hours later and the room is in darkness, but I can't sleep. Not without the *marabout*'s drink, and I haven't been given any tonight. Anyhow, I don't know if I want to see the crocodile yet. It will certainly be waiting for me, in my sleep.

The night is long. In the distance, a little way from the *jujuwoo* I can hear the metallic clang of the *Kankurang*'s machetes and in the darkness my mind replays every moment of the last few days: from when I was playing happily with Loli, sleeping – actual sleep without a crocodile to terrorise me – to when my mother woke me up and took me to Touray Kunda. Remembering the excitement, I think how stupid I was. Then waiting here in this hut, until it was time to go to the bush. I try to stop my mind thinking anymore, but the memories keep playing against my will; until I'm under that tree again.

In the very darkest part of the night, I can make out hushed voices huddling over where I think Aminata is. 'We must get the *Ngansimba*; she'll have the power to stop her being attacked by these witches.' *What about the* Kankurang, *why is he not able to chase the spirits away?*

'I told you from the beginning that we would have problems with the twins. They attract attention from the spirits and now, look – the younger sister is suffering!'

'Is she breathing?'

'Yes, but feel her head. She is full of fever. Light a candle, we need to see.'

'You've got to send for the *Ngansimba*.'

No! I draw the blanket up around my head to hide, more scared of her than the evil presences of witches in here. How can it be that the *Ngansimba* can help? She was the one who brought the pain in the first place. Is she the only one that can help?

Before, I thought I understood how things worked. Now that I am a woman – if that is what I now am – I have no idea. Is this what makes me a woman?

Somehow I feel less of me, not more. Those women didn't add to what I had...they took away.

The worried chatter around Aminata quietens on the *Ngansimba*'s arrival. 'The girl has been like this since last night, but it's worse,' one of them explains.

'I know! I see everything. I have been fighting this spirit and it is strong.'

From underneath my hiding place I peek from the corner edge of the blanket. The *Ngansimba* is holding onto a necklace, one with a tiny mirror sewn into the leather amulet.

'From this I can see into the spirit world. I didn't need to come in person, only to give you assurance. Let me see the girl.' The annoyance is evident in her voice.

The women move aside. The *Ngansimba* lifts Aminata's droopy head from the bed. She sucks on her teeth in disapproval and places her little head back on the pillow. She rubs some lotion into her hands and covers Aminata's face with them, while she chants some words. I'm terrified, but curious. The *Ngansimba* has to make a difference – I will her to – if that might help. Without warning, the *Ngansimba* withdraws her wrinkled hand, those long nails. She leaves muttering something, and disappears into the night.

At least for now, the *Ngansimba* is gone. I pull the covers back down and uncover my head. As I do, the metal bed where Aminata is lying begins to rattle. Her arms and legs jerk around. I hide under the blanket again away from the spirits, and someone calls to get her mother urgently.

By the time she comes, Aminata is quiet. I can barely bring myself to think it, but...is she dead?

211

'She was shaking...the spirits are trying harder. The *Ngansimba*'s power isn't strong enough.'

'I've got to take her to a doctor!' I know her mother's voice, even when it is panicked.

'How are you going to get a doctor to look at her? These things are secret!'

'I will just say the fever is malaria.'

'What will the *Ngansimba* say? She'll know we've taken the girl away from the compound.'

'But I've got to try something!'

I peek from the blanket in time to see Aminata's mother lift her slumped daughter into her arms. A tear falls down my face because I don't want Aminata to die. I do feel something after all. Some compassion is still there – something of me remains. No longer am I completely numb.

A thought quickly crosses my mind. Will my mother bother carrying me to see a doctor, if the spirits come? Or will she be too afraid of the *Ngansimba*? I don't realise I'm biting the inside of my lip until I taste the blood. My sore throat tightens, like I've swallowed an orange. Did Aminata's mother hold her down? Is this what mothers do?

Over the next few days, Aminata doesn't return. I want to find out, but I can't find a way to ask. The pain begins to ease, even when I pee, which make the days pass quicker – especially when we begin our lessons. It's not like lessons at school, although there's a lot to learn. The worst thing is that instead of a headmaster, we have the *Ngansimba* who threatens to arrive any time of the day or night. She brings fear into the room, quick to dish out beatings – for things such as not greeting her with enough respect, or not learning the secret songs correctly – and then there's the fear we all have at the recent memory of what she has inflicted upon us. Every time Hawa sees the *Ngansimba* she screams hysterically and hides under the bed. Sara tries her best to stop her, because the first time she did it the *Ngansimba* dragged her by the feet and beat her until she was quiet.

We've also got special dances to learn too, and it doesn't matter we are still sore. There is one song that I learn quickly, because I've heard it before and it plays all the time in my head. It's the one that the women sang, when I arrived here – the song of the crocodile.

Now it's my turn to learn it. To be ready when I hear the tune being hummed, to know that an initiation is planned and the *Ngansimba* is on her way. Only initiates understand this song, even men don't know it, but the words stick in my throat. When the *Ngansimba* listens to me, I have to force them out. I never want to hear this tune again, to know the crocodile is back for more cutting – how could I bring myself to join in the joyful singing? The *Ngansimba* beats me when I don't sing for her. Only when the beating is bad enough, do I sing. To learn it, to know this song, means to be ready to join with the initiation. One day she'll expect me to hold girls down for her too. Whenever we sing the song I feel dizzy and hot. I hate the song.

'Now you have met the crocodile!' the *Ngansimba* says one evening on her visit. 'Tomorrow you will leave the safety of this place and go back to your homes.'

The news ripples around the room with a stifled excitement because we don't want to be disciplined by her.

213

'You would be right to be careful,' she observes. 'This is the beginning of your journey, you will go back tomorrow full of respect and understanding. You have learnt a lot during your initiation. I will be back later to speak to you.'

In other lessons we've learnt about how to act as a wife. Like the discreet sign to show our husband not to invite his friends back if there isn't enough food to go around. I never want to get married. But I've been taught the sign to show my husband when I'm menstruating, something I've learnt about, since being here.

We've been taught about sex. There's a sign I can give if I want to sleep with my husband, but I will never need to use that. I never want a man near me. Near where I'm so sore. When we aren't having lessons, I fill the hours in the *jujuwoo* thinking up ways that I can remain unmarried, for as long as possible. The one lesson I liked best was finding out how to stop a man – that's not your husband – forcing himself on you to have sex. For that, I have to tighten my *fanu* through my legs.

'Do you think the younger girls understand?' I ask Sara.

'No. They probably join in this bit of initiation again when they're older.'

To spend time with the *Ngansimba* once is enough. I'm grateful I understand these lessons – never have to come back. As promised, the *Ngansimba* returns that evening, after we've eaten our meal.

'Remember the crocodile!' she starts.

How can I forget? I see it every time sleep comes.

'The crocodile can take you again, if she desires. If I hear of your insubordination, the crocodile will

214

visit you. Do you think the bush is only for the young and uninitiated? No! Why do you think your mothers respect me so?' The *Ngansimba* looks at us, sat around on the floor in a circle. 'You are now ready for your journey in life. You are stronger. You came to me as weak, disrespectful and undisciplined. Only wanting comfort. Life is not about comfort. You must now know you can survive discomfort and pain. That is part of life. You know you are alive when you feel pain! If you are hungry then good – it means you are not dead. Being thirsty will prompt you to look for water. Discomfort isn't to be shunned. Embrace it. The crocodile has shown you how strong you can be.' The *Ngansimba* pauses. 'Bring me some water,' she says and clicks her fingers at one of the women who instantly obeys.

'The crocodile has taught you strength. You have to be stronger than men.' She chuckles and waves her long index finger. 'They know that, but they never understand the strength we have. Without it our people would disappear. You have now endured your initiation. You will endure the pain when your husband enters you and the pain of bearing children.' The *Ngansimba* rises slowly to her feet and makes to leave. Then she turns back. 'Now you know you can endure anything. The crocodile has shown you the strength you have.'

I watch her leave and wonder how true that is.

Chapter 45

Binta

Preparations are being made outside the next morning. I can hear the noise of people arriving, a growing excitement and music playing, like at a naming ceremony. Just a normal party, anyone would think. When it's in full swing, the *Ngansimba* arrives and inspects us all, dressed in our new matching outfits.

'Together you are now a new *Kafo*. You will be there for each other for the rest of your lives. You will always have the support of each other,' she says. Her shoulders straighten and she raises her head, as though satisfied at a job well done. Today is about her as much as us. I can just imagine how people will be congratulating her on her esteemed role. How much money has she made from cutting us? Apparently, she cuts under the same tree each session and for each girl she makes a notch into the bark as a reminder how many girls have met the crocodile there. It makes me mad. With all the hatred and anger I can muster, I want to stare her in the eye. Instead, I just stare at her wrinkled feet, sticking out of her blue flip-flops.

We are led outside, given gifts and special honour at the celebrations. The expectation is that we're meant to feel good about being women, have fun, enjoy this special occasion, but I just want it to be over and go home. I hate people looking at me. I hate their gifts and congratulations.

'You knew what was going to happen here, didn't you?' I whisper to Sara, when we're sat in a corner together, quietly contemplating the activity around us. She nods.

'How come you knew so much?' I ask. My question is loaded with confusion.

'My aunt gave me the option to come. It wasn't easy to find information, but I managed to find some.'

'So why did you come and allow them to do this to you? You're already a woman. And you're from England. Why did you need to do this?'

'I didn't belong. Not in England – I'm too black. With my Caribbean friends I'm too African. I'm too Wolof to my mother's family, and too Mandinka to my father's. My aunt gave me a way to become fully Mandinka. To belong.'

'Are you glad you came?' I ask, making a point to look into her eyes. I know it is rude – to stare in someone's eyes – but I really want to see her answer.

She hesitates. 'I was so worried that my mother would find out about me coming here, and stop me.'

'Your mother would have stopped you?' I interrupt.

'Yes. But my grandmother and aunts were waiting for me when I arrived. I recognised my grandmother from photographs. They threw a party to welcome me.'

'A party like this?' I say, pointing to the people dancing before us with more scorn in my voice than I had planned.

She ignores my comment and continues, 'They were singing, saying how happy they were that I hadn't forgotten them. In the time running up to our initiation I felt at home. I felt like I belonged.'

'And now?'

Tears are forming in her eyes and she doesn't need to answer. Even the explanation she's given me about belonging doesn't seem enough. How can feeling that you don't belong make you want this? Then, as soon as I have the thought, I remember the time Malik called me 'E Solima'. Sara and I both wanted to belong – but only she knew what it really meant.

'Don't they know what we've been through?' I say angrily under my breath. 'What's there to celebrate?'

There are some boys in the corner near the large speaker, dancing and laughing at each other's moves. If the *Ngansimba* wasn't stood so close to it, I would throw the stereo over the wall to stop their stupid dancing. Then one of the boys turns: it's Yaya. I quickly move to hide behind Sara.

'Do you like him?'

'I did, but not now,' I mutter. I watch him and hate seeing him dance. 'I'm not sure about anything now. I did daydream about being his wife, but that was before I understood – it was a child's thought.'

I cover my head completely with my scarf, but, just as quickly, Sara turns and unwraps it gently, finding my face. 'My sister, back home we say "time heals". Perhaps you will still be his.'

I hide my face again. How can time heal? I no longer want to be a wife, not even Yaya's.

Chapter 46

Amie

I have been looking forward to this moment for days, to have Binta with me again. To hold her close, but as we walk under the moonless night sky and I take her hand, her fingers do not curl around mine. Within a moment she has freed herself from me.

There is so much I want – I need – to say to her, but I don't know how to put all that's required into words and we continue in a building, straining silence.

As we approach our compound, I suddenly know it will be too late to broach this subject again if I don't say something before we arrive. Everything from hereon, about what she has been through, will be known, but left unspoken. There are only moments left for me to voice something to her, but every sentence I form in my mind lacks the depth I need it to convey.

I know the hurt she feels and the confusion. Perhaps it is only in these last days I appreciate the sacrifice my own mother made to ensure my security: to be able to marry and have a family of my own.

'You have entered into your ancestors' strength,' I say finally. The words in the quietness seem louder than I'd expected. 'It will go well for you for the rest of your life,' I continue. Other words seem to want to come, but disappear on my tongue before they have a chance to be. What I have said seems so empty.

And then we are home and the moment to say anything more is over for good.

Chapter 47

Binta

It's so familiar. My compound, just as it was the night I left. The familiarity unnerves me, with the realisation that everything I ever knew was shrouded in a secret. How did I not see this coming? Were there signs that I missed? There must have been. Sara came to The Gambia knowing exactly what was going to happen. She chose to belong, even if it didn't work out like she'd planned. I didn't get to choose, and now I feel alone.

Since being home, all my energy has left. My very bones feel heavy. It's not just that I don't sleep, or if I do, I wake in a sweat. I've had nights before when I didn't sleep, because of the heat, or Grandmother's incessant snoring, but I've never felt this exhausted.

Each day I feel my body is trying to escape from me. I have to think hard to move it, to do normal things, and even thinking about doing stuff tires me. As much as possible I sit and watch things going on – the everyday things – and make myself believe things are normal. Although I want to see Jena and Isatou, I haven't yet. I prefer to stay around the compound; staying in one place feels safer. Besides, I don't want to be too far from home if I need to pee. It still's sore and I don't want to be embarrassed if I take longer and they ask why I've been so long. But I miss them. I think they've probably gone out of town as well these last couple of weeks, like they normally do in the summer holiday. Maybe when they return, I'll feel like seeing them.

Deep down I don't feel right. But I don't have anyone to talk to about it. I'm scared the way I'm feeling is some kind of bad juju. Perhaps the *Ngansimba* has put some curse on me. I would have talked to my mother before, but now there's no one; I just sit, numb. I close my eyes for a moment and imagine Jena and Isatou sat either side of me on the steps, their arms around my shoulders, comforting me.

One afternoon, I'm sat outside the *Fula*'s shop, on the corner of our compound on the steps. I'm watching my uncles mend a car, wiping their oily hands on their trousers and arguing with each other about what's wrong with the engine. It helps me keep my mind from darker thoughts and then I catch sight of my father approaching from around the corner that leads from the market. He stops and greets people along the road, his bag over his shoulder. The days of the week blend together in my head at the moment, but if he's home this early, it must be Friday.

'Binta!' he greets me. It takes a lot to make me smile these days, but I lift my head and make an effort to, because he's noticed me. He seems to see me differently since I came back. In the brief moment that I open my mouth to respond, my father has already gone up into *Fula*'s shop. I turn around and watch him walk into the

222

their place. Ibrahim's there behind the counter. He's a hard worker; he's always there, from dawn until after we all go to bed.

Ibrahim's wife Mariama is stood in the doorway of their living quarters. The *Fula*'s little boy holds onto his mother's *fanu* with one hand and sucks his fingers on the other. Ibrahim's smile is broad, more so these days. It's because his wife is pregnant, hidden under her loose-fitting clothes. At least that's what I think, but of course I won't ever say that aloud. But I'm sure.

They're a friendly couple, although they keep themselves to themselves. It's probably because they can't speak Mandinka – at least the wife doesn't. But I've learnt her name is Mariama from Ibrahim who does speak a little Mandinka. I like the *Fula*s. Not in the way my father likes them; a regular income from a shop that's difficult to rent this far from the road or market. I've heard him boast to his friends that he charges them too much. He justifies it by saying he's doing them a favour 'cause Ibrahim is a foreigner. He's from Senegal. 'Not everyone would give them an opportunity like me – supply and demand, it is just business sense,' he often says, gloating.

I like them because they're always smiling, even though I'm sure they know my father isn't being kind to them. And Ibrahim sometimes gives me a sweet from the basket on his counter and I think of the beautiful necklace Mariama gave me for *Tobaski*.

'*Salam Malikum* Ousman.'

'*Malikum Salam*, Ibrahim. How is business?'

'Fine, fine.' Ibrahim lifts a small section of the counter up, a hinged part built into the panel and goes into his living room. 'Just a moment.' He touches his wife gently on the shoulders, and eases by.

'He looks like you!' my father says, pointing to the child hiding behind Mariama as Ibrahim returns.

'Yes, that's what my wife says,' Ibrahim replies, handing over a rolled bundle of dalasi notes to my father. He doesn't bother to count it – Ibrahim wouldn't dare lose his shop for short-changing my father.

'Good man. I'll be back same time next week.' My father turns to leave.

As he does, Ibrahim quickly says, 'Ousman, I need to speak to you.' He lowers his voice. I'm not meant to hear and pretend to be busy fiddling with a loosened plait in my hair, but I'm listening carefully.

'When my wife, Mariama, had our son, we were still in our village. She had family around.' He pauses. 'She had women to tend to her.'

I twist a plait of my hair and strain my ear, as he continues. 'She had women to help and I think she has been worrying lately. You know, she doesn't know people here. Not well – and she wants to go home for a while.'

'Ah, no, that's not possible,' my father quickly replies. 'If you go, there will be too many others wanting to rent the shop. I can't keep it for you.'

I feel ashamed of my father's words knowing full well, probably as Ibrahim does, that he's lying. He's lucky to rent it at all this far away from the market square.

'But she has to leave to be with our people for some time.'

I glance from the corner of my eye and see my father nodding. The pretence of considering things, but I know my father well enough to know that he's unlikely to agree.

'I have the solution! You don't need to leave. I will speak to my wife, Amie – she will help her. Your wife will be fine here.'

'That is kind, Ousman...my wife would appreciate that. It's just that our *Fula* women have traditions and do things differently – she needs to travel home.' My father shakes his head. Ibrahim continues quickly, 'It would be just for a short time. I could even come sooner. You see I need to help her travel back, especially in her condition.'

I was right! She's pregnant.

'Once we get to Banjul we'll travel onto Dakar and our village is a two-day journey from there. Look, I promise I'd be back within just over a week.'

I can see Ibrahim's wife at the corner of the door, listening as well. Even if she doesn't understand the words, she might be working out what they are saying from the tone of their voices and she looks worried.

'Okay – if you want to keep the shop open, I need you to give me the rent for that time before you go.'

Ibrahim winces. 'Ousman, I'm not sure.'

'Look, Ibrahim, I need to know you will come back. I don't want to lose rent, see. You have a month – perhaps give me a little extra rent each week.'

'Ousman, it will be hard to get extra to you.'

'Okay, look. I'm a generous man. If you come back when you say, I will give you half the money back, and you can make it up to me over the next few months.'

'Thank you, Ousman,' Ibrahim responds, quietly. 'We will travel at the end of the month.'

A couple of nights later, screams resonate across the compound in the dead of night. At first, I think it's my screams, because I'm waking from another nightmare where the crocodile is lying across my stomach, not allowing me to move. It's pinning me down with its heavy body. Any movement will disturb it, so I lie still. But as I open my eyes, I hear the screams again. They're real, and the sound sends a tingling down my spine. Grandmother is oblivious to it.

The next piercing scream makes Lamin mutter in his sleep. He rolls over and his outstretched arm hits Grandmother across her snoring face. She shoos it away unconsciously, as though it's a mosquito.

It's a warm night, but suddenly I'm cold and shivering. There's only one thing – one person – that brings such terror: the *Ngansimba*. Before I have time to think, I slip into my flip-flops and I'm already in the darkness, walking across the yard. Then there is another shot of sound that makes my feet freeze. I'm stood right in the middle of the compound. What am I doing? I can't let the *Ngansimba* find me, just stood here.

As my eyes adjust to the dim light, I make out two people hovering outside the entrance of the *Fula*'s shop. I'm drawn to them: some safety being with others. I wander slowly over. When I get closer, I recognise the hushed voices as my aunts, and I pick up the pace towards them.

'What's happening?' I ask and pull a shawl over my shoulders, against the night draught, as I approach.

'We're not sure. It's the *Fula* woman. Ibrahim, her husband, ran to get your father. Your mother is on her way.'

Another scream, long and drawn, pierces the dark, still air. It conjures a wave of nausea, but I find myself unable to walk back to my room. The corrugated iron door of the shop screeches, opening fully. There is little light from inside the room, which shines onto the yard. My father appears in the entrance looking disconcerted.

It's a look I've seldom, if ever, seen on his face and his anxiety is contagious.

'What's wrong?' my aunts ask.

He ignores them. 'Binta? Is that you?'

'*Nam.*' It's me.

'Go get the doctor – Doctor Bojang.'

For a second I stand where I am, confused by how he's just ignored my aunts and spoken to me instead. No longer a child.

'Where do I go?' I ask, quickly dismissing the shock of him addressing me. The clinic only opens during the day; I have no idea where to find the doctor.

'Forday Kunda, near the market – do you know where that is?'

'Yes.'

'Go quickly, run if you need to – be fast.'

I do go quickly and head towards the market, forgetting the fear and concern. I try to blot out the screams that become more distant as I head away from our compound. I do hurry, but as much as I want to – despite my father's instructions – I cannot run: the *Ngansimba* has seen to that.

I follow the furrows and dips in the road caused by the incessant rain and walk as fast as I can. The main road is less hazardous, which is where I can make up time. Not surprisingly, Forday Kunda is silent when I arrive. It's only then it occurs to me that I don't know how to locate the doctor. Everyone is sleeping. I guess the doctor – the most honoured member of this household – would have the biggest room. I head towards what looks like the main part of the building.

'Doctor?' I pitch my voice at a level where I hope it's heard. But not too loud, as to wake the whole compound. Nothing happens. I notch my voice up a level. 'Doctor?'

A moment later, a bleary-eyed woman peers around the door. She disappears back into the house after I explain why I'm here. I figure this isn't the first time she's been woken for the doctor in the middle of the night. In the sky, stars shine brightly, accompanying the moon that appears from behind the cloudy night sky. It's majestic, but it also makes me feel so small. A scurrying in the sand startles me as a rat, half the size of a dog, scuttles across the yard. I jump up onto the first step of the building, just as the door opens.

'Doctor Bojang?' I ask, surprised, suddenly nearly face-to-face with a man in the dark.

'Yes,' he responds quietly. 'What's the problem?'

'I'm not sure,' I say, composing myself. 'Please, follow me,' I urge him.

When we arrive back at the compound, more people are standing quietly outside the shop. None are willing to enter. If it was a Mandinka woman they would have, but this is a *Fula* and they are probably unsure of their welcome. The small group parts to allow us through. Tentatively I push the metal door wide, holding it for the doctor. The warm light of a candle from inside the room catches the doctor's profile as he passes me and, without thinking, I follow him inside. It only occurs to me afterwards that I shouldn't have, but my father has already seen me. I brace myself and anticipate his telling off; instead there's relief in his eyes at our arrival. The *Fula*'s young son is asleep on a mat at my father's feet.

'Doctor! Thank you for coming,' Ibrahim says, and comes across the room to shake Doctor Bojang's hand. 'Please do something for my Mariama. The baby is

228

coming too soon. We didn't have time to go back to our home in Senegal. They would have known how to deal with this. You are our only help.' Ibrahim takes the doctor by the arm and ushers him towards the adjacent door.

'Try not to worry. The baby being premature can be a problem, but we will see what we can do.' Doctor Bojang speaks with authority and calm.

'No, you don't understand.' Ibrahim sounds panicked.

There is another agonising sound and I think again about the *Ngansimba*, immediately fearful that she's in the next room. The shop is only lit by a couple of candles. I inch my way towards the door, close behind the doctor. If she's here, I'll know to hurry back to my room – without being seen.

The *Fulas* have two small rooms. One is the shop, and the other is where they live. From where I'm standing, I can see a double bed and a small bedside table. The room is sparse, small. In the middle of that tidy space is Mariama. She's slumped across the straw mat on the floor in a contortion of pain, thrashing her arms. I watch her screaming. There is someone next to her, kneeling, attempting unsuccessfully to hold her calm. I know the person immediately.

My mother.

'Is the baby coming early?' Dr Bojang asks.

She turns around. I can see straight away there is fear in her eyes. 'Yes. But there's something else you need to know...'

Chapter 48

Binta

The bag is tan, brown, leather. Worn around the edges, particularly at the bottom where it has been placed many times on the floor. The doctor puts it next to him carefully, a precious cargo, his lifesaving tools inside. At least that's what I believe, in this moment – he has things inside that can help with anything. I've not had much to do with doctors, but I look hopefully at his bag. If *marabout*s have potions, the doctor must have something in there to stop Mariama's agony.

He kneels beside Mariama; she writhes around on the floor, like a snake fighting prey larger than it should have taken, unaware of anyone. I urge myself to look away, but I can't help staring at what is happening inside the little dark room.

'What is it?' Doctor Bojang prompts and looks at my mother, then to Ibrahim for an explanation when she doesn't answer. Instead there's an awkward silence. My mother just looks away. The doctor frowns and begins to examine Mariama's stomach, starting from near under her ribs, methodically working his way to her pelvis.

'The baby is low in the womb, definitely engaged to birth.' He turns to Ibrahim. 'Are you sure you need me here? You should really have called for a midwife.'

Ibrahim shakes his head. 'No, it's...it's not a job for a midwife. I need you.'

The doctor seems to notice the look that Ibrahim and my mother give each other. It is enough for him to continue, to undertake a job that he should not be doing. He shouldn't be doing women's business. Not birthing.

'Please,' my mother begs. 'Please help.'

Doctor Bojang nods, leans over decisively and draws Mariama's *fanu* up around her waist. 'Hold her legs.'

With effort my mother grabs her knee. The doctor takes the other. Between them they manoeuvre Mariama's flailing legs for him to examine her. He lets go immediately, starts to rise and tumbles back. His eyes are wide, his mouth open.

'Oh God!' he says and stumbles to sit on the edge of the bed. 'I've never seen this before.'

My heart begins to beat faster, afraid of what has caused the doctor to say that, fearful of the witchcraft that I feel filling the room. The exit is not far, just across the shop, but my legs don't move. I'm frozen in terror.

'Please, Doctor!' Ibrahim desperately pleads. He moves towards the doctor and puts a hand on his shoulder. 'Please try something!'

'I have to be honest – what I'm dealing with...is...I don't think your wife or the baby have much of a chance...'

My heart pounds hard in my chest. I think of Mariama's pounding to stay alive.

'Do whatever you can. Please!'

Doctor Bojang kneels beside her again, reaches for the well-worn leather bag and opens it. I'm expecting him to produce some medicine, some potion to work with. Instead, after rummaging around inside, he pulls out his empty hand. He looks past where Ibrahim is standing, and motions by a nod of his head. 'Got any razor blades in your shop?'

Ibrahim turns and finds them in an instant. 'Here!' He hands the doctor a couple of new blades encased in crisp, white paper. Doctor Bojang opens them and I notice his hands shaking.

'More light...I need more light.'

Ibrahim brings him two shiny new kerosene lamps from his stock. He fills them with liquid from a plastic yellow drum and lights them. The fumes overwhelm the air, acrid, almost choking me, but the light instantly illuminates the room. He places one lamp close to Mariama. Then he resumes his position and opens her legs again. My mother helps him keep Mariama steady, while he shuffles forward.

The doctor's back is huddled, blocking any view I have. From our lessons in the *jujuwoo*, I understand that childbirth is one of the other things us woman have to endure, but somehow I know this isn't right. Something is dreadfully wrong. It has to be for a man to come.

'I can't hold her and do what I need to do.' The doctor turns to Ibrahim. 'I need someone to hold her for me.'

Ibrahim stands in the doorway between the two rooms and looks over to my father. There is an unspoken understanding. This is women's work and they are already too close. It's enough for Doctor Bojang to be here. For men to be in the adjacent room.

232

'Binta, the doctor needs your help; go in with your mother,' my father says. I'm not sure I've heard him right. He has to tell me again and he waves his hand to gesture he meant what he said. His gentleness is so uncharacteristic that I'm taken aback and it's enough to encourage me to move.

At the bedroom door, the warm glow of the kerosene lamps fully lights up the scene. Instinctively I look to the doctor for reassurance, feeling helpless – despite now being a woman. I think he is surprised to see me coming to help, but his eyes are kind. I have a thing for eyes. You can tell a lot by them. Like if a person is evil, like the *Ngansimba*. It might be why we're not allowed to look at people's eyes – in case you see too much of their soul. His smile uplifts me, as though the ground feels more solid as I move forwards.

'Come!' Doctor Bojang holds out his hand. I take it and kneel down beside him. My hands are shaking, even more than his were earlier when he opened those razors.

'Good. Now, hold the leg here, that's right.' He directs my small hand in his, then he places it on Mariama's thigh. I'm doubtful that I can actually assist and I'm sure I'm not strong enough: not against her energy fighting the pain. I'm not strong enough either to fight my own demons, the images that settle in my mind. My mother is holding Mariama. Holding onto her thigh. Like she did to mine underneath the cutting tree. A sensation of rising nausea comes over me. The doctor places a hand on my shoulder, enough to steady me – enough to stop me running. I take a deep breath, and hold on tight to Mariama's writhing leg.

'Good!' the doctor quietly says to me, taking his strong hands from mine. With his hands now free he puts on white gloves, like I've seen the nurses do at the medical centre. He unscrews the top of a large, brown bottle from his bag, pours it over the razor and then over Mariama. The brown liquid pours over her, where the baby should be coming out.

'Antiseptic. It helps fight infection,' the doctor says, noting my interest.

I can't help but stare at the bulging skin between Mariama's legs. Some skin is pulled so tight it glistens in the light, which reminds me of Mamamuso's face where her tribal scars run down each cheek. Then I understand. The glistening skin is an old, large scar, which now rips in parts under the pressure of the baby.

Mariama's screams are replaced by long moans. The doctor wipes his forehead with his arm and carefully makes a small cut along where the bulge is biggest. My hands tighten around her leg anticipating her pain.

'The baby's head is very close,' Doctor Bojang says. He is concentrating on the cut he needs to make and I wonder if his hands are still shaking. 'I might cut the baby.'

'Do what you need to do,' Ibrahim says.

Doctor Bojang takes a deep breath and puts the razor where the bulge is and draws it slowly, deliberately upwards. Half the razor blade disappears into the skin, and instantly a trickle of deep red flows onto the mat beneath. I am transported to the bush. The doctor is the *Ngansimba*, and as the red liquid runs from Mariama, tears stream quietly down my face.

234

With my hands still gripping her legs, I wipe my eyes with my upper arm. Then I refocus, back in the present, in this room. There's the baby's head, full of wet silky black hair; it appears from the gap the doctor has made. By the time the shoulders are free Mariama is still. With a final pull, there is a gush of fluid and the baby's body slips free with a bluish thick cord attached at its stomach. The doctor cuts it and hands the baby, tiny and pale, to my mother. She wraps it in a cloth, then hands the baby over to me.

There is calm. Peace.

A baby is born, a new life, which I've watched unfold. It's amazing.

I think of my little sister, Mai, when my mother handed her to me for the first time. The look of utter joy she had and of happiness. It's the same feeling I'm expecting now, but as my mother hands the baby to me I register that her emotions aren't right – there's no joy, no excitement.

The baby weighs hardly anything in my arms. I sit on the bed, look down at it and cradle it protectively.

The doctor stands slowly, un-creasing his stiff joints and places a hand on Ibrahim's shoulder. 'I'm sorry. The baby's dead.'

Ibrahim's shoulders slump forward, and he nods in response.

It can't be! The head is a bit of a funny shape, but it can't be dead.

The doctor turns his attention to Mariama and holds her wrist in his hand. 'She's alive – just.'

I sit and look into the baby's sleeping face. It's not dead. I fold some of the cloth over its misshapen head, just leaving the face uncovered. It feels warm. I rock it slowly, like I do with Mai, and hum.

Suddenly there's panic in the room. Mariama shakes violently, causing a pot to smash when her arm hits the bedside table. I instantly know it's bad spirits – the same ones that came to the hut for Aminata. I stop rocking the baby and watch, frightened.

It's just like when the spirits came before.

Only, when Mariama is still, it's because she's dead.

Chapter 49

Binta

The next few hours merge into a blur of disbelief. I sob uncontrollably and there's a pain in my chest that won't shift, whichever way I turn over in bed. Ma took the baby from my arms and sent me back to my room. It was still dark then, but there was no way I could sleep. Tears eased down my cheeks onto the pillow for what felt like hours and I longed to see Jena and Isatou. Just to be with someone. To talk with them and try and understand everything that has been happening. I'm so confused, nothing seems to make sense and then a few more tears run down my face.

Dawn now breaks through the cracks in the wooden door and there's enough light for me to watch a spider scuttle across the ceiling, into a crack. For once I'm so glad to hear the Imam's call to prayer – it signals this horrible night is over. Grandmother snores, oblivious to the tragedy that has unfolded – normally I find it amusing, how she is deaf to things, but this morning it makes me angry. I know it's not her fault. But how can she not know what happened? How could she have just slept through it, peacefully – Mariama's agonising death? Her screams?

Since the bush when my life changed, I have thought how dying would be a way of escaping the pain and torment I face every day. But watching Mariama, seeing her struggle, her desperation to live, I feel differently this morning. I have to survive. More than that, I suddenly realise, I have to learn to live. I owe it to Mariama.

I slip out of bed and I'm drawn to find my mother.

It's the first time since the bush that I have had any thoughts of wanting to be near her but, apart from the doctor, we were the only ones in that room. I have to know I didn't just imagine it, that last night wasn't just another nightmare. My feet automatically move in the direction of her house. I need to see her; to seek some comfort in our shared experience. When I find her she doesn't look like she got much sleep either. Her eyes look tired, drained. Mai is strapped to her back, half crying, making the noise she does when she wants a feed.

'Binta,' my mother says quietly, with a gentleness that confuses my emotions. There's a note of surprise in her voice at seeing me unexpectedly at her door. It's not just because it's so early in the morning and everyone is still asleep, but because I've actively avoided her until now. I know she knows that. I've made a point only to talk to her when spoken to – and that's only to stop the crocodile disciplining me for disrespecting her – but it has been enough for her to notice, despite my careful subtlety.

'You did good last night.'

I don't say anything, but I allow her words to settle in my mind. I don't dismiss them, as I have been doing.

The words make me feel better, like ointment on a sting. I feel good that her words can still do that for me, but they don't draw me to move towards her, although part of me wishes I could walk across the room and allow her arms to enfold me once again. For a second I imagine it; I think of her embrace, of me being soothed by her voice from a nightmare to wake up in the reality I once knew. Then my heart quickens as I remember the last time her hands held me.

'I was just coming to get you,' she says. She walks to the corner of her room and picks up an empty bucket. 'I need you to do something. Come, fill this and meet me across at the shop.'

I do as she says; I carry the full bucket on my head across the compound and place it on the concrete slab outside the shop, where my mother is sat. Her top is exposed, feeding Mai, whose arm is wrapped underneath my mother's. Mai opens her eyes at me, her face content, blissfully unaware of the betrayal our mother has inflicted on me. She still blissfully enjoys her comfort and love. Then, without meaning to, I think of the dead baby in my arms.

The shop is closed and I really don't want to be here, but my mother stands before I have chance to walk away. She knocks on the door gently and there's no answer, which I'm relieved about. I'm ready to leave, but my mother opens the door.

'Come!' She turns to me and says, 'Bring the bucket!'

I try not to spill any of the water and follow my mother into the shop, past Ibrahim who is sat on a stool in the corner with his head in his hands. It looks like he might be asleep. Then I follow my mother into the back room. I hesitate at the entrance, but she pulls me in and closes the door behind us.

'We need to sort the room for Ibrahim. Here, take this. If you rub hard enough you should be able to get the stain out of the lino – use this cloth as well,' she says and hands me a scrubbing brush.

The evidence that last night was definitely real is there, right there – soaked into the floor. I want to ask where Mariama and the baby are, but the words don't make it further than my thoughts. It somehow seems wrong to ask.

My mother places a hand on my shoulder. 'I've got to go – I need to see to your brothers. I'll be back. I know this is difficult.' She pauses before she leaves, closing the door behind her and shutting me in with ghosts.

First I roll up the blood-soaked mat, then I begin working on the lino underneath. It makes a rhythmic swishing sound as I scrub through the scarlet to the blue, green and orange pattern beneath. When I dip the brush in the clear bucket of water it instantly changes colour. Crimson dances through the water, like it's bleeding.

'*Salam Malikum*, Ibrahim.'

The voice in the shop startles me. I stop scrubbing immediately, as I don't want Ibrahim to find me in here – for him to see me doing this. What would I say? How would I explain? Would he prefer to see the evidence of last night, or for everything to have disappeared as though it didn't happen?

'Doctor Bojang. Welcome.'

Doctor? I head over to the door and open it slightly, enough to see through when I put my eye against the wooden frame. Ibrahim is still slumped over his knees, but he is definitely awake now with his son sitting at his feet, naked, crying. Probably wondering where his mother is. The doctor takes a stool along the wall and sits in front of Ibrahim; he caresses the boy's head, trying to soothe him.

'I am so sorry for your loss. I did everything I could for your wife – and the baby.' The little boy cries again, this time louder. There's no placating him now. 'Ibrahim, when did the child last eat?' the doctor asks, picking him up from the floor and balancing him on his knee.

'Maybe late afternoon yesterday.'

'I'll get Ousman's wife to feed him. Where do they live?'

'Opposite.' Ibrahim points to where my mother will be.

This is a good chance for me to leave, to get out of the room while the doctor is out. I can say something to Ibrahim – to explain why I'm here. But then I look at the floor, still soaked and stained. I can't leave it for him to see like this. Also, I don't want to ever have to come back to this room again. That's what keeps me here more than anything else – otherwise my mother might send me back to finish it later.

'Ibrahim, let me bring you some bread. You need to eat,' Doctor Bojang says on his return.

'No, I don't have the appetite.'

'Well, let me bring you some coffee.'

If I scrub the floor, it's going to make a noise. Instead, I watch the men. A while later the doctor arrives back with mugs. He must have got my father to boil water on his gas stove.

'I wonder if you could help me understand some things?' he asks, and hands Ibrahim a cup of coffee. He brings his stool forward. 'Mariama was...there was no way for the baby to come out. I don't mean to ask to

241

offend you, Ibrahim, but I didn't understand what I was facing last night. As a doctor I want to understand, so that I might be able to save other women in the future.' Doctor Bojang pauses, takes a sip of the coffee, then asks, 'Why was she sewn like that?'

Ibrahim unfolds himself from his slumped position and sits upright; his fingers interlock on his lap and he takes a deep breath. I want to know too. I've got so many questions of my own.

'I shouldn't really speak of these matters, Doctor. It is a woman thing anyway and I don't know much, but what I do know is that it's sacred. I really shouldn't tell you anything. There is a curse for those who talk about it!' Ibrahim chortles a sarcastic laugh. 'Anyway I don't care about any curse – what else could happen to me? I'm on my own to look after a child in a foreign land. If I die it will be a blessing, not a curse now.'

'Ibrahim, you mustn't think like that.'

They allow a silence to settle while they drink their coffee. 'You may be able to help another woman?' Ibrahim asks and puts his cup down on the floor.

'Yes.'

'*Fula*s have different traditions – and some similar – to yourself. Our women have an initiation like your women. Both are – cut – during the ceremony.' Ibrahim goes quiet, the silence grows again and he puts his head onto his hands.

'A girl child was recently brought to me,' the doctor says. 'She'd been cut, here, in this town.'

Aminata! He must be talking about Aminata.

'The mother brought her to the clinic. She was only about five or six years old and she told me it was malaria. Malaria! That's been my enemy all these

242

years, ever since I watched my younger brother die. It's what motivated me to become a doctor.' He stands up and walks across to the window. 'You know what the clinic is like – everyone looking into my room – but we managed to put a bed sheet up over a broken screen to stop people seeing. I was horrified. She'd been cut badly. She didn't look like a girl should look. All the female flesh had been removed, and there were already signs of infection. I was able to stabilise her before she was transported to Serekunda.' The doctor walks back over to the chair and sits down. He sighs heavily and continues, 'She didn't make it – died a couple of days later.'

My head spins. There is a sudden wave of nausea that rises up from my stomach. I think I am going to be sick. Aminata? Oh God! No! Aminata dead? I bite down hard on my finger to stop from crying out and hurry over to the bucket, retching as quietly as I can into the bloodied water.

'In less than a month I've come across this issue twice. The girl was the first time I've dealt with it. Then last night – but your wife was different.'

I try to calm myself, desperate to hear what the doctor is saying. I go back to the door and wipe my mouth with the back of my hand. I need to hear more.

'I've always battled malaria, which has no conscience or agenda, but I've now seen there is something that I can truly put my effort into, to really make a difference. But, Ibrahim, I need your help to understand.'

'I don't know much, but I'll tell you what I know. When women are cut in our village, they are sewn together with thread. I've heard sometimes thorns are used to bring the wound together. In our village it happens with thread. A matchstick is put in place while she is sewn, you know – for urination and the menstruation time.'

I want to throw up again, but stop myself and take a couple of long deep breaths.

'But how can a woman get pregnant if she is sewn – I'm guessing that she is sewn for chastity reasons?'

'You know that your bride is a virgin. Sometimes the woman will go to the older women the night of the wedding and they will cut her open. Sometimes the husband will take his bride and cut her with the wedding guests listening outside, or force himself on her to break the scar tissue. I didn't want that. It took some time, some months – I didn't want to force myself on her. I hated to see her in pain. Little by little I tried until we were able to.'

'But she had a child already and she was still sewn completely. I don't understand.'

'When a woman is pregnant she is sewn up again to keep the baby from curses, and to keep the baby healthy. Then, before the birth, the woman will go to the midwife and they will cut her to give birth. After our son was born, I pleaded with my wife not to be sewn again. Before we came to this country she discovered she was pregnant again, and her mother persuaded her it was for the best.'

Ibrahim rubs his head with his hand. 'Her mother frightened her, saying that the baby would be exposed to evil spirits. The harvest had been bad in our village and with another baby I worried that we would not have enough food. That is when I decided we should travel here. We planned to travel back to Senegal in time for the birth. I didn't want her to be sewn, I argued with her mother. God, I wish I had stopped her.'

'It's sounds as though you tried, but you were fighting against your entire tradition, against fears, against curses. You loved her very much.'

I walk over to the bed in the corner of the room and push my head into the pillow and sob quietly for Aminata. I think of her climbing over me to sit with Hawa – how they became friends – and I think of her laughing. My head begins to hurt and I can't think. There's too much to take in, but the thing that I cling to most is hearing Doctor Bojang say how wrong this is – a doctor saying it. All of this is wrong. So wrong that he said he wants to fight against it.

Any thread of understanding to explain my mother's actions disappears. And as it does, it feels like something inside me breaks.

PART THREE

- After -

Chapter 50

Yari

It's the loud screech of breaks that immediately shatters my deep sleep. By the time I hear the thud of boots landing on the ground, my eyes are open wide, as I stare into the darkness for some clue as to what is happening.

'Sarko!' He hears the fear in my voice and the terrifying sounds heading towards the house. He quickly gets out of bed and moves across to the chair where his clothes are neatly folded from the night before. He balances on one leg and quickly pulls on his trousers, just before the sounds of heavy footsteps ascend the veranda steps and there is a quick triplicate bang on the front door, 'OPEN UP!'

'Who do you think it is?' I ask him and draw the blanket up around my chin in a feeble attempt to hide. The wood from the door splinters and there's a crash as it comes off of its hinges. I'm too shocked to scream; I cannot put the scene together in my head quick enough to react. At the sound of boots coming heavily through the living room I gasp, and Sarko runs across to block the bedroom door, but before he can get there it swings open and the shadows of men fill the open door frame. I find my voice and scream. It does nothing to stop them.

Immediately there's the sound of a dull thud as Sarko is hit across the face and he stumbles backwards, falls to the floor and lands with a groan. They head in my direction; one, two, three steps and then a hand covers my mouth and the screams filling the room; another grabs me around the back and under my arm. I'm dragged out of the bed, past Sarko who is being hauled up with two men behind him and out the bedroom, pushed through the living room. I kick furiously with my legs, trying to make contact with the soft flesh of the men around me and to grip with my heels; something to stop the propulsion in the direction of the front door. In the quickest of moments I feel myself being dragged down the steps, then the grit of the dirt under my bare feet as we cross the yard to the outside of the compound. Then my legs are lifted and I land with an echo onto metal. I open my eyes and realise I'm inside the back of a vehicle; from the slit at the back in the canvas I can see the night sky illumined by a slither of moon. Then the flap is pushed aside as Sarko is thrown in; he lands heavily, rolls on his side and moans in pain.

'Sarko!'

'Sshhh!' a man demands as he pulls himself up onto the back of the truck blocking any chance of escape. I swallow hard when I catch the outline of a gun in a holster on his belt. As the engine starts, the loud tinny sound of screws and bolts vibrating resounds all around, and as the truck lunges forward we are jolted to the side. Sarko lifts himself onto his arm as I edge over to reach him and help him to sit up. I touch his face and can feel a sticky dampness, which can only mean that he's bleeding, but it's too dark to see anything. With the guard looking over our every move, I silence the things I want to say and keep quiet.

The truck races and bounces over potholes as we zigzag through the back roads, accelerating towards the road that leads out of Kenji.

It can't be more than a few minutes since I was woken and it feels as though a dust of realisation is settling. In my mind I revisit every sound, every movement since this nightmare enfolded. *Who are these people?* It doesn't take much to figure out these are soldiers: the truck, the well-rehearsed raid on our home, the gun that I can't take my gaze from. But why – why would they want to take us? It must be a mistake. They came to the wrong home, got the wrong people. The words are inside to say just this, but apart from the shallow sound of my breathing no other sound travels out of my mouth. What have we done? I try to work out which way we are heading, but it's too difficult. I can only hear the sound of this one truck. There are no indicators to confirm that we are heading south. I assume that's where we are going – to the nearest police station.

After the attempted coup, the president put in place a curfew at night. At first there was a sense of seriousness and fear when we heard about it, but over the past few weeks they've become part of the humour in the town; women laugh as they remind their husbands to come home, rather than wander around in the middle of the night visiting mistresses. From the rumours the trucks drive through on patrol after dark and those arrested are taken to the next village, the one just on the border of Senegal, before being released the next day after checks are carried out.

But why take us? We were asleep in our own compound. If we were heading south I'm sure we would have arrived by now and the realisation of what that means makes my heart beat faster for the rest of the long journey. We are heading north and there's only one reason we would be heading that way. My heart continues to pound so that I can feel the pulsating in my neck and I swallow hard. We are heading north because that is the way to Mile Two Prison. And if we are heading there, we won't be released in the morning. Sarko is more alert and puts his arm across my body and squeezes my arm and I know by that he must also realise where we are heading. We both know the stories of people going in – and not coming out.

Chapter 51

Amie

There had been this growing tension for months that I thought would be over once Binta faced the *Ngansimba*. I agonised over what had to happen. Who wouldn't? To know you have to see your child face such pain, but to have no choice. I thought I would sleep again after it had happened, but now I often wake with a pressing in my chest and it's hard to breathe. To have to hold her was the hardest thing I have ever had to do, but I thought if she could feel my hands it might give her some strength. The days are passing by and she still doesn't look at me. That is what makes this the hardest thing.

To go against all that seems natural for a mother to do – to show strength to do what is needed even when it feels so wrong – I thought that was a demonstration of my love. But I saw the doctor's face. His disgust at Mariama's predicament – what had been done to her. Doesn't he realise though? However terrible it is, what other way is there? Mai stirs in the dark next to me on the bed; her arm stretches. We are so connected that even in her half sleep she is able to find me, and she latches onto my breast. Tears suddenly gather in a prickle in my eyes. What can I do? Mai will be grown too soon and I will face the same dilemma again.

I have tried to be strong, to do the right thing, but as the days pass I feel like there is a growing weight descending on me, crushing me inside. I feel more and more helpless. I thought that feeling of helplessness would lift after Binta went through this thing that we all have to endure. I thought the anguish of it would pass, but she is changed forever – I am too. Something of me has been broken seeing her cut. Taking her there – holding her.

Over the years I gradually accepted what happened to me at the hands of the *Ngansimba* was something that had to happen. There was no choice. It is what happens to women. Like childbirth; unpleasant, but necessary. And hearing it spoken of as such until it becomes part of my own mantra.

But I don't have relief from feeling trapped by circumstance. I just feel more powerless. It is worse than before. Mai pauses in her suckling as though sensing my internal dialogue. I hate seeing what this is doing to Binta. I hate what it's done to our relationship. But to know how this feels – and I will have to do it again with Mai.

Chapter 52

Binta

I take advantage that nobody is around and monopolise the living room. There's a dull pain in my stomach that doesn't ease. I climb onto my father's armchair, bring my knees up, bend them under me and clutch at my aching side. Each month, I'm unclean. I learnt this in the *jujuwoo*. It comes, always three days after the first darkest night when there is no moon. It's good that I don't have to do any chores at this time, because I don't think I could anyway. I don't think it's a coincidence that it happens when the nights are at their darkest, when spirits roam more freely. It didn't hurt like this before and I wonder if the *Ngansimba* has somehow cursed me as a reminder of her lessons.

Along the side of the wall of this room, there is a large, mahogany display cabinet. It dominates the space between my mother's and her co-wife's bedrooms. There's hardly anything on the shelves, apart from my mother's few cups and saucers and three schoolbooks I placed neatly on the bottom shelf at the start of the school holidays. My father likes to keep them on display to show visitors he's paying for me to go to school.

I think of how my mother persuaded him to let me continue my education, wanting something good for me. At the time, I thought she wanted the best for me. But all the time she was planning for me to meet the crocodile. I hate them. I hate her. I hate the illusion of it all.

I go over to the cabinet and carefully unlock the display unit and return to my place on the armchair. Since I last looked at a book, I've changed. I've learnt more than I knew there was to learn. Things that were never written, hidden in these pages.

'I see you found your books!' My father startles me and I look up. I'm more surprised when he comes and sits opposite me. 'I have a letter for you. Here.' He passes me a blue envelope.

'For me? Who's it from?'

He just shrugs, not because he doesn't know, but he doesn't look interested. This is the first letter I've ever received, I take it quickly and tuck it into the top of my *fanu* and expect him to leave. But he continues to sit opposite, poised, ready to say something. 'I have good news for you!' He reaches over and removes my books and places them on the coffee table next to him. 'You won't need to worry about these from now on,' he says, at which I look at him bewildered.

'You are going to marry Ibrahim!' He sits back in his chair, a smugness breaking across his face. 'That's wonderful, isn't it?'

I don't think I have heard him properly. I see his smile and watch his lips carry on talking, but it's like when I swam in the sea with Jena: the water muffled the sounds.

'Ibrahim, you know. My tenant. The *Fula*.'

I force the air out to make words, 'Mariama's husband?'

'Yes.'

'But she's only just died,' I manage to say.

'Exactly! He needs help with the son. It's a great idea – he'll stay here in the compound. You don't even have to leave here; you'll just be across from your mother in the shop.'

It gets worse. He wants me to marry Ibrahim *and* stay in that room, where I've just cleaned the blood off the floor – the room where I cradled their dead baby. My mouth is shut tight and I bite on my bottom lip. I know it's pointless to argue with him.

'...I've already spoken to the Imam. It won't take long to arrange things.'

I glare at my father in a way that would normally reward me a beating, but he doesn't notice. Evil words stick in my throat, words I can't ever say to him, because he's still my father. Besides, the things I want to say to him would make sure I'd see the *Ngansimba* again. As he continues to talk, the words blur as one droning sound and my eyes drift towards my schoolbooks that feel a million miles away. I don't really hear what he's saying. All I can think of is how my life is slipping away and it's like hands are holding me again. I'm out of control, someone else doing what they want with me. My focus returns to his words and all I manage to say in response is, 'Does my mother know?'

There is a brief look of puzzlement on his face. 'Not yet,' he says, waving the back of his hand dismissively. I don't think it's even occurred to him to say anything to her about this; not that she would care anyway.

He gets up to leave and points to the table. 'See, I told you – you don't need to worry yourself about books anymore!'

I watch him walk out the door and I have to fight the urge to scream. Then I reach across to the books – what was going to be my future – and push them, crashing onto the floor.

Chapter 53

Amie

There's been talk – Yari and her husband have been taken. The fact that nobody quite knows where or why fuels the speculation. Over the years I've heard the jeers others have made – the comments they've made about her. Trying to do things differently. We've all laughed at her ways – me included. Deep inside I am intrigued by her – the way she speaks, the different way she lives – but I've always hidden that from anyone else. I wouldn't have wanted anyone to question me, to make life more difficult than it needs to be.

I remember how she spoke with such confidence that day at the library in front of the elders, trying to get them to see that there were other ways of bringing our girls into adulthood. I admire her to be able to think differently. Some of the things I've heard her speak about over the years, I've wondered how she came up with such questions and opinions. I've grappled over and over until my head actually hurts trying to untangle these things.

To have thoughts that are your own. That's the benefit of education; it gives your brain freedom to grow thoughts.

At least that is what I thought before. But now I'm not sure. Look where Yari's thinking, her opinions, have got her. Arrested and gone. I thought she had strength against our traditions and ways, she was paving a new way of doing things. But that's not the case. She doesn't have strength after all. And I certainly don't.

Chapter 54

Binta

A few days later, when the ache in my stomach has subsided, I welcome the tedious chore my mother gives me to do. Slowly, I work my way through a neat pile of clothes to mend. Hems to sow, patches to cover holes. Even this task can't stop my mind racing. I can't get married! Not to Ibrahim, not to anyone. It's not been long since I was in the bush and I'm not even healed properly. I can't have a man near me, not ever. I feel ill and place my head in my hands, my elbows balancing on my knees. After a moment I feel better and know what I need to do. I have to go and see my friends. I feel strong enough now, I thought staying at home I'd feel less vulnerable, but now look at what has happened.

With all that has happened – facing the *Ngansimba*, witnessing Mariama's ordeal as she and her baby died, finding out about Aminata dying, this marriage to Ibrahim – I feel I'm at the bottom of a well. It feels as though there is no way out. I think about what Doctor Bojang said and for the first time in weeks, something makes sense. I'm justified to feel angry, to burn with hate and fear.

Something unexpected then happens. I cry, quietly enough so nobody can hear, but it comes from deep within. I sob into my hands for a long time and I feel some weight lift. Maybe there is a way out from this well after all.

When I wipe my eyes, I look up and notice rain clouds are gathering. They seem like they're dancing in the sky. Before long, they block the sun and the humidity rises to a point where it feels that the earth will explode. There's the distant rumble of thunder; there's going to be a break from this heat soon, a warm breeze blows. I'll wait until after the storm, then I'll go and look for Jena and Isatou, perhaps they are back in town if they did go away. A flock of birds suddenly takes flight before the first flash of lightning and then the raindrops bounce off of the dry ground, making individual splash marks. Heaven opens with a torrent of sound, rain hammering down with power against metal, tin and soil.

Beyond our compound wall, I can hear the delighted screams of children jumping into the quickly forming rivers, where roads were just a moment ago. The joyful sounds are so alien, so removed from how I feel; a different reality from mine. The squeals of happiness draw me to step outside into the back yard and I turn my head upwards towards the descending rain. It pours over my face, washing off the dust, cool and refreshing. I try to catch some of the pure water in my mouth and close my eyes. With my arms outstretched I stand there for some time until my clothes are soaked. Maybe it's because I've been crying or perhaps the way the rain has invigorated me, but when I go back inside I feel refreshed.

My wet clothes smell of the downpour. I wipe my face and hair with a cloth and sit on the edge of the bed to finish repairing the last of the shirts. The sound of the rain is deafening on the corrugated iron roof, but there's a distinct voice of a visitor just arriving. The constant pounding rain dulls some of the words, but I can tell that the voice belongs to an older woman. The voice is familiar, and when I push the door open with my hips – my hands are holding the pile of clothes – I see Mamamuso, Jena's grandmother. I'm surprised to see her here. She's not friends with my mother, and she's never visited us before.

'*Salam Malikum*,' I greet her, on my way to sit at the other end of the room.

Mamamuso pauses in her conversation with my mother and responds, but she hesitates until my mother says, 'It's okay. We can talk in front of Binta. She's a woman now.'

I feel awkward. Suddenly I need a distraction and move towards the cupboard to get out my books. I sit down at the far side of the room on the armchair and hide behind the open pages. It works, because Mamamuso soon seems to forget I'm here. As I flick through the open pages it triggers my mind to remember the conversation my father had with me earlier. I feel sick again to think that he wants me to get married. I would have once gone to Ma for help, but she's proven that she wants only traditions and that she doesn't care for my needs. I wonder if she knows yet of his plans. The words are hazy on the page; instead of seeing the text and pictures all I see is Ibrahim and his son. And me. My future. I thought things couldn't get any worse.

'That rain came down so quickly! Look, I'm soaking.'

'Can I get you some new clothes?'

'No, no. It's fine.'

Mamamuso exchanges some simple gossip about people my mother might know, but it's apparent she's not come here to discuss that and I turn the pages slowly, focusing my attention on her words. What does she want?

'Amie, I have come to ask for your help, with my granddaughter, Jeneba.'

Jena?

I force myself not to react and continue to fix my eyes on the book.

'She missed out before, but I've arranged for the *Ngansimba* to come and fulfil the duty.'

It's good that I'm sat down otherwise I know my legs would have made me collapse.

'What about Yari?' my mother asks hesitantly.

'Yari? Well, you know her with her different ideas,' Mamamuso says, waving her hand. 'She doesn't understand – for whatever reason. But you do. You understand the importance of these things. The mother is...away. So it's more than convenient.'

I try to focus my eyes on the page of the book, to hide my emotions – desperate not to stop Mamamuso talking. I need to find out everything about her plans for Jena.

'There is just one thing. The *Ngansimba* is willing as long as I get some help. I need a few women – I'm not strong enough to hold her. The *Ngansimba* is coming tomorrow night, which means I don't have much time to organise things and I want your help, Amie.'

I don't expect the reservation in my mother's voice. 'I don't know. If Yari isn't willing – something could happen.'

264

'Nothing will happen!' There's scorn in the old woman's voice. 'But if she's left uncut then who will marry her? What will she become? I only want for my granddaughter what you wanted for your daughter.'

Those words don't make sense, although I repeat them in my mind to process them slowly. I really want to believe it, to understand there's some explanation for my mother's actions. For a moment I want to hold onto Mamamuso's words, to understand that it was a necessary action – one of love. Something my mother had to do. But her hesitation in answering Mamamuso makes me more certain that it was wrong, like Dr Bojang said.

'There was a girl that was cut with Binta. She died.'

'But that wasn't anything to do with the cutting; there were bad spirits.'

My mother stands and faces Mamamuso. 'That may be. But there was a woman – the *Fula* who lived here in this compound. I watched her die last week. It was because of what was done to her. The baby was born dead too.'

Mamamuso raises her voice to my mother. 'That was a *Fula*! They do things differently. I'm talking about our ways. You must help me!'

In the pause between that and my mother's response, I feel every muscle in my body tense. The rain is easing, which makes her hesitation more noticeable. Mamamuso eases her ageing body from the seat and begins to head to the door. 'Think quickly,' she says. 'The *Ngansimba* is coming tomorrow night.'

Chapter 55

Yari

I'm sat with my back pressed against the wall of the prison cell and fear rises in me in waves as I piece together the extent of our situation. *Do Jena and Isatou know we've been taken? Did they hear the soldiers?* They must have done. The girls will be afraid. I close my eyes and try to picture the scene after the truck sped away, leaving only a plume of dust behind – with the commotion others would have woken and ran into our home to see what was happening. Sarko's sisters would have comforted my daughters and then they'll make plans to look after them until we are back; they'll make sure they eat well, get to school. For once I am glad that we live with Sarko's family and that they can do what's needed.

Then with the next thought I have the awful realisation: if we are gone, Mamamuso will find out. There will be nothing to stop her from taking Jena to the *Ngansimba*. To be out of control about what happens outside the prison walls is the worst part of this. I cannot do anything; the weight of helplessness

266

feels suddenly heavy and I hide my face in my hands and weep quietly, longing for some semblance of privacy in the corner of the cramped, hot cell.

'What were you arrested for?'

I wipe my eyes hurriedly and look up at the woman who is close enough to me that I can feel the breath of the words against my neck.

It's a question that has spun in my mind constantly since the soldiers invaded my home and I shrug my shoulders. I imagine it's because of my peripheral connections with the opposition party, but I've not been told formally. I'm not clear when I will know for sure. Or how long I'm supposed to be in here for.

'Are we in Jewheng Prison?' I ask. My voice struggles to get the sentence out where my throat is dry from thirst. I know what the answer is, but I hold onto hope that it might still be.

The woman laughs, which triggers a brief coughing fit. After a moment she sighs with an element of amusement, 'No. You are in Mile Two. Welcome to President Jammeh's Hotel.' The most infamous prison; where people disappear for years. And sometimes forever.

My stomach suddenly aches and the continued stench that seems to permeate from the walls seeps into the fabric of my clothes, every pore of my skin – it pollutes any hope I have of being released quickly. I press my hand over my stomach, willing the nausea to subside. If I'm ill, it won't make me popular, adding to the rank airless atmosphere in here.

I draw my knees up tightly to my chest, wrap my hands around my legs, bury my head into the ball I've made and sob quietly. I cry at the thought of my children without us. Of my discomfort and the injustice of this. And I cry through my fears of how Sarko will be treated. The rumours have rumbled like thunder over the years. We all know about the abuses behind the walls that stretch along the highway. At least the premise of what happens. The details have always been difficult to confirm, so terrifying that it generates conversations for weeks over whether they have been exaggerated. Oh Sarko! My sweet Sarko, what are they doing to you?

There's a crunching of metal keys connecting in the door barrel. Suddenly the heavy green door creaks on rusted hinges and three men surround the entrance; as it opens, a fourth steps forward and I look up and glance towards the woman next to me. The confidence in her eyes has been replaced by fear and I notice now how young she looks. I hold my knees tighter, desperate to stop shaking; to not let the guards see how afraid I am. Whatever will happen to me, I know Sarko will face worse. I have to be brave for him – for our girls. I close my eyes to shut away what is happening and wonder if I will ever see my family again.

Chapter 56

Binta

The place is tranquil. It was the first place I thought to come, but now I'm here I can't bring myself to enter inside uninvited. I remain hidden out of sight, behind the well. Now I'm here I don't know if I should've come, but when my ear catches the sound of buzzing bees overhead, my legs move quickly in the direction of the compound.

The sky is streaked in large strokes of pink, which signals darkness will quickly descend like a blanket. I tentatively hover at the compound entrance when I'm spotted.

'I haven't seen you all holidays. What happened?' Esther says as she runs towards me. 'I've missed you,' she says as she greets me with a hug.

'You too,' I reply, meaning it more than the words can really tell her. Things have changed so much since I last saw her. I hold her close and wish things were the same; I long for some semblance of what was before. It seems a lifetime ago, so far removed from what has happened that it's hard to think that really was me a short time back.

'It's nearly time for dinner…you will stay and eat?' Esther asks, as she releases me from her embrace.

'Sure. That would be nice, thanks.'

She takes me by the hand and leads me towards her family where they are sat under the tree on armchairs. We sit down just as her mother arrives from inside the house bringing a steaming pot of peanut stew and rice.

'Ah, Binta.' Hannah smiles. 'Nice to see you again.'

During dinner I hear the distant call to prayer. Although it's a good walk from the market, I think all of the town can hear it. But here the sound doesn't have the same impact as it does on my compound; no ablutions to make or prayer mats to unroll. It's the first time that I've seen people actively ignore the call. My grandmother is different. She doesn't actually hear it – at least she says she doesn't – which I think is probably true. Instead, we continue eating and I feel like I'm in another world, which is perfect as it makes me feel safer; detached from my reality. Exactly what is needed for what I have to do.

When the pink sky dissolves into the darkness, Esther's father, Moses, lights a kerosene lamp and places it on the table. It casts a warm glow upon Esther's family as they chat and laugh together. I didn't plan my visit like this, to be here for a meal. My mother will be wondering where I am, but I'll deal with that later. For now, I'm going to make the most of the *Karoninka*s' company and I want to stay for as long as possible. Besides, I can't leave until I've fulfilled what I'd planned to come here to do. I don't know how I'm going to start, and the more I think about it, the less I join in with their conversation. That's why, when Hannah asks me a question, she has to repeat it.

My greatest concern is the curse. I know that, by speaking of the things I need to discuss, people die. I don't know if it is a quick death, like Ibrahim's baby, or slow and agonising like Mariama's. With the possibility of death so close, I'm desperate to live. Not just live as in breathing, eating, being. But living like this family. Having fun again, laughing.

'You seem quiet, Binta. Is everything okay?' Hannah interrupts my thoughts. The question catches me off-guard and I hesitate and sense the family waiting for my response.

'There is something,' I say. I look at Hannah and then to Esther. I lower my voice and continue, 'Perhaps I can tell you later?'

'Of course.' Hannah nods and I relax knowing she has understood the sensitivity.

My appetite vanishes. I've set things in motion now and I'm not sure where it will lead. She might not want to hear about my secrets. The sky is now very dark, with only a slither of moon breaking through, which I'm glad of, because it's like a blanket covering me.

After the meal, once Moses and Esther's brother have left us, I feel the dynamics shift and I can sense the anticipation that Hannah has for me to begin. In the sky, there are glittering stars too numerous to count. Hannah boils water on a gas canister. 'I love tea!' she says. 'I spent some time in the UK with my husband. The English drink tea all the time. After I left I couldn't get enough tea! PG Tips is my favourite, but this will have to do for now.'

She pours some for us and adds spoonfuls of sugar. 'Mind you,' she says, 'the British don't have enough sugar in their tea – it makes it much too bitter!' She

271

chuckles to herself. If I wasn't so nervous, it might have made me smile.

'Binta, something seems to be worrying you. Can I help?' she asks and hands me a cup.

'I don't know how to begin... I shouldn't say anything. If I do terrible things will happen – there's a curse.'

Hannah reaches over and gently squeezes my hands.

It gives me courage to continue and I say the words quickly, 'I will be killed if I tell.'

It's too dark to see their faces in detail. Where it rained earlier the puddles are full of frogs calling to one another. I listen to their rhythmic chorus, which seems to fill the air. My mouth's dry and my heart pounds; for a moment I just focus on the croaking.

'I can see it is difficult, but I will help if I can,' Hannah assures me.

I look up at her and say, 'Our Mandinka ways are different to yours, you know.' Then I continue quietly, because I hope the spirits might not hear me, 'Do you know about our initiation?'

She nods. 'Yes, I know about – the cutting.' Hannah stirs her spoon in the tea, more slowly than I think she needs to, and says, 'It happened to me.'

'To you?' I say, a little louder that I intend. 'But you're not Mandinka.' Then I think of Mariama, the *Fula* and add, 'Or Muslim.'

She's still stirring the tea. The sugar must have dissolved by now. 'It isn't anything to do with religion, Binta. It's cultural. Common to many tribes.'

Suddenly I feel stupid, vulnerable and scared. She's just the same as my mother and I immediately expect her get angry with me for speaking of these things, but she doesn't. She takes a sip, looks over the cup at me and then says, 'I don't want it for my daughter, Binta.'

Esther doesn't seem shocked. I don't think this is the first time that Hannah has spoken about these things in front of her daughter; that's different to my mother who kept it hidden from me. My mind is hazy and I can't quite get my thoughts together. Christians are cut as well.

'How come you are okay to talk about it?' I ask, aware she doesn't seem worried about any curse.

'I've attended meetings and, over the years, I've become more aware of how wrong it is, Binta. We must talk about it so that others can know too but it's not easy.'

More pieces of a puzzle fit together. None explain to me why cutting happens. Just why not. If the horror of being held down and cut like that wasn't enough, there was Mariama's death. There's the baby, and little Aminata too – I know it wasn't malaria – and Doctor Bojang's conversation that I overheard. Now Hannah is adding another piece.

It's not just a few people that think cutting is wrong. There are others that want to stop it. I thought perhaps as time went by, as the physical pain lessened, I would understand why my mother allowed this. But I'm becoming more convinced of the opposite.

'You have been initiated?' Hannah asks, more as a statement than as a question I need to answer. I don't think she can see the single tear running from my eye, in the darkness, but still she says, 'I'm sorry, Binta.'

The warm tea is sweet on my tongue. I gulp it and prepare to speak. I need to say it quickly otherwise I won't be able to say it at all. Quickly, but clearly, so that they hear me first time: 'Jena is going to be cut. Tomorrow.' It solicits a combined gasp from both Hannah and Esther.

My words, bottled inside until now, continue to flow. 'I have to stop it. But I don't know how! Jena's mother is away and her grandmother is going to do it while she gets the chance. What can I do?' I wait for the curse, but I'm breathing. My heart is pumping. I know it is, because I can feel it beating hard in my chest. I'm still alive. 'There's something else – my father's arranging for me to marry. I don't want to, Hannah!' I try to steady the rising panic in my voice.

'Married?' Esther asks, incredulous.

'Oh, Binta,' Hannah says. 'Many difficult things on your shoulders. We'll think of something.'

'What are we going to do, Ma?' Esther asks. I'm glad she does, as I don't think I want to say much more.

'I don't know yet,' Hannah says. 'But you are brave to tell us, Binta.'

I nod, happy that I've shared my burden. It's going to be one thing figuring out how to save Jena – another working out how we won't get killed in the process. And if we could also find a way that I can avoid marrying Ibrahim, that would be a bonus.

'I'm glad I've got you both to speak to; it seems like we became friends for a reason.'

'For such a time as this,' Esther replies. Then she places her hand on my arm. I look down at her missing finger, wondering how long it took to heal. Wondering how long it will take *me* to heal. She gently squeezes my arm. 'Friends – for such a time as this,' she repeats, emphasising the individual words that they carry purpose and hope.

Chapter 57

Amie

Mamamuso returns for my answer the following morning, but as soon as she left the day before, I knew what I would say. Though I'm glad I had the night to practice the words in my mind, to build the confidence. I'm not like Yari. I don't know how she weaves around the arguments that elders present. When I think of the way she argues her points, it reminds me of when an animal evades a predator. The elders dart this way and that, trying to catch her arguments to put them in a cage and lock them away from the next generation, but they're never quite able to grab the issues. Instead the cage door remains redundantly open.

But that's not like me. Her arguments mull over in my head and for the first time I see the sense she makes – the way she tried to convince people at the library all those months ago. I wish I knew more then. Even though I feel a stirring in my conscience that we can do things differently, I don't know how to dance around and swerve the solid reasoning that has always been. That's why, when I hear Mamamuso arrive, my heart pounds hard. What if she dismisses what I say and somehow still draws me in to help with the cutting?

'I've come to get you. It's time, Amie,' Mamamuso says and steps up on the veranda just outside my door. She places her hand on the small of her back for a second before straightening up. I can almost hear her spine cracking as each vertebra realigns.

I wish I had Yari's confidence. Then I picture little Aminata and her empty space as the girls walked from the *jujuloo* back to their families. Mariama's screams echo again in my head as she tried in vain to give birth. I see the dead baby in Binta's arms. I swallow hard to dislodge the dry lump that seems to be building in my throat, so that my voice will be clear. That she will hear me.

'No, Mamamuso. I am not coming to help you.'

Chapter 58

Binta

The uneven ridges in the soil are a perfect hiding place for scorpions and the occasional cobra. It's nerve-wracking with only a little moonlight to shine the way. I try not to think about these things as I hurry back from Esther's home. Instead, I think about the plan we've come up with through the hours into the late night. We debated the difficulties, discussed the benefits and pondered the consequences...the reality of what we face.

The alleyway at the back of our compound is a precarious path that runs alongside the mud-brick bakery. The back way into the compound, away from the main entrance is my choice to avoid bumping into my father. He's likely to be sat outside enjoying the cooler night air, drinking his bitter *attyre* with friends. His barrage of questions, asking me why I'm coming home at this hour, scares me at this moment more than the scorpions and snakes.

I creep into my room and drop quietly into bed. I'm relieved not to have been spotted and for the plan to be over before it ever got started. Grandmother has her back curled with her arms underneath her head providing a pillow, snoring loudly as usual. In contrast, Lamin lies silently still on his back in a way that only small children seem to manage when they sleep. He is so still that it makes me put my ear near his mouth to check he's okay. The thought of Mariama's dead baby makes me jumpy. A gentle warm breath blows against my face and my momentary worry disappears in an instant.

As my eyes adjust in the darkness, I can make out the details of his face. I watch him, painfully aware this may be the last time I'm going to see him. I kiss his forehead and wish I could see my baby sister, Mai, one last time, but that's not possible. I can't believe my life has come to this junction – that I have to leave. I linger, wanting Lamin's warm skin to imprint on my memory, as though I will be able to take something of him with me. I breathe in his smell and I fight back the rising emotions of leaving. It's painful. But I can't lie my head on the pillow, sleep and pretend nothing is going to happen, otherwise Jena is going to suffer. *If I do nothing, knowing full well what is going to happen, how can I ever look at her again? I'd be just like my mother, allowing it to happen. It will be as bad as holding her down myself for the* Ngansimba *to cut. And if I stay, who's to say if I will remain here anyway? If Ibrahim marries me* – I press my hands against my temples to stop the thought progressing – *he could take me back to his family in Senegal*. I can't marry – it's even more of a reason to go.

The night passes slowly. The plan plays repeatedly in my mind. I analyse all possible flaws, of which there are too many. At best the *Ngansimba* will take me back to the bush. I see the cutting tree clearly in my mind, which is always there in my thoughts. Then there's the *Kankurang*. But, most likely, the *Ngansimba* will come after me and do more than cut. It's a good thing that Grandmother snores loudly. I'm on edge, ready to go.

The sky lightens and inevitably, it's time.

I kiss Lamin one more time and then kiss my grandmother on the side of her cheek. I know it's a risk, just in case it wakes her, but I can't help it. Tears well in my eyes – I don't think I'm ever going to see them again and wish I didn't have to go but I do quickly before I lose the little courage I have mustered.

I sneak out of the compound past the bakery where there is now a burning furnace. The baker is too busy placing the long dough into the fire at the back of the hut – as he does every dawn – to notice my dark shadow pass by his entrance. The warm dough scents the air and, as I move forward, it occurs to me how familiar the smell is – the aroma of my childhood – and I slow for a second, breathe deeply and continue.

By the look of the sky, I'm not sure I've timed it right. It isn't dark enough. It's going to be a race against the breaking dawn. I should have left earlier, but I guess I was just holding onto things for as long as possible.

The darkness is vanishing quickly. When I get to Jena's compound, I can already see the outlines of the buildings. I crouch low against the rough wall and debate whether to go through the window, to Jena's room, or across the open yard up into the house. I can't make out which window is Jena's. If I tap the wrong one, everything's going to be lost. In a quick decision, the door is my best option, but that means I've got to get across the compound yard. I move before changing my mind.

There's a chicken scratching around in the middle of the yard, looking for grains in the dirt, but apart from that there are no other signs of life in the compound. Everyone is still sound asleep for now. The chicken clucks, flaps its wings, and runs in zigzags, startled, as I make my way towards the steps on the veranda. The top one creaks under my weight and I freeze.

I hold my breath, anticipating the sudden actions that will come, alert to my presence. Silence continues. I'm aware for the first time that there are no sounds; even the crickets have given up their natural hum so close to dawn. I sigh in relief and turn the door handle slowly. My relief is short-lived when the hinge squeaks – everything seems to make a noise. Then a cough sounds from one of the rooms, which drains my courage instantly. I tense, ready to turn and run, but I hold my nerve.

Before I venture further, there's a moment when I think of all the punishment I'll face, if I get caught. It's not too late – I can be back in my room before anyone wakes. Then I think of Jena, due to meet the crocodile, and I slip sideways through the door. It's getting light, which means I can see where I'm going but it's not good because I'm running out of time.

Jena's room is at the end of the corridor, where hanging beads serve as a door. I push them to the side, expecting her to be asleep.

'Who's there?' she asks, the panic in her voice easy to notice.

'Shhh, shhh! It's okay. It's just me!'

'Binta? What are you doing here?'

I sit on the edge of her bed and her body relaxes. 'Who were you expecting?' Then Jena begins to cry.

'Soldiers,' she says between hushed sobs.

'Soldiers?'

'The ones who took my parents.' She sobs into her hands and her shoulders shake.

'It's okay,' I say and put my arm around her.

'But it's not! Every night I lie awake, listening for them to come back. I'm scared, Binta. I'm scared they're going to come for me next.'

'Sorry – I didn't know.' For a moment there is a pause as she wipes her eyes and I have dozens of questions I want to ask about what's happened to her parents, but the pounding in my chest, the fear I have of being caught stops me asking for now. Instead, I consider how I'm going to tell her what I know about the *Ngansimba*. It was so different in my mind when I had planned this and it unsettles me.

'My parents are gone. I don't know where they are – or if I'm ever going to see them again!'

'Jena, you need to listen to me. I don't know about your parents, but I know you are in danger.' I let the last word hang for a moment, for Jena to fully absorb it.

'How?'

I can make out the colour in the curtain as dawn is fast approaching. Just as the darkness of night comes quickly, the sun returns just as fast, like a switch on an electric light. I need to explain fast.

'I didn't know about the soldiers coming to your home. But I heard your grandmother is planning to initiate you while your mother is away.'

'Initiate me?'

281

There's slight excitement in Jena's voice. I'd forgotten how it was to be naïve, not to know about it.

'Jena – I've been initiated.'

'You?' There's a tone of disappointment in her voice. Perhaps because I've been included in something she hasn't, or because I didn't tell her. 'When?' she asks.

'At the beginning of the summer holidays. It's horrible, Jena. It's not anything we ever imagined. I shouldn't be speaking of it – there's a curse – but I can't have you go through it too. They make out it's a wonderful thing, the elders. But it's not.' I take a breath. Jena is listening to my every word and I have her full attention. 'They took us to the bush.' Suddenly I feel my heart beating, faster. I pause, battling against a panic that is coming over me. Is this the start of the curse? The words have a hold over me, as though I shouldn't speak them.

A distant cockerel focuses me; dawn is nearly here.

'They took us to the bush. We waited in a hut while we were each brought out, one by one. Then, I heard screams. It was of the girls that were taken out before me. I was so scared, Jena. I couldn't escape – there was nowhere to go, nowhere to hide.'

Jena holds my hand and squeezes gently, encouraging me to continue. 'They hold you down like an animal while the *Ngansimba* cuts all the flesh around your privates.' I know the words must be coming from my mouth, but I feel detached like I'm listening to them for the first time.

'Cut?'

'Yes. You need to believe me, Jena. Do I have to show you?' I say angrily. I don't mean to. I guess it's all the anger about what's happened, spilling out. I calm myself and tell her, 'She's coming to cut you today.'

'She's coming for me?' Jena gasps, lets go of my hand and jumps up from the bed.

'Yes. I overheard your grandmother planning it. She wanted my mother to help hold you.'

'God! I don't want to be cut. I wish Isatou were here.' The room is now lighter.

'Where is Isatou?' I was assuming she was in the room next door sleeping until the thought occurred to me.

'She travelled to see our cousin yesterday.'

I know I am expecting a lot from her, to just run away with me, but I must convince her – and quickly. Then I know what I should tell her. 'One of the girls died.'

Jena sits back on the bed, beside me, her back bent over her knees. 'I don't understand,' she mutters.

'I know. Neither did I. Your mother doesn't want this for you. And you remember what I said to you, when you were beaten with the cane at school – I'm not going to let you get hurt again, Jena; I'm not going to let you down.'

The Imam's call to prayer, louder than I usually hear it, startles me. 'We have to leave, Jena,' I say, getting up. 'There's no other way. Without your mother here, Mamamuso is going to do want she wants to you. You could die!'

'Where can we go?'

'I have a plan already. I'll tell you on the way, but we have to get out of here quickly, before Mamamuso finds us.'

'But what about my mother? What if I'm not here when she comes back?'

'She would hate this to happen to you. Imagine her coming back to find you dead? What use is that to her?'

The cockerel crows again. 'Quick!' I say, pulling Jena. 'Before Mamamuso finds us.'

Jena grabs holds of my arms. 'My grandmother is staying in my parents' room. Since the soldiers came, she's been staying in there to watch over us.'

The call to prayer echoes again and I hear Mamamuso waking in the next room. Obviously she doesn't have the same hearing problem as my grandmother. Through the draping beads at the door, I can see her carrying out a familiar ritual of absolutions. Then she begins prayers, prostrating herself on the floor, with her back to us.

'Come,' I whisper, pulling Jena again, knowing if we time it right we can get past the door before Mamamuso lifts her head from the floor. The Imam's call continues. The prayers will give us a few precious moments to pass unnoticed while the diligent faithful obediently observe the call. Back in my room, Grandmother will be snoring still, which is good, otherwise she'd raise the alarm that I've gone.

We run across the compound and out into the back streets that lead to the market. The sun is not quite up and the dim light gives us some cover. Usually, during the day, the street is lined with people sat watching the world pass by – they dutifully greet each other and exchange gossip – but now they are either praying, or asleep. A few figures hurriedly make their way to the mosque but, thankfully, most pray next to their beds.

I look towards the relative expanse of the market square and try to figure the best route across. For the time being, I crouch against a small wall while I wait for the bustle of men heading to mosque to subside.

'Let's go!' I say to Jena, before I lose my nerve.

We hurry across the wall of the mosque to the other side of the square. I take Jena's hand and lead her through the empty stalls to a small exit at the back. It leads to where the rubbish is brought each day from the market. Light is seeping into the day.

'Quick, this way!' I say, leading her along a path towards the field. Then Jena begins to run and because I'm holding her hand my legs follow. It's the first time that I've tried to run since I was taken to the bush. The tip of the sun is on the horizon in front of us. We weave across cracks and ditches, jumping up onto the path that goes into the forest. As we run further into the dense trees, the daylight is now bright enough to see the path clearly and we slow down.

'Where are we going?' Jena pants.

I take a moment to catch my breath. 'We'll head towards the beach. If we can get there quickly, we can avoid the fish sellers. Then north—' I pause, knowing that Jena's not going to like this '—to Serekunda.'

'Serekunda? That's too far!'

'I know! It's far, but we can't go by bush taxi.' I walk over to her and put my arm around her shoulder. 'People will see us. And my father will be on it. Nobody will expect us to leave the village, but if they do they will be waiting for us in the market to travel. This is the only way. Besides, once we get far enough north we can then get a taxi.' Jena follows me when I turn.

The forest appears calm; the tall palms move occasionally with a wisp of breeze that catches them from the sea. A small monkey scampers up the bark into the canopy, and sand begins to appear on the path. Although the dunes ahead dull it, there's the sound of crashing of waves.

'Nearly there!' I say, as we head out of the forest and run down a bank to the foot of a large dune. Exhausted, we collapse. The soft sand is already warm from the early-morning sun and I lie my head against the steep wall of the dune.

'Do you think they have noticed we've gone yet?' Jena asks and I can hear in her voice that she's nervous. I'm wondering the same, but I try to hide my fear – to be strong for both of us.

'Perhaps.'

The sky is so blue now. A single wisp of cloud travels slowly out towards the sea. I watch it as it drifts gently on its way and then I close my eyes and allow the morning warmth to sooth my weariness; I haven't slept most of the night.

'Binta!'

'What is it?' I open my eyes and the cloud has moved far away; I must have dozed off and there is a panic in Jena's voice.

'I heard something over there.' She points towards the opening of the forest.

The path is seldom used. Most people use the main road to the beach where it brings them directly to the stalls, the smoke houses and a kiosk where I sometimes buy a 7Up.

'I definitely heard someone!'

'Quick, hide.' We move behind the prickly branches of a bush, just big enough to hide us both. Tiny balls of thorns scratch our arms and stick to our skin and clothes.

I've got a good enough view to see a figure appear, but twigs are in the way and I can't get a clearer focus.

I hold my breath and hope the twigs hide us well enough, but the person is getting closer. Jena's fingers dig into my arm, where she's gripping me tightly. I would tell her to stop, but I can't expose us. I push my squished elbow into her side instead.

'Binta?'

I exhale and relief flows through my veins as I unhinge myself from my uncomfortable position. 'Esther?'

Esther takes a parcel wrapped in purple material from her head, puts it on the sand and gives us both a warm embrace once we have untangle ourselves from the hiding place. Jena looks to Esther, then to me puzzled. 'I told you there was a plan!'

'What do you both look like?' She laughs and removes a tiny ball of thorns from my hair. 'Here – I've brought you this from my mother.' Inside the material Esther uncovers three baguettes, a litre bottle of water, several small packets of individual biscuits and then she leaves the best until last; she unfolds a square of paper with smoked fish inside.

'There's this as well – look, you can open it like this.' She shows me a red penknife and opens the main cutting section. On the other side of the handle, there is a thicker metal edge with a curved shape. 'You can open drinks bottles with this one. It was my father's, but my mother asked him for it to give to you. You can keep it.'

Although we planned it, I can't believe Esther's here. Getting to the beach was the first part of our plan. The next part, to travel up country by foot is going to be harder, but I feel more confident that we can do it, now that we have got away from the town. Esther unpins a small leather wallet from inside her *fanu* and gives it to me.

'My mother wanted you to have this. There is twenty dalasi, enough for you to get some food along the way.'

'She is very kind. Please thank her for us.'

'Yes, you all are,' Jena says and reaches to hold both our hands in hers. 'Thank you.'

'I have to go,' Esther says after a little time, but I wish she could stay. 'Do you remember the place where my mother and I will be waiting for you?'

'I think so, at Kololi beach in three days.'

'Yes. You'll recognise the area when you get there. It should be enough time to get there from here – you'll know it when you get there. It's different from here – lots of tourists. There is a hotel going onto the beach, where my mother knows a maid. Take Care.'

Three days seems far away right now. I reluctantly let go of Esther's hand and watch her disappear back the way she came, into the forest. To distract my thoughts to what lies ahead over the coming days, I turn and size up the steep sand dune in front of us.

I pick up the parcel Esther brought us and grab Jena's arm, 'Race you!' My feet slip under the sliding sand until I drop onto my stomach at the top. Jena is close behind and nearly lands on me.

'Is it clear? Can you see anyone?' Jena asks.

To our left, there's the distant sound of an engine bringing the women to the beach. Most walk, but a few travel by bush taxi. They want to reach the shore to start work, cleaning the fish as early as possible in the morning. A handful of long colourful boats bob up and down in the water, the fishermen are casting their first nets of the day. Vultures already circle overhead, waiting for discarded fish heads. White smoke in the distance drifts up into the morning sky, where hundreds of fish are smoked each day, before being taken back to town to be sold. The thought of the smoky fish hanging in rows in those huts makes me hungry but we need to wait until the fishing village is far behind us before we can enjoy the ones that Esther brought.

In the other direction, towards the north, the beach curves and reaches as far as I can see. There are no people, just fine golden sand that stretches away around the headland. I'm sure we are far enough away from the merchants not to be seen. I hope the fishermen and the women are too busy to notice us: two tiny figures clambering down the sand dune, making our escape into the distance.

Chapter 59

Yari

During the initial twenty-four hours that I was locked up, time slowed to a point that forced me to notice every particle of dust floating slowly in the musty cell. It heightened my senses to the steaming urine warming in the corner, overflowing from the five-litre mayonnaise container. The sound of the cockroach's legs scurrying across the bare concrete floor, escaping a rat's pounce. The noises outside of my cell kept me constantly alert, the screams in the distance making the hairs on my arms and the back of my neck stand. It caused me to shiver, despite the lack of breathable air from far too many bodies in such a confined space. I lost count of how many hours merged into days.

But now here I stand at the entrance of Mile Two with two guards so close behind me that I can feel the warmth of their breath against my ear. I blink quickly in succession, the brightness gives a ring of white at everything I see and burns as I battle to open my lids fully. Midday. It must be midday; the sun is hot and high above. It could be morning though, or late afternoon. I quickly realise I have no bearing on time.

Although my eyes hurt, the heat on my skin feels wonderful. Because the guards are next to me, I suppress the immediate urge to wave my arms in circles to enjoy the space all around me once again. I also long to turn and examine the buildings from which we've just walked, to see if I can work out where Sarko is. I desperately want to see if his was one of the multitude of arms outstretched, as I passed the wired mesh that served as a small window for the forty men inside. What if he can see me from there? Will it encourage him that I'm being released, or will he feel more alone in this terrible place? Or perhaps – I suddenly cling onto a budding thought of hope – perhaps he was released already and is waiting for me?

A guard steps forward and opens the gates and allows me to leave. Just like that. No ceremony. As though I just popped by for a social call. No apology. No explanation. Just like that I'm free, at least physically. Inside I continue to feel that my soul has curled up into the smallest of space and it will take more than an opening gate to encourage it to unfurl. I step forward; the traffic on the Senegambia highway noisily reverberates through my bones as a lorry travels just in front of me on the way to Banjul. With the gate still open behind me, I feel as though I am standing between two worlds. There is the ordinariness, the normality of what I see in front; the cars transporting people to work, to the market, to see friends – compared to the condition of what I leave behind a few feet away. It doesn't seem possible. At that thought, I suddenly look back just as the guards push the gates closed and for the last time glance at the buildings in the distance. A stab in the pit of my stomach suddenly frightens me. There's a deep sense that Sarko is still within its hold.

Chapter 60

Binta

Directly above, with no shadow to shade us, the sun scorches the sand. It's unforgiving and burns my feet with each step I take. There's a little relief when I run into the breaking foam, into the shallow water where the waves gently ease up the beach. White golden sand stretches forever, before the curve of the land breaks up the coastline. Palm trees are dotted behind the sand dunes on my right.

'Let's get around that corner, and then we can rest.'

My stomach rumbles and reminds me how hungry I am. All my energy disappears, like water soaking into the sand and my pace slows. I'm walking like Grandmother does, urging one foot in front of another. It's not the only reason I've slowed down though. Far enough away from the fishing village, virgin sand stretches behind as well as in front of us as far as the eye can see. We're definitely alone on this part of this isolated beach, the only figures for miles and I feel safe enough, further away from the town, to futilely chase after the little hermit crabs that block our way, just for fun. They disappear at lightning speed into minuscule holes in the sand. They are too quick, making it seem like they are taking part in a well-rehearsed synchronised dance. Not one remains above ground, however fast we are.

'That must be the next village over there.' Jena points.

I cup my hand to my forehead to reduce the glare from the intense sun, and follow where she's pointing with my eyes. The land curves, revealing some fishing boats in the cup of the bay. 'I think it's Sanyang.'

'Is it safe to pass? Are there people around?'

'Perhaps we should wait until the evening.' We head over to a lone palm tree on the other side of a sand dune. 'Let's get some rest under that shade.

'Here.' I hand one of the fish to Jena. 'Best not eat too much of the smoked fish – it'll make you more thirsty.'

Before long, emotionally and physically drained from the past hours, I lie my head on the sand. Sleep comes easy. It's not until a bird chirps loudly in the warmth of the late afternoon that I wake. Jena's already stirring – the shade of the tree has shifted and is no longer covering us. Before my eyes have adjusted to the afternoon sun, I hear voices coming towards us. I shake Jena, waking her fully. 'Quick, into the bush, someone's coming.'

We hide just as several heads appear over the top of the dune. A small group of women are laden with their daily produce in baskets on their heads. Thankfully, they seem too busy to notice the bundled material I've left by the tree and the half-eaten fish.

'That was close,' I mutter, as the voices drift into the forest.

Jena rolls the palm leaf away from her shoulder. 'But they wouldn't have known us.'

'It doesn't matter; I don't want anyone seeing us. Someone might know your grandmother. We are still too close to Kenji. You know what it's like, someone always knows someone. Come on, let's get out of here, it's getting late.'

With the sky turning orange, I think we should head back over the sand dune to the beach. By the time we arrive at Sanyang beach, there are only a few fishermen around. Following another curve, the beach continues to stretch in front of us to the horizon, where the sun is moving lower.

'My throat is dry,' I say, and rub a finger across my chapped lips. It's a struggle to keep my legs moving, when all I can think about is sipping liquid, since we finished our bottles of water ages ago. I'm not even thinking about a fizzy drink, just the water from the well, complete with the bugs and dirt floating around on the top. Instead all I can do is allow a little saliva to build in my mouth and wet my lips before swallowing nothing, which makes my throat scratch inside wanting water even more.

'Look! Over there – a little tourist café.' Jena takes off and splashes through the surf, as she runs towards the place. I'm close behind, kicking through the waves, but not as fast as Jena. Not anymore. I used to outrun her every time. She thinks she's got faster, but I don't want to explain how my time in the bush has slowed me. I could still beat her, if things had stayed the same.

At the café there are *Toubab*s, pink from the sun. They carry on eating at their tables, as we walk past nervously. None greet us, which suits me fine.

Outside on a little wooden veranda I work my way to the bar and order drinks. They don't come a moment too soon – two bottles each to begin with, which I doubt will even touch my parched lips. The barman raises his eyebrows, questioning. I don't know if he's wondering why we are here, on our own. It's unusual for two girls to come to a café – especially a tourist one – without good reason. Perhaps he's just wondering why I am buying so many bottles. I ignore him and carry the precious treasure on a small tray over to where Jena is sat on a plastic white chair, which overlooks the sea.

From where we sit, I have a good view of the fishermen bringing in their boats for the evening. On the nearest boat to us, about twenty men jump from the vessel either side into the shallow water and each take a part of the crescent-shaped boat. They work together and drag it through the salty water, up onto the sand and on top of the rollers. Their arm and calf muscles ripple with the combined effort. It takes a few minutes for them to reach where they want to place the boat, not far from the café, next to other brightly decorated ones.

The activity on the beach begins to quieten. People are returning to their homes. I try not to think about how they are heading back to their town for dinner with their families. I focus my attention on the beautiful pink and amber sky, as the sun begins to set, and sip my cool Coke. When I squint, I can see the land where it disappears around the edge of the bay. It's more than a day's walk now, but I keep looking to see if anyone will appear around the headland – someone after us. I shudder at the thought of the *Ngansimba*.

'We ought to get going before it gets dark,' I say, and place the drained Coke bottle on the table next to the other empty one.

'Where are we going to sleep for the night?'

I spot the line of resting fishing boats. 'Over there.'

Boats are so narrowly parked that we are able to sit with our backs resting on one and put outstretched legs on the neighbouring one. The cramped space between the boats actually makes me feel safer, huddled tightly in between the wooden vessels. A few vultures wander around, ugly things, like evil old men. I throw a shell at one that gets too close, but there's a lot of them – too many to keep at bay all night. I hope they'll fly off before it gets dark.

I leave Jena behind, sat in between the boats and walk down to the breaking surf, drawn by pretty reds and oranges shimmering on the sea. I sit and put my feet into the breaking waves, but draw them back quickly when the salt stings the blisters on my toes. I pick up a handful of sand and let the warm grains trickle through my fingers forming a small hill, which an ant climbs up. I look out towards the horizon and my thoughts drift to thinking of my mother. Despite what she's done, I feel a deep sadness that I'm not going to see her again. An intense ache settles in my stomach; it's a physical dull pain that worsens as the hours go by at the realisation of what has happened. My throat tightens and I press my hands onto my closed eyelids to keep the tears from escaping.

Without much thought I find myself idly drawing some lines in the wet sand. The lines become figures of my mother, with Mai on her back; Lamin and Musa next to her, playing with a ball. A wave suddenly washes over the picture, and I'm left staring at the ocean taking my family with it. As I watch the picture disappear, I have a growing, overwhelming sense of being alone. The enormity of what I've done dawns.

Well, maybe not completely alone. I look over my shoulder to Jena and I jump up to re-join her, as the last rays of sun flicker on the sea. Within a few moments the sunlight disappears completely and we're shrouded in a dark cloak. After some time, a half-moon appears and a million stars glimmer across the sea; small lights bobbing up and down in the water. Heat has been sucked into the sea along with the sun and although the sand is still warm, there's already a chill in the air.

'Wrap yourself next to me.' I offer Jena the piece of material that she carried our food in. It's a thin barrier against the cool night, but it's better than nothing and the best I can do to cover us both. In the silence, above the soothing gentle breaking of waves, Jena sobs quietly, but I can still hear.

'Hey, don't cry. It's going to be alright.' I wonder if I mean the words, but it works and Jena's sobs cease. 'It's okay, Jena.'

The foaming surf is evident in the dim moonlight – the white standing out in contrast to the dark sea. Jena's voice unexpectedly breaks through the night air. 'I'm scared, Binta.'

I feel around in the dark and find Jena's hand and say words I know are true. 'Me too.'

I think of Lamin lying in bed next to Grandmother on the pink frilly sheets that felt smooth under my skin. I wonder how long it will take Grandmother to fall to sleep tonight, to enter into her snoring. She'll be worried about me. And my mother will be. A rock starts to lodge in my throat when I think of her. Why am I so sad? After all she's done? But the rock doesn't move, and gets worse when I think how I may never see her again. Or Grandmother.

I force myself to listen to the ocean's rhythm, to block out all the other thoughts that try to choke me. It only works for a while; everything is spinning around in my head keeping me from sleep.

And what about Mamamuso? What does she know? Does she know it was me that took Jena? She must do; she'll know my mother is looking for me and will put things together. Then there'll be the *Ngansimba* too. God, I can't think of her, and what she'll do if she gets those sharp yellow long nails back on me.

I open my eyes and look up at the slither of moon. A shooting star darts across the vast expanse. At this moment we're safe, which is more than I hoped for when I left the compound at sunrise, but all the same, I huddle closer to Jena.

The gentle motion of the waves splashing onto the beach, and the glimmering moonlight, give a disconcerting air of tranquillity.

I must have drifted off, but there's a tightening fear in my chest that soon wakes me from a fretful sleep – where the crocodile is coming for Jena while she's asleep and vulnerable on the beach.

I suddenly sit up and shake Jena awake, 'I think we should head off.'

'Now?' she says sleepily and rubs her eyes, drawing the material around her shivering body.

'We need more distance from the town.'

It turns out that it is easier to walk at night. The soft cool sand finds its way between my toes, while I swing my flip-flops in one hand. It's a relief to walk barefoot without the blisters rubbing, which helps us make good pace.

In the distance, where the sand dunes go into the forest, the sky is getting lighter. By the time we arrive at another fishing village, dawn is just breaking over the land. Boats line the shore waiting for fishermen to come and push them back into the water.

'What happens when we get to Serekunda?' Jena asks me.

'We'll meet with Esther.'

'And after that?' Jena throws a pebble into the sea.

'I don't know. Perhaps we'll wait with Esther's friends, until the *Ngansimba* has left town.'

'But Mamamuso will send for her again. I'm not safe until my mother comes home.' Her voice trails off.

'Jena, what happened to your mother?' I've been desperate to know, but it didn't seem right to ask her until now.

She sighs and takes a deep breath. 'I didn't know what was happening at the time. I was woken up by screeching vehicles and shouting. There were heavy footsteps coming into the house. It was really late at night, really dark and they came in the house with flashlights – I was scared, Binta. Really scared. I saw them from my bedroom, men...they were dragging my parents out. My mother was screaming my father's name because he was hit with something. I heard it too, a thud. She was crying. I didn't even move. I didn't call out to her. Isatou did, but they ignored her. I wish I could have done something, but it was all over with so fast. Now they've gone.' There are wet lines of tears on her face. 'I ran over to the window and saw them being thrown into a truck, it was really dark, no moon, but flashlights everywhere. That's how I could see it was soldiers.'

'Soldiers?' I interrupt Jena's narrative. What would Yari have to do with soldiers? 'But they'll know soon they've got the wrong people – they'll let them go soon.'

'It's been nearly two weeks though, Binta. There's no word. They're in prison – they have to be – but they've done nothing wrong!'

A thought comes to me. 'Do you remember, when we were at Esther's home, ages ago – her cousin came and told her father something about soldiers. Do you remember – he told Esther's father to be careful?'

Jena nods her head. 'I remember.'

'Maybe it's got something to do with that? Maybe Esther's parents might know.'

'Do you think so?' Jena looks at me, hopefully.

'Sure.' I'm not, but it makes her feel better. 'They'll be back before you know. Then you'll be safe. Don't worry.' I repeat the last bit again in English and carry it on automatically with a song my mother used to sing all the time, she only knew four words to it, but she'd sing it so often that whenever I hear any of the words I end up singing. It does the job, and Jena smiles a little.

'I'm never going to be safe, am I? Not from the *Ngansimba*?'

'When your mother returns, you will be,' I say, hoping it's true.

'What about you, Binta?'

'What do you mean?'

'When will you go home?'

'We've only been gone a night; I'm not thinking about going home yet!' A small lie. Thoughts of home present themselves, hovering above my head like a little cloud following me. I can tell Jena's not satisfied with my answer. 'I'm not sure I can go home. I'm frightened of the *Ngansimba* – what she'll do to me.'

'Will she really hurt you?'

'My father, my mother, even your grandmother, will beat me. But the *Ngansimba* – well, that's different. She can really do me harm.' 'Like I told you, one of the girls I was with died and she wasn't even trying to kill her.'

It is still too early, even for the first of the fishermen, which is good. We are still too near Kenji and my mother has relatives in the last village we passed from the Jaiteh clan. Kenji's full of Bojangs. And Tourays, Ceesays, and Sarrs, like me. All of them have family living along the coast. It'll be safer when we get to Serekunda, where the tribes are more diverse...if we make it that far.

With daylight breaking, ominous dark clouds hang heavy in the air. A storm is brewing. Waves are already crashing with more energy upon the shore, but at least the breeze takes an edge off the heat. Small mercies.

By early morning, I can see boats launching into the sea and there is a hub of activity on the beach. Dots moving in the distance that could be ants, but as we get closer, they grow into a defined a mass of colour, even under the dark clouds, separating out into individual figures. Women descaling and cutting fish, sellers walking along with refreshments in their baskets.

'There are a lot of people there. Perhaps we should wait?'

'No, we need to keep going. We can't miss Esther,' I say, trying to hide the anxiety I have walking through that crowd.

Vultures hardly bother to fly out of our way. They wander close to the women, who scrub the fish in large purple-and-green buckets. A mangy-looking dog reluctantly lifts its head, and watches us walk past. One ear is half chewed and covered in sores, where flies gather. They are disturbed briefly, but swarm back onto its open wounds when the dog lies its head back down onto the sand. As it turns out, the dog is more interested in us than any of the people are. I guess they've also seen that a storm is coming and they're busy packing up before it hits.

One thing that gives this stretch of beach some interest is the different type of birds flying above us, which causes the sky to fill with the colour of various flocks heading over the dunes. I've heard about a bird sanctuary. I hope the birds above mean we're near it, because that will mean we are on the outskirts of Serekunda. As we distance ourselves from the people I sigh in relief.

'Look, Binta.' There's a man walking towards us with cattle. 'Do you think that means another village is nearby?'

'I hope so,' I say. All I can think of is a cool drink. I could easily just run into the sea and drink my fill.

The cattle let out a deep 'moo' each time the herder's long stick whips down on their backs. The man is tall and skinny, with his dirty trousers barely staying up at his waist. He takes a long drag on his cigarette and stares at us. When he passes he raises a baseball cap and grins showing a yellow smile. It reminds me of a snake. Not that snakes smile. Or have teeth. Whatever it might be, something makes me think of a snake and I walk faster. I'm glad he's got to keep up with his cows otherwise I think he might stop. However hard I try to forget the *Ngansimba*'s words, there are some pieces of information that do stick closely in my mind and the one piece of information I'm now glad I know is: 'Some men are not to be trusted'.

I reach for the side of my *fanu*, ready to pull it tight – to make it difficult for a man – just like we were taught. Pull your *fanu* through your legs tight, the *Ngansimba* had said. And scream loud. What a joke. Screaming only makes your throat sore. Besides, I look around; there is nobody. As the man passes, I grab Jena's arm and pull her to the side. He slows, as much as the cattle allow him. Unmistakably I catch his gaze shifting straight to my waist, eyeing my behind with beady eyes. That's why I thought of a snake. It was his eyes. Horrible eyes. Thankfully, his cattle urge him on.

Still holding onto Jena's arm, we continue until the sun begins to set for the second night. Already it's getting cool with clouds threatening another storm. Soon the rain begins. It comes with little warning, just a few, large drops on my skin. The torrent comes quickly, before we can find shelter, and we are soaked to the bone. There's a sunshade sticking up out of the sand made of palm leaves. Several are dotted around the beach here, which means we are getting closer to the more popular tourist areas. It's not much of a shelter, but it's the only thing. The palm-leaf umbrella barely covers us, and when the wind picks up, the rain pours in sideways. We shiver with our backs to the rain, totally miserable and the only good thing is that the rainwater running off the leaves is good to drink.

The storm dies down just before dawn, before the rising sun breaks into the day. All night we've huddled against the beating rain, with no chance of sleep. Jena looks as exhausted as I feel. We begin another day's walk. Our footprints replace the dotted marks left by the rain throughout the night and soon the hermit crabs come out running in front of us, seeming to encourage us on a step at a time.

Exhausted, with blistered feet and hungry stomachs, we walk silently and slowly for a long time. Even chasing the crabs doesn't interest us this morning. Slowly we go on until the warmth of the rising sun seems to switch a thought in my head. It's already mid-morning.

'We've got to walk faster, Jena; otherwise we won't meet with Esther.'

'What if we miss her?'

'We can't.'

Chapter 61

Amie

The pain doesn't ease; whichever way I lie here in bed. There is an agony that feels like it's coming from my very core.

I play the scene over in my head, sometimes wondering if it happened, or perhaps if happened to someone else and I remember hearing the sadness of another's news. Then it feels as though I am falling from a height, my stomach flipping over and over.

'She's gone!' I put my hand to my mouth to suppress the sudden sobs that come. Has all these months of anguish come to this? I agonized over what I had to put her through, thought it was the only way – the thing that proved my determined loyalty to her future. It took everything for me to take her, to walk with the women to see her under the tree. I told myself I was being brave.

The weight I felt since that day that Binta was cut has never left. The guilt that settled so far inside will never dissolve. The fact that she's gone and I feel the grief that brings I also feel is somehow justified. The grief pushing against the guilt, crushing me in-between.

For the past three nights I have cried until tears no longer come. Will I cry every night now for the rest of my life? Three nights have passed already, slowly, every moment feeling like a day.

In the darkness I silence my sobs, immediately attentive to a creak of a door. I hold my breath and strain my hearing. 'Binta?!' I call out. A moment later there is another creak, but there's an accompanying rustle of branches outside in the yard from the palm tree. I exhale, not with relief, but with deep disappointment. I am too tired to resume my sobs. It was just the wind. Binta is still as far away as she ever was. Perhaps further with each passing day.

There has been talk already about where she might be, but as a mother I cannot deny the sparkle that left her eyes along with her childhood. I know it was supposed to change her, but to see her change from her outward, fun-loving personality to the one that was withdrawn deep inside her own head... What was she thinking? What was she planning? How desperate did she get?

What if I never see her again to tell her that I love her?

I thought I was being strong, but now I know it was powerlessness. If I could have seen what would have been afterwards, if only I could go back in time it would have given me boldness and I would have tried – even if it didn't make a difference. Even if she was still taken to the *Ngansimba* I would have been able to tell her I did everything I could.

Chapter 62

Yari

Idon't mind the walk. I don't mind the thirst that screams for water as I make my way along the highway, or the stares from people that I pass at my dishevelled appearance. The space behind, the expanse in front – it feels wonderful and I breathe the fresh warm air deeply until my lungs ache.

Eventually I arrive at the place I've pictured every night as sleep evaded me. To keep my hope up I would imagine the details of what I would do, where I would go when they released me. *When* was the word I had to keep forcing myself to believe, especially when despair rose in the early hours. Not when, but *if* they would release me, was what occupied my thoughts easily.

'Yari?' From the tone of Fanta's voice and the concerned lines that immediately form across the brow of her forehead, I imagine how I must look when she opens the gate. 'Come, come in.' She looks around behind me to check if anyone has seen me arrive. I knew it was a risk. The guards might have released me, just to follow and see who I am in contact with. But despite the possibility of putting her in harm, I admit I am desperate. This is my only option – I need help.

She takes me by the arm and leads me into the bedroom, walking at my slower pace and helps me sit on the bed. Oh, a bed! I run my hands across the covers. A bed, not the bare concrete or a urine-soiled and blooded thin foam mattress on the floor. Fanta opens a drawer, rummages around for a moment and pulls out a new outfit. A blue one with white-and-purple swirls from the cords tied when it was dyed. Then she opens another drawer and brings out a bar of soap and a towel. 'Here. The shower is out the back. Take your time. You must be hungry.'

It is as much as I can do to nod in response. 'Can I have some water?'

'Of course, of course.'

A moment later I put my hands around the cool metallic cup, and gulp the liquid which scratches against my throat. She brings me another cup. With this one I pause halfway through. 'Thank you, Fanta'.

A little while later we sit eating together. I can only manage a small helping of peanut *Domada* stew and rice, but it seems to give me the energy I need to voice the plan that I have mulled over continuously in my cell. 'I need to get back to Kenji. Can you help me? I have no money.'

'But is that a good idea, Yari? I've heard that soldiers have re-arrested people within twenty-four hours – makes it looks as though Jammeh has been gracious and then when people aren't looking, they are sent back to prison. Perhaps your home isn't the best place. People have fled over the border, even.'

I've heard those rumours too, but hearing them from Fanta someone outside the walls of the prison, makes them more real and the probability that it could happen seems more likely.

'I've thought about that. That's the other thing I need to ask. Can I stay with you for a short while – until I can find somewhere to live in Serekunda? I have enough money saved, but my bank details are at home. And if I do need to leave the country, I need my passport too. But more than that – I need to get Jena and Isatou.' I know I'm asking a lot and I pause. I hope she sees the desperation and the logic. 'I'd be careful, Fanta. The girls could stay in the compound and I'd be vigilant when I'm looking for a place to live – make sure nobody is following. As you say, they are expecting me in Kenji. If I come to Serekunda, although it's nearer the prison, nearer the Jammeh's men, there are more people to blend into the crowd. In Kenji I'm a sitting duck.'

I tentatively anticipate her answer, not wanting to jump to the answer, in case I'm disappointed. Then she replies, 'I'll ask my brother if he can drive you there in the morning and then you all come and stay here for as long as you need.'

Her kindness feels like a soothing cream cooling a burn and a couple of tears run down my cheeks. I take my hand from hers and wipe the tears with the inside of my wrist. 'Thank you so much. Thank you.' Then the part of the plan that I've revised over and over in the stillness of many stifling nights comes to my mind. 'If your brother is happy to take me, could we go in the night? I think the darkness will give us a better chance.'

Chapter 63

Binta

After walking for days, I can't believe that we have actually arrived. We are at the hotel, the destination that has drawn my every step, urging me forward when my legs were tired. This part of the beach is owned by the hotel, apparently. A private beach, the sign says: No trespassers.

I turn away from the sea and Jena follows me past *Toubab*s lying on little white sun loungers. Sand meets grass as we head towards the main hotel building, through luscious landscaped gardens. Palm trees are planted next to the path. They are not growing as they do in the bush back in Kenji, but in dead straight lines. They are planted alongside many glorious coloured plants, which pop up from different places – yellow, gentle pink and darker pink ones hanging from branches, others scarlet or fiery orange. When I briefly shut my eyes and breathe in deeply, the sweet fragrance flows through my lungs.

It reminds me of somewhere, but it's a moment before it comes to me. 'It's like your mother's flowers, outside your compound,' I say to Jena.

Spray from hosepipes rotate constantly, the water rises and falls mesmerisingly in a circle. Dodging the water, as it cascades back down, Jena runs through it. Her hair picks up droplets, which glisten in the sun. I follow her, catching the spray as the water comes down, which makes me giggle along with Jena. In that moment of laughter, for a second, I forget. Only for the shortest of time but, in that instant, I'm me again. Before everything. I forget that I've left my family. My home. I forget the *Ngansimba* for a moment. It is like something has lifted, just for a second, but it gives me a hope that there is more of me inside waiting to resurface. I giggle again, wanting the moment to last a little longer.

Up the path there are elegant whitewashed villas, with terracotta-tiled roofs, where *Toubab*s sit on the balconies, sipping. From what Hannah has told me, I guess they're drinking tea. I imagine sitting on the balcony in the cool evening air, watching the glowing sunset disappear into the sea.

'Where do you think Esther will be?'

'I don't know. She just said this hotel, at least I think it's this one.'

'But it's so big,' Jena says, looking around.

'Let's try that way.' I point.

We head further away from the beach, past the villas where sun loungers are placed neatly under the shade of straw parasols. I try not to stare, but there's a woman lying on her back, nearly naked. Only a tiny white piece of material covers her, unless you include the sunglasses and a large droopy hat, which covers her more than the material.

'Why would anyone want to lie under such a hot sky?' I whisper to Jena. The woman adjusts her hat and catches sight of us and I advert my eyes quickly.

'I want a lemonade!' she says and snaps her fingers. Then she turns over on her front. Jena's face screws up, about to laugh at the woman's arrogance; I have to put my finger into my mouth and bite to stop mine escaping. Jena manages to disguise her laugh into a strange cough, which makes me bite harder on my finger, because that's even funnier.

The sound of a deep voice behind us startles me, and I immediately forget what I was just about to laugh at. He asks if he can help us, in a way that isn't friendly, and doesn't actually sound like it means. I turn around and see a tall Gambian man in a finely pressed white shirt, complete with the hotel's logo on the chest pocket. A nagging thought comes to mind, something about a sign somewhere, something that makes me feel uncomfortable. Where was it? I've seen that logo before – on the beach, on a sign that was saying 'No trespassers'.

'No. We don't need help, thankyou.' I pause, trying to judge his response. I'm ready to run away – I don't have a good feeling about us being here. Then I'm suddenly inspired and say, 'The lady over there was asking for a lemonade.'

He looks over to where I'm pointing. For a moment he hesitates, trying to work out what to do with us and torn by two important duties – to serve his customer versus dealing with two trespassers. The woman decides for him, when she demands to know what's taking so long and he hurries towards her.

'Are you sure this is the right hotel?'

'I think so. Let's wait over there in the shade.' I point to a cluster of palm trees neatly planted at the edge of the beach. We sit and rest our heads against the bark. I don't know about Jena, but I'm exhausted and my feet are aching. This is where we've been heading for the past three days. I pull at a blade of grass and twirl it around in my fingers, trying to think what we should do if Esther doesn't come. Nothing comes to me and it is easier to try to push the thought away, but it is difficult.

'Do you know anyone in Serekunda?' I'm desperate for any ideas.

'My mother's friend. Remember – the one that lives near that prison?'

'Can we head there if Esther doesn't come?'

Jena shakes her head slowly. 'We can't. It's where I stole that bleaching cream from.'

Water spins from a sprinkler and dances as it's thrown into the air, and lands onto the very green grass. 'We could stay on the beach for a few nights,' Jena suggests.

I throw the blade of grass towards the sprinkler. 'No, it's too dangerous.'

'What do you mean?'

I'm thinking of the bumsters ready for easy sex, but I can't tell Jena that. 'Nothing, but I don't think it's a good idea.' Perhaps that's something to be grateful for – at least I know more about life from my time in the *jujuwoo* that I can use to keep us safe.

'It's been three days. Maybe my grandmother isn't as angry now. Do you think we could go back to Kenji?' Jena asks me, hopefully.

'No. The *Ngansimba* will kill us.'

'You really think so?'

'Well, she'll kill me. I don't know about you, but best not find out, hey? She nearly killed me once before, without trying to. We can never go back.'

Jena's eyes begin to glisten and I think she might cry. 'But don't worry. Things will work out.' I'm trying hard

313

to reassure her, even though I have a growing dread in my chest – but it works because Jena doesn't start crying. She even starts to smile, but then her eyes shift over my shoulder and the smile stops. Things happen too quickly to register that she has spotted something – or rather someone.

'Get up. Come with me!' shouts a man in a tone that I know demands action and obedience. He's already grabbing me under the arm, lifting me. I'm no match for him, no weight, and he handles me like a feather. He has Jena in the grips of his other muscular arm. It's the man from the hotel from earlier. The way he is moving us forward, I could nearly be flying – my feet hardly touching the ground.

'Where are you taking us?' I manage to ask, but he ignores me. His face is fixed forward, stern.

The *Toubab* woman removes her sunglasses and props herself up onto her elbows to watch, as we are led across the immaculate lawn. I avoid her glare, but still hear the 'tut-tutting' she makes under her breath. It's different to the sucking that Mandinka do through their teeth, but it's just as disapproving.

It's hard to keep up with the man's pace. I trip, but his arm tightens. We head towards arching white pillars at the end of a paved driveway, where he pushes me to the ground, hard. The tarmac grazes my knee and Jena lands next to me. Before I sit up, he's already walking away. As he does, he shouts, 'And stay out! If I find you in here again I will beat you.'

I dust my *fanu* down and look up at the words on the hotel arch. 'Well, I guess this is the right place, after all.'

Jena follows my finger, 'I guess. But now we're stuffed. How long will Esther wait?'

314

Words seem slow coming and I shrug in response. I think that our time is already running out. 'We've got to get back inside.'

'But you heard what he said, Binta.'

'We have to risk it; otherwise what else can we do?'

Jena shrugs her shoulders.

At the end of the driveway the planted borders lead to a clump of well-trimmed bushes. 'Follow me,' I say.

The landscaped gardens offer enough protection, until we come to the lawn. A path leads to the beach and I direct Jena to join me. We huddle behind one of the bushes.

'Where now?' she asks, crouching beside me.

I scan the open grass area and motion to Jena. 'Come on!' I say and leave my hiding place. I'm committed now. This time there's no sound of Jena behind. Something isn't right and I feel an immediate panic. From the corner of my eye, I see him coming for me. I used to be good at running, at dodging Musa. Left, and then a quick right turn. I always outwitted my brother. Only, this isn't my brother chasing after me in his bare feet. This is a man, in fast, polished leather shoes. And since the crocodile, I'm not fast anymore.

A blow comes from behind, catches me above the ear and sends me off my feet. In shock I cry out as the ground propels towards me. A ringing in my ear makes me giddy.

'I told you not to come back!' The hotel worker lifts me back onto my feet and drags me across the lawn.

'Where are you taking me?'

He's already halfway to the hotel building, dragging me by the scruff of my T-shirt, before he replies, 'I warned you. Let's see what the police have to say.'

I can't believe that after all I've been through – the endless walking, the blisters, hunger, thirst, and not to mention fear – it's all been in vain. The police will send me back to Kenji. And the *Ngansimba* will be waiting for me. In desperation I try wriggling free, but I'm at his mercy.

At that moment, the *Toubab* comes to my rescue. Not that she is aware, or even cares, but when she asks for another drink, I use the man's distraction to twist my arm away from his grip. He halts, perhaps deciding whether to come after me, but he goes towards the bar instead.

I recognise the path from earlier that leads to the sea and I sprint ahead until I find myself amongst a crowd of tourists on the beach. My heart pounds, not just from running, but from the fear of being so close to being sent back to Kenji.

'Binta!' I hear my name shouted through the crowd.

I'm already bent double, hands on my knees, trying to get my breath. Hearing my name only makes me breathe quicker. I can't see where the voices are coming from at first, but then Esther and her mother emerge, hurrying towards me. I'm too exhausted to cry with happiness – which is what I want to do – but manage to stand in time for them to wrap their arms around me.

Hannah kisses the top of my head. 'Let me see you!' She cups my face in her hands. Then she draws me to herself, where I press my face against her clothes, into her collarbone. There is her warm breath on my neck and I can feel the pulse of her heart. I close my eyes. In her arms I feel safe. I allow her to hold me, for as long as she wants. It makes me think of how I miss my mother's embrace, more than I realised. Hannah makes me feel she cares. When she does unfold me from her arms, I see Esther and she also hugs me, following with a hundred questions to go with it.

'All in good time,' Hannah interrupts.

I glance down at my feet and I realise something is missing. My flip-flops! It's slightly amusing for a second, before it triggers the series of actions in my head of how I came to be without them...the man, the police, the *Ngansimba* waiting in Kenji for me to return.

Now, with a question of my own, I slowly look up at Hannah and Esther, and ask, 'Where's Jena?'

The panic that rises in me when I think she's gone remains long after I spot her. She's there, some distance away on the beach. A bumster, one that doesn't look like he's got much to sell – not even himself, with dry skin and skinny arms – is moving towards her.

'I was just here!' Jena says, with surprise, when I approach. Hannah and Esther are directly behind. The bumster backs away, another lost chance of making money, or at least getting with a girl.

'I thought the police had taken you!'

'The police?' Hannah looks around, nervously. 'We need to head out of here. Follow me! I know another way to the streets – we'll get a taxi from there.'

'But what about my flip-flops?'

'We'll buy some on the way. We need to leave – now.' Within moments Hannah manoeuvres us through the crowded beach to the front of the hotel grounds and into the back of a taxi. Out of the back window the hotel gets smaller in the distance as we speed away and I allow myself to take a deep breath and inhale, relieved.

The taxi slows when we reach a quiet, smooth, paved residential road. It's lined with blooming flowers and

317

sprinklers are dotted amongst the communal gardens. The properties are tidy. No cracks in the paint or parts of the aluminium, or asbestos roofs hanging off as I'm used to and there is space between each of the compounds. They are not on top of one another, inching for space as in other parts of Serekunda. On our way, Jena tells us how she made her way to the beach, while the hotel man looked frantically for me.

'Here we are!' Hannah directs the taxi driver to pull over where we get out.

'Who lives here?' I ask, looking up at the metal gate as the car drives away.

'You'll see!' Hannah smiles.

Chapter 64

Yari

In contrast to the elongated hours that stretched out in that cell, as the car approaches Kenji I can't believe that it was only a day ago that I walked out of Mile Two. The road is quiet; only private cars travel this way in the dark. The last bush taxi would have arrived hours ago ready for evening prayers and we haven't seen another vehicle for nearly half an hour.

Mohammed drives slowly, and manoeuvres carefully around the potholes that are only visible a couple of meters ahead in the glare of the dipped car lights. I don't blame him for taking it steady to save his suspension as best he can, but energy pulsates through my veins at the thought that I'm going to see my children. The agonising moments away from them will soon come to an end. Inside I'm urging him to race, to bounce over every bump, to cause our bodies to bang against the doors of the car, make us grab onto the roof handles. But I need to be patient. It will soon happen. No more gaping void that I can't cross. Jena and Isatou will be in my arms and I close my eyes and imagine holding them in a tight embrace, drawing them back, feeling whole again.

When I open my eyes, it's hard to make out the landscape in the darkness. I'm on the edge of the seat and grip onto the dashboard. I squint to try and get a focus on how near we are to the town. 'Pull over here, we are close enough.'

The plan has been discussed, a couple of tweaks after thinking it aloud with Mohammed and Fanta in the car on the way. This is the plan: we'll turn the lights of the car off just before the edge of town and park. Then I'll walk the twenty minutes or so into the town, keeping to the back roads. I'll be back within an hour – hour and a half maximum – then we'll make our way from Kenji for good. My girls and me. It's more than a plan. It's what I have held onto to survive in my darkest moments. And now it's so close to happening.

I open the car door and sense the familiarity of my surroundings. With no moon there is complete darkness, as though these circumstances came together – were almost predestined – and it gives me courage as I step carefully towards my home. I know the route with my eyes closed, which is just as well, as the visibility is the same; there are the cracks in the road that threaten to twist an ankle, the piece of fence that sticks out, the tree stumps, and my heart races at the possibility of stepping on a cobra.

On the way a couple of people greet me as they walk past, and I pull my headscarf over my face. I know in the darkness they cannot tell who I am, but I just greet them back quietly and hope they don't recognise my voice. Not to greet them at all would be more noticeable. The fragrance of the flowers hanging over my compound entrance floats towards me and stirs a hundred and one emotions in a second; Sarko, the girls running around in the yard, doing their work at the kitchen table, our festive celebrations as a family. In stark conflict are more poignant memories; the image seared into my mind that night the soldiers came and tramped over the sense that home was somewhere safe, beautiful.

At the back of the compound, embers of a fire pit glow orange and inaudible voices drift in the air towards me. I can't tell if that is Mamamuso's voice, but I push myself against the wall and keep myself hidden and avoid the first step that creaks on the veranda. The smells of my home as I open the door fill my senses in a way I don't expect. The smell of normality, and for a second it is difficult to believe what happened to us. I make my way to the back of the house where the girls will be asleep. There's dryness in my mouth and my heart races with anticipation as I pull back the beads that serve as Jena's bedroom door. I've walked the three steps across to her bed thousands of times before; thousands of times I've quietly eased into her room, walked to her bed and stooped to kiss her head while she's been deep in sleep. The three steps from the door to the bed are so familiar they're ingrained. My feet easily guide the way in the dark.

I lean over the bed and touch where Jena's soft face should be only to find air and then the pillow. In a feeble attempt to find her, I pat down the bed in the unlikely event that she is curled up lower down, but my hands only find the bedding, still made up. There's a rush of adrenaline, a ringing in my ears as my heart rate picks up pace, anxiety pouring through me. Isatou. I have to find Isatou. My body switches to automatic, as my feet take me out of Jena's room. I turn right and into the next room. What if the soldiers returned and took my children? Would they do that? And a whole load of other questions rapidly fire in my mind, fanning the rising dread. 'Isatou,' I call in a desperate whispered urgency. 'Isatou!' I try again, approaching her door, and again as I reach her bed. Too dark to see her, but at the rustle of bedding, a creak of the bed I take a breath of relief.

'Mum?' Isatou's dreamy voice breaks the silence.

'Yes, it's me!'

'Mum!' She's now fully awake within a second. She jumps out of the bed and into the dark shape she can see of my arms.

For the most perfect of moments I stand there; she's nearly my height but my lips still settle naturally on her forehead, 'Oh, my lovely,' I say over and over, wanting to undo all the worry she's had, all the things that she's had to bare. Things she should never have had to deal with; and to have to do that without me. I feel that I've let her down again. I raise my hands to the faint outline of her face where I'm becoming accustomed to the dark. 'Where is Jena? She's not in her bed.'

At the fraction of hesitation before Isatou answers, I brace myself, knowing that she would have replied immediately if there wasn't anything to worry about.

'Tell me. It's okay.'

'Mamamuso wanted her cut; she got the *Ngansimba* to come.'

The shock and fear of that keeps me mute, which is probably for the best, as Isatou continues, 'She must have found out because the night before, she disappeared.'

'Disappeared? What do you mean? Where?'

'I'm not sure. But...' her voice becomes tentative.

'What *do* you know?'

322

'Binta has disappeared too – the same night – so it makes sense that they went together.'

Some thread to hold onto, to pull at gently to see what might be unravelled. 'Does Binta's family know where she is?'

'No – I saw her mother and asked because I thought she might know where Jena was too.'

'Do you know where they could have gone to?'

'No, but they've been gone for over a week already. Do you think she's alright?' The question hangs full of worry, needing hope for me to fill.

'Of course.' I hold Isatou to me and kiss her once again on the head, then as though a switch changes in my head, I become focused on what we need to do. 'We have to leave before anyone sees me. We're going to stay in Serekunda. I need to get a couple of things from my room. Do you still have that torch in your wardrobe?

'Um-hum.'

'Get that out, but be careful to shine it low so not to draw attention from outside. Fill a bag with a few things.' I pause. 'We won't be coming back.'

'Not ever?'

'No, my love. We need to start afresh. I'm not safe here, and now it doesn't look like your sister is safe either, what with Mamamuso's plans.' Then I hear her begin to cry and can just make out her shoulders shaking. 'I know, I'm sorry we have to leave,' I say, caught between being understanding and desperate for her to comply quickly.

'No – it's not that,' she says looking up, sniffing. 'Something awful happened – and it's all my fault.'

Chapter 65

Amie

At night the tears are less, but I only sleep because I'm exhausted. Sleep comes hours after my head sinks into the pillow, after my thoughts pass over different scenarios of what is happening to Binta: where she might be. Sometimes in the darkness I allow the gossip that I've heard in town during the day to seep into the silence. Taken to a foreign land with the *Fula* – Mariama's husband, they say. That's the theory that is spoken most and Ousman's elusive explanation and dismissive laugh neither confirms nor denies the fact. Out of all the speculation, it suits him for people to think Binta is now married.

It suits me best too. I imagine her happy with the *Fula*. He was a kind man. It's better than imagining and ruminating on snippets of whispers I've picked up. The version that Binta has fled with Jena because the *Ngansimba* was coming – if it was just that I would hold onto it with hope – that Binta will return. But I also hear that the *Ngansimba* is angry with them.

Insubordination. I can't even begin to think what she will do if she finds them, and I shudder.

That's why I refocus my thoughts on the *Fula*. Out of the two things most plausible, it's the one that I fear the least.

Chapter 66

Binta

A young woman dressed in denim jeans and a floral top heads along the paved path, past neatly laid rose bushes and ferns towards us, and enthusiastically waves to Hannah.

'This is my friend, Kaddy.' Hannah waves back, greeting her friend. 'You know my daughter, Esther, and these are her friends – Jena and Binta.'

'You must be thirsty, come through and I'll get you some drinks,' Kaddy offers as she unlocks the gate. She glances at my feet as I step over the threshold into the compound.

'I lost my flip-flops on the way here,' I say sheepishly.

'Don't worry,' she says, smiling, making me feel immediately at ease.

Inside the compound, we follow her through a small landscaped garden with a rockery, where a lizard is sunbathing, until we pass by and it scurries away at lightning speed. It reminds me briefly of the *Toubab* woman, lying on her towel at the hotel and I smile; she was like a little lizard, soaking up the sun.

'Come through – come and have a seat.' Kaddy motions to the cream leather sofas, as we enter her house. Her home is unlike any other that I've visited. I purposefully place myself down on one of two matching leather sofas, right under a rotating fan in the ceiling to benefit from the rhythmic breeze it spins.

'Coke?' Hannah asks, and after a moment hands me a glass with ice. Her nails are neat, and the varnish matches the flicks of pink in her top. I'm aware, when I take the glass from her, mine are chewed and sore.

'I'm glad you made it here,' Kaddy says, taking a drink for herself. She sits on the sofa opposite. 'I did wonder if you would be able to make it by foot and if you would find Hannah the other end. It was quite a plan.'

'It was far,' I admit, more aware now that I'm sat down of the pounding ache from the blisters on my feet.

'Thank you for agreeing to have the girls,' Hannah says to Kaddy. 'Esther and I will be leaving soon to go back to Kenji – it will be better if we aren't gone too long. I don't want to draw any attention to us being away, but I'll be back in a few days and then we'll think of something longer term.'

'No problem. It will be nice to have some company,' she says, which conveniently answers the question in my mind as to who else lives here. I assume Kaddy lives alone, which surprises me. I've never considered that a woman would – could – live by herself. I take a sip of the Coke and eye up the living room over the top of the glass. I was always taught that a woman lived with her family until she married and then she would live in her husband's compound. I have an uncomfortable feeling settling in my stomach. It seems so out of place with how I should be feeling. This is an amazing home, we've found our friends and we are safe. For a moment I mull over the disparity and then I realise it's because my world has shifted on its axis again. The reason I suffered everything that I did – the things that I was taught – was on the premise that there was no other way. There was no choice. Women are nothing without a husband. That's what I've heard, forever. But Kaddy is living proof what I was told was a lie.

By the time Hannah returns a few days later, I feel that I have known Kaddy for years. Over dinner, Hannah – who isn't one to usually bother with gossip – has gone out of her way to hear everything. 'Your name was being bantered around a lot, Binta. Apparently your mother thinks the *Fula* has run off with you, as his wife.'

'A wife?' Kaddy scoffs, in disbelief. 'You're much too young!'

'It's true,' I say. 'My father told me he wanted me to marry the *Fula*, just before I left town. To be honest, I'm not surprised the *Fula* left town. He was broken-hearted after his wife died; I can't even believe my father suggested that I marry him. He must have said it to him only days after she died. Can you imagine? Poor guy.'

'Your father is furious for not getting a bride price and even more furious for suggesting the *Fula* marries you in the first place!' Hannah tells me.

Serves my father right, trying to marry me off. I'm glad he's stewing on his own troubles.

'I think your mother is furious with him, for that as well. They are speculating whether they can find his village back in Senegal, but it appears that nobody really ever listened to the *Fula* – nobody knows where he is from exactly.' Hannah laughs; like me she's probably picturing my father getting himself confused and bothered over something that he put in motion for his own arrogance. Warmth rises in my cheeks as I think about how the whole town is talking about me – even if they're wrong. It's not nice being talked about and, for the first time since I left, I'm glad that I am not returning; that I don't have to face everyone and their gossiping and stares.

'It seems to have focused the talk for now, and for that you should be grateful, Binta, especially because...' Hannah stops.

'Especially because?' I look at her, trying to read her face.

'There was gossip about a girl being seen with Jena heading north on the beach.'

'How did they know?' Jena's voice is a pitch higher than normal, fear rising. 'We didn't see anyone on our journey, only tourists. We hid if anyone came near.'

There was the fishing village that one morning, but nobody noticed us then. I retrace our journey in my mind and then I suddenly remember. 'The cattle man! He must have said something. I knew he was sleazy!'

Hannah drops her tone more seriously, but she's not looking towards me now; she's looking at Jena. 'There is something else. I have some news for you – I'm afraid both good and bad.' Before Hannah says anything I'm trying to figure out in my head what it could be, but she's already continuing. 'I heard someone say that they thought they saw your mother, a couple of days ago.'

'Really?' Jena's face beams ecstatically. Suddenly she sits upright, her eyes are fixed on Hannah, ready to absorb every morsel of information. But Hannah continues quickly. 'They weren't sure, – the person was a lot thinner. But it's possible. I went near your compound to find out. I was careful that I wasn't seen. I didn't see her, but—'

The way Hannah pauses, and the way her face doesn't reflect the joy Jena has on hers, I instinctively know bad news is coming next. It seems clear that Jena's forgotten the news was twofold; she's too excited hearing about her mother.

'It's while I was near your compound that I heard something else.' She pauses, perhaps to carefully plan her words, or maybe to give Jena a chance to prepare herself. 'Your grandmother is dead.'

Immediately Jena puts a hand over her mouth, instinctively stifling the involuntary gasp, and then she mutters in bewilderment, 'My grandmother?'

'Yes,' Hannah says gently, and places a hand over Jena's shoulders as they slump forward and begin to shake as she cries, grief filling her being.

Empathically I instantly understand the grief and long to cry for my grandmother who I wonder if I will ever see again, but I'm also taken aback by the tears Jena sheds for the woman who wanted to hurt her. I grapple with the mixture of emotions stirring inside me and witness in Jena how complicated things are. Nothing is as simple as it should be. Even grief.

Chapter 67

Amie

I did think that the longer Binta has been gone and the more life goes on without her, the less they would talk about her. About what she might or might not have done. But in reality, the longer she is gone, the more threads are added to the stories and the more I notice the hushed voices as I walk past.

No longer do they want me to hear their thoughts. Instead I sense their disregard as they look at each other and slightly turn their backs. How can I not know what's happened? Why would my daughter run away? Or they wonder if I know more than I am letting on and have something to hide.

There has never been such a time when I appreciated the closeness of my *Kafo*. 'She'll be back, won't she?' I ask my friends sporadically, and they respond by rote that it's only a matter of time and to have hope.

How did I get things so wrong? I feel confused by everything that's happened. I hold Mai tight, rock her gently and sing to her. One of the things that has come to my attention is that they are blaming me for not getting Binta cut sooner. She was too old and I should have acted, not procrastinate like I did, they say. Now look at my situation. Perhaps Binta didn't even get married to the *Fula*, they voice. Maybe they just ran away together, the women at the marketplace scorn, just loud enough to hear before they discuss it in whispers.

The more I digest their words, the more I know they are right about not acting sooner. I hold Mai close, my nose on her hair and breathe in her beautiful scent. They are right. I sigh deeply: this is the time to act.

Chapter 68

Binta

When Hannah is due to return the following weekend from Kenji, Jena impatiently watches out for her, pacing around the garden and looking out of the gate until she catches a glance of her walking down the path. 'Is there any more news about my mother?'

'I know you are anxious to know, but let me get inside to have a drink first!'

'Sorry, I'm – I just can't wait to hear.'

'I know. Come inside with me.' Hannah sits down next to her on the sofa. 'I'm sorry, I haven't heard anything more. Jena, there's also been talk that your sister hasn't been seen.'

There is a hint of more in Hannah's voice, I keep listening rather than letting my thoughts wander back to Kenji and news of my family. 'I also heard the *Ngansimba* has left town.'

Jena suddenly looks up, her eyes wide. 'Do you think she's taken my sister? What does she want with her? She's going to cut her!' Panic rises in her voice.

I'm drawn to tell her what I know, now that I have met the crocodile myself. The facts are clearer than ever about what happened before to Isatou. 'No, she won't cut her,' I interrupt quietly, before I know my voice will fail to spill the words.

'How do you know?'

'Because—' I know I'm going to crush Jena with my words, and I wish it wasn't true '—she's already been cut.'

Even though I'm not anywhere near the fan, I suddenly feel cold and close my eyes in a futile attempt to escape the news that the *ngansimba* has left Kenji. I'm thinking about the *Ngansimba*. She must have found out that we were heading north. It wouldn't have taken her long to figure out I'm missing as well, especially with all that gossip going around about me marrying the *Fula*. Somehow, I doubt she'll believe I've gone off with him. If the *Ngansimba* left town it must mean only one thing – she's after me.

Chapter 69

Binta

In the silence of the night, as I lie awake, kicked by legs that either belong to Esther or Jena, I think about my mother and whether she really believes that I've left to marry; whether she really believes my father. I picture her like Yari, looking for me, wanting to protect me and a tear runs down my eye onto the soft pillow at the pain of what she did instead.

Suddenly I'm startled by a tapping on the compound gate, across the front garden. I sit up and wipe my eyes with the palms of my hand. I strain my ears and ease my breathing in order to hear clearer. Esther isn't as bad as my grandmother, but her snoring doesn't help me figure out the sound, but then it resonates across the compound again. I untangle myself from limbs that aren't my own, get out of bed and walk over to the open window. The tapping is crisply audible. Without thinking I know I have to wake Hannah and my heart races as I walk through the house to where she's sleeping, a dread rising through me at the thought of who it must be.

'Hannah!' I say, panicking, 'Hannah – someone's outside!'

'Show me!' Hannah says, blearily, becoming more alert by the second. She's on edge, like me. We're thinking along the same lines – the *Ngansimba*. On the way through the living room, she wakes Kaddy. 'We've got a visitor.'

From the way Hannah and Kaddy respond, I wonder if this is a scenario they've rehearsed in their mind. I wonder how it ends when they play it forward. Kaddy grabs a shawl on her way to the door, inching across the room with little visibility, and opens the door slowly, into the shadows. She slips out into the darkness. Quickly by her side Hannah follows, the door is ajar for me to come if I want, but there's an invisible force holding me back. Instead, I hide behind the door, watching. Not that I can see much. I can barely make out their silhouettes merging into the garden, becoming trees and bushes. There is no moonlight tonight. Seeing anything is impossible, but I clearly hear the gate tapping. Someone is there, and my hands start sweating.

Once they open that gate there is nowhere to run. The wall surrounds the house and there is no back garden, no back exit. I long to shout and tell them not to open it, but that'll be just as bad, giving up my position. Better keep silent, hidden. I hear hushed voices and the gate bolts slide, clanging into place, ready to swing wide.

I bite on my lip and cling tightly to the side of the door, peering round. When the gate opens there is an immediate sound of raised voices. My heart beats faster and my fingers press hard against the wood door, protecting me like a shield. I'm ready to run, to scream, to hide. My body is poised.

But then I'm confused.

The voice I hear is somewhat familiar, in fact I know it well, but it seems out of place. I can't picture whom it belongs to straight away. All I know – which is enough in this moment – is that it is doesn't belong to the *Ngansimba*. Surprisingly I cry out quietly, the relief unwinding in my chest. There's some blood in my mouth where I chewed the inside of my lip.

The shadows bob up and down towards me, their voices animated. This is not what I was expecting and I'm forcing my mind to make sense of it, even ruling out whether I'm dreaming.

'Hello, Binta!' the voice greets me. I still can't see into the darkness, to be able to confirm the face that's in my mind, but it just takes a flutter of a butterfly wing for me to realise whom it belongs to. Before I return her greeting, without thinking, I turn and run into the house.

'Jena, wake up!' I say, shaking her, laughing and trying to catch my breath. 'You won't believe who it is!'

Chapter 70

Binta

Jena jumps out of bed, waking Esther in the process, while Kaddy switches on the light. I'm still not used to having electricity and the immediate brightness hurts my eyes. I rub the stinging away and force my eyes to adjust quickly to whom I'm seeing. There, in the middle of the room, fully illuminated like some wonderful illusion, is Yari. Behind her is someone else I recognise and suddenly I feel a weight lifting inside, joy flooding my senses unexpectedly.

'Isatou!' I shout, rushing over to her.

After Jena unfolds from a long emotional embrace with both of them, I do the same. As Yari's arms wrap around me I notice how her collarbone protrudes; she's lost a lot of weight. Prison's done that. But there is still such a happiness in her eyes.

After a few minutes, our ecstatic laugher settles, although the euphoria continues to fill the room, pushing aside the familiar sense I've had of unsettled worry.

'Let me bring some drinks,' Kaddy offers. The fact that it is the middle of the night seems to have been forgotten as voices cross over, spilling news. Jena's sat between her mother and sister, holding onto their hands tightly as though they might disappear if she doesn't have physical contact. Jena's eyes seem to twinkle from where her smile fills every part of her face and then I notice a swift change; her shoulders straighten and she frowns slightly, then she asks quietly, 'Is it true? Is Grandmother dead?'

'Yes. I'm sorry.'

There's a stolen look between Yari and Isatou that I see, but Jena doesn't. I brace for some further news, the bad kind. Yari begins to say something, but Isatou interrupts, 'No, Ma!'

'She needs to know...no more secrets.'

Isatou nods; her eyes glance to the floor. Yari faces Jena in a manner that lets me know she's going to hear something that will remain with her forever. The times that has happened to me include when my mother told me I was going to become a woman and when Dr Bojang told Ibrahim his baby was dead. I wish I could prepare Jena, to soften whatever is coming.

'Your grandmother died, you're right. Only there's something else – she was murdered.'

'Murdered?' Jena cries out loudly.

'Mamamuso?' I utter, in disbelief.

'What happened?' Jena asks.

Isatou speaks. 'I was told to fetch you to bring you for the *Ngansimba*. I couldn't believe it when you weren't there. But then it was down to me to tell Grandmother you were gone. I can tell you, it wasn't pleasant, little sis.' Isatou manages a smile. 'I walked over as slowly as I could to Mamamuso. She was there, laughing with her friends, sharing honey bread...you know the one where the bees get stuck in the nectar? Then I had to tell her.'

For the first time I truly picture the aftermath of our escape.

'What did she say?'

'She beat me.'

'But it wasn't your fault,' Jena says.

'And while she was beating me she cursed Ma, saying if she was meant to be so educated then why didn't she understand how important cutting was? How Ma had all these miscarriages, because she didn't want to bless her daughters. They said some other stuff too, but it was really horrible.

'Afterwards, we waited together under the baobab tree for the *Ngansimba* to come. I was bruised. When the *Ngansimba* arrived, she came with a girl about the same age as me. I thought she might be getting initiated too, but it turned out she was her granddaughter and she was coming to learn the way of cutting. You were going to be her first, Jena.'

I'm feeling nausea hearing her story, but I'm unable to move; it has some unresolved ending that I must hear.

'The *Ngansimba*'s granddaughter looked terrified.'

'That's awful,' Jena says, her head in her hands.

'The *Ngansimba* was so angry, even when Mamamuso said they'd looked everywhere for you. Things got worse when Mamamuso offered to pay the *Ngansimba* double the money for wasting her time – it really made her mad. She was shouting at grandmother about it being about honour and respect.' Isatou hesitates. 'She said that she's going to find you and teach you a lesson, Jena. She vowed to punish you.'

Jena starts to panic, crying. It's a while before she's calm enough for Isatou to tell us what happened with Mamamuso.

'Late that night I was woken up. Since the soldiers came any little disturbance sets me off. That night I heard something and got out of bed to investigate. I crept in the darkness to the hallway. In the corner of the room I could just about make out Mamamuso sitting on the armchair. Then I saw the shadow of someone crossing the room towards her. Mamamuso woke up in her chair and asked who was there.'

Despite getting so far through her story, Isatou suddenly looks like she might stop, might leave the information hanging.

'Who was it, Isatou?' Jena asks.

'The *Ngansimba*.'

Noticing the lump that has formed in my throat, I gulp hard, trying to swallow.

'They argued about what would happen to Jena. Mamamuso was trying to talk her round to not hurting you, but the *Ngansimba* was furious. Then Mamamuso said how you'd fled town with help from another girl – Binta – and it was that girl that should be punished, not her granddaughter.'

My head is spinning. Nightmares and reality join together.

'The *Ngansimba* said how she was going to find both of you and deal with you in the bush – not just initiation. Mamamuso started threatening the *Ngansimba* then, saying how she would discredit her name throughout the whole of the Kombo South, saying she was no more than a thug. She kept on and on until the *Ngansimba* lunged at her in the

341

armchair, grabbed a cushion and pushed it down over her face.'

Tears are running down Isatou's cheeks. 'It was dark, but I could still see Mamamuso's arms thrashing around, and I could hear the strange sound coming from her. I just stood there the whole time. I didn't even scream for help, not even after the *Ngansimba* left – it's my fault.'

'That's nonsense, child,' Yari says, kindly.

'I was so scared,' Isatou says, muffled through her hands and sobs. 'Everyone thought Mamamuso died naturally. I didn't know who to tell.'

With more truth before me than I ever expected, I'm more confused than ever. Mamamuso was trying to protect her granddaughter from the *Ngansimba*, who she had asked to come. It doesn't make sense. How can you plan to hurt but protect the same person?

Then Jena asks, 'What about Pa? Is he okay?' I'm wondering myself if he's alive, and nearly dread the answer.

'I don't know,' Yari says, worry obvious in her voice. I take it as hopeful though. It's good to have hope.

Something has really been bothering me. 'How did you find us?' I ask.

'Isatou recognised Esther – Jena told me about how you were friends. We were in Serekunda already and she spotted her this afternoon getting into a taxi. It was a bit of a gamble, but we were desperate – I thought it was too coincidental to see her here. We jumped in the next taxi and followed you.'

'Why did you wait until it was dark to find us?' Hannah asks.

'I'm keeping a low profile after everything that's happened – with prison. We fled Kenji before anyone knew I was back. Soldiers can come again any time. I'm not safe, and then there's the *Ngansimba*. She'd easily blame me for Mamamuso's death, if her passing does start to raise suspicion.' People are more likely to believe her – especially as everyone knows we had our differences.'

Even though it's still dark out, I turn to look out of the window anxiously. 'Did anyone follow you? Were you seen?'

'No, I don't think so. That's another reason why we waited for dark.'

'Where are you staying?' Hannah asks.

'We left a couple of weeks ago and we stayed with my friend, but now we are staying in a small tourist lodge, by Bakau beach.' She puts her hand on Jena's and inhales slightly before saying, 'We won't be returning to Kenji.'

Jena's quiet for a moment, taking in the absoluteness of leaving her home.' 'Why?'

'Living in Kenji was only meant to be a temporary arrangement. We were due to live in Serekunda when your father got a teaching job, but then your grandfather died and we ended up moving to help Mamamuso. He got a job at the Middle School and well, then you both came along and months became years. But I need a new start – I cannot live there with the memories, or the threat of being taken in the middle of the night...And it wasn't only your grandmother that disagrees with my ideas. I don't feel you will be safe, Jena, not there. Not until you are older.'

'Where will we live?' Jena asks tentatively.

'I have some savings to pay for the room at the lodge and although it's been a while since I worked, I'm already looking for teaching posts. Then we can move into a small place when...' Yari's voice trails off; she finds it again by clearing her throat '...when your father comes back.'

'Can Binta stay with us?'

'Of course, that's the plan. We have a room with two double beds.' Jena lets out a slight squeal of delight and claps her hands together.

'But what about the *Ngansimba*?' Kaddy asks.

'I've been thinking about that,' Yari answers. 'There isn't any evidence to suggest foul play. Unfortunately it is unlikely anyone will take Isatou's word over a respected elder.'

'But she murdered Mamamuso, Ma – she can't get away with it – I saw her with my own eyes,' she says, exasperated.

'I know, but there is no other evidence to deem otherwise and I am not having you put at risk – what with your father in prison and the *Ngansimba* already angry with your sister. I can't risk anything else happening to my family, Isatou. I'm not having you put in danger too.'

'And what about her spiritual powers?'

'Don't be worrying about that, Isatou. She's as human as the rest of us.'

I look carefully at Yari to see if she believes her own words, because I don't. Isatou seems ready to argue, but thinks better of it and sits deeper on the sofa, dejectedly.

'It's late – we should head back to bed,' Kaddy says, seeing me yawn. 'I'll get you and Isatou a bed made up, Yari. Will you be okay on the sofas?'

'Anywhere will be great – especially after where I've had to sleep this past month.'

Chapter 71

Amie

Once I decided, I knew I had to put things into place quickly before I let fear stop me. That is something I learnt from before with Binta. Now that my eldest daughter has gone and the void left inside continuously aches, I hold Mai a little closer. It sometimes eases the pain. Perhaps it's because holding her close, there is a strength that seems to rise up in me. A maternal protectiveness that stirs, giving me a renewed energy where other times the lethargy from missing Binta seems overwhelming. If it weren't for Mai, I think every day would have been more unbearable.

The boys don't need me in the same way, they are getting older; but Mai – the dependence on me for her substance brings me out of sadness. Many times she latches on, suckling for milk automatically, and often by the time her belly is full, my shoulders are less tight and my gaze has been drawn to look into her adoring eyes. It's in those moments I keep being reminded that I let things go too long with Binta. I should have acted much quicker. The benefit now that I know more, that when

I look into Mai's eyes my resolve is more determined. I cannot let fear overwhelm me and take away my ability to act on my own terms.

I don't need many days to do what I have to do – and I will do it quietly, nobody needs to know where I've gone with Mai.

No more procrastinating.

I put Mai on my back, tie the material to secure her in place and set off.

It is time to act.

Chapter 72

Binta

The trees that line the avenue here are so tall that they offer little shade as we walk along the pavement. The grey asphalt road is wide with compounds hidden behind high whitewashed concrete walls, where I can hear sprinklers spinning on the other side.

'Here we are.' Yari directs us to a small entrance with signage either side, one for sparkling Vimto drink and the other with the name of the guest house and a large black arrow pointing to the bar and restaurant, as though we could get lost in the few centimetres from the path to the gate.

Given the compounds we passed on the way, I was expecting more. The single-storey tourist lodge looks like it has seen better days, the white paint is greying from dirt and some of the yellow square tiles are cracked on the veranda.

'Through here,' Yari says, leading us into a small reception area and past an unmanned desk to the back yard. Opposite there is a long outbuilding with five wooden doors and matching glassless windows with netted shutters to keep the mosquitos out.

'Isatou, take the girls to our room.' Jena and I follow behind Isatou to the far end of the block and for a moment, I'm aware that I feel a sense of calm for the first time in a long while. Being here with Yari – back again with my friends. There is something familiar – the fact that we are together again – that gives me a glimmer of hope that things might be okay: that I might be okay. Sometime, when Isatou is on her own, I think I might try to talk to her. I'm not quite sure what I'll say, how I will start the conversation, but I feel a bit stronger by the thought that one day we might be able to speak about what happened in the *jujuwoo*. We might have been at different times, but I know our experience is the same.

The room is large enough for two double beds. In the corner there is a chest of drawers and a freestanding electric fan – there's even a small sink with running water.

'Can we put it on?' Jena asks, going over to the fan.

'Of course.'

'Is this my bed?' I ask, eyeing it up invitingly.

'Yes. Isatou and I are using this one. You and Jena can have the other.'

I kick off my flip-flops and lie out flat on the bed. Jena has found out how to work the fan and every few seconds the breeze drifts over me and I close my eyes and enjoy the feeling of rest. Not just physical rest, but mentally: my shoulders sink deeply into the bed underneath me and I consider how much safer I feel with Yari by my side.

'And the restaurant has lots of different food – the omelette is good,' Isatou says. 'He doesn't do Gambian food though, just European.'

'Talking of food – how about we take Jena and Binta on a trip to that café – that cake shop we found, Isatou?' Yari says, smiling, already picking up her handbag.

We head to the end of the long avenue where traffic fills the busy main road going into Serekunda, but we don't get a taxi; instead we walk and Yari assures me it's not far. After only a few minutes, we are in a part of town where there are various buildings including a small church, a bank and electrical shops. We cross over the road, timing our steps to avoid the oncoming vehicles that refuse to slow for our benefit, and arrive on the other side as the sky unleashes a torrent of rain. The rain will leave as quickly as it's come, but for a few moments everything is saturated. A few sellers take large plastic sheets to cover their goods, while they take the full onslaught of the storm themselves. Others are taking shelter in the doorway of the shops, including the café where we're heading, which means we have to push past a growing, huddling crowd as we enter the shop.

Eventually, with Yari's determination, we squeeze inside but for a moment it is too crowded and we stand near the window. I push my nose against the glass, causing it to steam up under my breath, and proceed to use my fingers to make lines in the droplets.

It's while I am squished up against the window that I see a face across the street that makes my knees nearly buckle. The noise from the shop immediately silences around me; all I can hear is my own heartbeat and a scream inside that doesn't escape. Opposite, sheltering in another doorway, is a face that's embedded in my memory.

'Yari!' I whisper in a panic; it comes hoarse and I nod in the direction in which my widening eyes are staring. 'It's the *Ngansimba*!' I want to scream, but it materialises as a husky squeal and the words fail.

Beads of perspiration line my forehead, but I feel an immediate chill run through my body and I feel my stomach flip over in absolute terror like I've been punched hard.

My vision blurs, but through the window I see the hazy outline of her walking towards the café; my throat throbs, feeling like it's constricting. I grasp at my chest, attempting to slow the painful beating of my heart, and my knees buckle under me. Yari catches me as I slowly slide down the wall.

I need to warn her – tell her that the *Ngansimba* is just about to come through the door – but I'm struggling to get enough air into my lungs to breathe, let alone speak. My heart beats harder, so hard that I can even hear the pounding of blood in my ears, feel it in my neck throbbing. The sounds in the café, strangely now mute, convince me that I am leaving this world.

I can't slow my racing heart. And although I tell myself to breathe, something that should be easy, my body doesn't obey and I feel I am distant from myself. My juju catches my finger as I desperately grab at my neck, focusing my thoughts. Things are clear suddenly; I feel like I am dying, sat with my back against the wall, my legs crumpled underneath me and it's because of witchcraft. It must be. The *Ngansimba* hasn't even entered the café yet and she is having this effect on me – her spiritual powers at work. I'm terrified of what she will do when she is present in front of me.

An image of a python comes to my mind, constricting around my chest, holding me fast. Suffocating me.

Holding me for the crocodile to come.

Then I see the door open and, with a ringing in my ears, the room spins, my chest hurts with the effort of getting air into my lungs and I'm sure I'm going to die.

Chapter 73

Amie

It seemed a good idea at the time to come alone, but now I wish my *Kafo* were here. With Binta gone the constant tide of grief and guilt come together, overwhelming my senses until I feel numb. Perhaps that is why it has been easier to take action this time for my other daughter. With Binta, I agonized over what I had to do. I unpicked and wrestled with arguments that had been set in place generations ago, but it did me no good. At the end of the day, thinking too much about what I had to do just made me feel more powerless.

I am powerless.

There is strength in that admittance. To face the truth that however tall I stand, I am still facing something bigger than me. There is also some relief. Perhaps it is only relief and no strength at all. I'm just deluding myself to think I have any strength. Yes, maybe it's just relief. That I come to the conclusion that I just need to act. Not think and ruminate on it too much. Feeling numb helps. I just have to take one step after another and see where it leads.

Today it leads me here.

I'm almost surprised to find myself here. That my feet have taken over, but now I slow and watch the women moving in the same direction, some in front of me break out in joyful singing and dance as we move. The rhythm of their melody seems to bring something to life inside of me, it rises in my chest spurring me forward.

This time I will be stronger. There are things a mother must do for her daughters, even if there are consequences.

No longer will I be swept along like the River. This time I set the course. I will determine when things happen. Mai might not understand why I am doing what I am until she is older, but at least I will say it was my decision.

Chapter 74

Binta

'Look at me, Binta! Look at me!'
The authoritative words somehow connect with me and I raise my eyes, my face gently cupped in Yari's hands, who is now kneeling in front of me. Yari's worried look relaxes, as my eyes register with hers.

'That's right, Binta. Good. Now breathe – no, slowly, that's it. In. And out. Again.'

Yari's hands let go of my face and she puts her hand under my shoulder to lift me up. I have to put my hand behind me to feel the brick, to feel the security of the wall and to support my shaking legs while I stand. My mind has gone numb and I'm dizzy.

'Come, let's go here,' she says, directing me towards a table, emptied for my benefit as we move towards it. I assume it's because the three women sat there a second ago fear whatever curse I've got. Yari eases me down on the white plastic bench and sits next to me; Isatou and Jena shuffle along the bench on the opposite side of our booth.

I hardly register the Lebanese café owner coming to our table with four coffees and as many cakes. 'Thank you, that's kind,' Yari says to him. Then she passes a cake with pink icing on top towards me. I try to thank her, but it comes out as a whisper and to be honest, the briefest wisp of the sweet smell makes me feel a touch nauseous.

'You need some sugar – try a bite,' she says after a moment. My hand shakes as I reach out to put it in my mouth. I'm grateful that when the sticky icing touches my lips the nausea eases. By the time I have finished the coffee and placed the cup into the saucer, I notice my hands are steady too.

'How are you feeling, now?'

Part of me wishes Yari hadn't asked; I feel embarrassed and I still feel people are staring at me, but I'm also glad because it gives me the opportunity to ask cautiously, 'What happened, Yari?'

Isatou pauses sipping her drink and Jena leans forward, her arms resting on the table, attentive to her answer.

'I think you had a panic attack.'

'A what?' I hear the word 'attack' and it confirms what I thought. 'Witchcraft.'

'Oh, Binta. No!' Her voice softens and she puts a hand across my back, placing her hand around my shoulders. 'No, not witchcraft. Sometimes the body is overwhelmed by fear and it reacts. But something triggered it.'

Immediately I remember; the fog in my thoughts now settled and I turn around quickly in my seat to scan the café, to watch the door. 'She was coming in! She was here! Where is she?' My heart is pounding again and without realising it, I am gripping Yari's arm tight.

'Shhhh, it's okay, Binta. She's not here. She didn't come in.'

'But...?' Tears are building.

'You're safe.'

'I saw the *Ngansimba*,' I say, crying, tears running down my cheeks.

'It wasn't her, Binta.' Yari draws me across the bench and brings me close, protecting me, placing my head on her shoulder. 'You're safe.'

By the time we arrive back at the tourist lodge the rain clouds have dispersed, leaving a glow of oranges with the setting sun.

'Good day, ladies?' the owner, an old *Toubab* man, asks. He walks into the entrance hallway and places a basket of small gardening tools down by his feet. For some reason I notice clearly his white socks and muddied sandals.

'Yes, thank you, Mike,' Yari replies, the café incident left behind. I didn't think she would tell him, but I'm still relieved when the conversation moves on.

'Yes, planted some more this afternoon. Used to have a gardener, but he didn't know the difference between a weed and a perennial.'

Yari laughs, obviously understanding the joke that passes me by.

'Anyway, I'm just putting these away—' Mike lifts the basket of tools and looks at his watch '—and then it will be time to serve dinner.'

'Lovely, thank you.' We follow Yari through the hallway, out to the back yard where the raised white painted concrete flowerbeds run the perimeter of the property. Our room is located in one of the three out-buildings; we manoeuvre between the white plastic patio chairs and tables where a handful of European tourists are drinking beers, sat under the shade of the Coca-Cola umbrella parasols.

Once inside the room I immediately flop onto the bed, all my energy waned. I rest my head on the pillow and soon my exhausted mind begins to wander and for some reason, my memory settles on the time we crossed the wasteland by Jewsang Prison. I remember the fear that rose in my stomach as we walked and how exposed I felt. To think Yari actually stayed inside one of those cells. I imagine she slept on a hard floor with rats nibbling at her feet. Why should Yari experience such hardship, while the *Ngansimba* gets away with murder? I don't expect a reason to form in my head giving the answer. I am now getting just to disorientating, unanswerable questions that fill my mind since becoming a woman. I miss how life was once simple, predictable and clear. When things made sense.

'Don't get too comfortable, girls,' Yari says, interrupting my thoughts. 'You need to go get showered before we eat. The light doesn't always work, you see, Binta. Best get showered before dark. Isatou, go take Binta and Jena and show them where they need to go.' Reluctantly I peel myself up from the soft bed and follow Isatou out into the yard, along the side of our outbuilding and around the corner to another smaller building where there is a room with silver pipe plumbing running up the wall from the ground and out from just under the roof. 'Here's soap - and you can dry with this.' Isatou hands me a piece of folded material. 'Just turn that tap there, on the wall. Sometimes it's warm, but usually not.'

'Thanks.'

After she's gone I stand under the pipe ready to shower and turn the tap. A gurgling starts to sound from the far side of the room, and I look up at where the water will come. From the tinny noise building in the pipes, it should gush out right about now, but instead a little dribble a water drops with effort. I stand waiting, just about to walk away, when I'm saturated with a cold jet of spray that takes me by surprise and I gasp.

Not trusting the water to continue I work fast to get the grime of the day from my skin. I close my eyes, tip my face upwards and let the water trickle over my forehead, willing it to wash away my thoughts, and the fear I felt in the café today, for good.

The lathered soap runs off my body, a bubbly stream from my feet to the little hole in the tiled floor, disappearing. I wish it would take all the grime I feel with it too: the shame of everyone talking about me back home. The pain of missing my family – the constant emptiness I have knowing I won't see my grandmother again. The memories. The fear. The nightmares of the crocodile.

But sadly I just watch the soapy bubbles being drawn into the plug, leaving my insides feeling exactly the same.

Chapter 75

Amie

Before, I imagined being swept along like the river does – taking anything with it in its way. I do feel that I'm being swept along, but instead of powerlessness, this time I feel as though I'm being carried. The women around me with their energy propel me. I don't have to put effort in, I can even close my eyes and allow the river to take me where I need to go. It is invigorating. I am beginning to feel alive!

There are many more women here than I realised there would be. This is going to be a big event. For a moment I pause, squint against the midday sun at the figure of an elderly lady. I recognise her – definitely it's her. The *Ngansimba* from my sister's village, she was there at my niece's celebration when they came from the *jujuwoo*. I'm surprised to see her though, not least as this is a long way from where she lives. It's seeing her that makes me suddenly aware that I really don't understand the extent and significance of today.

Maybe, I shouldn't really be here. My pace slows. What am I doing here? Then a new crowd of women ease past me and I begin to go in the same direction again. As we near our destination, my heart begins to pound. The river has carried me and here I am.

Naïvely I thought I could keep it all quiet, but now I realise that I will have to be brave enough to tell them what I've done for Mai; otherwise, what will be the point of all this?

Chapter 76

Binta

A week later, Isatou, Jena and I sit chatting in our new favourite place: a worn wooden bench at the front of the guesthouse entrance. There's not as much to watch here; not like at Mr Janneh's shop with all the comings and goings. The guesthouse is off the main road and it's quiet. It's one of those roads you have to know about. A little lizard catches my interest on the wall, bobbing its head up and down with its front leg momentarily poised, soaking up the late-afternoon sun.

Yari appears through the gates, paper under her arm, a wide smile filling her features.

'I have fantastic news!' she says, laughing, and waves the paper as though it already explains.

I glance at Jena and she shrugs, just as her mother begins to dance to herself, silent music loud in her own head. Yari's joy is infectious; I haven't seen her like this since before – well, for a very long time. I suddenly remember a different life, where there was laughter, singing, dancing – fun.

'Make room!' Yari says. Just in time we shift apart as she lands on the bench and sighs deeply.

'What is it, Ma?'

'I will tell you, my dear Isatou. Today is a wonderful day. I have a job!'

'Amazing!' I say, and clap in delight.

'Congratulations! Where?' Jena asks.

'At the high school, a supply teacher for a term with the likelihood of a contract from next term. I start on Monday. And if that wasn't enough, look at this...' Yari takes the newspaper from under her arm, unfolds it, turns a couple of pages and places it carefully on Isatou's lap. 'See, read here.' She points to a section towards the bottom right-hand part of the page.

'"Bumsters congratulated for encouraging tourism—"'

'No, here!'

'"Ten men arrested over the past two months...due to be released." But Ma, it doesn't say who, or what they were arrested for,' Isatou says.

'You're right, but after I saw it, I visited my friend – the one who has connections; they know a human-rights lawyer – and he seemed to be optimistic that it was referring to your father.'

'Really?' Isatou and Jena jump up and down, unable to contain their excitement.

'We can only hope, but it is possible it will be as soon as late next week. I guess we will find out then. My friend's lawyer-friend is going to keep us informed of any developments.'

It's nearly dark by the time we are all sat at one of the plastic patio tables, a series of bulbs on a string illuminates the yard in a warm glow, making it difficult to read the menu, but Yari already knows what she wants. The guesthouse owner is stood next to her, a small paper pad in the palm of his left hand, a pencil poised ready to write down her order.

'Two large pizzas and side salads.'

Joyous friendly chatter drifts across the yard from the tourists at a table behind us.

'The tourists that come to places like this are seasoned travellers, students coming on a budget or ex-patriots that like to avoid the larger hotels with package holiday-makers. You know the type. They like to think they know the country after a couple of days by the swimming pool,' Yari laughs.

Soon our food arrives.

The owner dispenses the plates in front of us, the aroma rises, sparking my appetite. 'What do you think of your new home, Binta?'

With a mouth full of pizza, I swallow, anxious to answer, 'It's great, Yari. Thank you.'

'Well, now I have this new job the next thing I need to do is find us all somewhere more permanent to live. I'm going to be busy tomorrow looking. Isatou—' Yari pauses as she picks up another slice of pizza '—I want you to go with Jena and Binta in the morning to a list of schools that I'll write down for you – see if they have spaces.'

'Ma, what about the school fees?'

'Just find out first and I'll worry about that later. Anyway, when your father comes back to us, things will be better and I'm sure things are going to change soon – I can feel it. Things are changing for us.'

'You mean, I can go to school too?'

'Yes, Binta! There is much more for you to learn.'

'Thank you,' I say as I finish my pizza quietly, chewing slowly, digesting Yari's kindness as well as the food. My own father wasn't prepared to keep me in school, but here is Yari, doing that for me, and I hope her faith for the future is true.

'Anyway, eat up, don't be long getting to bed – you've got an early start tomorrow.'

Before long our plates are empty and Isatou and Jena stand and push their chairs back and both walk around to where Yari is. Together they say goodnight and jointly give her a hug, before they head to our room.

'Night girls,' Yari calls after them, and then shifts in her seat expectantly for me to follow; but after just watching Yari with her daughters there are a sudden plethora of questions rising in my mind. My body seems weighed down by them, stopping me from moving.

'Yari, do you think I'll see my mother again?'

She turns in her seat to face me fully. 'Oh, Binta.' The brief pause that follows focuses my senses on the lump in my throat and the prickling tension of building tears. She takes my hand and holds it in hers. 'I don't know,' she says quietly.

'Why did she want me to go through it, Yari? You didn't for your daughters.'

Yari sighs. 'I wish I could tell you – and if it was just simple to explain, but it isn't, I'm afraid. It doesn't mean she doesn't love you.'

The words spark a battle inside making my emotions mix, unsettling me. I want to believe those words, but how can my mother love me and hurt me? Some of the tears that have been building fall onto our hands.

'Binta, let me ask you something.'

I let go of Yari's hand, and wipe my eyes with the back of mine, sniffing as I do. Then I look at her, ready for her question.

'Did your mother choose her life – her husband?'

I shake my head slowly, knowing that Yari knows my mother, wondering why she's asking.

'Did she choose when to get married?'

'No.'

'Did she choose when to have children, or how many?'

I just look at Yari, puzzlingly, wondering where she is going with her questions.

'Does she have the power to choose what happens in her own compound, in her home?'

'No, not really – it's up to my father and grandmother, I guess.'

'Does she decide when to cook?'

I think about it for a second and reply, 'Well, she knows which week she has to do all the chores and when her co-wife is on duty or my aunts.'

'What would happen if she decided not to cook on that week?'

'The other women would get cross with her, make her life difficult – call her names, probably. My father would get mad.'

Yari pauses again as though she wants to continue, but needs to wait. 'Do you see a pattern, Binta?'

'I'm not sure.'

'Your mother married when she was a child. She has lived her life being told what to do, when and how. What voice does she have? What power do you think she might have thought she had to stand up against anyone? You told me if she changed the cooking

366

rota that it would create difficulties – how much more if she were to stand up, not just her own family and compound – but everyone she has ever known? *Everything* she has ever known?'

I begin to understand what Yari is trying to say and some of the churning inside me subsides as I ponder her words, only for other thoughts to quash it.

'But when you love someone, Yari—' I try to form the sentence that will explain what I want to say, but it leaves me more frustrated '—it's not just standing up to a cooking rota!' I raise my voice so that the chatter from the table behind diminishes and I can tell that they are looking over to me. 'You stood up to it,' I say, lowering my speech.

Yari looks over my shoulder to the other table that has gone back to their conversation, clinking as beer is poured into glasses. 'It was different for me, Binta. I have had the privilege of education, of a husband I chose to marry who supports me and who shares my values that I have had the opportunity to explore and challenge. Even then, look – what good was that when Isatou was taken...?' Yari's voice falters and she coughs slightly. 'If it wasn't for you, Binta, the same would be true of Jena too. It's difficult in our society. Your mother managed somehow to keep you from this until you were much older – how many others were your age at the initiation?' My mind switches to that hut, images of us sat together, before I have a chance to stop myself thinking about it. Apart from Sara who came from England, I was the oldest, although it didn't occur to me at the time – probably because I was caught up in the fact that Sara was older than me. It didn't cross my mind, but now that Yari has pointed it out, I'm puzzled. 'If my mother stopped it from happening until now, why didn't she stop it happening at all, Yari?'

'I don't know how your mother prevented you from being cut earlier on – most girls would have been cut before, but your mother – imagine, this woman who was a wife about that age – managed to postpone that for you. Change isn't easy, Binta, but know your mother loves you.' She squeezes my hand, as if to emphasise the point.

I nod slowly. 'I wish it were true, Yari.'

'The truth is like a needle, an old man and a young man can pick it up,' she says, putting her hand gently on my cheek.

'What does that mean?' I ask.

'It means, the truth doesn't belong to just one person. Anyone can know the truth. Now, you need to get sleep. We all have a busy day tomorrow.'

'*Suto Yediya*.' I say goodnight to her and leave. I consider what Yari has told me – for the first time I see my mother from a different perspective. She prevented this happening to me for as long as she could – I determine that I will hold onto that fact because, as I do, I feel the ball of pain inside of me soften very slightly.

The lights from the yard throws enough glow into the room when I open the door that I can see Isatou sleeping, curled up on the bed that she will share later with Yari. Jena has her back along the wall on our bed, a sheet covering her, deep in slumber. Quickly, I close the door behind me to stop insects from coming in and shut out the light as I do. It takes a second for my eyes to adjust to the dark, but the bed isn't far from the door,

I sit down and the metal springs squeak. Fumbling at the foot of the bed I feel around for another sheet to pull over me, more to keep any insects at bay rather than the chill.

I lie my head on the pillow and I replay the conversation that I've just had with Yari in my mind. My mother cares – loves – me, she said. She didn't have a way to stop it, even if she wanted to. I close my eyes, now aware of how utterly exhausted I am. I'm so tired that I only half-heartedly attempt to draw the sheet up around me against the recognisable monotone buzz of a lone mosquito.

The café is empty and aside from the bright moonlight filtering in through the window, I'm surrounded by darkness. Sat with my back against a wall, I face the door and my racing heart pounds hard in anticipation for what is about to happen. I try to move, but my body is a dead weight; my legs a burden and I am helpless. There is a shadow across the frosted glass in the door. The handle moves and the door creaks open. My eyes are fixed where I'm expecting her to be, but they instantly drop to the reptile that is now halfway across the threshold with its scaly, powerful body; the moonlight leading a spotlight across the floor to where I am. Every part of me wants to scream, but if I do it will come for me for sure – if I am silent it may walk by and I try to stop the fear escaping under my breath, the air too loud from my lips. The creature is large, the nails scraping over the floor, halfway to me already.

My heart is about to explode through my chest – it is pounding too fast – and then, to my left, my hand rests on something wooden, a stick perhaps. Clouds cover the

*moon dimming the room; as though synchronising with
the impending doom I anticipate, the crocodile's tail
swishes from side to side, knocking chairs to the floor.
It comes nearer and I can hear its crackled breath, I
smell the rotting flesh in its mouth as it opens its jaws.*

*In the moment it moves to me, the clouds move on
giving me clear sight and in one swift motion I bring
the stick from the floor connecting it hard across its
bony snout. Tonight, for once, I determine – it will not
devour me.*

'Binta! Binta!' I open my eyes to the dark around.
Disorientated for a second, my body tenses in readiness
for the crocodile's bite, but then two worlds seem to
part when I recognise Isatou's voice in the dark. 'You
were having a nightmare – you sounded frightened.'

I unclench my tightly gripped hand and expect to
find the stick still there. I lift myself up and reach for
the dark shape of Isatou and I hug her, making sure –
needing her to be real.

'I understand, Binta. I have these nightmares too,'
Isatou says, brushing a hair away from my face. It's the
first time the subject has been broached and her words
are powerful, as though giving me the permission to
feel the hurt and betrayal. 'You're okay now,' she says
soothingly, 'but I'm going to get my mother.'

I don't really want Isatou to leave me, but she's back
within a moment with her. Somehow my sobbing hasn't
woken Jena, who is curled up on our bed nearest the
wall, blissfully still sleeping: without nightmares.

'Oh, Binta,' Yari says when she arrives, she sits with
me on the bed and cradles me in the way my mother has
on many occasions and comfort combines with feelings

of missing her. Isatou hugs me too and then makes her way back into bed opposite, seeming confident that Yari knows how to care for me.

After a few moments Yari says, 'It might help – to talk? Tell me about what scares you – about your nightmares.'

I don't answer, but consider her words. I think she's right – but I can't. I wouldn't know what to say, where to start, the words don't come. This is something I will have to fight on my own: the memories of the crocodile, my nightmares that come at night and now the panic attacks that come by day.

'You know, Binta, these things that have happened – if you can find a way of getting through them, it will make you stronger. For me, it was finding a voice.'

I pull away from Yari's chest, where she's been holding me tenderly, and look at the shadow of her face in the dark. 'You really think so?'

'I do.'

I glance over in the dark room to where I can see the now sleeping outline of Isatou. I feel sad that Isatou went through this too, but at least she has her mother to talk to about things. 'Yari,' I begin tentatively, 'how did you forgive your mother?' I am aware that I am asking personal questions that perhaps I shouldn't, but hidden in the dark, it gives me the security of asking without seeing her reaction, her possible disapproval.

'My mother – like yours – had little opportunity, education or voice.'

I am relieved that she's not offended by me asking.

Then she continues, 'I have come to understand that what she allowed for me, even as much to say what she wanted for me, was what she thought was best.

You have to know, Binta, apart from being caught up completely in a society that demands you behave in a particular way, they are told lies: that you have to be cut to be healthy, happy and to have a prosperous life. What mother wouldn't want that for her child? Once I started to understand that, I saw her actions were part of something bigger than she could decide on her own. I pitied her even.'

'But, Yari, I feel so angry.'

'That's not a bad thing! Use that anger, Binta. But direct it in the right place. Use it to change things.'

'How?'

'I'm not going to tell you—' she pauses and I feel disappointed, until she adds, 'but in a few days I'll show you.' Yari strokes my temple and kisses me on the forehead.

'Show me?'

'Yes!' she whispers.

In the darkness of this room, with her holding me, I feel safer than I have done since before I met the crocodile. She places my head on the pillow, arranges the sheet over me before I search for her hand to hold again. I don't want her to go, not even across the two steps to her bed. Yari stays sat on my mine and as I listen to the sound of the crickets outside, I close my eyes, my fingers wrap tightly around hers and as I drift back to sleep I think I sense some of the strength she has being passed onto me.

Chapter 77

Amie

I adjust Mai on my back, not because she's crying or
I'm uncomfortable, but because I need this moment
to hesitate and gather my resolve. I look up and see
the women ahead walking towards where I need to go.
I straighten my shoulders and feign confidence, my chest
aches from the quick pounding of my racing heart.

'It's time, Mai,' I quietly tell my daughter.

It's time.

Chapter 78

Binta

The downpour was sudden and intense. As we get out of the car and walk towards the white concrete pillar entrance gates of the grand hotel, the heat begins to rise from the asphalt road and there is a familiar post-rain scent in the air.

An expensive black Mercedes passes us, splashing through a drying puddle. It slows and pulls up outside the lobby entrance of the hotel. A doorman moves forward quickly to open the back passenger door and assists a smartly dressed woman to get out.

'She's from the government.'

'The government?' I whisper, suddenly aware of what that might mean given Yari's recent imprisonment.

'Yes, there are lots of important people here today,' Yari answers, infuriatingly still vague, but she doesn't seem concerned. In equal measure I'm relieved and curious. She still hasn't explained to any of us what we are doing here, just that there was somewhere important for us to come today. Yari speeds up her walking. 'You three are slower than grandmothers.'

She laughs over her shoulder to us – she seems energised and motivated by whatever the draw is within the gates of the hotel.

Another car, a dark-grey Land Rover pulls up outside the entrance lobby, where we are nearly at now. A lady in her late twenties gets out of the passenger seat and closes the door behind her, before the driver pulls away. She is wearing jeans and a white T-shirt with pink writing on, but from this angle I can't read what it says. The doorman opens the glass lobby door and greets her, expecting her arrival, it seems. He continues to hold the door as a stream of women filter through. There is anticipation, an excitement that I overhear in the chatter around me. I'm even more intrigued now as to why we're here.

Yari directs us to a queue that is beginning to form and we ease slowly forward to a desk where a couple of women are busy checking forms and handing out T-shirts.

'Look, do you think we're going to get one?' I ask Jena.

'I think so, everyone's getting one.'

'Wonder why?' I say, more to myself as Jena is distracted. She's looking up at the grand staircase.

'That's called a mezzanine,' Yari notes.

'Mezzanine?'

'The balcony-type thing that goes all the way around there.' Yari motions with her arm, smiling. She's enjoying the way we are absorbing it all. My own eyes are drawn to the reflection of the lights on the polished marble floor. We inch towards the desk, but before the woman looks up, Yari quickly turns to me and takes my hand. 'This is what I wanted you to understand – when we spoke the other night. It wouldn't have been the same if I just told you about this. I wanted you to see for yourself – to experience women coming together to bring about change.'

I feel foolish when her face is expectant of me suddenly understanding, but instead I know my eyes give away my continued confusion.

'This—' she smiles and gestures widely with her outstretched arms '—a combined voice speaking up against the traditions that harm our girls.' Yari doesn't get to see the recognition forming on my face as the woman at the desk asks her to register and draws her attention from me. I look around the hotel again; now, instead of wonder at the grand décor, I'm taken aback by what Yari has just said, and suddenly I see the people here with fresh understanding. They are not just individuals, but they have come together for a common goal. One purpose. For a second I begin to feel something inside rise above the confusion and hurt from everything that has happened. As though a little butterfly has found its wings and is about to soar high above the clouds.

Isatou looks over to me and we have a mutual understanding that Jena doesn't notice. I wonder if she's also feeling the same as me, feeling the beginning of a healing that I didn't think was possible. That people care. That what happened to us wasn't right. 'Here!' Yari turns and hands us each a neatly folded white T-shirt. Others around us are putting them on over their flowing kaftans, combining African and Western dress in the same outfit. It's not until I take mine to wear that I notice the pink writing across the front and I hold it up to see the slogan properly.

Gambia Annual Conference
Women against FGM

I put the T-shirt over my head; my thoughts are racing. Before I can ask Yari, she's already moving towards where people are being greeted and invited into a large room. Inside there are green leather-backed chairs and comfortable red fabric ones set out in rows filling the room and most are already taken. The hum of chatter fills the air as Yari leads us towards the middle, where there is still a sprinkling of empty seats at the end of one of the rows and we follow her and find one to sit in next to each other.

Yari puts a hand on the chair's back in front, leans across Isatou to Jena and me. 'There are women here from all over The Gambia – even from right up river. Some have taken hours to get here. Isn't this fantastic?'

I look around the room and can see a couple of women behind us with tribal markings on their face; I can tell they're not Mandinka.

'How did you know about this, Ma?' Jena asks.

'I've been before and also it was advertised in the paper last week. As soon as I saw it, I knew we must come.'

A microphone suddenly squeals into life, the sound bounces from the speaker, silencing the chatter in the room like a gun. An expectant pause descends in the room directed towards a woman who now stands on the platform at the front of the room.

She takes one step towards the microphone and begins, 'Welcome to our annual conference on FGM in The Gambia. Today, you will have a chance to hear what work we have been doing to push for the end of traditional practices. We have speakers from the health profession and we are honoured to invite our guests in politics.'

A round of applause erupts and the woman on stage has to wait for it to subside before continuing, 'If you look at the booklet you have been given on your way in, the agenda today also covers a question-and-answer session as well as hearing about our strategies and how we plan to implement these in the coming months.'

'Yari.' I lean over Jena and say quietly, 'What is FGM?'

'It stands for female genital mutilation – cutting.'

'Oh!' I lean back in my chair, absorbing the atmosphere – the room is filled with all sorts of women coming with one purpose. I think of the strength I felt when Yari soothed me back to sleep after my nightmare and I feel something like that again: a strength coming from being here with women saying that change is possible.

'Room for another two?' a familiar voice whispers from behind my shoulder and turning around I'm surprised to see Hannah and Esther here as well.

'What are you doing here?' I ask Esther as I shuffle along the empty chair to my right.

'My mother tries to come each year. This is my first time though, but I didn't want to miss it, especially as I thought you would all be here.'

'Shhh!' Yari puts her finger up to her mouth and I turn my attention back to the speaker.

'...Raising up a new generation...a voice within schools...needing young women all over the country... will you become a peer educator? Could you tell your story?'

By the time the speaker has finished, energy is running through my veins in a way I have never experienced before: I nearly stand up and shout 'Yes!' in response to her, but then she walks off the stage and another speaker takes her place. Then the excitement I felt is immediately replaced by waves of nausea as I imagine myself telling my story. Voicing any of what has happened. My senses are turned inwards so that all I am aware of is my heart racing, my palms so sweaty that I rub them on the edge of the fabric seat. It takes effort to focus on the speech, but as I do calmness returns; I become more absorbed again and my heart slows.

'All need to do our bit...nothing will change if we don't take action...'

It's as though the woman knows the thoughts that are budding in my mind and her words rise up against every fledgling reason I think about why I couldn't ever speak out. Maybe – maybe my voice could join with theirs too? My whisper to combine with others to make an undeniable roar. I ponder this as I watch the woman leave the stage and the chatter in the room increases, which seems to release something inside of me. Emotions – ones I'm not quite sure what they are – rise in me and make me feel bigger than I am.

'They are selling drinks at the back – it's a break now. Do you want something?'

'Sure. Thanks, Hannah.' I watch her and Esther make their way through the crowd to the back of the room, and continue to absorb the atmosphere of being here.

It's as though being in this room I am becoming something new, or maybe it's just releasing what was already there – only hidden. Suddenly I feel lighter; that what was crushed in me is now unfolding, not tight and dead. I sit upright in my chair, a vertebra in my neck cricks quietly, my shoulders relax and I take a deep, deep breath.

Chapter 79

Binta

I turn around to see Hannah hurrying back towards me down the aisle; she moves to the side to avoid bumping into some women who are wandering in her direction, deep in conversation. The way she is making her way to me with purpose immediately alerts my curiosity.

'Binta! I need to talk with you. Come with me!'

I ease out of my seat and she takes me under the arm, 'Quick. We have to be quick.'

'What is it, Hannah?' We are already halfway towards the back of the room where the majority of women are congregating. She slows for a second and turns to me. Despite the hurriedness she now seems hesitant to tell me.

'I've seen your mother, Binta.'

A lump suddenly fills my throat and I swallow hard in order to be able to ask, 'Where?'

'She's actually here.'

'In Serekunda?'

Hannah takes a momentary breath, 'No, here at this conference.'

'Here?' I let out a quiet cry. My legs immediately feel shaky beneath me and from every angle questions bombard my mind – What is she doing here? Is the Ngansimba with her? Is she going to try and take me home? – Along with the questions, a flurry of mixed emotions rise up in me; the constant bubbling anger, worry at her reaction towards me, but most of all – and confusingly – a relief that I can see her once again.

'Where is she, Hannah? Is the *Ngansimba* here too?' My eyes scan the women, desperate to separate the individuals from the crowd. My heart races, already dreading spotting the *Ngansimba* – and there are too many women hovering across the entrance, which means I'll be trapped in here. I'll have to face her.

'Calm yourself. No. It's just your mother. She doesn't know you're here.'

'She doesn't know? Why is she here then?'

'How about I take you to her and she can explain.'

'I don't know, Hannah. What if she tries to take me home?'

'You are safe – do you trust me?'

I think about it and how much Hannah has risked helping me and I know I have to trust her. The overwhelming need to see my mother again is enough for me to nod.

'Come.' She takes me gently by the arm. 'She was over there, towards the back.'

I look, but can't locate her and I'm suddenly anxious that we might not meet. My heart begins to race at the thought that I might not get to see her again. Ever.

Then I spot her from a distance; I know the blue, purple and white tie-dyed outfit she's wearing is her special outfit. She's stood on her own, looking out of the window seeming to be out of place and uncomfortable, with Mai asleep on her back.

I move slowly towards her through the bodies in front of me, and I lose sight of her a couple of times. Time seems to change, seconds like hours and with every second, the possibility that my mother will move away and I'll lose sight of her completely. And then she is only a few steps away. She hasn't seen me and now she's close enough I take a breath to pause, gathering courage to open my mouth to speak. 'Ma,' I say as I step towards her and she turns around, a dozen emotions show on her face at once. Her eyes widen, as does her mouth and then her face lights up with joy. 'Binta!' she says, and takes a step to me to close the void, and puts her arms tightly around me. 'Binta! My daughter!'

Her reaction is an instant relief, and I feel my body relax into her embrace.

She pulls back from me, her hands still on my shoulders and she looks as though she wants to ask a hundred questions. Her hands move to cup my face, like she needs to register it's me, but she doesn't know what to say apart from repeating my name.

'How is it that you're here?' I'm the one that speaks first.

'Binta, I've missed you. I've been worried about you – where have you been?'

'I had to leave – the *Ngansimba* was after me, Ma, because I helped Jena escape.'

'I thought so.'

'Really?'

'Your father thought you left with Ibrahim to get married, but I wasn't sure. Then I heard about Jena going missing and it made more sense.'

'I can't come home, Ma – I'm not safe.'

'I know.'

'I can't go back with you – please don't ask me.' I know she can tell the panic that's there in my voice.

'It's okay, I'm not – anyway, your father wouldn't allow it either. He would be made to look foolish if people knew you didn't end up getting married. He lost a tenant and told everyone how he had married you off. He'd look silly if you turned up again with a different story. He couldn't bear the embarrassment.'

'So why did you come for me?'

My mother's forehead creases as it does when she looks confused. 'I didn't know you were here, Binta. I'm surprised to see you – but I'm so happy.'

'Then why are you here?'

She doesn't answer immediately, but turns and glances again out of the window where the hotel garden boasts a sprinkling of bright colours. It reminds me of when Jena and I hid amongst the bushes when we were escaping being caught and sent home. The irony – that I'm now stood, invited, on the inside of a grander hotel for the very reason I ran away – doesn't escape my thoughts.

My mother slowly turns to me again and I notice how her eyes look watery. 'Binta, I'm sorry for what happened. I didn't know things could be different. I'm sorry you were taken to the bush.' Then she avoids my eye and looks over my shoulder to the women dispersing back to their seats. I don't know what to say in response for a second, but then the question seems to flow without me thinking. 'What brought you here today?'

My mother focuses her eyes and looks to me. 'After everything that happened – before you went to the bush – I was always told it was for our children's own good, for your health, but then Aminata died. And then we watched Mariama die in front of us – how awful that was.' I nod in agreement. 'Then you left. There were many nights I thought about what happened and I – I miss you. Binta, it made me question if things were right, the way I'd been told. Then I heard about this conference and I know I had to find out more for myself. I cannot lose another daughter. I don't want to make the same mistakes with Mai. But I don't know how to do it differently.'

Yari's wise words resonate in my mind and I begin to see my mother caught in a society where she has no voice, no strength to do anything alternative.

'Ma, I'm glad you came,' I say, taking her hand and holding it in mine. 'I missed you too.'

The sound system pierces into action, signalling that the conference is recommencing. 'Come, Ma. Come and join us – we're over there,' I point. She allows me to guide her across the room, following the flow of others heading back to their seats.

'Binta, I can't believe I've found you,' Ma says, holding onto me and I realise how nervous she seems and it occurs to me that she has never been in a hotel like this before, never in a grand room surrounded with educated and influential women.

'Yari,' I say. She's sat at the end of the row and I get her attention. 'Look who I found here at the conference!'

'Amie?' Yari turns around looking as surprised as I was. She stands and looks quickly at me and I can tell that she's unsure of my mother's motive.

'It's okay,' I respond quickly, noting her hesitation. 'Ma has come here because she wants to understand more – for Mai's sake.'

Yari exchanges a quick understanding look with me, and I know she's thinking of the talk we had a few days ago.

For the rest of the speaker's presentation the words wash over me, despite my best attempts at keeping them floating away, because all I can think of is my mother; seeing her again and what she told me. It's more than I could have ever imagined.

With my mother here, Yari's words echo in my head about forgiveness. I'm not sure about forgiveness, at least not at the moment, but as I watch my mother sitting attentive to the words of the speaker, I realise that she really has never had a choice. I really can see that she still loves me.

She came to this conference on her own, looking out of place and tentative but now, sat in between Yari and Hannah, she looks strengthened. I sense it too; similar to the night Yari held my hand, settling me after the crocodile came to me again in my nightmares. I found strength from her, but now it is magnified – a whole community of women surrounding me. Surrounding my mother. I look across at her and it dawns on me that her actions, by coming here, are more powerful than any words she could have ever said to me.

Mai stirs, her head turns and her beautiful dark eyes open and blink; she focuses and looks in my direction, recognises her older sister and smiles. I reach over and touch her little hand and her fingers wrap around mine. I can't believe how quickly things can change. In the course of today, how much I've learnt. How much the future seems different. Not just for me, but also for my little Mai. I stroke my thumb over her smooth wrist. Suddenly a thought fills my mind and I feel a lightness inside that I haven't felt for a long time. Mai will not experience the beating drums that will leave her heart pulsing in fear. Ma's hands will not have to hold her down.

She will never have to hear the song of the crocodile.

The crocodile will not come.

ACKNOWLEDGEMENTS

'It takes a village to raise a child.' This African proverb seems particularly fitting when I consider how many people have helped to shape this story into what it has become.

It seems a long time ago now, but thanks to those in the writing group who encouraged me with the first baby floundering steps; especially Joy, who has been by at my side through every draft and rewrite, listening patiently as I developed the plot.

A huge, huge thank you to agent Madeleine Milburn for believing in the importance of Binta's story, and for all you did along the way. I still smile at the way your team surprised me with the colourful cardboard crocodile and the dozens of paper cut-out people featuring quotes from my novel around your office. They were reminders to me when the journey got tough that this is still a story that needs to be told. Thanks to Hayley Steed at the agency for all your help along the way, and to Anna Hogerty for the final polish.

Thank you, Donna Hillyer, for your skills as an editor, ensuring the narratives of all the women in the story work cohesively.

Jem – as everyone knows, we shouldn't judge a book by its cover … but we all do - I love your design and Steve Foot worked on the typesetting to make it ready for both print and ebooks. Thanks to both of you for your advice on getting the book ready.

There have been many kind people that have taken the time to read various drafts and were bold enough to give me honest feedback, including Linda, who proofread the very first draft. As well as those that have read early copies of my book, thank you also to the people that have spent time promoting it. A special shout out to Tina, who always amazes me in how she spreads the word everywhere she goes – I really appreciate that – and to everyone who has read, reviewed, blogged, used their influence, re-tweeted, told their friends and family, their work colleagues and suggested it at book clubs. I am immensely grateful for how you help to promote the novel.

Writing this story made me reflect on the special women that journey along life with me. Friends that share both struggles and laughter; they are immensely treasured and are true rocks: Julie, Kathy and Lynda. The special bond Binta feels for Mai is a dedication to my own big sister, who would have been the first to organise a big launch party along with an appropriately decorated cake for me. And to my most honest critic, but also my biggest fan … my mum – you really made the dream happen! And to the rest of my family – especially my wonderful boys – thank you for all the support you give me. You are stars. The achievement in writing this book pales in comparison to the privilege of being your mum.

Finally, the biggest acknowledgment is to the women and girls that have met the crocodile, or live with the reality of meeting it one day; and those too who tirelessly campaign to end FGM. A special mention to survivor, author and activist Hibo Wardere – thank you for the encouragement and support you have given me. You are all brave, courageous, wonderful people. I dedicate this book to you, and truly hope in some way it will help to make a difference.

AUTHOR'S NOTE

Unfortunately, Binta's story is not unique. Although the story is set within the historical context of President Yaya Jammeh's rule in the early 1990s, Binta's story is just as relevant, if not more so over twenty years on. It reflects the experience of nearly 200 million women worldwide today. In the UK alone, 20,000 girls are at risk each year of undergoing FGM.

For some readers, Binta's experience might bring to the surface their own memory of 'meeting the crocodile'. You aren't alone, and my purpose in writing the book was to contribute towards helping to end the practice, not to re-traumatise those who have experienced this first-hand. My book is dedicated to you and all the women that have gone through FGM, and I hope it will help to reduce the numbers of girls that the book will be dedicated to in the future.

I am also aware of how traumatising the story is for other readers. Many people have commented that they weren't expecting how they would feel afterwards. Thank you for continuing to read.

My biggest motivation for writing this novel was to help raise awareness within education, protection services, social and health care. If you are a professional working with girls potentially at risk, contact your Local Authority safeguarding hub. Teachers can find support from their designated safeguarding leads. Within the UK there is now mandatory reporting for certain professionals. Each Local Authority has a Local Children's Safeguarding Partnership (LSCP) which can also offer information, training, guidance and support. In cases of immediate danger, please contact the police.

For updates on how this novel is being used to raise awareness around FGM, for additional resources to use in schools and book clubs and for links of organisations involved in ending FGM, please visit authorcarolinelisa.com

Thank you for reading.

#fgmnovel
#endfgm
@authorCLisa
authorcarolinelisa.com